Treasure

in the

Library

Treasure in the Library

Win Day

TREASURE IN THE LIBRARY

ISBN 978-0-9952082-5-4

Copyright © 2017 by Win Day
Published by Creative Implementations
106 Garrison Square SW
Calgary, Alberta T2T 6B2
Canada

This is a work of fiction. Names, characters, places, and incidents are products of the author's imagination or are used fictitiously and are not to be construed as real. Any resemblance to actual events, locales, organizations, or persons, living or dead, is entirely coincidental.

NOTE TO READERS

This was the book that started it all.

I have always been a storyteller. I was shy and quiet as a child (I can hear my adult friends laughing hysterically as I write that). It was hard for me to speak up in front of people I didn't know, and even harder to speak up in front of people who knew me. The only way I could get through it was to practice, practice, practice until delivery became automatic, just as a storyteller practices her delivery.

Everyday incidents became stories to tell.

Eventually I outgrew my fear of speaking up and speaking out, although it's still harder for me to speak in front of five people I know than five hundred I don't. But I never outgrew my love of stories and storytelling.

As I got older and life got busy, I relegated the stories that bounced around in my brain to the back burner. I got married, raised kids, built a career and then a business. But the stories wouldn't go away. Sometimes they were just snippets of dialog; sometimes they were full scenes; always, they hinted at characters I wanted to know more about.

Then in a coaching program for entrepreneurs, I met a book coach. A book coach! Who knew there was such a thing? Maybe she could help me take those voices, those characters, those stories and get them out into the world.

And so she did. I started writing *Treasure in the Library* in 2013, with her guidance in the early stages. Then life got in the way, as life frequently does. It took me three years to finish the first draft. And when I did, I promptly shoved it under the bed. It was choppy and disjointed and needed serious revising—and I was too close to it to even start.

Instead I got involved in a group project with ten other writers, and wrote and revised and published my first book in eight months. *On a Whim* came out in October 2016.

I poked around at starting other projects after that one. Researched two, even started plotting one. But this book kept calling me back.

And I'm glad it did. Revising it, rewriting the parts that needed rewriting, editing the parts that needed a lighter touch, were much easier given all that I'd learned since tucking it away.

I'm still very fond of the story. I like writing about smart women who figure out where they belong and discover the one they belong with while they're at it. (And what reader doesn't love looking at pictures of gorgeous old European libraries? And gorgeous young European men?)

So here it is: Emily and Nik's story. There are books and secrets and family drama, and finally love.

Enjoy.

DEDICATION

To my parents, who taught me young the value of a library.

Chapter One:
Nik argues with the King

Nikolas Kuliç was not a happy man.

He should be happy. He had everything a man could want, didn't he? What's not to like about—how did the Yanks say it—"faster horses, younger women, older whiskey, and more money"?

To Nik, "faster horses" meant more horsepower. He frowned into his glass, thinking of the Ferrari 458 Spider currently garaged at his villa near Florence. Too bad he had flown from Italy instead of driven. Muscling that powerful beauty around the twists and turns of Dubrovia's mountain roads was always a pleasure, and a much-needed distraction.

"Younger women"? Well, maybe a little younger. Thoughts of Italy brought up the image of Helena DiSalvo, his current mistress. He might have a year or two on the lovely Helena. She was stunningly beautiful, socially polished, and sexually experienced. He shuddered at the thought of a naive virgin or shrinking violet. No, thanks.

"Older whiskey" was spot on too, Nik thought, as he held his glass so the light shone through the amber liquid. He'd acquired a taste for good Irish whiskey during his Oxford days and still preferred it to the locally produced port as his after-dinner sipping drink. Or his pre-discussion-with-the-king sipping drink. He eyed the crystal decanter over on the sideboard and sighed. Better not top up until after he had spoken with his uncle.

Which brought him to the last phrase: "more money." Who wouldn't want more money? He was proud of his financial accomplishments. Dubrovia's economy had made great strides since he had taken over the governance of their external trade. He also managed the personal finances of the royal family, and now raised his glass in salute to the recent improvements on that front.

But it took money to make money. He had been both clever and persistent to take Dubrovia's slowly growing profits and turn them into real gains. So why now were his plans being thwarted? This week he'd had to make more than one pitch to the king and Council to keep reinvesting the bulk of last year's profits in the largest contributors to their growing economy—the winery and the new spa resort.

He scowled at the dregs of his drink, then tossed it back. *Dammit,* he thought to himself, *we need to keep moving forward, or we'll fall behind. Can't they understand that? I wasn't trained to be king or even crown prince, but I'm damned good at business.*

He pushed himself out of the chair behind his desk and set down the tumbler at the knock on the door. Tomas, master of the royal household, entered and gave him a respectful nod. "The king will be ready for you in a few minutes, Your Highness."

"Thank you, Tomas." Nik shrugged into the jacket held for him by the older man. "Is he still in the breakfast room?"

"No, sir, His Majesty is in his personal sitting room."

Nik grabbed a manila folder from his desk, wincing inwardly as he followed Tomas out of the den and through the main library. Bad enough having to argue his case in Council. He didn't want to fight with his uncle, but this might be the last chance to get his point across—and his funding back.

Oh well. It is what it is. He took the stairs two at a time. *Better to get it over with so I can fly back to Italy, and Helena, and the wine distribution contract negotiations with her father.* Sometimes it was better to cut your losses, and save your strength for the battles you stood a better chance of winning.

He knocked briskly on the door to the king's sitting room.

"Enter, and welcome, Nikolas," said King Filip as Nik crossed to join him in the stuffed chairs by the fireplace. "Pour yourself a glass of port. Or there's some of the Irish you like."

"Good evening, Uncle Filip. Thank you, I'll have the port." Sharing a glass of port had been a tradition among the men in his family for as long as he could remember, and he wanted to strengthen his connection to his uncle. "May I top yours up?"

The king glanced at the door to the queen's chambers and shook his head regretfully. "I think not. Your aunt decreed that one glass of port is quite enough for me of an evening."

He waved Nik into the chair across from him. "Why don't you sit down, Nik, and we can talk about this afternoon's Council meeting?"

"Uncle Filip, I—"

"I did listen, my boy, and I agree with you for the most part. It's the priorities of the investments I wanted to discuss tonight. I am proud of you, Nikolas. You've done remarkable things in the last ten years."

The king looked down at his port and swirled the liquid around in the glass. "Your mother and father, may God bless their memories, would be so proud of what you've accomplished—for Dubrovia, for your family, for yourself. None of us—Council, the queen, and I—imagined how our little country would be thriving financially the way it is today."

Nik sipped his drink and wished it was whiskey instead. "Thank you, Uncle Filip. It means a lot to me to hear you say that. But that's the point I was trying to make in Council. We really need to keep looking forward and investing in our future."

"And you see the winery and the spa resort as our future."

Nik moved abruptly, jostling the glass balanced on his knee. He caught himself before spilling his port. *Didn't I say that all along? How could they still doubt?* "Of course. We make excellent wine, and we offer a fantastic resort in a beautiful location. That's what people want, what they'll pay for."

"Yes, Nik. Commerce is the engine that keeps our little country running. But Niko, if we focus only on commerce, we run the risk of forgetting our culture and losing our heart. That is why," he continued, raising his hand to stop Nik from interrupting, "that is why Council voted to fund the restoration of the royal library."

There wasn't enough port in Nik's glass to cut the taste of his disappointment. "The library? Uncle, why the library? Revitalize the State Orchestra. Put Dubrovia back into the circuit of museums that lend and host traveling art exhibits. Maybe that will bring some tourists, who will stay at our resort and buy our wine. But the library? Who cares about the library?"

"Yes, the library. We have sadly neglected it since before the First World War, and we were not terribly careful with it for several generations before that. We really don't know much about its contents except that they are ours. I assume you read the file? Minister Janko has corresponded with the universities and the governments of Croatia and the Czech Republic, and we realize that restoring the royal library is the first step to bringing our culture back to life."

King Filip leaned forward, his elbows on his knees. "Niko, if we do not guard our culture, our heritage, it will be lost. If we ever do join the European Union, we must be strong and confident in what we represent. Otherwise, we shall be overshadowed by the crowd, and we will lose what we have and who we are."

Nik stood. He had to move, had to pace. He couldn't sit and listen to his uncle, his king, endorse a choice that might result in unwelcome consequences.

He walked to the window and peered into the night. Closing his eyes, he breathed deeply. How to respond without insulting the man who meant so much to him?

When his eyes opened, instead of the gardens outside, he saw his uncle's reflection, rippled and uneven in the old glass. New threads of silver winked at his temple and in his beard. When had King Filip grown old?

Nik turned back to face the room and studied the older man. Filip was still strong, still powerful, but he had definitely aged since his son's death. Was this focus on the past a natural product of that aging? Nik wondered.

"Well, Uncle, I'm disappointed, of course, but I see that I will not be able to change your mind. I wish… Well. No matter. Do you have a plan to proceed, or shall I ask my contacts in Italy and France? I can reach out to my old dean at Oxford, ask if he knows someone."

"Janko assures me he's already found the best person. The final contract isn't in your file? No? Ask Janko to forward it to you. Last week he hired Dr. Emily Charette. You remember her, don't you? She lived with Stefan and Kate in Fredericton? She had some family arrangements to make before traveling, but she arrives tomorrow."

A flash of honey-brown hair, liberally streaked from the sun. A glimpse of blue-gray eyes that gazed soberly at the world. And the memory of one far too young, far too innocent, for the likes of him. Dangerous, dangerous territory.

His uncle was still speaking. "We had thought to hire both the Doctors Charette, Emily and her father Edward. They have done some excellent work in Ireland and Belgium. But Edward is recently retired, and only Emily is available. Apparently she is the one with the expertise in Slavic languages anyway. And hiring only one expert at this point will help keep the first phase's cost down."

"And how high would that cost be, now?"

His uncle named a figure. "That's for the initial assessment, of course. Dr. Charette, Emily, will provide a detailed budget and schedule for the entire scope after this initial phase."

Uh oh. "How long do you expect this whole thing to take? And how much money are we talking about in total?"

"Well, we don't know yet. We provided some preliminary photos and measurements of most of the rooms—except, of course, your office in the den—to give her some idea of the scope. But the whole purpose of this first phase is for her to do an accurate count on which to base the estimates for the remaining work."

Nik studied his half-full glass. "Uncle Filip, are you asking me for my approval? Because I'm still not convinced of the value to Dubrovia, not in comparison to expanding our wine distribution or ramping up the marketing for the spa and resort."

"I know you don't agree, my boy, but I hope that you will come to support the project. Since your office is in the den and the den is in the main library, I ask you to respect their work and their space, as they will respect yours."

"I think I can manage to stay out from underfoot of a little librarian," Nik said wryly. "It's more a matter of—"

He recognized the ringtone as soon as he heard it. He tried to ignore the gradually increasing volume of his cell phone, hoping the caller would hang up and try later, but he had to at least take the phone out of his pocket to silence the persistent thing.

"I'm sorry, Uncle Filip. I forgot to turn this off before we started."

He'd deal with Helena later. She'd likely be in a snit over his refusing her call and would expect a present, preferably something sparkly. He frowned as he pocketed the phone again. *When did I become so well trained?*

"That's fine, Niko. I think we've covered everything. Unless there is something else you wish to discuss?" The king raised his eyebrows at Nik, who shook his head.

"Well then," Filip said, rising from his chair. "I will let you get on with your evening. I'm sure you want to return to Italy and your negotiations. We'll host a small reception and dinner tomorrow night, but you are not required to attend."

He walked with Nik to the door. "You court the DiSalvo family for their wine distribution channels and their contacts in the wine community. Does this"—he gestured to the phone in Nik's hand—"mean that you also court the DiSalvo daughter?"

"No!" exclaimed Nik. *Marry Helena? Where did Uncle Filip get such an idea?* "I enjoy Helena's company, obviously, but do not intend to marry her."

"You must choose a wife someday." His uncle chuckled, clapping Nik on the shoulder. "But your aunt and I would hope that you choose someone you care for. We are not in such dire straits that you must marry for a dowry or a place in European society. So if Helena is not to be the one, perhaps you should start casting your eye elsewhere?"

Nik said good night and walked quickly to the grand staircase, heading for his suite. Marriage? Not now, not yet. He could almost hear the cage door swinging shut.

And certainly not with Helena! Although, now that he thought about it, had she and her mother been dropping hints, making comments? Had he been ignoring important clues?

He slammed into his sitting room, yanked off his tie, and tossed it onto a chair. It felt like a leash, choking him, holding him back.

He stabbed at the buttons on his phone but stopped before completing the call. Whiskey first. *Take a minute, take a breath, take a drink. Then call her back.*

Nik poured himself a generous three fingers and paced around the room. Maybe he was overreacting. Maybe his uncle saw what he wanted to see. Hell, maybe Helena and her mother saw what they wanted to see.

Either way, perhaps it was time to nip this thing in the bud. How to do that, though, without jeopardizing the contract negotiations with Helena's father? That would take some more thought, and more whiskey.

And he would be sorry to lose her as his mistress. He enjoyed her company, most of the time. She was a glittering jewel on his arm at social functions, and she was a truly excellent bed partner, he thought as he swallowed the last of his drink. Perhaps a gift was in order. To smooth things out for now. But not jewelry.

There. He had it sorted in his mind, and reached again for the phone as it rang. Helena, of course.

"Hello, Helena, *cara*. How are you this evening?"

"Nikky. I am wondering why you are there and not here. And I am wondering why you do not take my calls. My father is holding a party on his yacht in a few days. I think you know about this, yes? And we are attending together, yes?"

Oh yeah, she was in a snit. "Calm down, Helena. I will be back in Italy in time to escort you to your father's party. I told him I would be there, and I keep my word."

"Oh yes, the famous 'word' of Nikolas Kuliç. My father values your word very highly, do you know that? I am wondering why I should also. But you do not give me your word, do you?"

"Helena, I just told you that I will return in time. Do you doubt me?" He was careful to speak in English. His Italian was passable, but he wanted no misunderstandings and his English was better than hers.

"Oh, I do not doubt that you will attend," came the petulant reply. "I am wondering how much more you care for my father's contracts than you care for me, if a phone call from your uncle can send you scurrying back home."

Her voice turned sultry, seductive. "Do you not want to be here with me? Remember that lovely negligee you brought me the last time? I am wearing it right now, because I thought of you and how much you liked untying all the little bows and ribbons and taking it off me, as if you were unwrapping the best present..."

"Helena, enough. My uncle is also my king. As crown prince, I do not ignore a summons from my king. I am first and foremost in service to my country. Do not forget that."

"I do not forget!" she snapped. "I am wondering if my father's contracts are more important to you than I am. I—" She stopped and took a breath; he heard how much effort it took for her to change tactics. "I am wondering also if you forget some of the duties of a crown prince. Perhaps I can help you with a few?" she purred.

Nik pinched the bridge of his nose and pressed. Hard. If only he didn't need her father's contracts! "Helena, I will be there late tomorrow. We will talk then."

"Oh, Nikky, you know it is because I miss you so. I want everything to be perfect between us. And how can it be perfect if you are so far away from me?"

"Helena, you—" he started, then stopped to take a deep breath himself. "Helena. Tomorrow. I will arrive tomorrow. Remember my responsibilities here. We will talk more when I am in Italy."

"Oh, yes, Nikky, I will be so glad to see you! And my mother and father will be happy you are coming to their party. I will see you tomorrow, then. Think of me," she whispered, "when you go to bed tonight. I will think of you."

Nik broke the connection and threw the phone on the chair next to his tie. The glass almost followed, but why waste the whiskey?

Wonderful. Now he had to juggle easing back from Helena without pissing off her father and blowing the negotiations. He needed that wine distribution contract!

Hell, maybe popping in and out of Dubrovia to keep an eye on this library project would be a welcome distraction. It would certainly be worth it if he could keep the king and Council from throwing too much money down this particular rabbit hole.

And surely he could avoid one young librarian who triggered memories and an attraction he would rather avoid. Dangerous, dangerous territory.

No, Nik Kuliç was not a happy man.

Chapter Two:
Emily arrives in Dubrovia

The airport was hot (which she expected) and busy (which she didn't).

Emily stood in line to enter the terminal building. She was drooping, swaying-on-her-feet tired after more than twenty-two hours of travel. Finally, finally, she was here.

So this is Dubrovia. She lifted her braid to cool the back of her neck as she gazed around. It was hotter and more humid than she expected. She stepped forward with everyone else, dragging her wheeled carry-on, her messenger bag slung over her shoulder. It was so great to be out in the air for a few minutes, after so long inside airplanes and terminals.

And the air smelled different here. *Green,* her tired mind thought. More than just grass: she could smell trees and flowers and other growing things through the jet fuel and hot pavement smells typical of every airport.

Hitching her bag higher on her shoulder, Emily shuffled forward a few more steps in the long, slow-moving line. As she moved closer to the door and the possibility of air-conditioning, she fished around to find her passport and work visa and a copy of her contract.

The papers looked almost as worn as she felt. Her quick shower and change of clothes in Amsterdam was many hours and many miles ago. Her usually crisp cotton blouse and dress slacks, her favorites for traveling, were limp and creased. Even her shoes felt wrinkled.

She stifled a yawn and rooted around in her bag again for her bottle of water. She uncapped it, took a long swig, and sent out a fervent wish for a place to grab a cup of coffee inside the terminal before she was whisked off to the castle. Coffee would be good. Coffee might revive her enough to keep her coherent for a little while longer.

"I'm not ready for this," she mumbled. She glanced around furtively, hoping everyone else was too caught up in their own personal stuff to hear her talking to herself.

Oh, yay. It didn't look like anyone noticed. Not this time, anyway.

Her father had noticed yesterday morning, when she stopped in to say goodbye on her way to the airport. "You never will be ready till you go do it. You've spent your whole life at a university, Em. It's time to step out into the real world and discover what's out there," he'd told her.

Emily huffed out a breath, getting irritated again remembering. This wasn't her first trip, for Pete's sake, or even her first time living away from home. Granted, it was her first major project. And yes, she thought as she capped and stowed her bottle, she had lived at or around a university for her entire life. She *liked* universities. And libraries. And books.

She welcomed the familiarity of a library and books—preferably a big library with lots of books in all sorts of languages: anything from medieval Latin, to ancient Greek, to formal court French from the pre-Napoleonic days, to local dialects and everything in between.

She remembered with pleasure some of the books and illuminated manuscripts from previous projects in France and Belgium and Ireland. All different, all beautiful, all treasures in their own way. What treasures, she wondered, would she find in the long-neglected royal library of Dubrovia? That would be the fun part. *It's the castle part I'm not so sure about. This particular castle, in this particular country. And the people inside it.*

It felt a little weird, being here like this. Emily had never anticipated doing a project in Dubrovia. As a very young undergrad, she'd lived with the former crown prince and his family for a while when they'd attended university in Canada, almost a dozen years ago.

She had heard when her friends perished in an accident, an avalanche in Switzerland that had buried their car along with so many others traveling the same road. Just as Princess Diana's death made the headlines, so had Stefan's and Kate's. But Emily's own mom had just died of ovarian cancer, and she needed time to deal with her own grief and with her devastated father. She'd had no time to worry about sending condolences. The royal family had pretty much retreated out of the public eye afterward; she rarely read about any of them.

Except for Stefan's cousin Nikolas. She heard plenty about him; he was the only celebrity she made a point to follow. Nikolas, whom she had met briefly a couple of times while she lived with the Kuliç family. Nikolas, who was way too big, way too male, way too intimidating, way too... everything. Nikolas, who was now crown prince.

And won't that be fun, when I run into him again. He's going to be so happy (not) when he finds out that the scrawny, awkward teenager who couldn't look him in the eye back then is camped out on his turf, working on a project with mixed acceptance from the Royal Council, of which he's a vocal member. She closed her eyes with a grimace. *Oh, peachy.*

At last, she grabbed the door handle from the man in front of her and moved through the entrance, holding it for the person behind her. They were inside the terminal building! Now to make her way through customs and immigration, find a bathroom and a cup of coffee, and locate her ride.

Craning her neck as she looked around, she almost ran into the fellow ahead of her, who'd stopped short. "Oh, I'm sorry, pardon me," she said, first in English and again in Czech. She repeated it in the local dialect when still he didn't move.

She peered around him, trying to see what was holding up the line (besides the crowds—who knew there'd be so many tourists visiting this little country?). She could barely peek over the heads in front of her. A very large man holding a very small sign worked his way back through the line, looking for someone.

Looking for her, apparently. His face lit up when he saw her. "Dr. Charette, I am glad to find you! Let me help you with your bags." He grabbed the handle of her wheeled carry-on and eased the messenger bag from her shoulder. "Please, if you would follow? The car is waiting outside."

Emily scrambled to keep up as he pushed his way through the crowd. "Don't I have to clear customs and immigration first? I've got the forms they gave us on the plane, and my work visa—"

"Not to worry, miss," her escort said over his shoulder. "We go over here and they'll clear you right away. No need to go through the lines with the others."

Huh. Well, that's different.

She followed him to a door over at the side and into a small room with a single person who seemed to be waiting just for her. Sure enough, the officer stamped her passport and visa without really looking at them, welcomed her to Dubrovia, and practically shoved her out the door.

Her driver was already loading her carry-on into the trunk of a long black limo. "Wait!" exclaimed Emily. "What about my luggage? I checked a bag back in Edmonton."

She'd no sooner gotten the words out of her mouth when an airport employee approached with her larger suitcase. He handed it off to the first man, gave her a small bow, and retreated into the terminal.

"All taken care of, miss. Now, can this go in the trunk or do you need it with you?" He held up her messenger bag.

"Oh! With me, please. But listen, could I duck back into the terminal for a minute? I'd like to grab a coffee and freshen up before we get going."

"There's water and juice and fresh coffee in the car, miss. And if you follow me, I will show you to a private washroom through that door." He managed to point with his chin as he closed the trunk on her luggage, then led her over and unlocked the door for her.

Suitably refreshed, Emily exited the building once more and got into the open door of the limo. Sure enough, a thermal carafe of coffee waited for her, accompanied by fine china cups emblazoned with the royal seal.

The driver poured her a cup and introduced himself as she added cream. "My name is Havel, and I am pleased to welcome you to Dubrovia. I am one of the drivers at the castle; if you do not choose to drive one of the cars yourself, I will be at your disposal while you are here. Now, if you are ready? It is about a forty-minute drive." He closed Emily's door and got into the front seat.

She gazed outside as he started the big car and pulled away from the curb. Holy smokes, they were even going to get a separate exit lane, especially for them.

Personalized escort through the airport, priority clearance through customs, and now a ride in the fanciest car she'd ever been in, including the stretch limo at a friend's wedding. Dark gray leather seats, plush black carpeting. Fresh flowers in little crystal bud vases on the pillars between the doors.

Emily shook her head. Now this, this was a far cry from catching the bus and the train to the Edmonton airport yesterday (was it only yesterday?) and schlepping through the various airports in between. This was unaccustomed luxury. She hoped she could live up to the expectations implicit in the royal family's treatment of her, sight unseen.

She breathed in the steam from her cup and took a careful sip. It was good, it was strong, and with any luck there was enough in the pot to keep her awake for the forty-minute ride.

Chapter Three:
Emily at the Castle

The castle was perched partway up the hill, a brooding sentinel guarding the river and the small city below.

Emily choked down a snort, then glanced at her driver in the rearview mirror. At least he hadn't seemed to notice. God, could she be any more clichéd, any more pretentious? Good thing she was arriving late on a sunny afternoon. Couple more hours and in full darkness, "It was a dark and stormy night" would be running through her brain.

Her tired, jet-lagged brain. After journeying for so long, all she wanted to do was shower off the travel grime, crawl into a bed, and sleep till tomorrow. Not likely, though, if she remembered correctly.

She pulled her itinerary folder out of her messenger bag and forced her weary eyes to focus. Yes, as she recalled, there was to be a small, informal reception that evening, sort of a "Welcome to Dubrovia, who the heck are you?" event. Letting the papers drop to her lap, Emily leaned her head back on the seat and fought to keep her eyes open. The coffee was wearing off.

The scenery outside the powerful car was a good distraction. She was glad not to be making the drive herself, at least the first time. Being driven gave her the chance to look around, get her bearings.

They were coming up on the capital city of Cerina now. Like many European towns that had been only lightly touched by World War II, it was a mix of well-preserved old and sleek, functional new. More old than new, she mused, and wondered how that mix would be reflected in the people.

Their road kept them out of the center of the town, running along the river and then into the countryside. Emily turned back around to catch a last glimpse of Cerina. From this angle, she couldn't see the newer sections that had sprung up on the edge toward the airport, and the little city probably looked much as it had for a hundred years or more: filled with narrow streets paved with cobblestones, and tall, skinny buildings with intricately carved wooden doors and shutters. There were flowers everywhere; every window had a box, every doorstep had a pot or two, and baskets hung from every telephone pole, the only modern additions Emily could see.

She turned her gaze forward again, leaning a little to catch a glimpse of the castle, which was now playing hide-and-seek through the trees as the limo started up the twisty road. Havel drove them past well-tended fields edged in banks of more flowers. Although they were climbing into the hills, the area was more open than she had expected. The edge of the forest didn't start till they were nearly on top of the turnoff to the castle drive. Emily rolled her window down a couple of inches, enjoying the cooler, fresher air.

On the other side of the road from the gated entry to the castle grounds was a second arching gate, this one with a sign for the winery. The curves and hollows of the rolling landscape prevented Emily from seeing much of the acres of plantings, but she could hear the buzz of bees, the hum of workers' voices, and the occasional clang of equipment. From her research she knew the area was thriving agriculturally, but it was gratifying to see it in person. Too often she had seen communities barely scraping by; for such people, restoring and archiving their cultural heritage took a back seat to survival. The fact that Dubrovia had a growing, thriving wine and tourism industry, coupled with its older mining and agriculture, meant both time and money were available on a national scale to spend on nonessentials. Which was good for Emily as this first phase of the project was likely to last for months.

The car swept up the long drive, giving Emily a few minutes to collect her belongings and her thoughts. Jet lag was certainly doing a number on her concentration. When they rolled to a stop under the porte cochere and she got her first glimpse of her welcoming committee, she had a few seconds of panic when her tired mind couldn't immediately identify the man who stepped to the door of the car to help her out.

"Dr. Charette, it is good to see you again! Welcome to Dubrovia. I trust you had a pleasant journey?" he asked with a smile, shaking her hand and signaling to the driver to collect her bags.

"Yes, thank you, Minister Janko, although a long one." Minister Janko, that was his name. He'd been one of two dignitaries from Dubrovia who had come to Canada looking for someone to work on their library. Looking for her, as it turned out.

"Here, we will bring your things in for you," he said as he led her into the entranceway. "For now, let me welcome you to Castle Cerina and introduce you to Tomas and Marta, master and mistress of the royal household."

An older couple stepped forward to greet her in heavily accented English. Emily replied in the local dialect, "I'm pleased to meet you, Tomas, Marta." Their eyes lit up as she spoke in their native tongue.

Janko continued, in the same language, "Tomas will show you later what automobiles are available, so you can choose one to use while you are here if you would like. But for now, Marta will show you to your rooms." He nodded to the staff. "We know you traveled many hours to get here, and we truly appreciate your making such a journey to help us. We want you to be comfortable during your stay, yes? There is a reception and dinner tonight at eight, but in the meantime I'm sure you will want to freshen up and perhaps sleep a bit. So, I will leave you in Marta's capable hands, and I will see you later this evening."

Emily stared after him in bemusement as he bowed and walked away. She'd been dumped off pretty quickly. While she was quite accustomed to being underestimated and dismissed, it didn't usually happen quite so fast.

Marta stepped in and filled the breach. "Mademoiselle Doctor, will you come this way?" she asked, gesturing for Emily to follow her through the hall. "Minister Janko has asked me to prepare a guest suite for you. I can show you now. Or I can perhaps take you on a small tour of the public part of the castle, if you prefer?"

"A tour would be lovely, thank you, Marta. If I nap now, I might sleep right through the reception and dinner tonight."

As she followed Marta through the main reception hall, Emily craned her neck around, trying to look everywhere at once. The hall was magnificent, an outstanding example of Central European architecture and design. Originally built in the mid-1300s, Castle Cerina was more a fortified manor than a castle and wasn't particularly large, as palaces go: it had some two hundred rooms covering about two hundred thousand square feet on five floors, including a basement.

They did a circuit of the ground floor, which was elegantly finished in panels of carved black walnut and whitewashed plaster, with massive walnut beams above. Everywhere Emily looked there was color: on wall hangings, tapestries, paintings, upholstered furniture in rich, deep reds and blues and greens. And of course in the ever-present flowers.

Marta led her down a hallway that came off to the left of the reception hall. "This is our tapestry gallery, and it leads into the royal library. As you can tell, the library materials encroach into this area. These are the newer works, as those shelves and seating areas were added in the 1940s and 1950s."

Okay, now she was curious. She was hired to assess and possibly restore a library. But if so much work was done sixty, seventy years ago, what could they need now?

And then Marta threw open the doors of the main library, and Emily knew.

THIS was more like it.

Oh, it was still a beautifully appointed room. Pillars of carved walnut separated the banks of shelves, and there were lovely multipaned windows across from the door, and an enormous fireplace with a heavy stone mantel on the wall to her left. A spiral staircase, with detailed sides and open treads, took up one corner farther to her left and led to the second level.

She saw tables and shelves piled haphazardly with loose books and scrolls. The room didn't smell overwhelmingly musty or mildewed, thank heavens, but neither did it smell of the pleasant beeswax and lemon polish of the tapestry gallery. It smelled of books, and age. *This* was what she had come here to rescue.

Marta walked over to a doorway to their right. "The den is used by Prince Nikolas when he is in residence," she said, touching the door without opening it. "I cannot show you without speaking to him first, you understand."

"Is it part of the library, then, or just his personal office? I mean, are there books in the den that would be included in the general catalog, do you know?"

"I'm sure of it," said the older woman as she led the way to the spiral staircase in the opposite corner. "There are many shelves, but most are behind locked screens, and only Prince Nikolas and his staff have the keys. My girls do not clean in there unless supervised. You must speak to him about access."

They made their way up the spiral stairs and through a series of stacks. It was like winding through a maze of books, Emily thought; far more interesting than a boxwood maze in a garden! The upper gallery ran all the way around the room, including over the tall windows of the lower floor. Emily mentally doubled the rough estimate of books—and the time needed to count and index and catalog them—that she had made based on the early photographs Minister Janko had shown her in Edmonton.

They passed through an open doorway and entered yet another room. Marta pulled open the heavy curtains on one of the tall windows. "The upper reading room is directly above the den and is accessible only from the second level. No one uses it much. I understand from Minister Janko that it will be made available to you as a place to work while you are here."

Emily turned in place, getting her bearings in the large space, her space. "It's a beautiful library. I can see why your king and Council want to restore it."

Marta led her back the way they had come, eventually leaving the main library and walking through the tapestry gallery. "Yes, I'm sure you will be told all about that tonight.

For now, I will take you up to your suite. Your belongings should have arrived."

Back in the reception hall, they started up the grand staircase. "The king and queen's royal residence is on the second floor," Marta explained as they continued up to the third floor. "There are more family suites and some guest suites on this floor, including yours."

They came out of the staircase into an open area that looked more like a comfy living room than something Emily expected to find in a castle. "Princess Rose's wing is down that hall, and—"

"Princess Rose?" Emily stopped in her tracks and turned to Marta, stunned. "I thought she had died in the accident with her parents."

"No, poor child. She was badly injured, so much so that she is now in a wheelchair and keeps mainly to the castle these days. The king and queen had an elevator installed for her down at the other end of her wing, by the schoolroom."

Rose was alive! How could Emily not have known that Rose had survived?

Marta continued, "Crown Prince Nikolas's wing is just down that way. And these are your rooms." She opened the door. "Sitting room, bedroom, and bath through that door. And here is Anja, who I believe has just finished unpacking for you. She will be taking care of you while you are here, so if you need anything, use the house phone to reach her. Or me or Tomas.

"Now, the reception tonight is at eight in the salon, followed by dinner at nine in the breakfast room. It will be a small gathering this evening: King Filip and Queen Elspeth, Ministers Janko and Bartak, whom you met in Canada, their wives Adriena and Margo, Minister Rikard Asanovic, and Princess Rose. Will you need Anja to run your bath now, or to come back and bring you down at eight?"

Her head was still spinning with the news about Rose. But even confused and jet-lagged, Emily knew she didn't need anyone to run her a bath! Having a servant at her beck and call felt weird. "No, thanks, Anja, is it? I'll be fine from here. Thank you for taking care of my things. And thank you, Marta, for the tour. I'll see you later, then?"

"Yes, Dr. Charette, Tomas and I serve at all receptions and dinners here." She shepherded the younger Anja out ahead of her. "Again, welcome to Dubrovia and to Castle Cerina."

Chapter Four:
Rose waits and watches

"C'mon, c'mon, c'mon…"

Her mutterings sounding like a prayer, Rose cautiously fed power to her wheelchair, reversing at an angle. If she was careful, she'd be able to extricate the front wheel from where it was jammed between the rails at the side of the short ramp. And if she was very careful indeed, she'd manage to do so quietly enough that no one would realize she wasn't in her room studying.

It's not as if she couldn't scoot around the castle on her own. It's just that she was so tired of everyone making such a fuss. She wasn't running away from home, for Pete's sake—although the thought occasionally crossed her mind. She just wanted to be able to go places by herself sometimes. If she said something to Jacquie, her physiotherapist would have insisted on accompanying her "just in case." And Lidia, her caregiver, would simply have wheeled her wherever.

She was so tired of being babied! So of course, what does she do but get the stupid wheel on her stupid wheelchair stuck in the stupid railing on the stupid ramp. "What a great way to prove I can do this myself," Rose mumbled in disgust as she wiggled in her chair, hoping to bounce herself free. She would *not* call for help. She'd rather sit here all night and wait for someone to find her in the morning.

Rose eyed the slope of the ramp and the angle of her chair. Maybe she could get herself out of the chair and down to the ramp and free the wheel that way?

No, that won't work either. While she could probably ease her way down to the floor herself, she knew perfectly well that she wouldn't be able to get back up. Not without help. Which she didn't want to ask for.

Okay, now she was really starting to get mad. Mad at not being more careful on the ramp. Mad for not realizing the wheel was the perfect size to get stuck if she slid into the railing just right. But mostly mad at the entire situation.

It wasn't FAIR that she was stuck in this stupid chair, she thought, banging a fist down on the arm of the chair. Not FAIR that everyone treated her like a baby because she couldn't walk. Not FAIR that her mom and dad died in that snowslide.

Rose stilled her movements with a gasp and squeezed her eyes tight. *No, no, no. Don't think about them now. It won't help.*

She clenched her hands hard in her lap, trying to still their trembling. If her hands were shaking, she'd never be able to make the joystick move the tiniest bit needed to get herself loose.

Her breathing under control again, she opened her eyes and gently, *gently*, wiggled the stick from side to side. She let out a sigh of relief as the wheel finally popped free, then straightened herself and her chair and continued down the ramp and into the observation room. From here she could see out the front of the castle and watch for the limo to come back up the long drive.

She heard footsteps in the hallway as she eased through the narrow opening and closed the door behind her. *One thing about stone floors and high ceilings, they sure give you plenty of warning of someone coming.* No way anyone could sneak up on her. She, on the other hand, could do plenty of sneaking in her electric wheelchair.

Unless she got stuck on a stupid ramp again, she admitted, wrinkling her nose. And the elevator was a telltale giveaway, when she went from floor to floor, since most everyone used the stairs except her and her grandparents. Or the staff when they carried something.

Rose rolled over to one of the big bay windows. This part would be tricky. She couldn't get close to the glass in her chair; she'd have to climb out and perch on the built-in window seat. She carefully set her brakes (then checked them again) before easing her way over onto the padded surface.

But from here, she could see. She eased back the heavy velvet curtains, sneezing at the dust loosened by the movement. *Sheesh, when was the last time anyone opened the drapes in here?*

Probably not since the last time she and her parents looked at the stars together. Rose missed them a lot, and stupid little things, like moving the drapes and dislodging a ton of dust, triggered the memories.

"Look up, Rosie. See those stars? That's the Little Dipper. And the bright star at the end of the handle? That's the North Star. It's the same North Star that Nanny and Granddad can see from Ottawa. So when you look up, and they look up, you're connected. The same starlight touches you both."

After her parents died, and she was so badly hurt, she sometimes begged her nurses to move her bed over to the window at night. Somehow, seeing the stars, watching the moon run through its cycle, made her feel like a part of her parents remained with her. Just as six-year-old Rose could connect to her grandparents, sixteen-year-old Rose could feel closer to her mom and dad.

Too bad Uncle Nik went back to Italy last night. We could have looked at the moon tonight. It was close to full and so bright they wouldn't see many stars when it was up, but it was pretty.

She grinned as she remembered the conversation she'd overheard last night. Okay, she'd *eavesdropped*. But it was fun to listen to Uncle Nik; he knew the best curse words! Why, at this rate, she'd be able to swear in four languages! Not that she would, of course—not out loud, anyway. But sometimes she got so FRUSTRATED by everything. Spicing up her vocabulary, even if she never said the words out loud, sometimes helped cheer her out of a bad mood.

Being in a wheelchair sucked. Losing her parents two years ago sucked. Being stuck in this castle for the rest of her life would REALLY suck. So she listened, and learned, and hoped she might overhear something to use as leverage to get herself out of here.

She didn't learn much last night, though. Her uncle slammed back into his suite after a conversation with her grandfather, the king. She'd heard him because she'd been fetching her iPod from the upper reading room of the library, and his rooms were right above, and his fireplace flue just happened to connect to the one in the reading room... Anyway, he hadn't been happy when Helena called him. In fact, he was downright grumpy. *Hurray! Maybe he'll dump her. Helena's a really nasty person. I don't know why he lets her stick around.*

Well, she did know, actually. Even though NO ONE EVER TOLD HER ANYTHING, she'd managed to learn that Uncle Nik was trying to get some contracts or something with Helena's father. So maybe that was enough reason to not dump the nasty witch.

Rose surely hoped not. She hoped he figured out how to get his contracts without having to marry Helena. That would be the most awful thing ever.

She'd listened to the end of his phone call, but he never told Helena why he came to Dubrovia, only that he was going back to Italy. Rose knew of the plan to restore the library—it was no secret, when the maids had spent the last few days getting one of the guest suites ready.

She even knew who was coming, and wasn't that a surprise? The last time she'd seen Emily Charette was back in Canada. Emily had lived with her and her mom and dad for a few years when Rose was little. The Mountie teddy bear Emily had given her for her third birthday still sat on her bed.

And now she's a grown-up. And she's coming here to restore the library. Today. Any minute now, in fact. Will she remember me?

She reached over and pulled the blanket from her chair. Better cover up her legs and prop up her back, so she didn't get too stiff to climb back over. She leaned against the glass and settled in to wait.

Chapter Five:
Welcome dinner

Emily found her concentration slipping as dinner segued into dessert. Paying attention to multiple conversations in multiple languages was always tiring. Coming at the end of almost twenty-four hours of travel, as was the case tonight, it was exhausting.

Minister Janko was speaking about the library project again. She quite liked the minister and his wife, Adriena, seated across from her. They reminded her of Santa and Mrs. Claus. Emily half expected little elves to pop out from under the table.

Whoa. No more wine for a while! She reached for her coffee cup and took a grateful sip. The hot punch of caffeine might be enough to keep her on her toes and speaking coherently. She hoped. Almost as much as she hoped the evening would end soon and she could get some sleep.

"We have no idea what all our library contains," Janko said, repeating what he had told Emily back in Canada when they had interviewed her at the university. "Over the years, we preserved it as best we could. But no one has sorted and cataloged it all since before the turn of the last century." He shrugged in rueful apology. "Our kings must focus on keeping Dubrovia free and independent. It is difficult, being a small country next to more powerful neighbors. It is only in the last ten years or so that our agriculture recovered to grow more than we use ourselves."

Another voice broke in from farther down the table. "Yes, and the reason those ten years were so fruitful is because we kept our focus on important things, like agriculture. And our tourism and the winery. That's why I support Prince Nikolas's expansion proposal and not this waste of time and money. In his absence, I feel I must speak for him and for those of us who support him and all his work to keep our economy afloat."

Emily turned in her seat. The disapproval in the man's gaze sent a ribbon of cold down her spine and made her cheeks flush. What was his problem? Rikard Asanovic, the youngest of the councillors here this evening, had had it in for her from the moment they were introduced. It was weird, she thought, for the older faction to support her more than the younger. Sometimes she ran into this sort of dislike and disapproval from the older men who took issue with her gender and age. The younger ones most often ignored her, but this was the first time one had actively worked against a project of hers.

Was it because it was *her* project, and not *their* project? The subtle difference was one reason why she missed her father so much. On their joint ventures, once she'd moved from assistant to partner, his presence created a buffer for her: he took care of the social obligations and the political maneuvering, and she took care of the books and cultural artifacts. But she was on her own here, and would be from now on.

Best not take the bait. Emily turned back to Minister Janko and smiled. "I live in Canada, remember?" she replied, forking up another bite of dessert. "We know all about being the mouse next to the sleeping elephant, but we have never been in pure survival mode, as you have." She saluted him and the king with her fork and popped in the mouthful of a most excellent strudel.

"Being in survival mode, as you said, for so long caused us to perhaps not value our heritage as much as we should," said King Filip. He raised his eyebrows at the younger Asanovic. "Trade and agriculture are essential, of course. But we should not lose sight of the bigger picture, the legacy we want to leave to our children and our children's children. Crown Prince Nikolas is well aware of our feelings in this matter."

Emily didn't want to make an enemy, but she did want to make a point.

"Your library may not be organized, Your Majesty, but it was well cared for. Believe me, I've worked in places where the first thing we had to do was fix a leaky roof or chase out the mice. Yours is in good physical condition, and we'll work to make it a national treasure again."

Asanovic snorted as he set down his wineglass. "That's all well and good for you to say. We're paying you a pretty penny to sort through some old books. What is the point? How is that going to help Dubrovia?" He turned from Emily to the king, dismissing her again. "I still think that we should be investing in the winery and expanding our distribution into North America instead of pouring money into the library! Prince Nikolas—"

"His Highness Prince Nikolas is not here," reprimanded the king. "His business ventures keep him away as often as not," he explained to Emily. "But he agreed to this project, even if he does not necessarily see the point of 'chasing down our history,' as he puts it. He is much more interested in chasing down our future."

"Your library could well hold a window into your future as well as one to your past, Your Majesty. That's one of the amazing things about private and royal libraries. They reflect the tastes and interests of their owners, and they end up being repositories for all sorts of things over the years. I never know," she enthused, "what I'll find when I start digging. It might even be something that benefits your winery. There are questions and concerns among some EU countries about Czech and Croatian wine varietals and the wines themselves. For example, Croatia must change the name of its prosek if it wants to export it into the EU, because Italy complained that the name is too close to their prosecco although the wines are nothing alike.

"I don't know your wines that well, although we've had some lovely ones tonight," Emily said as she picked up her wineglass again and raised it in salute. There may be Dubrovian wines that will encounter similar problems when you join the EU and come under their scrutiny as you expand your exports. But sometimes, in these sort of cases, age and precedence win. Wouldn't you like to find documentation proving the lineage of your grape varietals and the wines themselves? I'll bet it's in there somewhere."

She gestured again with her glass. "That gives your wine industry one solid reason to want to support restoring and cataloging your library. And other items I might find— documents, artifacts, art objects—will likely be of interest to historians and linguists and sociologists. You may find yourselves overwhelmed with requests from scholars all over the world, including North America"—she nodded to the young councillor as she put down her glass again—"who will pay dearly to study here."

"Oh, come on. You really think that old books and dusty junk are going to bring more people, more money, than wine and a luxury spa? I don't know who you spend time with, although I can guess," Asanovic said with a smirk. "But I can guarantee that the rich and famous, the powerhouses of society, aren't going to come here to wander through the bookshelves."

"You never know," she countered. "Cultural exchange between the newer EU members is becoming a big business these days. In Canada and the US, folks whose families immigrated generations ago are trying to trace their heritage back to their roots. Why do you think those river cruises are so popular? And bus trips into the mountains of southeastern Europe, and through the old Soviet states? Dubrovia is a little jewel, tucked away here. Yes, you have worked hard to build your economy's solid footing. But it *is* stable now, which is more than some of your neighbors can say. And there's more to Dubrovia than a winery and a spa, as profitable as those are."

Emily looked around the table. "My father and I worked in some lovely little libraries over the last four or five years. Every single one is now a profit center. It can take a couple of years to become profitable, but it does happen. We went through a château in Bordeaux that had been terribly neglected for years. Remember I said we had to fix a roof? The place had been badly damaged in World War II. One whole wing was gone, and the others were falling down. We couldn't restore that library in place; we had to move everything out while the roof was fixed and do the cataloging in the old cow barns because they were in better shape than the château. But we found some amazing artwork: paintings and illuminated manuscripts, first-edition books, even some glass pieces that had survived the bombings. Once the château was restored and everything put back in place, the owners were able to list with the French government as one of the highlights of an art tour that now runs every spring and fall."

The king and queen looked intrigued. Asanovic just looked annoyed. "We can't tap into resources at that scale to back us up and bail us out. Every penny we sink into the library is money we could better spend elsewhere. And Bordeaux wine is more important to France than Bordeaux art tours!"

Emily knew it was only the presence of the royals that kept Asanovic's disagreement civil. She despised the current trend toward belittling culture and education. To her it was a short-sighted and potentially dangerous position. Asanovic was no scholar, nor did she expect him to be. But she had hoped he would at least take pride in his own culture and heritage. The fact that he was an avid supporter of the absent Nikolas didn't give her a warm and fuzzy feeling about the reception she would receive from the crown prince whenever he next decided to visit.

Facing off against one of them at a time was unpleasant. Dealing with them both together would likely be brutal. Especially the Nik half of the "Rik and Nik show," as she had started to think of them.

Ever since Dean Smithton, her boss at the university, had approached her about this project, she had kept a firm lock on the archive in her mind where she stuffed unpleasant or uncomfortable memories. Once in a while, though, a strong thought would pop out and clamor for attention.

She had met Nikolas Kuliç only a few times when he'd visited his cousin Stefan, then the crown prince, in Canada. She remembered him vividly: he'd been a devil-may-care twenty-one-year-old student from Oxford, even then a world traveler with an eye for pretty women. Emily wasn't sure she had managed to say more than a handful of words to him then. With any luck she had been so unremarkable that he wouldn't remember her or connect this Dr. Emily Charette to the shy and awkward fifteen-year-old who babysat his cousin's daughter. Ruthlessly she stuffed the memories away again, hoping they would stay buried indefinitely, and rejoined the conversation.

"We would like to expand our university," King Filip was saying when she tuned back in. "Mostly our young people go abroad to further their education. What we teach here is the basics: engineering, education, health care, agriculture, business. We've focused on aiding our country and our people to function in the world. If scholars become interested in us for what we find in our library, then the world will become more interested in Dubrovia."

"Which gives us a stronger footing in the EU," continued Janko. "And the stronger we are in our culture, the better our bargaining position for getting our wines and other exports accepted and protected."

"We can also keep more of our young people here if our university offers more programs and more advanced degrees," added Queen Elspeth. "It is disheartening when your children study elsewhere and choose not to return. We were fortunate in Stefan because not only did he return, he also brought back a wife and daughter. And while Nikolas spends a great deal of time outside Dubrovia for now, he will return for good someday. But how many families scraped and saved to send their sons and daughters off for a better education than we can offer here, only to lose them to foreign opportunities afterward? And then we do not retain enough highly educated, highly skilled people of our own to do the work we need done here."

She's sad, thought Emily. Grief recognized grief over dessert and coffee. The queen obviously missed her son and daughter-in-law just as Emily missed her mother. And she refused to think about her father, how his slow, steady decline was almost harder to bear than her mother's brief fight against the cancer that killed her.

The entire table rose as the king and queen did.

"Ladies, gentlemen, we thank you for your attendance this evening as we welcome Dr. Charette to Dubrovia and to Castle Cerina. We are certain," King Filip said, "that you will all afford her whatever assistance she requires in her work." His gaze swept the table and then lingered on Asanovic. "Ministers, we shall continue this discussion in Council in the morning."

Chapter Six:
Emily and the Queen

Emily winced inwardly as she stepped away from the table with the others. As she said her good nights, part of her mind was going over the conversation, especially her exchanges with Rikard Asanovic. His departing nod was as curt and unfriendly as his greeting at the reception a couple of hours ago. Oh well. With any luck he would dismiss the whole evening as of little or no consequence and not go running to Prince Nikolas with stories of the crazy library lady wanting to turn the Dubrovia economy on its ear.

She turned to the king and queen to make her own farewells for the evening.

"Dr. Charette? A word, if you please, before you retire," said Queen Elspeth as the other guests made their way out of the room. "We can adjourn to the music room. Marta will bring tea."

"Of course, Your Majesty."

Emily followed the queen into the music room and took a seat in front of the unlit fireplace as Marta wheeled in a serving cart with a lovely old tea set. Emily was no expert on fine china, but she was willing to bet she was going to be sipping from an antique teacup that was likely older than Canada and worth more than her car.

"Thank you, Marta, that will be all. I'll pour, shall I?" said the older woman as she deftly handled the teapot. "I wanted to speak with you and get to know you a little better." She handed Emily a cup and saucer. "Stefan and Kate spoke highly of you all those years ago when you lived with them. I was glad my son was able to make friends during his stay in your country."

"Well, since he married a Canadian, I'd say he made friends pretty easily!"

"Oh, my dear, you don't know how pleased we were when he told us he had met the girl of his dreams and wanted to marry! Stefan had always been so quiet, so shy, so immersed in his books, not at all like his younger cousin Nikolas. It was never as easy for Stefan: he was so studious, so serious. Kate was quite the breath of fresh air that he needed. And Rose! Well, Rose is our joy."

"You must miss them very much."

"Every day. And for Rose, to lose her mother so young. It is a hard thing, to grow up without a mother."

"I was twenty-seven when my mother died." Emily had to swallow hard to continue. Thinking about her mom still choked her up every time. "I don't think it gets any easier as you get older."

"It is a hard thing for a mother to lose a child—children," replied Elspeth. "And it is a hard thing for a country to lose a crown prince, for a king to lose his heir."

"Prince Nikolas is the heir to the throne now?"

"Yes, he is. He was named so after the accident when Rose was so badly injured. And he will be a strong king for Dubrovia, I think, when he decides to settle down and spend his time here. But this library project, as you heard at table, is not where his interests lie."

She sighed. "It would have been close to Stefan's heart, closer than it is to Filip's. Stefan would have made a fine, quiet king. Dubrovia would have grown slowly and steadily under his influence. He never had the interest in charming the rest of Europe that Nikolas does."

"So restoring the library is kind of a memorial to Stefan and Kate?"

"Partly, I suppose. But mostly we do it for Rose." The queen picked up the teapot, raising her eyebrows at Emily to ask if she wanted more. When Emily shook her head, she poured into her own cup and set the pot back down on the trivet. "Rose's disability will make it hard for her to attend university away from home. Not impossible—nothing is impossible—but difficult nonetheless. If we can start expanding and improving our university here, she can stay home."

"Would Her Highness not want to follow in her father's footsteps and attend university somewhere else? If not in Canada, perhaps someplace in Europe?"

"She may, but we are hoping not. She has not yet expressed interest in a particular school. We'll support her in whatever path she ultimately chooses, of course, but it would be lovely for us if we could keep our granddaughter closer to home. And even disregarding her disability, she is the heir to the heir. Until Nikolas changes his ways and takes more of a hands-on role here, it would not be wise for them both to be out of the country for extended periods, you see."

Emily did see. Well, sort of. She understood the queen's concern about keeping safe the succession, and about protecting her granddaughter. But the line between protecting and smothering was a fine one, and trying to keep a teenager bottled up in the castle would likely be an exercise in futility. She thought about her father, and how he had pushed her out of the proverbial nest when he talked her into taking this project. How different her life was from Rose's!

As different as a scholar's and a princess's could be, she supposed. Emily would prefer to stay in her libraries, safe among her books, if she could, rather than travel and work on projects far away from home. But royalty stayed home to rule. Except for Nik, who hadn't "settled down" to his responsibilities yet. *And that is none of my business. So what's the point here? What does the queen want from me?*

She didn't wonder for long. "I know my husband, the king, had originally intended to hire your father, the other Dr. Charette. For me, I was pleased to learn it would be you and you alone who would be coming to Dubrovia."

"Thank you, I'm sure, Your Majesty. Might I ask why?"

"Because of Rose. She and her mother were so close. Now that Kate is gone, I worry Rose does not confide in anyone," came the sad reply. "I miss Kate and Stefan every day—for myself, but even more for Rose. The girl isn't likely to come to her old grandmother for a heart-to-heart talk about schools or boys or the future, now, is she?

"My hope is that your work in the library, and our dream to expand the university here, will help convince Rose we can bring part of the world here to her. I see her becoming restless, discontent. Oh, she rarely complains, but there's something... unsettled about her heart and spirit. This is her home, and we want her to be happy here."

Oh well, no pressure. Just restore the library and kick-start the university. And make friends with a sixteen-year-old girl who may or may not remember you from more than ten years ago. All on your own, with Dad failing and becoming more fragile by the day back home. Piece of cake.

Nervous didn't come close to covering the way she felt. Lonely; missing her dad and the familiar environment of her university home; afraid of falling short of everyone's expectations on this, her first solo project; apprehensive about meeting up with pieces of her past, some of which were better left there—those were the feelings swirling around inside of her.

Her cup rattled in its saucer as she carefully placed it back on the table. She didn't care that she'd been training for such an opportunity for years; she wasn't ready for this! But she wouldn't let her father down.

"I'm looking forward to meeting Her Highness again. It's been such a long time. Do you know, she's older now than I was when I first met her and her parents?"

"Yes, it is unfortunate she was not able to attend this evening," answered Elspeth. "We hope that having you here, showing her what a young woman can achieve, will inspire her to follow a scholarly pursuit."

Emily caught the return of the royal *we. Nope, no pressure at all.* "I don't know if I can be anyone's inspiration, but I am of course willing to speak to her about university or careers or anything else she may want to ask me."

"Good. Rose needs a friend, and we want her to learn more about her country's culture. She likes her books, and she spends time in the library, so perhaps she will be the one to take responsibility for it in the long run. It is an appropriate project for a princess, after all, and it needs a royal champion."

"Will Princess Rose be involved in the restoration?" In other words, would Emily be dealing with one more royal who didn't want her in there?

"We have not raised that possibility with her. She knows, of course, there will be work done, and by whom. But we felt it would be better if the two of you found your own way to work together. Just as we expect you and Prince Nikolas to find your common ground, so to speak. You understand he uses the den within the main library as his office, do you not? While he is not here at the moment, he will be in residence off and on over the next few months. There may be times when he will ask you to confine your work on a given day to the upper stacks, if he needs the larger space. Rose can help you there as well, as she and her uncle are quite close."

Oh, boy. Just what she needed. She could only hope Rose's reaction was a mite friendlier than Councillor Asanovic's. If everyone Emily worked with or around every day was against the restoration work, her time in Dubrovia was going to be rather unpleasant.

What was protocol here, for exiting what had turned into an informal chat? she wondered. Should she wait to be dismissed, or take her leave and bid the queen good night?

"Your Majesty—"

"We do not stand on ceremony when in private conversations here; we are not so formal as all that. I'm sure you have had a very long day and would like to find your bed." Elspeth set down her own cup and rose gracefully, drawing Emily up as she did. "I am glad you are here, my dear. And if sometimes you can spare a few minutes to share memories of your time with my son and daughter-in-law, I would be grateful. For now"—she squeezed Emily's hands—"I bid you good night."

Emily walked back to her rooms, deep in thought. She was eager to get started in the morning, but a little worried about how and when Rose would appear. How was she supposed to make friends with a girl who may not want her there, and who may not even remember her? She had fond memories of Rose as a child, but the last thing a teenager wanted to hear was tales of her childhood.

And Nik… well, Emily would rather not think about Nik at all.

Chapter Seven:
Rose watches Emily

It's been such a long time. Will she remember me? She looks a lot different than before. She looks like a grown-up! Kind of reminds me of Mom, her clothes and stuff. I don't remember her like that. I remember her more, well, like me. Except not in a wheelchair. And blonder.

Rose ducked her head to look through the spindles of the railing rather than over the top, and rested her chin on her hand with a sigh. So far, it didn't seem like much happened, just moving some papers and stuff around, although her grandparents were sure excited about the whole project. Rose rolled her eyes. Of course they were. Not much ever happened in Dubrovia. Anything or anyone new grabbed everyone's attention.

She felt unsure about someone mucking around in her library. She could spend hours in the upper reading room and be quite happy all by herself with her books and her music. And Papa and Nana said that restoring the university followed restoring the library. That was both good and bad, she thought as she maneuvered herself to a better spot to watch from. Good because maybe if new professors came, younger ones who didn't mind talking to girls who weren't quite old enough to attend yet, maybe she could find someone else interested in astronomy and physics. Bad because she really, really, REALLY wanted to go somewhere else for her degree.

Maybe she'd go to Vienna, or Oxford. Some of the astronomy books she snitched from the library and brought to her room were published by Oxford researchers.

Uh oh. Books from the library. She had a pile in her room at the moment. Maybe she should bring them back before anyone missed them. She always put them back exactly where she got them from, but as she watched Emily in her white gloves carefully moving piles of books and manuscripts, Rose realized that she didn't take as good care of them as she ought to.

She eased back from the railing and headed toward the corridor. *Since Emily is so busy downstairs, now would be as good a time as any to bring back the books I have from up here. And I can do the ones that belong in the main library tonight while the grown-ups are having dinner.*

"No one ever misses me at those dinners anyway," she said under her breath as she sorted through the books in her room. She felt a little guilty about having piled the books any which way on her desk and shelves. As she turned back to the door, balancing the ones she wanted to return right now on her lap, her freshly made bed caught her eye. Well, not the bed so much as the old teddy bear nestled into the pillows.

The bear was old and worn, a beloved childhood toy that had seen much use and abuse over the years. Its Red Serge jacket was soft and faded, the rim of the brown Stetson was crumpled in places where little hands had grabbed and held, and one brown leather boot was missing a heel. One arm had been restuffed and sewn back on years ago, and the other was about due for the same treatment.

She picked him up from his place of honor and cradled him in her arms. Emily had given her the Mountie bear the first Christmas she lived with them, when Rose was not quite three. Bear had been her constant companion, traveling everywhere she went. Even as she got older, he sat on her bed during the day and on her bedside table at night.

When Rose's mom and dad brought her back to Dubrovia, Emily told her that Bear would always remind her of Canada. Just like the stars connected her to her Canadian grandparents, that stuffed Mountie bear would connect her to her Canadian big sister.

Many nights after the accident, she cried herself to sleep holding Bear. When she was all alone at night, when she hurt so much she couldn't sleep, somehow hanging on to him helped. And when she came back to her room after a painful physio session, she turned to him for comfort.

She didn't hesitate. She would bring him to the library to show Emily as a way to revive that link, that connection. She tucked him down beside her and steered her chair back to the library's upper level.

But first, the books had to go back where they belonged. "Sorry, sorry," she apologized as she inserted them into their homes on the shelves. "I promise I'll be more careful with you next time."

She held the last volume in her hands and stroked the embossed brown leather of its cover. She loved books, she did: the smell of them, the feel of them, and most of all how they could take her to new places and show her new things. The stars she watched with her parents seemed closer when she read about famous astronomers and their discoveries. How she would love to visit a real observatory someday! Her dad's binoculars gave her a taste of the night skies, but she wanted to go deeper.

The book she held was one of her favorites, a history of European astronomers. Some of the most famous ones had lived and worked near Dubrovia. Johannes Kepler commissioned a Czech astronomer and optician for the lenses in his famous telescope. Who's to say they hadn't stopped in Dubrovia on their travels around Europe? Castle Cerina contained an observation room, although it wasn't used for much anymore except looking down over the valley and the city below. A lot of castles probably had a way to observe the stars, though, even if just from the battlements or towers. Astronomers needed high places, and lots of times castles were built up high. And Rose knew that scientists back then relied on private and royal patronage to fund their studies.

Kind of like Dr. Charette, she mused as she tucked the book onto the shelf and left the gallery. *She's here because Papa and Nana are funding her work. Wonder how she gets paid when she isn't someplace like this? It must be great to be able to travel like that.* Rose daydreamed all the way to the main library about the many places she wanted to see.

As she approached the threshold from the tapestry gallery into the main library, she heard a slither-thump-clang-clatter from the far end by the spiral stairs to the upper stacks. She grinned at the muttered curse. It sounded as though Emily had dislodged a precariously balanced pile of papers and other debris from one of the long tables pushed right up to the stacks.

Rose hurried into the library and came to an abrupt halt. The tableau at the far end of the room was not what she'd expected to see: Emily, for sure, sitting almost underneath a table and rubbing her head, but also two unexpected visitors.

What's Uncle Nik doing home? And why, oh why, did he have to bring Helena with him?

Chapter Eight:
First encounter: Emily

The morning sun left pools of warmth on the flagstone floor as Emily settled into her daily routine. After a few days, she knew that the first level's assessment wouldn't be a quick study. This library was a mess.

Oh, not so much physically. There was no fire or water damage like she and her father had encountered in France a couple of years ago, when they'd waded through piles of disintegrating paper and leather for days as they raced to salvage as much as possible before it all rotted down into a soggy mass. This building, this room, hadn't sustained damage like that.

But neither had it been treated like a library. It fell somewhere between an art gallery and a dragon's lair of treasure gathered over centuries. The woodwork was polished to a high gloss. No dust bunnies hid in the corners. Emily grinned. Dust bunnies weren't permitted in Marta's tidy universe.

She lifted the top book from the stack on the table and sneezed. Emily knew she needed all of the first week of this term of her contract to sort and sift through the loose stuff scattered on the tables on the main floor. She didn't harbor any illusions about getting deep into the stacks this time around, but only a rough count would be possible. She sighed. Unless she drafted some help, she faced a much longer contract term than she'd anticipated.

One more pile sorted, one more table done. It was amazing how mixed up and confused this place had gotten. If a logical order or a written catalog ever existed, Emily had yet to see evidence of it. She found tax assessments and land deeds from the late 1800s mixed haphazardly with first-edition theological writings from the fifteenth-century Czech philosopher Jan Hus and a hand-copied treatise of American statesman Samuel Johnson's 1752 *Elementa Philosophica*. And all that sat on top of a stack of British newspapers from the 1950s.

Even more amazing was the excellent physical condition of material handled many times over the years by many people who didn't understand its value. Well, that wasn't quite true, she thought. Value was relative, after all, and a kingdom focused on survival would tend to mine their library for whatever help it could provide in a crisis. And that sort of physical data mining could wreak havoc on an orderly collection of books and papers.

Emily stood and stretched, removing her dusty gloves and stuffing them into her messenger bag. Time to finish up these tables and move on to the stacks. One more set to tackle, but these would be the worst. She eyed the pair of long wooden tables pushed into the corner beyond the stairs, then pulled on another set of gloves and went to the other end of the room to grab a cart. She intended to unload the mess from the tables to the cart; so much stuff obscured the surface, there was no room to do the usual shuffle from one pile to another.

The cart had a sticky wheel and took a bit of effort to muscle around. She nudged the back wheel with her toe to get it rolling again. *Good thing the floor is marble. I can slide it if it gets stuck.*

It was like steering a wobbly shopping cart in a grocery store. The thing had a mind of its own and refused to travel in a straight line. As she reached her destination, the cart gave a lurch and banged into the edge of the nearest table.

Emily held her breath as the precariously balanced mess shifted, papers slithering against each other. "Don't fall, don't fall…"

With a screech and crack of rending wood, the back leg of the overloaded table collapsed.

"No, no, no, no!" Emily made a grab for the edge of the table, but couldn't stop the inevitable tumble. She watched in horror as papers, books, and a metal-bound box slid faster and faster toward the floor. Slither-thump-clang-clatter, and it was all over but for the dust puffing up in the sunlight and gently wafting back down.

"Oh, dammit." The flotsam and jetsam of the wreck of the table lay at her feet. Emily fell to her knees, pulling the cart within reach and scooping first the papers and then the buried books into piles on its shelves. It reminded her of playing pick-up sticks, or digging something out from the side of an unstable sand dune. Every time she removed something, the rest of the mess on the floor shifted to hide the layers underneath.

It couldn't get any worse. She'd stood there all smug in her opinions of library owners whose treasures lay forlorn and neglected for generations. "So what do you do? You dump them on the floor like last week's old pizza boxes," she scolded herself as she eased out another handful, straightening the papers and laying them on the cart. "Great way to take care of the treasures, Em."

She worked her way under the leaning table to fish out the debris that had rested against the library shelves. The papers had scattered, but the heavier books had slid straight off and onto the floor. Which was better for the books, because no bouncing meant less damage, but made them harder for her to reach. "At least Marta isn't in here. She'd have my head. Actually," mumbled Emily as she went back in for a few more books, "she'd just look sad and disappointed. How could it get worse?"

It could get worse.

"What is she doing under the table? Nik, are your servants always this careless?" Light feminine laughter accompanied the questions.

Emily jerked upright and banged into the table. "Oh, ow," she said, rubbing her head as she landed hard on her tailbone. "I'm sorry, I didn't hear you come in."

As she looked up from her seat on the floor, she caught her breath in shock. Her heart, already beating a little fast from the noise and the accident, gave an odd lurch and settled into a hard, thumping rhythm.

"I can see that," drawled the man in front of her. "Dr. Charette, I presume?"

Oh, boy, could it get worse.

As often as she'd worked in the homes and official buildings of the rich and famous, she'd never gotten used to their version of casual clothing. Here she sat on the floor in a pair of dark slacks and a light blue Oxford shirt, loafers on her feet, her hair pulled back into a loose French braid and fastened with a purple scrunchie. And there they stood, the perfect couple: the elegant golden-haired woman in a floral silk sundress and delicate sandals teetering on four-inch heels, diamonds at her ears and throat, her hands clasped around the bicep of her partner, himself tailored and polished in a stone-gray suit, tie loosened and collar unbuttoned.

Emily eased out from under the table and grasped the hand he extended to her, careful not to bump the table again as she stood. The instant flare of heat when their palms met startled her, and she let go as soon as she regained her feet. "Thank you," she said, glancing up, then dropping her eyes again to brush off her slacks. "Yes, I'm Dr. Charette, Your Highness. And I apologize for the mess. I can promise you that it won't happen again."

"Oh, Nik, seriously? This is the threat you came back to take care of? Surely someone else can manage one incompetent librarian?"

Emily knew the light murmur in Italian was not meant for her ears. Gee, that gave her a lot to choose from, didn't it? A threat or incompetent. Terrific.

She breathed deep and kept her face blank, fighting to not react. She was pretty sure the woman was Helena DiSalvo, which made her the crown prince's current… girlfriend? Lover? Potential wife? Didn't matter. Emily's only concern right now was to not look like an idiot and to ease whatever concerns Councillor Asanovic may have raised about her work in the library so these two would leave.

"Is there something I can do for you, Your Highness?"

Please, oh please, say no. Say you were just stopping by, wanted to say hello, have to run, see you next time. She looked down at the piles of stuff still on the floor. Maybe if she avoided eye contact they'd take the hint that she just wanted to pick up the pieces and get on with things?

Chapter Nine:
First encounter: Nik

He strode into the library, his attention split between the woman on his arm and the tablet in his hand. Nikolas hadn't planned on being back in Dubrovia this soon, and certainly not with Helena, but Rikard's increasingly strident emails and voice mails had piqued his curiosity. Apparently in less than a week Dr. Emily Charette had managed to become a Dubrovian favorite. King and Council, staff and locals—everyone talked about the restoration of their library, the rejuvenation of their culture, and the delightful Canadian who led the charge. At this rate Council would dump even more money into the mess on her advice.

Rikard wanted him back for damage control. Nik wanted to see for himself. Was she as manipulative as his ally in Council made her out to be? Nik's experience with women told him that was a distinct possibility.

Helena was a prime example. He hadn't meant to bring her along with him on this trip, had he? He'd intended to fly in, talk to Rikard, check on the library, and fly back to Italy. But somehow she had teased and cajoled her way past his security and weaseled and wormed her way onto his private jet this morning. All with a naughty smile and a promise to take care of him so he "had some fun and didn't worry so much." Which was Helena-speak for great sex followed by a shiny, expensive gift. The old ritual no longer appealed.

So here he was, fresh from his meeting with Rikard. His ally on the Royal Council had been so incensed he was almost speechless. Who would have thought that some mousy little librarian could rile a grown man so much? It would be laughable if not for the amount of money at stake. But the stakes *were* high, and Rikard was worried, and so Nik had come to investigate. And once that was done, he could leave and return to the real action in Italy, schmoozing wine distributors to open their ports and shipping contracts to Dubrovia.

He tuned out most of Helena's chatter. As usual, she kept up a running commentary about the castle ("horribly old fashioned"), the staff ("surly and inefficient"), and the councillors ("cold and unwelcoming"). Good thing he had no intention of marrying her; she would never fit in here.

So far, he hadn't caught a glimpse of the elusive librarian. Where was the girl hiding? He needed to find her, make sure she made headway on the library without intruding on the lives of his family and his people, and fly back to Italy. He could hear someone speaking; was she talking to herself? Because there didn't seem to be anyone else here.

They had almost reached the far end of the room before they turned a corner around a stack and he spotted her, just as the heavy cart she wrestled with jerked and bumped into a table. The screech of rending wood made Helena jump and grab his arm tighter. *Why did women wear those ridiculous heels if they couldn't walk in them? Oh, right: legs up to here...*

"What is she doing under there? Nik, are your servants always this careless?" Helena said, the Italian suiting her cultured voice.

He winced as Emily jumped and cracked her head on the underside of the table. That had to have hurt. So did the apology she offered for being careless, and the shock of recognition that flashed across her expressive face as she rubbed the back of her head.

"Dr. Charette, I presume?" His turn to feel embarrassed, this time for how ridiculous he sounded. Who else would be sitting on the floor of the library, worried about papers and books falling off a table? He offered her a hand up.

Where their palms touched, heat arrowed up his arm and down into his gut. *What the hell was that?*

Nik withdrew his hand as Emily stood, careful to hide his unexpected reaction from Helena. The last thing he wanted was for her to go into a snit. As she made fun of the little librarian in Italian, he once again entertained the fleeting thought that this relationship, casual as he kept it, had reached the end of its useful life.

He lost patience with all things female. Nik looked at the broken table, at the scattered papers and books, then back at Emily. He eased Helena's hand from his arm (not without some resistance) and reached for the library cart, moving it out of the way so he could check out the broken table leg.

"You're going to need some help here to move the broken table out of the way and recover the rest of the books and things. Call Tomas and have him send someone from housekeeping. In the meantime, why don't we step over there to the chairs and you can give me a status report?"

Neither woman appeared pleased. Emily looked anxiously back at the mess in the corner as she walked to the chairs by the window. Helena just looked angrily at him.

He turned her aside and addressed her in English. "Helena, I don't expect this to take too long. You are welcome to stay here with us, or you can go back up to my suite and wait in the sitting room, if you'd prefer?"

She released a small sigh and answered, in Italian of course, "Oh, no, Nik, I can't imagine that this will take much time, surely. I would be delighted to stay with you here for a few more minutes."

This would cost him a visit to her favorite jeweler in Rome before heading to her father's yacht party. Nik made a mental note to have his assistant call ahead to make sure they were immediately presented with a selection of earrings. But this would be the last shiny, sparkly present, he promised himself. Time to close this thing with Helena out.

He turned back to Dr. Charette, who was still looking at the corner, biting her lip. Her very pretty pink lip in her very pretty face. Once again he felt an unexpected rush of... something. He didn't want to call it lust, or even mild attraction. She was so definitely not his type! How could he be attracted to this quiet, delicate woman? He decided he simply appreciated the female form. Nothing to worry about.

"Dr. Charette? Would you mind explaining what it is you are doing and how much longer you expect it to take?"

Before she could reply there came a cry from the other end of the room. "Oh, no! What happened? My telescope!"

Nik spun around as his young cousin attempted to wrestle the heavy table away from the wall. She was light, the table was heavy, and they both tipped toward the floor.

No! He pushed his tablet into Helena's hands. Visions of Rose's accident two years ago flashed through his mind as he raced over to the corner, grabbing the handles of the wheelchair just as it started to tip up onto one wheel.

"Let go, Rose! Or you'll fall too. I'll find your telescope, I promise." He stood the chair upright again once she released her grip, pulling her back away from the table as it crashed to the floor.

She trembled, and Nik knelt down next to her, scanning her for injuries. "Oh, Rose, you gave me quite a scare! Did it hit you on the way down?"

Rose shook her head, looking teary eyed at the mess on the floor. "No, no, I'm fine, Uncle Nik, really. But my telescope! The old telescope that Dad and I used to use was on that table somewhere. And now it's on the floor, under all that stuff, and I can't see it, and I really, really hope it's okay. It can't be broken!" She reached for the table again, her breath jerky and hitching as she fought back tears. "Nana

71

and Papa will kill me if I broke it. It's so old. We don't know how old, but they always told me to be so careful with it, and now it's down there, and—"

"Rose. It will be all right. We'll get it out from under, and you can check for yourself." Nik brushed his hand over her cheek, wiping away the single tear that had trickled down. His heart warmed for his young cousin. Since her accident, she avoided talking about her parents in any context, and they had all let her. It pleased him to hear her refer to her father, even if she talked about the telescope. Stefan had always been one for stargazing when they were boys growing up in the castle. Looks like Rose had inherited one of his passions.

"My, such excitement over some books and papers!" Helena shook her head as she and Emily approached. "Good morning, Princess Rose," she continued, speaking slowly and loudly. "Do you remember who I am? My name is Helena—"

Nik frowned at her. What was that all about? "Helena, of course she remembers you. You met her at dinner with the family just last month. And you know that Rose is neither deaf nor stupid, so you need not speak to her like that."

He turned back to his cousin as she tugged up the afghan on her lap to cover something tucked beside her in her chair. He raised his eyebrows as he saw her stuffed bear. Helena already acted as if Rose had some sort of mental disability. No point in drawing attention to a leftover childhood behavior.

"So, Rose, where do you think the telescope ended up?" he said with a wink at her blush.

"Under the far corner, r-right by the shelves," stammered Rose. Helena was frowning, flustering her.

Rose bit her lip as she rolled backwards to give him some room. "I'm sorry, Uncle Nik, I should have stored it someplace safer."

Emily moved past Helena to help Nik as he leaned over to lift the table, and she nodded at Rose on the way by. "Actually, Princess, it's my fault the table collapsed. I bumped it with the cart. So if anyone is to blame, I am." She reached for the other end of the table, and she and Nik heaved it up and out of the way.

He took a good look at her while they were muscling the furniture around. She was older now, obviously, a little taller, a little curvier. Quiet and contained. Still with the sun-streaked dark blond hair he remembered, and still shy with him, as she kept her focus down on her feet and the table they were moving, never glancing up to catch his eye. He wasn't sure if that was down to nervousness or embarrassment at the current situation, but it made Nik want to say something, do something, to make her look up. To look at him.

Helena spun her bracelet around and around on her arm. From much experience, Nik knew that the gesture preluded a tantrum.

"She's quite right. This is her fault, and her responsibility. So someone else on staff can help her clean up this mess, Nik, and help the little princess," she said with a false smile for the girl. "Surely you don't need to do this yourself?"

"Why should I call someone in to do something as simple as this? Here, Dr. Charette, push that cart closer again," he said to Emily. He worked his way through the piles on the floor, handing her first papers, then books. Emily kept pace with him by loading up and then moving the cart, and together they gradually cleared their way back to the shelves.

Nik kept one eye on Helena, hoping she had the sense to keep further comments to herself until they were closed in his office and away from Rose. And Emily, for that matter. Neither one deserved to be on the receiving end of one of her tantrums.

He tired of them himself. Yes, he was a prince, the crown prince. Why should that make him incapable of picking up some papers and books and helping Rose find something? Why should Helena insist on calling in a staff member? And what kind of help did she think Rose needed, for God's sake?

His hand brushed something with hard, cold edges when he cleared the next armload. Nik pushed aside the last few papers to find the end of a brass-bound wooden box about as long as his arm and about as heavy as a big book. Or two.

The metal edging showed a few dents, but the hinges and clasp were undamaged. He fished it out from underneath and showed Rose. "Is this what you're looking for?"

"The telescope! It isn't broken, is it?"

"Let's have a look." He flipped up the hasp and tugged on the lid. It stuck, just for a moment, and then popped up.

The box and its contents were old. They had the characteristic smell of a museum display, but everything was surprisingly clean and well tended. Rose, as her father before her had done, took good care of the instrument.

"That's it? That's what you were worried about?" Helena asked incredulously. "I thought it might be a new, expensive telescope, the way you went on and on. This thing can't be powerful. Don't tell me anyone still uses it!"

Nik placed the box in Rose's lap and turned to face the woman. "It isn't the power that gives it value. Right, Rose?"

"It's really old. Dad always thought it might be one of Kepler's own telescopes. He spent some time in Prague, so he might have come here too, or one of his students maybe. We never found any books or anything about it, though." She touched the scope with reverence. "We had a newer one when we lived in Canada, I remember. But Dad found this a couple of years after we got home, and then we always used this one."

"Why don't you check the lenses, make sure they weren't damaged in the fall?" Nik eased to his feet as Emily dropped down to take his place, kneeling beside Rose to steady the box as she fiddled with the interior clamps.

He looked down at them. The expressions on their faces were remarkably similar: a mix of reverence and eager curiosity. Rose had found a kindred spirit, which made him glad for his young cousin. He knew she'd been lonely, the last couple of years, as the only Kuliç under the age of sixty left in the castle when he traveled. And he traveled a lot.

So maybe if there had to be someone here, in his space, pre-empting his project funding, having that person be Dr. Emily Charette wasn't the worst thing in the world.

He eased back more and took Helena's arm, turning her away from the tableau in the corner. "Helena, why don't we leave them to it? You said you wanted to talk to your father. You can call from my office while I finish reading this report from Asanovic." He took his tablet back from Helena and turned it off, tucking it under his arm.

Emily's head came up with a start. This time she caught his eye and held it, although he could see that it cost her. "Prince Nikolas, I—"

"I'll be back in Dubrovia next week, Dr. Charette, and we can discuss his report then. In the meantime," Nik said, "before you try to do it yourself, ask Tomas to send someone to see to the damages in here."

He bent down to kiss Rose on the cheek. "Try to stay out of trouble, hmm?" he murmured in her ear, tugging on a lock of her hair.

He straightened and walked Helena toward his office, hoping he could get her behind a closed door before the fireworks started. She paced stiffly and silently next to him, but that wouldn't last long. Good breeding kept her behavior just on the side of polite in public. In private, she had a tendency to let fly.

He looked back at the corner to see Emily now bending over Rose to peer at the telescope. Getting a good look at her heart-shaped rear gave him a punch to the gut. Who knew those dusty dark slacks had been hiding such an enticing shape? His eyes slid sideways to the well-dressed blond on his arm. She might have a more expensive wardrobe, but a fancy dress couldn't hide the fact that she was model thin. And as cold and hard as the diamonds she preferred.

He opened the door and waved her in before him, glancing back as Emily's warm laugh reached him. No diamonds for that one, he mused. He stopped in his tracks when she looked up at him. From this distance he couldn't tell if she blushed again, but she looked back down at Rose and the telescope quickly enough to make him think so.

Nik closed the door. Time enough next week to figure out what that little flash of heat meant. For now, he'd deal with getting Helena to Italy, and figure out how to leave her there.

Chapter Ten:
First encounter: Rose

"I don't think she likes me much." Rose's hands were on the telescope case, but her eyes followed Helena as Nik escorted her into the office at the other end of the library.

Emily gave a rueful laugh. "I'm not high on their list of favorite people either." She stood and deliberately turned her back on the couple. "I try not to think about stuff like that too much. People are hard; libraries and books—and telescopes—are easier." She leaned over to examine the telescope case.

"Oh, yeah," Rose agreed, rolling her eyes. She peered around Emily and saw Nik look back at them. "Especially some people."

Rose balanced the case on the arms of the wheelchair. Since Emily was facing her, she hadn't noticed Nik looking at her, his eyes narrowed in speculation—but Rose had. *Now, isn't that interesting? Maybe Helena isn't such a sure thing, if Uncle Nik is interested in Emily over here with me and not Helena over there with him?*

She straightened in her chair again. "Do you think my telescope might be a treasure? Dad always made me think so, but we never knew for sure. Could you check and tell me what you think? I don't care if it's worth a lot of money," she assured Emily, "but it would be so cool if it belonged to Kepler or somebody like that!"

Emily looked down at the box in Rose's lap. "This reminds me of a violin case. The lining and clamps are kind of like that too. It doesn't have any markings? Let me steady it while you close it. I want to look at the outside."

Rose obligingly shut the case and tipped it up so Emily could see. "Here, see for yourself. We never found anything, but we didn't know what to look for."

Emily examined the case but couldn't see any identifying marks. She looked at Rose. "Maybe if we go over by the windows? The light is a little better. And it's kind of dusty back here still," she continued, as Rose sniffled and sneezed.

Rose shrugged as she found a tissue and wiped her nose. "Sure. Uncle Nik keeps a magnifying glass in his office, if you want one."

"I've got one in my kit here." Emily grabbed her messenger bag on the way over to the windows and dropped it onto one of a pair of wingback chairs. She handed Rose back the case as she rummaged through her bag to find her magnifying glass.

Rose started to hand over the case, but Emily stopped herself before reaching for it. "I'm sorry, Your Highness. I was so excited about the telescope, I'm getting ahead of myself. We haven't formally been introduced." She held out her hand. "I'm Dr. Emily—"

"I remember you." Rose clutched the case close. "Don't you remember me? You didn't use to call me 'Your Highness' back then. You called me Rosie Posie."

"I—"

"You lived with Mama and Dad and me. In Canada when you were all in school. And you played with me, and you read to me. You taught me how to make snow angels, and how to make maple syrup taffy on snow. Here, hold this for a minute," she said, shoving the case at Emily and rummaging between the arm of her chair and her leg. "You gave me this, when I was still a kid. Don't you remember Bear?" she asked, pulling the stuffed Mountie bear from under the afghan and holding it out.

Rose shrugged, embarrassed but determined. That bear was a leftover from her younger days, and a reminder of her time in Canada—her time with Emily. "It's kind of a baby thing, I guess."

"Oh, Rose." Emily sat down in the other wingback chair, set the case down on the floor, and reached for the toy. "You still have Bear." She handled the old stuffed animal with care. He had been well loved, but the marks of various repairs over the years were clearly visible, as was the inevitable wear. She looked at Rose, who was twisting her afghan in her fingers. "He's held up pretty well, hasn't he?"

Rose nodded without meeting Emily's eyes. "When I was hurt, Uncle Nik brought him to me in the hospital. He was the first thing I saw when I woke up. Uncle Nik told me to hold on to him when it hurt, after my surgeries or physio, or when I missed Mama and Dad, because Mounties are so brave, and I had to be brave too. I don't think Uncle Nik thinks about how old I am, even now." She huffed out a laugh. "Maybe it would be easier for him if I was a boy. Maybe he would tell me to suck it up or something. I think teenage girls frighten him to death. Little girls and teddy bears, not so much."

Emily touched the crumpled brim of the bear's brown Stetson and smoothed it back to almost its original shape, then she handed Bear back to Rose. "I hope it helped. You did have to be brave. I know how hard it is when your mom dies, and you were hurt on top of that. I lost mine about the same time you lost yours. It's still hard. I miss her every day."

Rose looked up sharply and sucked in a breath. "I didn't know about your mom."

"She died of ovarian cancer, a couple of days before your accident. That's why we didn't contact the king and queen or send any messages about your parents. My dad, well, it hit him hard. I had to make all the arrangements because he couldn't cope for a while. I heard on the news, about your accident, the day of Mom's funeral. The report said you were in the car, and we heard about your parents and your great-aunt, but no one ever mentioned you. I thought... we thought you died in the car with them because we never heard anything different. And then I had to deal with Mom's funeral, and my dad, and everything. I didn't think to reach out afterward and ask." Emily reached over and touched Rose's hand. "I'm so sorry, Rose."

Rose shrugged a little and blinked hard to stop a tear from falling. "It's okay. I'm sorry too. I remember your mom from when she came to visit when you lived with us. She smiled a lot, and she always brought flowers for Mama." She sniffled and gave Emily a watery, embarrassed smile. "Not how you expected to spend your morning."

Emily squeezed her hand, then let go and sat back. "I'm so glad I've met you again, Rose. When you didn't come to dinner the first night I was here, I wondered whether having me here would be hard for you, because I used to know your parents. And Her Majesty the queen has told me that you spend a lot of time in the library. The last thing I want is to push my way in and make you uncomfortable, here in your own space."

"That's not why I missed dinner," Rose replied. "Or not the only reason. I had a long PT session that day. Sometimes my back hurts too much for me to sit in my chair for a long time, especially at night when I'm tired and if I've had to work hard with Jacquie that day."

A sheepish expression crossed her face. "I was kind of angry about you being here all the time, though. I sort of hide in the upper reading room sometimes. It's the only place I can be by myself for a while without someone coming to find me, as long as I tell Jacquie or Marta where I am. I guess they figure I can't get into too much trouble up there."

She fiddled with the stuffed animal. "So, yeah, I kind of think of it as my space. But it isn't, not really. It's part of the library, and I know you'll go through everything up there."

"Part of my job description is to be unobtrusive," said Emily with a wry smile. "I fade into the woodwork and become part of the space I work in. So I can give you a choice: if you're certain that I'm not getting in your way too much, I can work up in that room when you're available to be with me. Or if you'd rather *not* be right where I'm working, if you want privacy, I can arrange to work in that room when you're somewhere else, and work out here when you're up there."

Rose shrugged. "No, it's okay. I don't mind if you're there when I am. Or when I'm not."

"As long as you're sure. If you change your mind or you want me out of your hair that day, just let me know. Believe me," Emily said, huffing out a breath that blew her bangs up off her forehead, "there's enough to keep me busy out in the stacks."

Rose tucked Bear back next to her side and pulled the afghan up again to cover him up. She didn't share Bear with everyone. At the advanced age of sixteen, she felt a little embarrassed to still want her stuffed animal—but not embarrassed enough to have put him away with the rest of her childhood toys.

Emily touched the vintage watch on her wrist, one Rose remembered seeing her mother wear. Rose might keep her animal close, for comfort; apparently Emily wore her mother's watch, for remembrance.

Once she had sorted herself out, Emily reached down and picked up the telescope case and her magnifying glass. Raising one eyebrow at Rose, she said, "Are you ready to start looking at your telescope again?"

"Of course!" Rose pulled her chair a little closer to where Emily was angling the case toward the light streaming in through the big windows. "Is there anything on the outside? Can you see any markings? What are you looking for?"

Emily peered through the glass and went over every inch of the outside of the case. "Sometimes we'll find maker's marks on pieces of silver and gold plate that are so worn you can't see them without a magnifier. Sometimes I'll find one more by feel than by sight. I was hoping to find something like that on the brass bindings or the hasp or the hinges, but I don't see anything."

"What's a maker's mark?"

"It's a mark the silversmith or goldsmith uses to identify their work. It's like a signature," Emily said absently, turning over the case to examine the back. "Have you ever seen someone at a state dinner turn over a fork or spoon, or even a china plate, to look at the mark on the back? They're looking for something to identify the artist or the manufacturer."

Rose rolled her eyes, then glanced at the office door to make sure it was still closed. "Helena did that at dinner, that time I met her," she said. "Most of Uncle Nik's girlfriends do. She was just the most obvious."

Emily huffed out a laugh. "Guess she wants to figure out how much he's worth before she marries him."

Rose shuddered in horror. "Oh, gag, she can't marry Uncle Nik! That would be awful! She'd come to live here in the castle. And I'd see her every day. And I'd have to be NICE to her!"

Emily set down her magnifying glass, balancing the telescope across the arms of her chair. "Well, he has to marry someone, doesn't he? Isn't she the latest candidate?"

"Oh, boy, I hope not. She's lasted a long time, though. Most of them don't. And there's been a lot. I think he wants some sort of business deal with her father. I hope he can sign the deal without having to marry her, and find someone better."

And wasn't that interesting again? Uncle Nik had looked back at Emily, and now Emily wanted to hear about Uncle Nik and potential brides, while blushing. Rose watched as Emily kept her face averted, focusing on the case and fiddling with the latch until her flush faded.

"I'm sure he'll do what's best for Dubrovia. I could wish he was a little happier with the idea of the library restoration, but, well. Anyway." Emily took a deep breath. "Items like this make my job fun. I wish there was a table here by the window, though. Natural light is the best for seeing textures and marks that are almost rubbed off, or are covered in years of tarnish or dirt."

"We could go upstairs," offered Rose. "There are a couple of tables in the bay windows in the upper reading room. I like to do my homework there cause it's so bright in the afternoon."

"Are you sure, Rose? I know you said it would be okay to work up there, but I don't want to impose…"

"No, really, it'll be good!" She bounced excitedly in her wheelchair. "I can show you my space, and you can see what's up there. And we can examine the telescope too."

"If you're sure," said Emily, hefting the case and setting it back on Rose's lap.

"Yes, please! I have to go down to the other end of the castle, though, and use the elevator. There isn't one at this end. So it'll take me a couple minutes to get there."

"Tell you what. Why don't I find Marta or Tomas or someone to take away the broken table and stack up all the stuff that hit the floor, you head down to the elevator, and I'll meet you in a few minutes?"

* * *

They left the main library together. Rose peeled off to head down the corridor for the elevator while Emily stopped the first staff person she saw, who was polishing a wood bench in the reception hall outside the library's gallery extension. The man returned with her to the main library, where she explained what had happened and was promised that it would all be taken care of immediately.

Emily headed up the spiral stairs in the corner of the room and wound her way through the second-floor stacks to the upper reading room. She beat Rose by a couple of minutes and took the time for an impression of the room.

It was a much cozier space than the big hall downstairs, with a lower ceiling and warmer colors; thick woolen rugs scattered around on wooden floors instead of flagstone (with obvious paths for a wheelchair); a pretty fireplace flanked with overstuffed chairs; and big, bright bay windows that invited the visitor to stop and stay awhile.

No wonder Rose spends so much time here. And is that a star map on the wall?

It was a painting rather than an accurate drawing of the night sky. Emily realized it must be by a local artist, because the stars were a little different than the way they looked in Edmonton, so much farther north. It was also amazingly detailed for something that had been created hundreds of years ago, from the date on the little brass plaque on the frame. Someone here had spent a lot of time outside at night, long ago.

She pulled out her magnifying glass again to look more closely at it as Rose rushed in. "Sorry I took so long! I passed Jacquie on my way; I need to go down for physio in about an hour, so I can't stay the whole afternoon."

"That's fine, Rose. We'll either spot something quickly or we won't. Before we get started, though, do you know anything about this painting?"

Rose wheeled over to the biggest table by the windows, skirting the edges of the rugs with the ease born of great familiarity, placed the case in the sunniest spot, and came over to the painting. "Not so much. See the date, 1589? The family has always supported painters and sculptors and musicians and such, so there's a lot of artwork scattered all over the castle, but we don't know much about the stuff that old—or I don't anyway. There was a lot of religious upheaval in this area during the Reformation. We're kind of tucked away here, so things never got as violent as they did in other places. A lot of folks kind of made their way here and never left. I think this painting was from one of those guys." She shrugged. "Is it important? Nana might know more. She's into art and such more than I am."

"I don't know if it's important, as far as your telescope goes. But it's interesting that astronomy is so important to you, and was to your dad, and then there's this painting here. So it's been important all along, hasn't it?" Emily said as they moved back over to the table and the telescope case.

"Does this kind of thing happen often when you work in old places, where you need to identify stuff that isn't books or documents or artwork?"

"So many interesting things end up in libraries! Let's look inside and see if there are any identifying marks there. Open it up, Rose!"

Inside the box was a wooden tube with brass ends, one holding a large lens, and one holding a smaller eyepiece tube and lens. The telescope was nestled and clamped in a padded frame covered with worn blue velvet. Around the edges of the box were nestled smaller brass pieces, replacements for the eyepiece tube and both lenses. Tucked under smaller clamps in the lid were some cleaning cloths and a small vial of what looked like oil that might be for conditioning the wood.

Emily gently released the clamp around the main piece and lifted it from its bed. "Let's take a look at you, shall we?"

Chapter Eleven:
Emily reports to Nik

He was hearing voices.

Granted, his ears were still ringing from Rikard's blustering rant as they'd walked together to this morning's Council meeting. "It's ridiculous! They are completely taken in by this foreigner, this woman. Not only has Council approved the money for this first phase of her project; they are seriously considering moving forward with the rest! Without seeing an estimate yet! I tell you, my friend, if you want to be able to expand next year, you must do something about her."

Nik had leaned against the wall and considered his colleague. "Don't you think you're being a little overdramatic? No, I don't support the project. Yes, I wanted the funds directed to revamping the resort and spa this year and expanding our wine distribution next year. But the contract was awarded by a Council vote, and with the king and queen's full support. Are you suggesting I go against their decision?"

He pushed off the wall, gave one hard look to the red-faced man, and turned on his heel. Over his shoulder he'd said, "Choose your words with care, Rikard. And remember who I am."

Now, Nik strode scowling through the halls, shaking his head. After Rikard, there had been the Council meeting itself. He hadn't asked for the keys to the crown jewels, just a status report and accounting on this damned library project. Apparently questioning the advisability of committing so much money to a single project (one with no commercial viability, in his opinion) was tantamount to questioning Council's judgment on every decision, every purchase ever made.

As the crown prince—hell, as the king and queen's nephew—as long as his family's actions didn't jeopardize Dubrovia, he felt obligated to support their decisions even when he didn't agree with them. Throwing money at the library might not be the wisest move, and not his first choice, but protesting now served no purpose. All he wanted was an accounting, dammit!

Nik really needed a drink. And since he didn't want to be fussed over, he headed toward his office in the den rather than to his suite. Somehow even Tomas and Marta's son Anton, his faithful aide of more than ten years, acted as bedazzled by this project and besotted with its shy little librarian.

He wanted to lock himself in his office in private, pour himself a couple of fingers of Irish, put his feet up on his desk, and contemplate the ceiling for an hour. Or two. That might put him in a better frame of mind to open up the latest report from Dr. Charette and determine if her budget estimate was as outrageous as Rikard claimed.

He wanted to hear nothing for at least an hour. Instead, he heard voices.

Not just any voices either. Female voices. Multiple female voices. And did he hear a male voice as well?

Who the hell was in his library?

His footsteps slowed to a stop as he strained to listen. He moved quietly to the spiral staircase leading to the second floor, pausing occasionally, trying to make out words and identify the speakers.

He grinned as Rose's clear laugh pealed out. When had he last heard his cousin's laughter? Far too long ago, by his count.

So Rose spent time in the library? He reached the top step and listened again. The marble floors and wooden panels and stacks of books bounced the sound around some, but he thought it came from the section on the other side of the cavernous room, almost directly above the door to his office.

He rounded the corner of the farthest stack and came to an abrupt halt. There were Rose and Emily, huddled in front of a laptop. He saw the other speaker now, on the screen: a man, blond, maybe late twenties.

Nik still couldn't identify the language, but clearly Emily knew it. Her conversation partner said something that made her spin around, her expression a mix of surprise and guilt.

"Your Highness!" She jumped to her feet, nearly knocking over her chair. "I'm sorry, we didn't know you were there."

"I could tell," Nik drawled. "What's all this?" He ignored the little stab of something hot, something sharp, deep in his belly.

"Sir, we were just—"

"Oh, hi, Uncle Nik!" Rose said cheerfully, swinging her chair around. "Come and meet Pétur Tumason. He's Emily's TA. He's from Iceland! Isn't that cool?"

"Mr. Tumason." He nodded to the man on the screen, then turned to Emily. "Dr. Charette? A word, if you would?"

"Of course," Emily replied. She looked at the screen, looked at Rose, and bit her lip. "Rose, want to finish up for me today?"

"Sure!" Rouse bounced happily around to face the screen again, then glanced back over her shoulder. "See you later, Uncle Nik!"

He raised his eyebrows at Emily as she gathered up her messenger bag and followed him out through the stacks. "Is that appropriate, do you think? Leaving the princess there to converse online with a strange man?"

"He's not a strange man. I taught Pétur as an undergrad for a couple of years. Now I'm his thesis adviser and he's my teaching assistant. And Princess Rose has spoken to him a number of times over the last couple of months." Emily slanted him a glance as he motioned her ahead of him. "So have both your aunt and uncle, the king and queen."

Nik barely heard her. He was distracted, watching her step carefully down and around the winding stairs. She wore a casual outfit compared to the clothes worn by women of his acquaintance, but the khaki skirt hugged her bottom and stopped just above her very pretty knees. He found himself regretting they were traveling downstairs and not up; he would have enjoyed watching her slender calves flex on every step.

As they reached the bottom, she asked, "What did you want to speak to me about, Your Highness?"

"We can talk in my office." He put his hand on the small of her back when he stepped off the stairs, intending to steer her across the room.

The motion was offhand, made in passing without thinking, and he would have made little notice of the slight touch—except Emily stiffened and pulled away.

Now, isn't that interesting? He kept his hand in place as he escorted her across the room.

By the time he unlocked and opened the door to his office, Emily looked well and truly flustered. Her face was flushed, her breathing uneven, and she'd increased her pace as they crossed the open floor, as if trying to get away from his touch.

This was her fourth rotation in Dubrovia, he knew, and he hadn't seen more of her than the occasional glimpse as he went in and out of his office. Her reports, written and verbal, had gone to Council. Any comments he wanted to make went back to her by way of Rikard Asanovic. *I might have erred there*, he mused. He reached around her to open the door. Rikard's hard-line approach was more extreme and less effective than Nik had anticipated. Time for a change? A more hands-on method?

Speaking of hands-on: in all these weeks, there had been no direct contact between them. And now all of a sudden there was *contact* contact. Hand on her lower back or on her elbow contact. Escorting her into his office for a private meeting contact. It was… intriguing, he decided, as he stepped into the room behind her.

And stopped abruptly so as not to run over her.

"Whoa." Emily had come to a dead halt just inside the door.

He skirted around her and walked over to his desk, then turned around and leaned back on the surface, watching her. "Haven't you been in here before?"

"Oh. Wow. No, I haven't." She turned slowly to look at more of the space. "And there weren't any pictures in the preliminary package of information we received."

He watched, amused, as she let her messenger bag slither to the floor and moved toward the shelves. Her eyes widened and her head swung from side to side as she tried to take in as much of the room at once as she could.

Funny how you take a place for granted when you grew up there. He imagined she must feel much the same about her home as he did about his.

He tried to see it as she would. The den was a beautiful room, much different from the other spaces in the library. Like the rest, it was richly appointed, but instead of stone or exposed wood floors and big, bright windows and towering wooden stacks, this room welcomed with all warm colors and softer surfaces. Not a cathedral to learning; rather, a decadent refuge. His refuge.

It was paneled in alternating carved oak and wine-red silk. The curtains were a deeper red, more a cabernet sauvignon than the pinot noir of the walls. An acre of jewel-toned tapestry carpeted the floor. Shelving ran around the bottom half of the fifteen-foot walls, with breaks for the curtained windows and walk-in fireplace. Row after row of books peeked out from behind intricate brass scrollwork. Above the bookcases were scattered paintings, assorted weaponry, and the odd bit of taxidermy, punctuated by working gas sconces.

The big overstuffed chairs and sofas clustered in front of the fireplace were covered in deep brown leather. The desk, large and ornate, managed to look masculine and imposing in spite of the panels carved with flowers and intertwining vines.

He supposed the place suited him well enough. It was comfortable and familiar. Helena had always found it stuffy and old fashioned, or so she said. It certainly wasn't a woman's room, what with all the weapons and dead animals. She worked to get him out of it as much as possible.

Emily Charette, on the other hand, looked like she could settle in and explore for a while. She walked in front of the banks of shelves, running her hand along the brass screens that protected each one, occasionally stopping to peer more closely at a particular offering. To Nik she appeared as fascinated as another woman might be in a store full of sparkling jewelry.

She wandered, and he watched. She had a very expressive face, he realized, and a trim little body. He sucked in a breath when she crouched down to peer into some bottom shelves. Her khaki skirt rode up well above her knees as she lowered to the floor—as did his eyebrows at the smooth expanse of thigh thus exposed.

The bolt of heat to his gut surprised him. Her clothing wasn't provocative by any stretch of the imagination. You could almost call it drab. He couldn't imagine any other woman of his acquaintance being caught dead in a similar outfit. And yet he couldn't stop looking. And wanting. And wondering.

Okay, now, enough is enough. She just about had her nose pressed up against the scrollwork. Did a bunch of old books really fascinate her, or was she avoiding talking to him? Time to find out.

Nik cleared his throat. "Dr. Charette? Emily? Do you mind? I expect to take a call in an hour or so."

She flinched and tripped over her bag as she swung back to face him. "Oh! Sorry. This is my first time in here. I didn't realize it would be so different…" Her gaze wandered again, this time to the shelves across from Nik's desk, and her feet followed her eyes back to that end of the room.

He poured two glasses of sparkling water from the chilled bottle always on his sidebar, then crossed over to place one in front of her as she dropped down into one of the overstuffed armchairs by his desk. "Now. Let's start with your latest report, shall we? You were not at the Council meeting last week; I hoped to discuss your progress then."

"Last week was my regular rotation back home. Three weeks here, a week in Edmonton was what we negotiated into the contract."

He swirled the ice and sparkling water in his glass, wishing for whiskey. "I wondered about that. It seems a rather inefficient way to manage a project such as this, no?"

"It was a compromise," said Emily. "Your Council originally proposed that I be assigned here full-time. Dean Smithton and I asked for two and two. We settled on three and one." She shifted in the chair, annoyance flashing over her expression before disappearing, smoothing out into her usual calm demeanor. "I have personal and professional obligations in Edmonton. If Dubrovia had been adamant on having someone here full-time, I would not have taken the project."

"This is neither the time nor the place to dispute the contract. Those are the terms of your employment. While I may not agree with Council's approach, it is nevertheless what we must deal with. I'm sure you can understand I am simply trying to protect Dubrovia's interests in this matter." He shrugged, perching against the edge of his desk. "It is always disappointing to discover one's own project may not rank with the same priority to others as it does to ourselves, yes?"

"Your Highness, I can assure you the project to catalog and restore Dubrovia's library is of high priority. And while I must fulfill other obligations, during the times I am not here Pétur continues with the count. That part can be done remotely."

"Perhaps I need a better understanding of what your work here entails. I know from your reports the entire project is in three phases. I would like to know more of what is involved in each phase."

He pushed off from the desk and strolled over to a large globe nearby, spinning it idly. Her fresh and floral scent, light though it might be, crept into his awareness, distracting him.

"I would be happy to explain again, Your Highness. I spent some time going through the process with Ministers Janko and Bartak when they came to Edmonton, before we signed the contract. I have the presentation my dean and I made to them in here on a flash drive." She started to reach into her bag, now visibly annoyed. "I can show you—"

Show. She could show him. But not with some sort of electronic presentation.

"I think that's a grand idea. You can show me what you have been doing for the last three months, and what you will be doing going forward. But not with a presentation," he said. He closed the distance between them in one step and caught her wrist before she extracted the drive. "You can show me in person."

She froze in place. Nik wasn't sure whether to be flattered or insulted.

"In person?" she exclaimed, leaning back in an attempt to free her wrist. "What do you mean, show you in person? I understood that you insisted I file a report with Council every week instead of once a rotation. If you've been reading them, you know how much progress has been made and what is left to complete this phase." *And if you don't read them*, her tone implied, *why do I bother to write them?*

The more he thought, the more he liked the idea. "Indeed, in person. In fact, we will trade this showing. I will spend a day with you here in the library, and you can walk me through what you do here. Then in return, you will spend a day with me touring the vineyards and the winery so that you can see what I try to do there."

He released her wrist, allowing her to return the flash drive to her bag as he crossed to sit behind the desk and reach for his calendar. His palm tingled from the brief contact. Emily, he noticed, cupped her wrist with her other hand, looking down as if she held something precious. Then she looked up and blushed, dropping her wrist and tucking her hands in her pockets.

Nik smiled as he opened his leather-bound daybook. Her pulse had jumped under her silky skin. So she wasn't unaffected by his touch. Was it just annoyance, or perhaps something else?

"How does Wednesday sound?"

"Wednesday? This Wednesday? Your Highness, I—"

"Wednesday, and then Friday," he said, glancing at his schedule. He'd have to move a couple of appointments.

"Wednesday in the library, Friday in the winery." He caught her eye, amused at the flush still covering her cheeks. "That gives you tomorrow to prepare for me the next day. And I will arrange for us to visit one of the mountainside vineyards and tour the winery across the road. And talk over lunch."

Nik stood from his chair and circled the desk. He extended his hand to raise her from her seat.

"Of course, Your Highness. As you wish. I am at your disposal," she stated flatly, placing her hand in his and standing. That brought them close enough for him to feel the heat from her body. Her cheeks may have flushed from annoyance, but he was willing to try and change that over the next few days.

He continued to hold her hand as he walked her to the door. By the time they had crossed the ten feet or so, she pulled at him, trying to free herself.

"And I think we can dispense with the formalities, hmm? If we are going to spend a couple of days together 'Prince Nikolas' and 'Dr. Charette' gets to be a bit much. I think we can be Nik and Emily, yes?"

"Your Highness, I'm not sure—"

"That's all right, I am." Nik opened the door and leaned against the frame. As he still held her hand, he took the opportunity to brush his thumb over her knuckles.

He smiled at her quick intake of breath. "I will meet you Wednesday morning, around nine." He released her hand, gave her a small bow and a smug smile, and closed the door behind her.

He whistled as he returned to his desk. Gulping down the rest of his water, he retrieved the bottle of Irish whiskey from the sidebar, poured a shot into his tumbler, and tossed it back. Then he reached for the phone. He had appointments to reschedule and an excursion to plan.

Chapter Twelve:
The library tour

Emily Charette was not a happy woman.

The morning had started out well enough. She got to the library about a half hour before she was supposed to meet with the prince, early enough to have the space to herself for a little while.

Emily loved the library in these early hours. The castle hadn't yet geared up for the day, so there were no cleaning staff rushing around, making noise, adding their own brand of smells. She took a deep breath and smelled... home. Books, paper, parchment, leather. The slightly sweet scent of beeswax candles in the decorative sconces and freestanding candelabras. The fresh fragrance of the lemon polish Marta's crew used on the wood stacks and shelves. The heavier perfume coming from the bowls of lilies scattered around on the tables.

Dropping her messenger bag on a nearby table, she moved to the French doors at the far end and swung them open to the garden. More scents flooded in: fresh-cut grass, lilacs and roses in bloom, even the slight tang from the stables at the far end of the gardens.

She closed her eyes and listened. The deep hush of a book-lined room. The slight swish of the draperies in the breeze from the open doors. One voice, likely a grounds-keeper; the clang of a tool, and an answering laugh.

The decisive click of leather dress shoes on marble floors warned her that Prince Nikolas was coming. He slowed and stopped, then headed in her direction. She dragged in one more deep breath of the fresh air from outside. Turning back into the room, she pulled the doors almost closed, leaving them ajar to the morning. Time for today's performance. *Stay cool, don't get flustered. This isn't about you, Emily, it's about the project.*

Less than an hour later, she shrugged off the first interruption. When Prince Nikolas's phone rang, they had barely gotten started. They were standing in the upper stacks, at the edge of where she had left off yesterday. Emily unpacked her tablet and digital camera as she spoke. "In this phase, the intent is to do an accurate count and get a feel for what's here. The purpose isn't to dig into the books and papers deeply, or try to identify unknown works at this point. Although sometimes—"

The prince pulled his ringing cell phone out of his pocket and looked at the screen. "Please excuse me, I need to take this. I won't be a moment." He turned aside and spoke softly into the phone. "Helena? I thought we said…"

Emily stood for a second, camera case in hand, as he moved farther away and she could no longer hear his hushed conversation. Perhaps Helena wasn't so much an ex-girlfriend as Rose wanted her to be. Wishful thinking on the princess's part, maybe? Emily shook her head and continued to unpack, getting the camera out of its case and checking the battery and memory card.

By the time he returned, sliding his phone back into his pocket, she had her laptop and tablet booted up and ready to go.

"My apologies for the interruption. You were saying?"

"Sometimes I see titles and authors I'm familiar with from other projects or from my studies, and I'll make a note of those as I go along. But in this phase, what we do is count. Best way to do that is with pictures. I make my way around all the stacks and shelves and tables, making a high-res photographic record." She stepped around him and grabbed the tall ladder, sliding it along the track that suspended it from the ceiling.

Emily felt his eyes on her, as tangible as a touch, as she went up the rungs. Thank goodness she had the foresight to wear slacks today rather than a skirt. Now all she had to worry about was pantie lines, not whether she was inadvertently flashing him! She climbed up carefully, very aware of the pull of her clothes against her skin.

And still he watched without speaking. The back of her neck prickled and got hot, and she kept a good hold on the ladder and her camera with her suddenly damp hands. She froze when his hand reached up and held the side rail right next to her leg.

She had to clear her throat to make any sound. "You don't need to hold the ladder, really, Your Highness. It's got brakes on the bottom that hold it still when there is weight on it," said Emily, continuing the rest of the way up to where she could reach the top shelf.

"That's all right, I don't mind," Nik replied. He did look very comfortable there, when she peeked back down, leaning against the upright ladder with his arm hooked through a rung. "And I thought you were going to call me Nik, not Your Highness?"

Emily cleared her throat again and aimed her camera at the first row of books. "Yes. Well. I'll work my way down the ladder, one bay of shelves at a time, and then transfer the photos to my laptop. That way I keep them labeled correctly."

He moved to the side as she stepped down, clicking away, but didn't let go of the ladder till she stepped off. "So a lot of your time is spent climbing up potentially unsafe ladders? Is that why the university suggested that you lead the project and not your father: because he can't climb the ladders anymore?" He moved with her to the table, where she connected the ends of the cable to the camera and laptop. "I never thought a librarian's career would carry a physical fitness requirement."

"I'm an archivist, not—"

She was interrupted by the appearance of Rikard Asanovic around the edge of the nearest stack. "My prince?" he said, holding a sheaf of papers out to Nik. "Could you look at these?"

Nik raised his eyebrows. "This couldn't wait?" He tapped on the table, an impatient sound. "Excuse me, please, Emily. I'll be right back."

Rikard smirked at Emily as Nik moved to another table and started flipping pages. "Don't expect him to spend the whole day with you in here, you know. He has far more important things to do than follow around a librarian."

Emily transferred the files from camera to laptop, removed the cable ends, and moved the ladder over to the next bank of shelves. "I'm an archivist, not a librarian," she said, climbing up without looking at him. "And this was his idea."

Nik came back and handed the papers back to Asanovic. There was a hushed exchange of words, and then the other man spun on his heel to leave.

Making her way back down to the floor, Emily reached the table with her laptop the same time Nik did. She glanced at him before linking up her camera. "Most of this phase looks kind of boring. I take pictures; I transfer them to my laptop and note where they're from. When I finish a collection of shelves, I enter the photos and the locations into the database to count and see if I can make a preliminary identification of any of the material. Princess Rose helps with the counting sometimes, during her free time in the afternoons, after her classes."

"So that is what she was doing in here with you on Monday, then? Counting from the photos?" He leaned close over her shoulder to observe.

Emily stiffened, holding her breath as she eased over to the side and tipped the laptop so he could see the screen. Why did he have to smell so good? "No, not then. We were talking to Pétur, my grad student, about some of the books I had found a couple of weeks ago. When I was home last week, he asked me to examine a few in particular and send him scans of some of the inside pages. They might be relevant to his thesis, so he'll be putting in a formal request to come and view them in place when we reach the next phase."

"Why the next phase? Why not now?" Nik asked as he moved with her around the table.

She sidled away toward the ladder. *I wish he'd stay put! It's distracting, the way he keeps following me. I bet he doesn't even do it consciously. I wish I could ignore it...*

The thought made her foot slip as she stepped onto the bottom rung. She caught herself with a gasp, easing out of his grasp as he reached out to steady her. Emily stepped off to stand on the other side of the ladder. Being on solid ground improved her balance, but did nothing to settle her fluttery stomach. "Rather than spend the next couple of hours taking pictures, why don't I walk you through a sampling of the rest of what we've accomplished the past few months? Then we can move on to the next two phases, if you want."

"If you prefer. I want to get a sense of what the entire project will entail. After all," Nik said, raising one brow as he followed her back to the table, "we hired the leading expert to work on our library. It would help me to understand what an expert librarian can do for us."

"Archivist," she muttered.

An hour later she regretted her change in plans. At least going up and down the ladder had kept some distance between them.

Down here, on the other hand, sitting side by side at the table, he touched her. A lot. A hand to her shoulder, a brush of his fingers when she handed him a printout. Even the lean of his shoulder against hers when they were both looking at the screen. Emily kept her head down as much as she could, to hide her continuous blush.

The third interruption was almost a relief. This time it was his personal aide, Anton, who pulled the prince aside with a look of apology in her direction.

She took the opportunity, when he stepped away to deal with whatever this one was all about, to take a deep breath (or two) and settle herself.

Instead of the calm, almost meditative state the familiar scents of a library usually triggered, she found herself more aware of his scent, swamped by the feelings it invoked.

No, no, no! She was not that gangly, impressionable sixteen-year-old anymore, crushing on the exotic prince who came to visit her housemates. She was a well-respected college professor. She had a doctorate, and grad students, and internationally published papers, for heaven's sake! And she was here to do a job. Not to go tripping down memory lane, especially when the memories weren't her most comfortable. And certainly not to, what? Crush all over again? At almost thirty, she was way too old for crushes.

Even if he was the single most gorgeous man she'd ever seen.

"Focus, Em," she said under her breath.

She jumped when Nik responded from right behind her, "Pardon?"

"No, sorry, I—never mind. You asked before about the phases and what happens after the accurate count and some preliminary identifications. We move on to indexing. We're still not digging deep into the contents of the books yet, or at least the project lead won't be. During the indexing, though, there will be a team in here, examining every book, every document. We'll be looking at authors, publishers, dates, provenance, trying to establish when and why each item was added to the library, where it came from, how it fits in here, and who around the world might be interested in it. The library still won't be open to the general public, but you should at that point be thinking about starting to invite particular scholars here." She slid out of her chair and headed back to the shelves, camera in hand. Maybe a few more trips up and down the ladder would settle her brain. And at least that would put her out of touching distance. She hoped.

"I'm confused. If the materials in this library are as valuable and as interesting as you think they are, why are we delaying inviting those scholars and experts here? Would it not be more efficient if they arrived as you work?" Nik followed her over and leaned on the ladder again.

"Sometimes we do," Emily agreed. "In larger libraries like this one, where there is enough room to keep us from tripping over each other, we might bring them in partway through the count. But when we negotiated this contract, your Council chose the three-stage approach. In fact," she said, looking down from her perch, "I was under the impression that you were the deciding factor there, Your Highness."

"Me? Why would I object? Any effort to move this along faster must be a good thing, no?"

She frowned down at him, confused. "But the proposal, the contract, says—"

"Yes, I know what it says. I read it over last night. I am asking why it says that, why there are three phases instead of only two."

"Because that's what you preferred? In the grand scheme of things, adding in outside scholars and historians at this point probably wouldn't change the overall time line. It can actually slow this phase down a little, if I get pulled away from what I'm doing here," she said, gesturing toward the shelves with her camera, "and become more involved with the books as books and not simply as items to be inventoried."

She hooked an arm over a rung and turned sideways to face him. "My understanding is that when Ministers Janko and Bartak were in Edmonton negotiating the schedule, they were getting direction from Council, from you, to make a minimal impact on the day-to-day routines in here, because your office is in here."

"Direction from me? There was no direction from me. I was not informed of this project at all until after the contract was signed and you were scheduled to start work. If there was direction, it came from Council. But not from me."

"I can't tell you what happened on this end, Your Highness. I only know what happened on my end. Either way"—she shrugged—"the scope and phases were negotiated with the University of Alberta, not with me. I only had input on the actual schedule, because I needed to work out my personal—"

"Personal and professional obligations," he interrupted. "I remember. But I researched you, you know. Your track record, you and your father's, is filled with the discovery of items of value above and beyond their interest to scholars and historians."

"Yes, we have found objets d'art, and long-lost music manuscripts, and scientific instruments and treatises. In some places, though, not all. And I won't know till I look, will I? The whole point of this phase is for me to take that quick inventory of everything."

"I'm not sure I understand. You made a case before Council that this work, this project, will help Dubrovia by giving us more exposure. And yet here you are, hiding away in all these books, working so quietly that people in the castle barely know you are here, let alone outside scholars and historians. And not others who may find value in your discoveries and launch them onto the world stage."

Emily had never come down a ladder so fast in her life. "I'm not hiding! This is where I work. This is where the history is. This is where *your* history is! Have you ever heard the expression, 'we are the sum of our experiences'? This library, all these books and documents and records—these are the sum of Dubrovia's experiences," she said, moving to stand toe to toe with him. "That may not be important to you. I keep hearing that your focus is on Dubrovia's future. But how can you plan for the future if you don't understand your past?"

She was shaking inside and out by the time the words came out of her mouth. *Great. Way to piss off the employer.* At least these shakes were caused by anger and not by some indefinable emotion she didn't care to examine. "Look, I—"

And his phone rang. Again. Nik stepped back, looking down at the screen as if to decide whether to answer it. Unbelievable. Emily turned away from him as Rikard Asanovic rounded the corner of the closest stack. Un-freaking-believable and heading toward surreal.

She glared; the councillor smirked. "Making any progress?" he asked. He took a seat at her table, leaning back in her chair and idly jiggling her laptop mouse to bring up the screen.

Emily reached over from the other side of the table and swung her laptop around. "Don't touch that, please."

He shrugged and turned to glance at the prince, who was still murmuring into his phone and jingling the change in his pocket, then swung back to face Emily. "Not that it matters. I'm sure you are starting to see the point of this little exercise, yes?" He moved to the shelves and pulled a book at random, flicking through its pages of photographs.

She pulled out a pair of cotton gloves. "Here. If you're going to handle photographs, wear these."

"No, thanks." He dropped the gloves and the book on her table.

Emily rescued the book and gently returned it to the shelves. "All these interruptions were to prove a point? What point?"

"Why, that Prince Nikolas has more important things to do than spend the day buried in piles of books, of course. What else? Did you think he wanted to spend time with you?" Rikard laughed.

"I already knew how little value you place on my work. I didn't need that point proven to me. And this whole job-shadowing thing, this 'trade a day in the library for a day in the winery,' was his idea."

Emily quietly seethed. Okay, not so quietly. It was hard to sit and listen to someone disparage her work. She didn't much care what Rikard Asanovic thought of her personally, but she wasn't sure how much influence he had on the crown prince, and she'd be damned if he would discount the entire project because he didn't like her (or maybe just had a problem working with women?).

"I realize that what I'm doing here may not seem exciting and glamorous to you. But it's important. I was explaining to Prince Nikolas about how vital understanding Dubrovia's past is to taking her into her future."

"Oh, yes, I'm sure that musty old books and ancient documents are going to be a big help in improving our balance of trade or expanding our wine distribution or renovating the resort and spa to attract more tourists," Asanovic said, his tone dripping with condescension. He moved back to stand across the table, looming over her. "Why are you really here, Doctor? What are you hoping to prove, from all of this?" He waved his hand, dismissing the entire library with his gesture. "This, all of this, is not going to help Dubrovia. So how does it help you, hmm?"

Emily stood and glared across the table at him. "You can't know that nothing in this library will help with your plans, with Dubrovia's plans, for the future. You have no idea what's in here that can make a difference somewhere! And until I take at least a first glance at everything, neither do I."

"So this is all for Dubrovia, then? You expect us to believe that? No one does anything for nothing. I'm wondering what a mousy little librarian hopes to gain out of this," he growled. "I'm wondering whose interests you are truly promoting."

"Promoting? What promoting? I have no vested interest here." Good. Her voice was low and steady. She may be shaking on the inside, but she refused to let him know it.

"Ha!" exclaimed Asanovic. "And you expect us to believe that? Isn't it your goal to stay here as long as you can, stretching out this project so you are paid more, in the hopes that you'll earn a gold star on your résumé? I think you love being here in our library, pretending it's yours. Do you sometimes pretend to be a princess too? Or is it all about the feather in your mousy little librarian's cap, and coins in your coffer?"

"Rikard. Enough."

Two words. That's all it took, two words.

"My prince, I—"

"I said enough. She's right; it was my idea to spend a day here in the library and familiarize myself with her work. However, it was not my idea, nor my intent," he said to Emily, "to be interrupted so often and so persistently. I am sorry for that." Nik gave her a little formal quarter bow, more than a nod of the head but less than the half bow she had almost gotten used to getting from the staff every time one spoke to her.

He continued, "Apparently my request that we not be disturbed except in an emergency was not strongly enough worded. Or my people exaggerate what constitutes an emergency." He frowned at Asanovic, who looked as if he were biting his tongue. Hard.

Nik turned back to Emily. "At any rate, I offer my apologies. I must excuse myself for the rest of the day and deal with matters. I would like, however, to continue our session tomorrow, with my promise to dedicate at least four solid hours, either morning or afternoon, if you could please choose which you prefer?"

Emily breathed a sigh of relief. Maybe by tomorrow she'd have regained her composure. "Of course, Your Highness. Tomorrow morning would be fine, if it suits your schedule. That way I can still work with Princess Rose in the afternoon when she finishes her schooling." She kept her eyes on him, refusing to look at the simmering Rikard.

"Good. Shall we say tomorrow, at nine a.m. again?" At her nod, he turned to go, motioning Asanovic to accompany him. "And Rikard," she heard as they walked away and around the stacks, "tomorrow I expect my request to be honored. I will not brook such interruptions as happened today."

The other man's response was too soft to hear, even if she tried. She dropped back into her chair, put her elbows on the table, and rested her chin on her hands. Argh! She'd have to go through this again tomorrow!

She hopped back up to watch them walk away through the upper stacks and down the spiral stairs in the opposite corner. "Damn," she said under her breath. The little tingles she had tried to ignore all day flared up into a heat that washed through her as the two men parted on the main library floor, Rikard heading out into the hallway and Nik turning toward his office door right below her.

Emily ducked back behind the stack, grimacing, listening for his office door to close, glad he hadn't caught her watching him. She would be more careful tomorrow, and again on Friday when they did the other half of this exercise, the winery tour.

Enough for now. She didn't understand why Nik wanted this big production in the first place. She figured he'd be underwhelmed since she hadn't made any earth-shaking discoveries in the library. (Or at least not yet; there were still those astronomical texts that Pétur had asked her to examine.)

Time to pack up and be someplace else for a while, and try to think about how she might impress the crown prince tomorrow. Or at least not bore him to death. "And if he doesn't understand that a lot of this step is the boring part," she muttered under her breath as she packed up her things, "then he should just read the stupid reports, and not come in here, and get in my way, and, and keep TOUCHING me so much!"

She stomped her way along the stacks, grinding her teeth and taking deep breaths. Maybe a swim would calm her down. If nothing else, it would cool her down.

No, Emily Charette was not a happy woman.

Chapter Thirteen:
In the pool

Flip, push, turn into another lap. The cool water of the pool ought to have cooled off her temper by now. Not so much.

Emily had the place to herself, although she half expected Rose and Jacquie to show up at some point. They hadn't eaten lunch together today or met up during the afternoon so Rose could do her homework while Emily was up and down the ladder photographing more books on more shelves.

No, instead she'd spent this afternoon getting ready for tomorrow and the second installment of her dog and pony show with His Royalness Prince Nikolas. She had first gone through the contract signed by both sides, focusing on the schedule for this phase. Then she'd reviewed all her work, all her reports, all her notes from the Council meetings to date.

Flip, push, turn into another lap. She'd been at this awhile; might be time to start thinking about getting out and drying off.

Instead she swam, and she seethed. It was all so clear! Her initial proposal. The contract negotiations, with input from the king and Council (and said Council included Crown Prince Nikolas). The final contract, specifying her rotations of three weeks in Dubrovia alternating with one week in

Canada. Her weekly reports. And her notes from the one Council meeting a month she attended.

So why did he act as if he never knew they could combine the first two phases, could invite outside scholars and historians at this early date, could start opening up Dubrovia's royal library to the world? Had he never read *any* of this? What the heck had Rikard Asanovic been telling him, then?

Flip, push, turn into another lap. Her strokes, so smooth and regular when she'd started, were getting choppy as she tired.

Apparently nothing. Either Rikard hadn't told him or Nikolas hadn't listened. Or the project was so far down his priority list that he had ignored it from the beginning, except to complain about the money being spent on the library instead of on his precious winery or spa resort.

A spa resort? That's what he thought would make the world sit up and take notice? Well, they might notice, she thought, digging deep for her next stroke, but how could anyone take you seriously when the best thing you had to offer was a playground? What value did he think that added to the world? For someone who seemed so concerned about his country's image, she thought he would want to keep Dubrovia's culture alive and well. What was a country's culture, after all, if not outside validation of its identity?

Flip, push, turn into another lap. Her arms and legs were burning now.

So what would change his mind? Projects like these always started slow. A lot of groundwork remained before progress was apparent. She'd found nothing of major import yet because working alone meant she was stuck counting everything. If Pétur were here to help, she could explore the more promising pieces.

Flip, push, turn into another lap. She dug deep with her leaden arms and struggled to keep her strokes even.

Ha. Prince Nikolas was so opposed to her being here, Council would never approve bringing Pétur here as an intern. Another body meant more money, even if only to cover room and board and travel.

Could she influence his opinion at all? Not on the intern, necessarily, but on how important this was for Dubrovia? Or was trying to change his mind like swimming laps in the pool: burning a lot of time and energy but not getting anywhere?

And could she try to influence him professionally without it getting personal? Because if feelings got involved, she knew which one of them was going to get hurt.

Emily slowed to a stop in the middle of the pool and rolled over onto her back. She floated, letting her breathing even out, staring up at the tiled ceiling. Her body was almost still, her hands just gently sculling to keep her afloat, but her mind moved rapidly. Too bad movement didn't result in any clever ideas. Maybe a soak in the hot tub would relax her enough to allow a plan to form.

* * *

Rose eased her back against the jets of the hot tub and sighed in relief. This was about the only place she could move her legs herself without it hurting a lot. "Oh, boy, that helps. Thanks for bringing me down here, Jacquie."

"No problem. After a session like that one, you need to keep your muscles loosened up. And I know it's a lot more fun to soak in the hot tub than to do another half hour of stretching exercises!" Jacquie replied. She pushed Rose's pool wheelchair over to the side and out of the way before climbing in herself.

"Don't I know it! I wish I could get in and out of this myself. I'd be down here every day."

Her physiotherapist grinned. "Ah, ah, ah, you can't avoid stretching every day. Once in a while is okay, but while the hot water and the jets feel good, they're no substitute for the real thing."

"I know, I know," Rose grumbled. "Stretches and exercises and more stretches. I can move my legs more, and they don't cramp up so much, but it's so slow! I hate not being able to stand up and walk around. I hate when I have to ask people to do stuff for me. I just want to be normal again!"

"Rose, I don't want to discourage you, but—"

"And my back is getting better, isn't it? I haven't needed pain pills in months now."

"Only you can tell whether you hurt less. I can keep you moving, and yes, I have seen some improvement, but I don't want to raise your hopes. Physio isn't going to be a miracle cure for your injuries, I'm afraid."

"No, I know. That's why I wish I could talk to my grandparents about what Dr. Bergner said. She showed me some cool reports from surgeons in the UK who worked on people who were hurt like I was. Some of them can walk again now!"

"Do you have the reports? Would you want me to talk to the king and queen about them?"

Rose sighed, passing her hand back and forth in the stream of bubbles coming from the jet beside her hip. "No, don't talk to Nana. I don't want them mad at you too. Nana got upset at my last checkup when Dr. Bergner mentioned surgery. On the way home she talked to Papa about finding a new doctor, if all Dr. Bergner was going to do was recommend more surgery."

She looked up at a faint splash from the pool. "Emily's sure swimming a long time today. Usually she only does laps for a half hour or so."

"Is that what we're waiting for?"

"I want to hear how her meeting with Uncle Nik went this morning. I thought they were going to spend the whole day in the library today. I was kind of surprised she was down here already."

"From what I heard, it didn't go well," Jacquie said as she switched to the submerged seat across from Rose.

"Ooooh, what did you hear?" Rose said as she leaned in eagerly.

"It's not that it didn't go well—it's that it didn't go at all. Seems everyone kept interrupting. Eventually Prince Nikolas called it off for the day. They're supposed to try again tomorrow."

"I bet that won't go over too well with Councillor Asanovic. He's not happy about this library stuff. And I don't think he likes Emily too much. Of course, I don't think he likes me too much either."

"How can you say that? You're the princess; everyone loves you."

"Not everyone. Not him, and not some other people. To some people I'm in the way." She squirmed down under the frothing water, refusing to meet Jacquie's eyes. "If I had died when my parents did, then sure, I'd be the princess that everyone loved to remember. But I didn't. I'm still here. I'm still a princess, but I'm not *the* princess. I'm not the heir, and I can't do most of the usual princess stuff, like travel around and be an ambassador for Dubrovia like Uncle Nik's been, or even stuff like host receptions here or greet visiting dignitaries. A lot of people act embarrassed around me, or something like that. They don't talk to me. They barely see me. It makes them uncomfortable, me being in a wheelchair. They don't know how to treat me or what to do with me. Or about me."

Rose shrugged. "No one would ever say anything to my face. It's more the way they look at me sometimes, you know? You've heard the expression 'an heir and a spare,' right? Well, I'm the spare, at least for now, until Uncle Nik is married with kids of his own. But having me as princess is like having a spare tire in your trunk with a bad puncture: not exactly useful."

"Rose! I can't believe you think that!"

"I can't believe it either."

They hadn't heard Emily approach; her footsteps on the wet tile were muffled by the bubbling water. As she set down her towel and started to climb the steps into the tub, she continued, "I don't believe you feel useless, do you, Rose? You haven't found what you want to be useful *at*, more likely."

"Yes! That's why I want to go to university somewhere else. I want to travel out of Dubrovia and see what's there, what I can do. I can't be queen here. I don't *want* to be queen! I want to DO something."

Rose was vibrating, she was so excited. Emily understood! They'd talked sometimes, in the library while Emily was taking her inventory and Rose was doing her schoolwork, or over breakfast or lunch; Emily joined Rose for at least one meal a couple of days each week.

"Have you looked at the astronomy programs we talked about? Any sound appealing?" Emily asked, ducking down farther into the water.

"The ones I like best are in the US. I'm not sure my grandparents will let me go so far away. And with my back the way it is, I'm not sure how to manage the living away part, not on my own. Which is why I want to check into surgery again, like Jacquie and I were talking about. And my grandparents don't want that."

"Have you asked them?"

Rose sighed, looking down and swishing her hand back and forth through the stream coming from the jet by her side. "Last time I tried, Nana cried."

"What about Prince Nikolas, Rose? He must have gone away to university. Do you think he would talk to your grandparents for you?" Jacquie asked.

"Maybe, but I don't know what he thinks about my going away. He gets kind of overprotective, like the only place I'm safe is here. If I go anywhere, I might be in another accident." She rolled her eyes. "One thing about Uncle Nik: he thinks he knows what's best for everybody. I mean he doesn't *tell* you that, but he manages to get things done his way most of the time. And when something gets in his way, well… I'm glad I'm not the one he's mad at."

Emily pushed her wet bangs off her forehead. "Ha. I can vouch for that. He certainly wasn't happy this morning."

"We heard." Rose giggled. "Anton told Jacquie, and Jacquie told me. He really let Councillor Asanovic have it."

"Oh, man," moaned Emily. "I am not looking forward to doing it all over again tomorrow."

"Was it that bad, working with Uncle Nik?"

"I don't know, honestly. We never got past getting started. And getting started again, and again. We kept getting interrupted." She leaned back and closed her eyes. "Having an open-door policy can be a good thing when you're the boss. It makes you more approachable. I have one with my students; they can come talk to me whenever I'm in my office. I wish my dean's door were open more often! But today was ridiculous. It wasn't an open door, it was a revolving door!"

"So? Close the door."

"Kind of hard in the big open library, don't you think? Other than posting a guard to direct people away, I can't keep them out."

"Not if you guys worked in his office. Think about it," Rose urged, leaning forward. "You said the whole point is to show him what you're doing in this phase, every step, right? And you haven't worked in his office at all because no one goes in when he's not here. So everything will be new to you. You can treat it like starting a brand-new project from scratch. Well, except for the database and reporting already being set up and all. But the space would be new, right?"

"Yyyesss," said Emily slowly, "but—"

"No, listen!" Rose sat up straighter. This was a great idea! She had been watching Uncle Nik watch Emily, and Emily watch Uncle Nik, when each didn't think the other one was looking. Why not lock them in a room together for hours and wait for something to happen? "You want to see what's in his office, right? And he wants to see how you work, so he can understand why it takes as long as it does. So the best place to show him that is a place where you aren't familiar with anything. It'll go slower than the stacks. There's lots of different stuff in there, not just books on shelves."

"How do you know that?" asked Jacquie. "You don't go in when he's not around, do you?"

"No, not anymore. But sometimes I went in with Dad or Mama, before, when it was Dad's office. I liked looking at the big globe. And there's a really neat orrery that I used to play with sometimes when I was little. An orrery is a mechanical model of the solar system," she explained in response to Jacquie's puzzled expression.

Turning back to Emily, she continued, "So, what do you think? If you go in and close the door, then Anton can stand outside and turn people away if they come looking for Uncle Nik. He does that sometimes, when Nik has a meeting or a phone call and he doesn't want to be interrupted. You could get a couple of hours in at least. I don't know how long the whole room would take, but maybe you could get kind of an idea? And then you could arrange with Uncle Nik for other times when you can get back in?"

"Well, that might work," said Emily, her brow furrowed with indecision. "I'm still not sure it's a good idea, to be in there with him. I didn't think he was comfortable with anyone else invading his space."

It was going to work—it had to! The more Emily and Uncle Nik worked together, the less Councillor Asanovic would make trouble for Emily. And Uncle Nik would have less time to spend with Helena, or even think about her. Maybe if Rose pushed a little harder…

"Do you want me to ask him for you? He's having dinner with Nana and Papa and me tonight—"

"No! No, don't ask him. Let me think about it. No, really, I will," Emily protested. She swallowed hard and climbed out of the steaming water. "It's better if it comes from me."

Chapter Fourteen:
Nik clears his plate

"They'll never go for it."

Nik snatched at the folder Rikard had tossed on his desk before it slithered off the edge. "No, likely not this version. It's a starting place for our talks next week, though. I flagged all of the no-compromise points; everything else is open to negotiation."

"But you took the biggest incentive for them to sign off the table!"

"Perhaps, and perhaps not. I am not interested in signing away exclusive distribution rights to our wine in perpetuity." Nik shrugged. "Actually, I am not willing to sign away anything in perpetuity. Not now, and not to the DiSalvo family. And not without understanding what drove them to insert that clause into this latest contract."

"Oh, come on. It's pretty easy to understand, isn't it? They've had exclusive rights for almost ten years now, but we've only been signing a year at a time. They want more certainty in their business. So do we, for that matter. So why shouldn't they ask for a longer term? And why shouldn't we sign?"

"Rikard, this is not open for discussion. My job—no, our job—is to make sure Dubrovia's interests are best served. Granting exclusive rights forever to anyone other than a Dubrovian company under direct control of the

Crown is not in Dubrovia's best interests. And no one here is in a position to take that on."

"That's my point! Locals don't have the contacts and the shipping infrastructure in place. So why not give the DiSalvos what they want? It sounds like a win-win to me."

"Because I'm not convinced we can't do better. There are other distributors, in Italy and elsewhere, who've expressed some interest in our wines, and we can't explore those options if we are tied to a long-term, exclusive contract."

"So you're willing to destroy a business relationship that has served us well for the past decade, because you think there *might* be another option out there? What about our non-business relationship with the DiSalvos? Or wait," exclaimed Rikard, standing abruptly. "Is that what this is all about? Helena pushed for marriage and you don't want to marry her for some reason, so you want someone else to distribute our wine so you don't have to deal with her?"

"My personal relationship with Helena DiSalvo is her business and mine. It has no impact on these negotiations."

"If you believe that, my friend, you are a fool," Rikard said, shaking his head in disgust.

Nik leaned back in his chair, bracing his hands against the edge of his desk, and stared at the other man. "Say that again?"

Rikard tried to backtrack. "Look, Nik, you might not see the connection between the two, but you can be damned sure everyone else does. Especially Papa DiSalvo. He wants his little girl happy, and he wants exclusive rights to Dubrovian wines, and he gets both if you marry her."

"I am not interested in keeping Salvatorio DiSalvo happy. And when Helena was here on Monday, I explained quite clearly that a marriage has not—will not—be offered," he stated. "And I ended it with her. If she has not yet informed her father, that is her issue, not mine."

"Are you serious? You cut it off? Without talking to Council? You—"

"And why should I talk to Council? This was none of their concern. My personal life is not a topic for discussion. Her expectations were unrealistic, and it was time to make that very clear, to Helena at least." Why was Rikard so caught up in a possible marriage to Helena? Nik didn't think he had given anyone reason to expect a royal wedding anytime soon.

"I imagine things will soon be clear to all parties. Perhaps," Nik said slowly, thinking aloud, "perhaps it would be best if I were not so involved personally. In fact, perhaps I should remove myself from this stage of the negotiations altogether. Yes, I think that would be best for all concerned."

He handed the contract folder back to the other man. "Here. You do it. Enlist Vidor Estok; he's handled the legal end for the last few contracts, so he's familiar with the situation. Start from this position, negotiate the financial terms only, no concession on exclusivity except possibly the distribution within Italy—and hold that back as a final resort—but not anywhere else. And for no more than two years. Just don't commit to anything until I've had a chance to review it."

Rikard took the folder without looking at it. "They're expecting you."

"So? They get you and Estok instead." He came around the corner of his desk and clapped his hand on Rikard's shoulder, steering him toward the door. "Dealing with the two of you instead of with me should clear up any misconceptions about my personal involvement. This contract is with Dubrovia, not with me. Are you telling me the two of you cannot manage to negotiate the terms of a contract?"

"No, of course not. We can take it all the way to signing, in fact."

"That won't be necessary. Council must approve something of this magnitude, and I want to review it thoroughly before they give it their stamp of approval," Nik said as they reached the door.

"So now that you've officially broken it off with Helena, are you sure DiSalvo is still willing to handle our wines? I thought a crown for his daughter was going to be one of his stipulations."

"No crown. No marriage. And no contracts, if you don't start negotiating!"

"I'll see what I can do. Here's hoping she'll find another target. Or at least starts amusing herself far from home. If she's not under Daddy's nose, he may be more agreeable."

Rikard opened the door and almost ran into Emily's knuckles as she started to knock.

"Oh! I'm sorry, I didn't think—"

Rikard looked at Emily in surprise and turned back to face Nik. "Is this what has distracted you?" He shook his head in disbelief. "I can't believe you're putting the future of Dubrovian wine at stake for a mousy little librarian!"

Emily's "I'm an archivist, dammit, not a librarian!" came at the same time as Nik said, "Emily's project has nothing to do with the wine contracts."

"No? Then why are you spending so much time on the project and on her? Or maybe she didn't realize you would be here yet." Rikard turned from Nik and stepped right up to Emily, a smug smile appearing on his face as she stepped back. "Did you think you could convince someone to let you into his office before he arrived? It's early," he said, glancing at his watch. "Is that what you were thinking, Dr. Charette?"

Emily stood her ground. "No, of course not. I hoped to speak with you before we got started at nine," she said to Nik.

"Oh, and what about, if you please? What makes you think—"

"Rikard, enough," Nik said, his expression stern. He pointed at the other man, and then out into the main library. "Go. Find Estok. Start on the contract revisions. I will speak with you both later." He reached for Emily's elbow and started moving her into his office.

"But she—"

"It wasn't—"

She finished her sentence from the inside, facing the closed door. "—my idea."

He kept his hand on her arm, pulling her gently but steadily away from the door and into his office. "What wasn't your idea?"

"Oh, well, I—" She stopped dead and tried to extract her arm. "No, that's okay, I know I'm early. I can come back later. I don't want to interrupt anything. You wanted to start at nine?"

Instead of letting go, Nik tugged her toward the chairs in the sitting area near the fireplace. He was set on keeping hold of her. He liked having her a little off-balance. And he liked having her in his space, which was something to think about later, because usually he tried to keep intrusions to a minimum. Certainly Helena had not been a welcome visitor. Not that she liked spending time in the library or his office; Helena had never been content unless she had a crowd of people around her.

"You're here now. And you're not interrupting. Rikard and I had just finished our discussion, and I can start now." He gave up trying to steer her to a chair when she planted her feet and pulled her arm from his grip. "So, tell me then, what wasn't your idea?"

"This whole thing where you spend a day with me in the library, and I spend a day with you in the winery."

Emily held her arm where his hand had rested. He wasn't sure she realized she was doing it.

She turned in place, looking everywhere but at him. "I'm not sure what you think you'll discover by watching me take pictures and count books."

He raised his eyebrows. "Surely there's more to your job than just counting books? Isn't that a job for an intern, or at least someone more junior than you? I'm surprised you're spending your valuable time on such low-level tasks."

"Normally I wouldn't. But your Council wanted me here for the entire project and didn't want to pay for me to bring one of my interns with me. So I'm who you've got, at least here. Pétur Tumason, one of my TAs, is back in Edmonton double-checking my counts and doing some pre-screening, at least as much as he can from photos. And Princess Rose helps out some afternoons."

"Still, there must be a better use of your time than this! If we are to do this project, and it seems as if we are, then we should be doing it properly."

"The first stretch was a bit different than what I'm doing now. I spent the first few weeks, my first rotation, going through all the loose items on the tables, on and in the lecterns and scattered around in boxes and baskets. There was an awful lot that never made it to the shelves because no one knew where to shelve them! Working through all that material, and doing a quick walk through the shelves to see if any of it did fit somewhere and simply hadn't been put back, gave me a fair idea of what all is in the public spaces. Once that was done, though, it became a matter of counting."

Emily waved her hand, indicating the shelves in the smaller room. "All this was a surprise, of course. Which brings me to what I wanted to talk to you about before we got started today, Your Highness. I was—"

"Nik."

"Sorry?"

"I thought we agreed you would call me Nik? 'Your Highness' sounds so stuffy and formal, don't you think? If we're going to spend a couple of days together, we might as well be comfortable. I find people tend to work better when they're comfortable, don't you? Isn't that why you dress like that, to be comfortable?"

He indicated her clothes: dark brown pants, a deep green Oxford shirt, brown shoes, brown belt. As plain as plain could be, on first glance. But the pants were a tailored fit and cupped her rounded bottom, tucking in at her waist and highlighting the subtle flare of her hips. Her shirt, while a simple button-down in style, was made of silk, not cotton, and draped softly over her very nice breasts.

Nik caught his breath and shifted his stance. He was sure her clothes were comfortable for her. Right now they were making him uncomfortable. He was used to women who dressed and moved to attract. Who knew he could have such a physical response to a little brown sparrow who apparently tried to remain unobtrusive?

Emily stared at him for no more than three seconds. "Yes. It is. I never know whether I'll be down on the floor or up on a ladder. I'm not sure how what I'm wearing is relevant." She closed her eyes and took a deep breath, and opened her mouth to start speaking again. "Here's the thing—"

"Before you start, why don't we come over here and sit down?" Nik interrupted. He crossed to one of the big stuffed chairs by the fireplace and pointed to the other. "At least put down your bag. You had breakfast with Rose this morning, correct? Would you like coffee, or no, you drink tea, don't you? I can ring for some."

"No, thanks, I'm fine for now. Tea later, maybe," Emily said as she placed her bag on the floor and stood awkwardly by the indicated chair. "Look, I—why are you doing this?"

"Doing what?"

"Being so nice, offering me tea and all. I'm intruding in your office. We both know you don't want me here, that you don't want this project to go on at all. So I'm not sure what you want from me."

Nik sat and motioned her to sit too. "The project contract is a done deal, is it not? So why not make the best of things? You have a job to do, and I want to understand what you do and how you do it. So why don't you tell me what you came to my office so early to tell me, and then we can go out into the library."

"That's what I wanted to talk to you about." Emily eased down and perched on the edge of the chair. "I think we should work in here today."

He leaned forward, elbows on knees, studying her. "Why in here?"

"I understand this is your space and you like to work by yourself in here. But that's the good thing, don't you see? People are used to you coming in here and shutting the door and working, so they leave you alone. We were interrupted so many times the other day, we never managed to accomplish anything."

"This is true, but—"

"I have another reason too," she continued, interrupting him. "You're right, the taking-photos-and-counting-books phase is boring. And if we work out there in the main library, that's what's left. But in here?" She jumped to her feet, unable to sit still. "This place is like a treasure box! I don't know what's in here. It's so different from the rest of the space. The start of a project—that first time through a library, that glimpse into the unknown, the possibilities of discovery—that's the most exciting part. The counting and even the documenting that will come later, those are necessary steps. But this? Exploring this? This is the fun part!"

Chapter Fifteen:
The library tour, take 2

It was as much fun watching her face, Nik decided, as it was paying attention to what she was doing. He leaned against his desk as Emily turned the key in another lock, eased open the filigree brass door, and stood for a minute looking at the books on the shelves. She slowly ran her fingertips along the spines, tracing the gold lettering on one particularly large volume before pulling it out.

"You have a lot of books about Italy in here, did you know?" She tilted the cover toward him. "Here's one on northern Italy. They produce a lot of white wines in the north, don't they? Are the Dubrovian whites similar?"

"Some are," he confirmed. "We make a sparkling white that is similar to a prosecco, produced with the same fermentation methods and close in taste." Nik shook his head as she returned the book to its place and reached for her camera. "You can read Italian too? How many languages do you speak?"

"Oh, I can muddle along in a bunch," Emily said absently, focusing and clicking her way down the stack. "Most of the major European languages anyway. I grew up in a trilingual household, so languages come pretty easily to me. I don't have a good ear for the languages of Asia, though. And I can't read them at all. Which is why I stick to libraries in Europe, mostly."

She reached the bottom shelf and sat right down on the floor. He was used to that by now: when something grabbed her attention, the rest of the world disappeared.

When the tea and coffee service was delivered midmorning, he had to almost drag her out of the far corner and over to the table to fix herself a cup. He never did convince her to sit and drink it; she wandered the perimeter of the room, teacup in hand, looking at the tapestries and stuffed heads mounted above the shelves, asking questions about the heraldic arms and weapons scattered around.

"Your tea is getting cold," he reminded her at one point.

"That's okay." Emily looked into her cup, tipped it up and swallowed the rest of the contents. "I'm used to it. I end up drinking far more cold tea than hot when I'm working. Just not usually in the library itself!"

She placed the empty cup on the tray on the table and returned to where she had left off examining the bottom shelf of the set to the right of his desk, across from the door. He couldn't get over the expression on her face. Or more accurately, the expressions. Awe. Delight. Nerves. Reverence. Excitement. And a host of others, coming and going in quick succession over the course of the morning.

At first she had almost danced through his office, flitting from one thing to another so fast he thought she should be dizzy. Questions came fast and furious, most of which he could barely answer.

He never thought about his office as a potential treasure trove. It was simply the place where his father had worked, and then his cousin Stefan, and now Nik himself. Sure, there were lots of old bits and pieces scattered around, some on the walls, some on the shelves, some standing on their own pillars and plinths and pedestals. He moved some of those out of the way the first time he had more than two people in here for a meeting. For the most part, he ignored it all as part of the scenery.

So when they first started working today, he watched Emily look around, poke around, and generally investigate everything she could without unlocking the brass grates over the shelves. When she got to the big map chest across from the door and pulled open the first drawer, she made an exclamation of dismay. "Look at all this! Do you have any idea what's in here? Or how long it's been here?"

She rummaged around, shifting the top pieces to the side to uncover the layers below. "Oh, man. You've got World War II–era maps mixed in with land grants from the 1800s. The mess is as bad as the tables out in the main library." She slid the drawer closed with a bang and glared at him. "This is your space! Weren't you ever curious to know what's here? How did it get into this condition?"

Nik raised his hands defensively. "Don't look at me! I haven't touched anything except the desk and the closest set of shelves since I moved in here two years ago, after Stefan died. It was his office before mine. I doubt anyone has done anything to organize this place since long before I was born." He narrowed his eyes at her. "Isn't that the point? We know it's a mess! We called you in to fix it."

Emily winced and turned away, back to the shelves. "Sorry. You're right, of course. It just breaks my heart when I find such valuable materials so neglected."

"You make it sound like we abandoned a baby! It's books: paper pages and leather covers. And maybe some artwork. Besides the fact they might be worth something because they're old, what makes them so valuable? Why is this so important to you?"

"Well, partly it's the age of it all, because I'm from Canada. We don't have the sense of history of place that you do here. Dad says—"

She stopped and took a breath. "My father used to say that to Europeans, a hundred miles is a long way, and to Canadians and Americans, a hundred years is a long time. When we lived in Calgary we thought nothing of driving eighty kilometers to Banff, in the Rockies, for lunch. But there isn't much in Edmonton, where we live now, that was built before 1900. In Cerina, there are headstones in the cathedral's cemetery with dates in the triple digits! So yes, anything old has intrinsic value just for its age."

"But that's not all. Not for you."

"No, it isn't." Now she moved over to the shelves and ran her fingers over the brass grill encasing the first bookcase. The key was in the lock; she turned it and eased open the door, tugging a little against the slight resistance and smiling at the squeak of unoiled hinges. "It's history. It's where you came from as a people, how you got to where you are now. What drives you as a country. What's important, what's changed, what you fought for, or fought against."

"So you think you can make judgments about people or predict their behavior based on the history of their country?"

"Well, no, not exactly. No more than you can predict someone's behavior by studying their parents and grandparents. But knowing someone's family history and the environment they grew up in can at least give you some insights into how they'll act or react. You recognize patterns, if not specifics."

"So your analysis of our history resembles doing background research then, like the due diligence I do on a company I want to invest in." He was starting to see her point. It never occurred to him to evaluate his country's history, or any country's history for that matter, in the same way he evaluated business opportunities.

"Yes! It's not so different. The scope I examine here is broader than economics alone, and I look back further, but you get the general idea."

Nik thought about that while she worked her way through that bookcase and into the next. By the time she moved on from the set of books on Italy, he was contemplating turning Rikard loose in his office and telling him to look for anything that could be useful in Dubrovia's external trade negotiations. Except Rikard's written comprehension of languages other than English and Czech and their local dialect might not be good enough to catch subtleties and nuances. Hmm. He'd need to hire an interpreter. Or two. Maybe—

He brought his mind back to the present with an effort. He could barely see Emily's head where she had sat down on the floor. He crossed over to behind the desk, wanting to see what she'd find next. And to see her when she found it.

But not right now. The old clock on the mantel caught his eye. He would have been more aware of the time had he not turned off the chimes years ago. Right now he said, "Are you ready to take a break?"

"Hmm, sorry? What?"

"I said, are you ready to break for lunch? It's after one thirty. We've been in here for hours; we should step out and have something to eat."

"One thirty? Oh, no! I need to make a phone call. If it's all right with you, I'll make my call and duck down to the kitchens for something quick and meet you back here... when?"

"Nonsense. I can wait for you to make a call. And then we can take a real break with a proper lunch. Have you had any meals down in the town yet? There's a lovely little café on the edge of the university grounds. I'll phone them and let them know we're coming and arrange for a car while you make your call."

You'd have thought he had suggested flying to Paris rather than driving down into the city from the expression on her face. "I can't go to lunch in a café with you!"

"Whyever not?" He crossed back to his desk and picked up the phone. "You have to eat. I have to eat. I suggest we eat together, and you can tell me more about these potential treasures in my library that you seem to think you will find."

"No, really, that's okay." Emily grabbed her messenger bag from the chair where she had dropped it. She backed toward the door even as she rooted around for her phone. "Honestly, I'll call home and meet up with you later."

She was through the door before he could stop her.

Chapter Sixteen:
In the vineyard

Emily shaded her eyes with her hand. The early-morning sun shone bright on the side of the mountain, burning into her eyes as she gazed downhill. "That's a lot of grapes. I knew about the vineyards down by the castle, but I had no idea they came up this far."

"This vineyard is fairly recent. My grandfather converted this side of the mountain to grapes before I was born. The vines don't yield as much fruit as the ones we passed on the way up, but these grapes make superior wines."

"What was up here before the vines?"

"Mostly soft fruit—cherries and apricots, I think. And apples. But we had a fire, a forest fire. See there?" Nik reached in front of her to point down the hillside, gesturing at the bank of taller trees. They crossed a small river, not much more than an overgrown creek, before climbing the last stretch of incline. "The fire went down the mountain, turned at the river, and kept going all the way down to that ridge."

Somehow as he described the course of the fire, his other arm found its way over her shoulder to point her in the right direction. She eased out from under the light touch. *He's even more touchy-feely this morning than usual. What's going on?* Yesterday he'd started out almost distant, although he'd warmed up as the day went on. She wasn't used to the masculine attention.

And this was Nik. The man she'd crushed on so many years ago. She felt her cheeks warm and decided to blame the strong sunshine if he noticed.

Fortunately he didn't, or didn't appear to, so she decided to pretend it never happened and asked, "What started the fire? We have forest fires in Alberta every year, and grass fires on the prairie. Scary stuff."

"I don't know if they ever determined the cause. My grandfather and great-uncle were up here; they got caught up in it and ended up taking shelter in the old tower up on the ridge."

"What tow—oh, look at it! It's gorgeous! Is it still in use?"

"The shepherds sometimes use it in bad weather. We pasture sheep and goats just over the ridge in the summer." He touched her arm to turn her to face away from the sun and toward the side of the mountain. "But only the ground and second floor are used. I don't think the stairs are safe anymore."

"Oh, too bad. I bet there's a tremendous view from the top."

"There is." His brilliant grin caught her off guard. "Stefan and I used to climb it when we came up to work in the vineyard during the summers."

"You used to work in the vineyards?"

"You sound surprised. Yes, we worked in the vineyards. And in the winery. We used to have water fights with the high-pressure hoses used to clean the crushing vats." He chuckled, obviously enjoying the memories, then shook his head. "Life was a lot simpler then, when all I worried about was whether I got the vats clean to my mother's standards." He opened his mouth to say more, but turned at the sound of voices.

"Niko! You're here! It's so good to see you! And look, everyone, he brought a girl!"

A grinning face appeared from around the nearest row of vines. The older man, his back bowed by long years of hard work and his face lined from the sun, caught Nik up in a hard hug.

"Gabrial, you old rascal! It's been a long time. How are you? How is Antoinetta? And your boys? You have two in college now, don't you?" Nik pounded the older man on the back.

Emily was floored. This was Crown Prince Nikolas, the elegant-suited, formal businessman who intimidated underlings and escorted a beautiful woman on his arm every time the press photographed him? This man, comfortable in well-worn jeans and rubber boots and a snug black T-shirt, dirt on his knees from crouching down to check the grapes and the condition of the vines? This man, who greeted the work crew with obvious affection and no little familiarity?

He was certainly not the man to whom she had defended her project, not the man whose business acumen took the small country's foreign trade to the heights it currently enjoyed.

How could she reconcile his many facets in her mind? She remembered Nik as the young, carefree cousin of her good friend. Then, doing her research about Dubrovia before taking the contract, she'd read about the successful businessman and the globe-trotting playboy. And she'd met the stern, disapproving prince with the power to shut down her project, or at least sour the opinion of Council and sway them from moving forward with the remaining phases.

She never expected the warm, approachable, likable Nik who stood in the center of a laughing group of men, trading jokes and insults and generally having a wonderful time.

And she felt like an outsider. She belonged down in the castle, in the library, not up here in the vineyards. She started to edge back toward their truck. Maybe she could just—

"Niko! Who is this lovely young lady? I thought you were dating that skinny blonde. This one looks much more the thing, eh?" The first man to greet Nik came over to her and shook her hand with great enthusiasm. "My name is Gabrial Vavra. And you are?"

"Hello," she replied cautiously, with a sideways glance at Nik. He just stood, grinning, and let her make her own introductions. "I'm Dr. Emily Charette, and I'm here—"

"Oh, you are the famous professor who is here to save our royal library! Dobromil, Josef, come and meet Niko's professor! She's the one Elisa told you about, you remember?" He turned to Emily, beaming. "Our queen is most certain that with your help, our university will recover its former glory. And then perhaps our young people will not be so eager to leave, yes?"

This was an unexpected twist. Queen Elspeth had said something of the sort on Emily's first day in Dubrovia, but no one had mentioned it since. She felt unqualified to even comment about their university, let alone make any sort of recommendations about changing it!

"Yes, I'm a professor, but I'm here for the library, not the university," she tried to explain.

"Nonsense. It's all part of the same thing, isn't it? You agree, don't you, Niko?" Gabriel turned to address the younger man.

"Dr. Charette is making her mark on the library. We're lucky she came here. She and I spent yesterday in my office, the den, and found all sorts of references and old documents she will want to spend more time studying. Isn't that right, Dr. Charette?"

He was teasing her. Teasing her! But not in the slightly nasty way she was used to from him and from Rikard Asanovic. This teasing was the teasing of a friend, one who understood her work and took her seriously.

The conversation drifted to more general talk of university and travel. Apparently most of these men had children, or grandchildren even, who were out of the country attending school somewhere else. At least that was a safe topic; everyone always wanted to talk about their own children, and she could deflect the more personal questions by talking about her school and travel experiences.

She didn't want to think about the questions they were peppering at Nik about her. The men all spoke to her in Czech, and she responded in the same language. If she was careful, they would never realize she also spoke their local dialect, and she could dodge the more intrusive questions.

Because Nik did just fine in that regard. No, she wasn't his girlfriend. No, he wasn't going to bring the "skinny blond one" up here. Had he ever? And more importantly, yes, he was back home to live here for good.

That last one cost him, she could tell. Emily couldn't imagine how it must feel to give up his lifestyle, the life he'd built for himself, to come back here and take on the responsibility of being crown prince. The perks and privileges of a prince probably weren't substantially different from those of an international business magnate, but the increase in responsibilities was huge.

He extricated himself from the crowd and made his way over to where she stood a little off to the side. "I am sorry for the interruption. I didn't expect them here; I thought they were working farther down the hill today. That's why I came up this far, to show you the vines and the mountain without having to deal with them."

"Don't apologize. They're wonderful. I didn't want to get in the way. They wanted to talk to their prince. How often can they do that?"

"More often than you might think, but not as often as they would like. Or I would, for that matter. I like to touch base with them all at least a couple of times a year. They've been working the vines longer than I've been alive, most of them. If there's a problem anywhere, they'll know. And many of their kids study agriculture and viniculture and come back with fresh ideas."

"And do you take their advice?"

"Sometimes." He smiled at her, walking with her back to their truck. "Sometimes not. Somebody has to be the boss; that's my job. But I like to think I listen and let them have a say."

He held the door open for her, and closed it gently after she climbed up into the cab. "What do you say we head back down the hill? I'd like to show you the vineyards close to the castle. Those are our oldest vines, there with our olive trees."

Chapter Seventeen:
The winery tour

She felt the skin on her face loosen and relax. Inside the winery buildings it was cool and just the slightest bit damp, quite a change from the dry, dusty heat out in the vineyards. Emily wasn't sure if it was really damp from moisture, or whether it was the residual evaporated wine in the air that made everything a little clammy. Certainly the vaulted rooms full of barrels smelled more like wine than like wet stonework.

In fact, if she took a deep enough breath she could feel the alcohol catch in the back of her throat. "I never realized that the barrels let so much of the wine escape."

Nik took a deep breath himself and closed his eyes. "Mmm, yes. The angel share, we call it—the little bit of wine that evaporates during the secondary fermentation in the barrels. You don't want to light a match in here. One reason why so many wineries are built in or near caves, and why our barrels are stored underground, is because the temperature stays constant pretty much all year round. We don't have to heat down here except in the coldest part of the winter. And for that we have fired heaters that blow barely warm air in through the vents."

He pointed up at the ceiling. Emily could hardly find the openings in the stonework. The rooms were kept dim by her standards: only one or two ceiling fixtures in each row of barrels was shining. "Is that why you have so few lights, to prevent sparks?"

Nik nodded. "And lights can throw a lot of heat too. We try to keep the conditions down here as constant as possible. About the only time we switch all the lights on in a room is when we're turning barrels, or loading and unloading. When we test we'll bring a flashlight so we can read the instruments."

They walked through the echoing room and back up into the sunlight just as a small van drove up. "Oh, good," said Nik. "They're here."

Nik's aide Anton got out of the van, waved at them, and then walked around the vehicle to open the passenger door on the other side. He ducked down, and several minutes later Rose's wheelchair whizzed around the side and rolled toward them.

"Hi, Uncle Nik! Hi, Emily! Thank you so much for inviting me to come to the winery with you! I'm not able to come up here very often anymore."

Emily turned to Nik. "You invited Rose?"

"I did. Do you mind?"

"Mind? Of course not! I think it's a great idea. She loves to get out of the castle. And if she stays here on the grounds, she doesn't need to have bodyguards trooping after her. I know how much she hates that."

"So do I. I thought she could have a bit of a treat." He raised his voice to include the girl. "Rose, did you bring lunch with you?"

"Yes, I think Anton has it in the back of the van."

Anton was already retrieving a pair of rather large picnic baskets. "I think my mother has sent enough for an army, so I hope your morning in the vineyards has made you hungry," he said, hefting his load up and closing the door.

"You are welcome to join us, if you'd like," Nik said, taking one basket from him and leading the way over to a pair of tables sitting under a tree.

"Thank you, but I think I had better return to the castle." He pulled Nik aside, and the two men conversed quietly.

"Emily, look at all this! Can you help me get the cloths out of the baskets? Or put them down on the bench, where I can reach? The table is almost too high." Rose was trying to open the nearest basket without tipping it over on herself.

"Of course." Emily hurried over to help Rose all the while keeping half an eye on Nik and his aide. Was Nik going to have to leave and not finish the tour of the winery with her?

She had mixed feelings about that. On one hand, this morning had been a little intense. Not seeing him laughing and joking with the laborers in the vineyards; no, that had been enjoyable, if unexpected. What had made her uncomfortable had been more the physical stuff. He liked to touch: the small of her back when he walked alongside, her elbow when he steered her in one direction or another to look at something. Even her hair, when the breeze had whipped up and loosened some strands from her braid. Her hands had been full, juggling her camera and grabbing her hat so it didn't blow away, so he had just reached out, brushed the tendrils away from her eyes, and tucked them behind her ear.

And he liked to stand close, close enough that she felt the warmth radiating from him over and above the heat she felt from the sun. Close enough that she smelled his scent— a little spicy, a little woodsy—on top of the perfumes of the ripening grapes and the blooming roses at the end of each row of vines. Close enough that she was always, always aware of him.

Meeting up with Rose here at the winery proper was both a relief and a letdown. She liked having the buffer, but she missed the closeness, the intimacy of the morning, more than she expected to. More than she wanted to. She didn't want it to end, but she didn't want to repeat it either.

On the other hand, if he left now, would they have to pick up where they left off yet again, and finish touring the winery on another day? Emily wasn't sure that was such a great idea. So far, Nik hadn't seemed to remember her from before. Which was a good thing; no one wants to be reminded of how young and stupid they once were. Everyone had their adolescent crushes, didn't they? As long as she played it right, played it cool, she'd be safe.

Nik walked back to them, smoothing the slight frown from his face and smiling at his cousin. Emily caught her breath. This was a different smile, a different Nik, yet again. Not joking-with-the-guys Niko, the one she saw this morning in the vineyard. Not big-business Nik, the powerful, controlling CEO who had called her into his office to report on her project. Not even Crown Prince Nikolas, who sat in on Council meetings or led them in his uncle's absence. This smile, this Nik, was affectionate and warm. *Family Nik,* she thought as he teased Rose about the spread of food she had wheedled from the kitchen staff.

Her heart gave a little bump. Oh, no. No, no, no. She was not going to turn all gooey inside about Family Nik. He wasn't her family. She didn't *have* family, not like that. She had her dad, and that was enough. It had to be enough.

* * *

"Elias tells me that we have a new litter of puppies," Nik commented to Rose as they repacked the picnic baskets with the remains of lunch.

"Not new, Uncle Nik. They're a couple of months old now. He said he'd bring them out once we finished eating." Rose turned to Emily. "If that's all right with you?"

"I should warn you," Nik said, "they're rather large and slobbery. If you don't like big dogs, we can take ourselves into the winery and finish up while Rose visits with the puppies."

"No, that's fine, I like dogs." Emily turned to face the scrabbling and barking of what sounded like an entire pack of young wolves rounding the corner of the building. "Okay, that's a lot of dogs."

At least a dozen barking, yipping, jumping pups surrounded their feet. Some tried to climb up onto Rose's lap as the girl giggled and pushed them off. Some snuffled around Nik's boots and tried to chew on the edges of his jeans. And a couple leaned against Emily's legs, yapping for attention.

A man about Nik's age came trotting around the corner after them with an older dog, the pups' mother, at his heels. He whistled sharply. About half the pack spun around and tore off in his direction. The others milled around looking confused until he whistled again and they ran to join their littermates.

"Well, at least he's got them half-trained." Nik laughed.

"Half of them trained, or all of them halfway trained?" Emily asked as she brushed at her jeans. The morning's coat of dust was rapidly turning to mud on her legs. Oh well.

"Both, and neither. Rose," he continued, turning to the girl, who was still giggling, "did you want to play with them for a while? I want to take Emily through the blending and bottling areas."

"Yes, please, Uncle Nik. They can't climb up on my lap yet, and there are too many of them to hold even if they could."

Nik retrieved one of their tablecloths and spread it on the ground. He carefully lifted Rose out of her wheelchair and placed her with her back against the tree they had been sitting under. At his signal, Elias released the pups with a voice command. They raced over to sprawl and bounce on the cloth and on Rose.

"Is she going to be all right under all those dogs?" worried Emily.

"Sure. Elias will make sure they don't misbehave." Nik motioned to the man standing off to the side with the older dog. "Elias, meet Dr. Emily Charette. She is heading up the restoration of our royal library. Emily, this is Elias, one of our principle vintners. He handles the whites and sparkling wines. Elias, why don't you tell Emily about them while I speak to Rose for a minute."

"Pleased to meet you, miss." Elias switched the dog's leash to his other hand and shook hers. "I hear you spent the morning up in the vineyards?"

"Yes, but I think we saw red wine grapes up in the hills."

Emily listened as Elias chatted enthusiastically about his grapes, his wines, the upcoming harvest and Harvest Festival. But a good portion of her attention was on Nik. Kneeling down on the tablecloth next to Rose did interesting things to his jeans as they tightened around the long, lean muscles of his thighs and the tight, round muscles of his butt. And talking to his young cousin did interesting things to his face, softening his smile and lighting up his eyes as he laughed with her.

No, no, and no again! This wasn't the Nik she knew, or thought she knew. It wasn't even the Nik she remembered from fifteen years ago. Was this the real, true Nik, the one with the heart? And if it was, had she been doing him an injustice by not seeing, not recognizing that heart?

It didn't matter, she decided, as he rose from his crouch and came back to where she stood. Whether this was a new, unfamiliar side to the same man, or a side that had been hidden all along behind the CEO and the prince, it didn't matter. It couldn't matter. He was still her boss, he still had the power to shut down or at least cripple her project. She refused to be attracted to him. Nope, not going there.

And then he picked up one of the pups and dropped it into her arms. "Here. You look way too serious for an afternoon of picnics and puppies. Hold him while I talk to Elias for a minute, and then we'll go inside and tour the rest of the winery."

And her heart gave that funny little bump again. Not good. Not safe. Not wise.

* * *

Emily watched Nik rinse and dry the hydrometer and nestle it into its case. "You're a different person down there," she said.

"What, in the barrel rooms?"

"No, down in the castle. Not like here or up in the mountains."

"What do you mean?" he asked, looking up, a question in his eyes. He latched the little wooden box and replaced it on the shelf near the sink before turning to face her. "How am I different? I'm the same person, always."

"Well, underneath, sure, I guess. But up on the mountain, or here in the winery, you're... lighter, maybe?

Freer? Less serious? Down in the castle, there's this, I don't know, distance between you and everyone else. Or a layer, maybe. It's harder to see you under it."

Now he was scowling at her. "I don't wear masks. I hate masks."

"No, not a mask." Emily shook her head in frustration. "I'm not explaining this very well, am I? Look, let's head back outside and find Rose. And I'll try to think of a better way to describe it."

He ushered her out of the small lab area and back into the big underground storage room. They walked between the rows of piled barrels and toward the stairs that would take them back to the upper levels.

And people. She wanted to make her point before they came within hearing distance of other people. And before he had a chance to stew about what she had said, since it was clearly a sore point.

At the bottom of the stairs, she paused and said, "Not a mask. More like a… a cloak. A weight on your shoulders. Like you have to be the one responsible for everything."

"That would be because I *am* responsible for everything. Not only am I the business manager of the winery, but I am also the crown prince. This whole kingdom is mine to care for." He motioned her up the stairs ahead of him.

Emily hurried up the stairs; she wanted to watch his expression, and she couldn't when he was behind her. And maybe looking at her ass again. Although, he was annoyed enough at her comments that right now his focus might be more on what she'd said than how she looked.

Or not. She reached the top and swung around in time to see his eyes lift up to meet hers. She blushed, as she had every time she'd caught him looking at her today. This time, though, this time his face was expressionless.

"Nik, I know the whole kingdom is your responsibility. But up on the mountain, or here in the winery, you're not directly involved in the day-to-day as much as you are in the castle or in public." She waved her hand in a broad arc, indicating everything beyond the walls of the vaulted room.

"No, I'm not up in the vineyards or here in the winery every day. Not now, anyway, although there have been times when I was younger that I was." He brushed past her to move on through the next set of barrels.

Emily hustled to keep up. "And those were some of the best times you had growing up, right? Up on the mountain this morning, when you were talking to all the workers, they laughed and joked with you, and you laughed and joked right along with them. You were a part of their lives when you used to spend your summers in the vineyards. You're still part of their lives. You know their names, their partners, their children, their grandchildren. They remember that, and they love you for it."

"They're mine." He shrugged.

"Yes, they are. They all are." Emily stopped him with a hand on his arm. "You've shouldered the entire weight, the vineyards and the winery, all Dubrovia's business and trade, and now you're heir to the throne as well. I guess I just never realized how hard that would be for you. I guess I thought it was just kind of an extension of what you already did."

Nik looked down at her hand, but he didn't pull away. "I never wanted the throne."

"I know. I remember that from when I met you all those years ago. You were happy even then that your cousin was the heir, not you." She squirmed a little. "I overheard you talking to Stefan and Kate one night, when I lived with them. I'm not sure if you remember me from then. I used to help take care of Rose sometimes. I was upstairs putting Rose to bed and you all sat in the kitchen. Kate was teasing you about... well, your lifestyle and how you were a bit wild and how you and Stefan were so different. And you laughed and said right out that you were glad Dubrovia was going to be his responsibility."

He made a noise somewhere between a grunt and a laugh. "I remember that night. I was on a break between terms at Oxford, so I went to Canada to visit them." He covered her hand with his, and tightened his grip when she tried to pull away. "And I remember you."

"Oh, well, I wasn't sure you did. It was a long time ago," Emily stammered, "and I was a lot younger than you. I didn't think you noticed me at all."

"I noticed. It was not wise of me. Stefan warned me about you."

"Warned you? About me? What about me?"

He pulled on her hand and swung her around to face him. "That you were too young, too innocent for someone like me."

She couldn't quite catch her breath. He stood very close, closer than he had that morning when she became so physically aware of him. Down here, in the cool and the damp, where the wine barrels towering over them gave off fragrant hints of fruit and alcohol, his heat and his scent overwhelmed her senses.

"I…"

He nudged her bangs out of her eyes and behind her ear. "You what?"

"I think… I think this isn't a smart idea."

His fingertips moved lightly down the side of her face and along her jaw and behind her ear again. He cupped his hand around the back of her neck. Gently, so gently. She could have moved away anytime. So why didn't she? Instead she closed her eyes and breathed him in.

Just before his lips brushed over hers, she heard, "I think it's a marvelous idea."

Chapter Eighteen:
Emily gets some help

Emily cracked open the door with a sigh of relief at finding Nik's office empty. Anja had told her, when she delivered Emily's breakfast, that Nik had left early, heading back to Italy. Castle gossip (of which Anja was a dedicated follower) placed him neck-deep in contract negotiations again.

Anton had instructions to allow her into Nik's office in order to finish her count in his absence. So here she stood. Counting. Glad he wasn't there to look over her shoulder, distract her, make her laugh, kiss her again.

But it hadn't been a real kiss, had it? He'd barely brushed her mouth with his. She couldn't control the sharp little intake of breath, the thump of her heart, the flutter of her eyelids, as she'd waited for him to do it again. Wanted him to do it again.

His breath, warm, tasting of the wine they'd shared at lunch, had feathered over her lips as he approached for a second pass. Which never happened, because at that precise instant she identified the faint drumming in her ears as not the beat of her heart but the clatter of footsteps.

She'd sprung away, almost knocking into a tower of barrels in her haste to gain some distance. Nik reached for her, to steady her so she wouldn't fall, but she gave him a quick shake of her head and backed up another step. Her fingers crept up to touch her mouth as he threw her a frustrated look and turned to face the arriving Anton.

"Sir! Sir? I'm sorry to interrupt, but if you could please come outside…" Anton was out of breath and apologetic. He glanced quickly at Emily, winced, and looked away again.

"What is the problem? I gave orders not to be disturbed today."

"It's the DiSalvos, sir. They arrived about an hour ago and insisted on seeing you. My father called from the castle to say Miss DiSalvo is on her way to the winery, with Councillor Asanovic."

"She's on her way here? Why? And with Rikard? He should know better." Nik turned to Emily, reaching for her hand. "This won't take long. I'll send her back with Rikard, and we can finish our afternoon here."

"No, no, that's all right. You go and… well, do whatever you need to do. I'm sure Anton will take me back to the castle. I can ride back with Rose." She extracted her hand and nervously tugged on her braid. The scrunchie holding the end came off in her hand, and she pushed it onto her wrist.

Nik frowned at her as Anton nodded rapidly. "Yes, of course, sir, miss. I will make sure Princess Rose and Dr. Charette are transported back. But, sir, if you please—"

"All right, Anton, I'll be right there. No," Nik said to Emily as she turned to follow his departing aide, "a word with you first, please."

"No, you need to go. I'm sure there's a problem, or Councillor Asanovic wouldn't come here with Miss DiSalvo. No need to worry about me. We can forget this ever happened. Right?"

Emily knew she babbled, but what else could she say? The near-kiss was a mistake. It shouldn't have happened. She shouldn't have let it happen. He was her boss, sort of; at the very least he was a client, and it was inappropriate for her to have shared a kiss with him, not to mention unprofessional. What would her father think, if he ever found out? He couldn't find out!

"We need to talk about what happened here. But," Nik acknowledged with another frown, "not now. Now I need to find out what's brought the DiSalvos to Dubrovia today. I told Rikard to schedule a meeting for next week, in Italy."

She might not know what had brought Signor DiSalvo here, but Emily was pretty sure she knew why his daughter had tagged along. And it wasn't to tour the winery, contracts or no contracts. Helena DiSalvo's arrival reminded her why talking about the near-kiss was a bad idea, let alone repeating it. Emily knew she had no business thinking about confidential talks or kisses or anything else with Crown Prince Nikolas Kuliç.

She put more distance between them, edging toward the door. "We don't need to discuss anything. Whatever this was, it isn't going to happen again. It's not only a bad idea but also inappropriate of me, and I apologize."

"There is nothing for which you need to apologize. You did nothing wrong. We did nothing wrong." He caught up to her just before she got to the end of the row of barrels, and stepped in front of her before she could escape out into the sunshine.

"I hope I haven't jeopardized the work I'm doing for Dubrovia. I can promise you I will stay out of your way in the future. I'll work out in the main library mostly, but if you're willing to let me get into your office with Anton present, then I'll finish up in there while you're away."

"That is not necessary."

He stood in her way, his speech as stiff and stilted as his body language. She mentally shook her head, not wanting to get distracted by his speech patterns when she needed him to move. The woman waiting outside for him wasn't known for her patience. Emily could hear Helena's voice, although she couldn't yet make out the words.

Maybe if she gave him something else to think about, he'd focus on that and not on her. "Or maybe I should bring in someone else, someone—"

"You intend to leave? You do not intend to finish your work, to keep your commitment?"

Okay, bad choice of words. He was now focused on something other than today's events, but not in a good way.

"No, no, of course not. I meant since we spoke about bringing in some help, someone to take over the counting, now is the time. I can get a grad student or two here in a couple of days, and they can finish up in your office. Or would you rather I hired someone local?"

The voices outside were getting closer, getting louder. Emily winced at a particularly shrill complaint.

Nik stared at her, his expression blank. "Do either. Do both. Whichever you think is best. I would not want you to be uncomfortable working in the library. And it seems you will be so, if you were to work in my office now. Yes?"

"I—yes. I would be a little uncomfortable working in your office right now. I think it would be best if I brought in someone to help. It would allow me to focus on examining some of the more interesting works as well as, well, adding some distance."

"Fine." He turned and walked to the doorway, then spoke over his shoulder. "But we are not done with this."

That was two weeks ago. Since then, she'd seen him every once in a while, coming and going from his office, sometimes with Rikard Asanovic, sometimes with his uncle, the king. Always in a hurry, always looking at least stern if not downright annoyed.

As he did the day she introduced her assistants, new and old. With the dean agreeable to the reassignment of her teaching assistant, Pétur flew in from Edmonton on the weekend and started right in on Monday morning. And she hired a student from the University of Dubrovia in Cerina, an IT undergrad with more of a focus on the information than the technology and a passion for local history.

The two of them took over the photographing and counting, freeing Emily to start a more in-depth study of some of the texts that had caught her eye. Their enthusiasm had made a good impression at their first Council meeting, when they presented the overall status while she talked about the astronomy texts she was working on translating. Even Nik was civil if not welcoming, although she avoided looking directly at him during the session.

Emily felt like a bit of a coward, then and now. She made a point of working in the far end of the upstairs gallery as much as possible ever since their day in the winery. The odd time when she and Nik crossed paths, she smiled politely and kept moving. Each time as she walked away she could sense his eyes on her back (she hoped on her back, anyway).

So here she was, counting again. While she was authorized to be in Nik's office in his absence, her students were not. They worked in the upper reading room at the moment. The sound of voices drifted down through the fireplace flue from the room above: Pétur, of course, and Ivan Machacek, her local student hire, and Rose, by the sound of it. It was great to see Rose blossoming under the attention of two young men. Even if Pétur was very gay, and very married, Ivan wasn't. And he was closer to Rose's age: nineteen to her sixteen.

Caught up in her work, half listening to the voices and laughter from above, Emily missed the opening of the door. She didn't miss the scent of coffee, though, and said absently, "Thank you, Anton, could you leave it on the table?"

"Not Anton, and I'll put it on the table, but I'd rather you joined me," drawled a familiar voice.

Emily froze. He wasn't supposed to be here. He was supposed to be in Italy! "What... what are you doing here?"

"This is my office, remember? I work here."

The lazy amusement in his voice surprised her. The last time they'd spoken, as they stepped out of the secondary fermentation room at the winery and into the sunshine, she'd been sure he was annoyed. Annoyed at Anton for nearly walking in on them, annoyed at Helena DiSalvo for arriving and interrupting them, and annoyed at Emily—for pulling back from the near-kiss (the responsible move!), for suggesting she bring in help to work on the library (and he'd agreed, right?), for avoiding him ever since (okay, so maybe that hadn't happened yet, but it was justified).

And yet here he came, bringing in coffee, looking as if he wanted to settle down for a cozy chat, acting as if nothing had ever happened between them.

Well. All right. Apparently he would follow her lead and step back and not push the situation. No more kisses. Even if it hadn't really been a kiss at all. That was a good thing, right? The proper thing, the professional thing to do? What she wanted? So why did her insides feel a little hollow?

She turned off her camera and walked over to the table. "I'm sorry. I thought you'd left for Italy this morning. If I knew you were still here, I—"

"You would have worked at the other end of the library as you have for the last two weeks whenever I am in my office. Yes?" Nik handed her a cup of coffee. "Here. Marta tells me you usually take coffee this time of day."

"Yes. Thank you." Emily buried her nose in the cup and breathed deep of the rich, dark brew. He'd added the right amount of cream (how did he know?). The coffee's scent wafted up, strong enough to mask his, especially if she stayed on this side of the table.

He poured himself a cup and sat on the long leather couch, indicating the chair across from him. "Why don't you sit and tell me how things are going? Is your assistant from Edmonton enjoying his work here?"

"Pétur? I think so, although he misses his partner. But he and Ivan help a lot; with them assisting, we're on track to finish the first counting phase right around Christmas." She eased herself down into the big armchair and sipped at her coffee. "That should please you. We'll be out of your hair before you realize."

"Mmm." He made a noncommittal noise as he added cream to his own cup. "While I appreciate getting my office back"—he smiled briefly at her—"I am more glad that with their help doing the counting, you'll be able to do what only you can do here, which is to start the in-depth study of the materials you've uncovered."

Where was the crown prince so focused on his winery and spa resort that he dismissed her work out of hand? She was confused.

"Prince Nikolas—"

"Nik. I thought we were beyond the formalities?" This time his look at her fell somewhere between amused and pained. "I am sorry if my actions made you uncomfortable the other day in the winery."

"Not uncomfortable, exactly... Okay, yes, I was uncomfortable. What happened was a bad idea. I—"

"Why?"

"Why what?"

"Why were you uncomfortable?"

"Well, because... because..." Emily stopped in frustration and set her cup carefully on the table. "May I speak bluntly?"

At that, he laughed outright and sat back, more at ease than at any time in the last two weeks. "Now you ask permission? Have you not been?"

"I—yes. All right." She sat farther back in her chair, still somewhat stiff and awkward. "My behavior was highly inappropriate, to say nothing of unprofessional. I'm not like that. I don't make a habit of, of..."

"Kissing men?"

"I didn't kiss you!"

"No," he said, teasing her now, "I kissed you. Was that truly such a bad thing? I told you at the time I thought it was a marvelous idea."

179

"I… you… we can't. I can't. I'm young for this position. And I know you and your Council would probably be more comfortable if my father were here, managing the project. To tell you the truth, my university would have been more comfortable too. But his health made that impossible. So, this is my first major solo project, and I can't afford to screw it up. I can't afford any sort of shadow on my record, any hint of poor conduct."

"And this project is so important to you?"

"My reputation is everything to me. This project is crucial for my reputation, my professional standing." She shifted uneasily. "If I led you to believe anything else, I'm sorry. I never intended to."

"And so you did not." He shook his head when she started to speak. "No, truly. You did nothing wrong. And while I don't necessarily agree with your position," he continued with a wry smile, "I will honor it. And I will treat you, and your work here, with the utmost respect. You've earned that, I think."

"Th-thank you. It means a lot to me."

"However," he said, raising his hand as she drew in a breath. "However, I would like to wind the clock back a little. I thought after spending those few days together, observing each other, we perhaps moved a little beyond a strictly professional relationship. Into a friendship, at least, for the duration of your time here."

Friendship? With the crown prince of Dubrovia? If she hadn't been friends with his predecessor, his cousin Stefan, she would never consider it. But she had been friends with Stefan and Kate and Rose.

So maybe she could be friends with Nik too. She only had to remember that they were JUST friends. There could never be anything more.

Chapter Nineteen:
Rose sees a way out

Rose fought to keep her mind on her assignment and her eyes on her book. But it was hard! Pétur and Ivan were over at the other end of the upper reading room, her favorite homework space, arguing cheerfully about hockey. Strange—hockey wasn't particularly a popular sport in Dubrovia, and she didn't think of either Pétur or Ivan as athletic. But apparently wherever two or more guys gathered, there would be arguments about sports. Even Uncle Nik and that nasty Rikard Asanovic talked about hockey and football.

She sighed and forced her eyes back down and turned the page. The microeconomics of post–World War II manufacturing in central Europe bored her more today than usual. If she had to study the time period, why not read about scientific developments, the space race, computers and electronics, or biomedical advances (although some of the descriptions made her a little queasy)?

She wanted to roll her chair over to where the guys had set up in the far corner and help them with their counting. She'd worked with Emily before they both got here; she knew how to keep the records! Yeah, most of the work was kind of boring. But with a couple of hot guys to talk to? Not boring. Not boring at all.

Rose sighed again. Not that either one of them would ever look at her. Pétur talked a lot about his partner, Sean, back in Edmonton, which put him out of the running: committed AND gay. Not that she was interested in someone so old! But it would have been nice to at least be *looked* at sometimes, as something other than a sort of little sister.

And Ivan avoided looking at her at all. Which kinda sucked, because he was cute in a geeky sort of way. And he was only three years older, which wasn't so much of a difference, was it? But she was a princess, and he was a commoner. Not that she cared! But he seemed to. He spoke so formally to her, calling her Princess or Your Highness. At least Pétur called her Rose, except when other people were around who might be a pain about titles. Like Councillor Asanovic, who had given both guys lectures about protocol and proper forms of address last week, in her hearing. Since then, Ivan barely seemed to be able to work in the same room as her.

Should she pack up her stuff and go back to her rooms? He seemed to be okay today, laughing and joking with Pétur. So no, she'd stay. And maybe in a little while she would go over and offer to help.

As she finished reading this chapter and answered the essay questions her tutor had sent, Rose scowled down at the book in her lap. She loved taking her courses online because now she got to pick her own classes and learn more interesting stuff. But she missed being in a classroom with other kids. When you were the only one your teacher focused on, you couldn't have an off day and not pay attention, because there wasn't anyone else to hide behind.

How had Emily been able to stand it? She was always so much younger than the other pupils in her classes. Everyone always knew who she was; she couldn't hide either. Even when Rose had attended school down in Cerina before her accident, and everyone knew her as the crown prince's daughter, they had all tried to pretend she was just another student. She hadn't received preferential treatment.

She missed that. She missed the activities, missed the other students. Although she had been shy, with only a few close friends, there were a couple of girls that she used to have lunch with or do homework with. When she got hurt, though, and stopped going down for classes every day, she lost touch with them. They weren't comfortable coming up to the castle—or they weren't comfortable being around a girl in a wheelchair, maybe.

Nope. Not going to go there. She vowed again that she wouldn't always be in a wheelchair. She just had to put up with this for a while. Even if she hadn't succeeded in convincing her grandparents that more surgery for her back was a good idea, they wouldn't be able to stop her once she turned eighteen. Two more years and she would be of legal age and could take control over her trust. Then just watch her.

She jumped at the touch on her shoulder.

"Hello, Rose. How's the schoolwork coming today? My guys aren't making too much noise for you, are they? I can ask them to tone it down if you want."

Rose closed her book with a thump, grateful for the distraction. "Hi, Emily. No, they're fine. I was thinking about going over to see what they're working on today."

"Are you sure? I don't want you to get in trouble again for skipping out on your assignments," Emily said, trying to look stern and failing.

"That was one time, on their first day! And I made up the work the next day." Rose laughed and pushed her book onto the table by the window. "Let's go over. I want to see what they did today."

"Oh, sure, it's all about the work, and not about the guys, right?" Emily teased. "And it can't be Pétur, so it must be Ivan you want to see. Not that I blame you," she continued softly, bending down to speak directly into Rose's ear. "He is pretty cute, isn't he?"

"Emily! He's way too young for you!"

"And believe me, I never thought I'd see the day when I could say that! I've always been the one who's too young."

Pétur turned as they approached. "Who's too young? You? Never. Straight men like younger women, don't they, Ivan?"

Emily punched Pétur's arm as the university student flushed pink. "Don't tease him, Pétur."

"Who said I was teasing him? Maybe I should ask you about older men, hmmm? Especially that hottie of a crown prince." He pointed at Emily and laughed as she turned a brighter pink than Ivan. "Ah, ah, ah," he said over her sputtered protests. "You know I'm right. You're not going to do anything about it, though, are you? Miss Scaredy-Cat, Miss Doesn't Date? I bet your social life is more boring here than in Edmonton."

"Hey, I'm here to work. As are you. It's work back home I came up to talk to you about, though. We need to sort out some class schedules. Ivan, you can take over for a while, can't you?" Emily said. "Pétur, I've got a conference call in about an hour with Dean Smithton, and…" Her voice trailed away as they walked off.

Rose sneaked a peek at Ivan. He still blushed, but he looked at her. Really looked at her. He gave her a little shrug and a half grin. "Dr. Charette says you used to help her count, before Pétur and I started working for her. Would you… would you like to help me? The work goes faster with two people."

"Yes, of course! I can't climb up on the ladder, but I can transfer the photos from the camera. And I know how to use the database software."

"Okay, then. If you can do that part while I take the pictures, it would be a real help. If that's okay with you?"

"Sure!"

They worked in companionable silence for a while. Then Ivan asked, "Why don't you go to classes down in the city anymore?"

"Oh!" Rose fumbled the memory card he handed her, and caught it before it dropped to the floor. "Well, after my accident, my grandparents decided it was better if I studied here." She inserted the card into the laptop without looking at him. "How did you know I don't go to school in Cerina anymore?"

"My cousin Maria—Maria Beran, do you remember her?—is your age. She told me you used to be in some of her classes," Ivan replied. He perched partway up the ladder and looked down at her. She could feel his eyes on the top of her head.

"Of course I remember Maria. And I miss going to classes and seeing everybody every day. But the problem isn't only my grandparents. St. Anna's isn't set up for someone like me." Rose fought to keep the bitterness out of her voice. "It's all stairs and narrow doorways I can't get my chair through."

"I never thought of that. I thought maybe you didn't want to go to gymnasium there, or that the local school was okay for primary school but not now you're older." He came down the ladder and pulled out the chair across the table from her. "It's the tradition for your family to attend school somewhere else, after primary, isn't it?"

"My father and Uncle Nik did, sure, if that's what you mean by tradition. I don't think it goes back any farther, though." She fiddled with the memory card, pushing it into the slot and popping it back out, till she realized what she'd done. She pushed it in firmly and took her hands away, folding them carefully and placing them in her lap.

"It's not that I don't want to go back. Besides it being hard for me to get around there"—she shrugged and looked across at him—"they'd send bodyguards, and I'd probably have to bring Jacquie, my physiotherapist. It gets complicated."

"Okay, so maybe you couldn't go back for all your classes, and I can see why not at St. Anna's. But you're taking some advanced-level stuff, right? The physics book you had the other day, that's university level. Can't you take a course or two at the university?" Ivan asked, leaning forward earnestly. "I think they're more set up for wheelchair access. And you could see your friends."

"Oh, I would like that." Rose sighed. "I would like so much to be able to leave the castle more. I feel so stuck here! And if I could prove to my grandparents I could handle a couple of classes now, like this," she added, waving her hand to indicate herself and her wheelchair, "maybe they'd listen to me about going away to university."

She beamed at him. "I can't believe I never thought of that! It's a good idea. I could ask Emily to help me find out what courses I should take to qualify for a physics or astronomy program somewhere. And I can ask Uncle Nik about talking to someone at Oxford."

She frowned a little. "Maybe not Uncle Nik. I don't think he thinks it's a good idea, me going someplace else for school. But he did! And my father did."

"But that's not for a couple of years yet, right?" Ivan asked. "So you'll still be here for a while?" He smiled at her shyly. "I would like to see you sometimes, if you came to the university for classes. If you agree. And your grandparents of course."

"Oh! Yes, I, I would like that too." Rose knew she blushed, but she didn't care. Ivan wanted to see her, and not just here, and not just because he worked in the castle now! How cool was that? She hoped she didn't come across like some little girl with a crush. He was older but only a little bit. And maybe he liked her a little more than a little bit. "I can ask my grandparents—"

"Your Highness! What are you doing here, alone with this person?"

Oh, terrific. Just who she didn't want to hear. How had she missed Councillor Asanovic's approach? He was the sneakiest person she knew. Honestly, he gave her the creeps. No wonder Emily didn't like him.

Well. She *was* the princess, so she could tell him to get lost. And while she'd been taught to be polite, she struggled right now. Why was he snooping around up here? Shouldn't he be working with Uncle Nik, or meeting with Council, or doing anything else, anywhere else?

Rose raised her head to look down her nose at him. Which was hard, considering she sat and he stood. She remembered what her grandmother the queen looked like the last time she had been annoyed at someone, and channeled her. She hoped it worked. "I am here because I live here in the castle, Councillor. And Ivan is here because he assists Dr. Charette in cataloging, and today they are working in the upper reading room."

The older man made a point of looking around. "I do not find Dr. Charette here. So she has decided to leave her work to her assistant? And she leaves you alone with him? Where is your attendant?"

Sheesh. You'd think she was six instead of sixteen. She started to speak, but caught Ivan's subtle headshake and held her comment.

"Councillor Asanovic, if you want to speak to Dr. Charette I'm sure she will be returning soon. She stepped away to make a call," Ivan said. He started to gather up his things. "And I can leave, if you think it is inappropriate for me to be here with Her Highness."

"No!" Rose exclaimed, grabbing hold of the laptop. "You don't have to leave." She turned to Asanovic. "You can leave, Councillor. This is the twenty-first century, not the seventeenth! I don't need a chaperone in my own home, and I don't need an attendant. Until I have more surgery, I'm stuck in this chair, and I'll need help getting around if I go anyplace else, but here I can manage." She glared at him.

"Surgery? Now, Your Highness, you know your grandparents have not sanctioned more surgery for you. It's far too dangerous."

He truly was slimy. Oh, he sounded all sincere and solicitous, but she had overheard him once talking to Uncle Nik's old girlfriend. Then he had been all for the surgery, even with the risks. Maybe she'd die, maybe she'd end up paralyzed, or maybe she'd not improve any. He didn't care, as long as her condition didn't distract Uncle Nik from— well, she wasn't sure what from. Or maybe her condition was *supposed* to distract him? She'd not been able to tell (which happens sometimes when you eavesdrop, she'd found).

"And it's none of your business," she told him. "It's between me and my grandparents, so you can leave. Go find Dr. Charette if you want to speak to her. Or you can talk to Anton and make an appointment to talk to her some other time."

"Anton?" His voice went up in disbelief. "She is using Crown Prince Nikolas's personal aide to book her appointments now? We'll see about that!"

He stormed off with barely a nod to her. Ivan, he ignored completely. Just as well, as her friend looked very relieved to no longer be the center of attention.

"Well, that was fun." She spun her chair away from the table and back again. "I hate him!"

"Princess—"

"Okay, *hate* might be too strong. But I really, really, really don't like him. And neither does Emily. I can't figure out why Uncle Nik is friends with him," she finished under her breath.

"Well, sometimes we're friends with someone for a long time, and they change and we don't. Or the other way around," Ivan said. "May I ask you something, though?"

"Sure, as long as it isn't about Councillor Asanovic."

"No, it is not. And you do not have to answer if you don't want to talk about it. But I wondered about… when you were hurt. You're in a wheelchair now, but you're not paralyzed? Your legs still work?" He gestured at her legs and blushed again. "If they work, why do you need more surgery?"

Man, he was cute when he blushed. "They work," Rose answered, "but they hurt a lot if I stand or walk. I have physiotherapy every day to make my legs and back stronger, but I'm not getting any better. I'm getting stronger, but without more surgery my spine won't improve."

"But the surgery is risky? And this is why your grandparents do not give their permission?"

"Well, sure. Any surgery on the spine is risky. It could make things worse, or at least not improve anything. But there's a good chance they can take some of the pressure off the nerves and make the pain less, even if I don't ever walk much better than I do now."

"Are you not afraid of such a risk?"

"Sure, I'm afraid. I'm scared I might get worse. But I'm tired of being stuck, and tired of being a burden. I want to travel! I want to be able to go to university someplace else. I want to study physics and astronomy with the best people in the world. There's so much to see, and so much to learn, and I can't do it STUCK IN THIS CHAIR!"

Chapter Twenty:
Rikard warns Nik

"**D**id you realize she spends her afternoons in the library with that student? That is, when she's not following Dr. Charette around."

Nik blocked out the sound of the irate man, focusing instead on the contract draft in front of him. It had taken Rikard and the lawyers almost three weeks to get to this stage, but it finally looked like something he could endorse. He read through the last few clauses again and signed on the last page.

"There, that's done. Make arrangements for you and Estok to present it to Salvatorio DiSalvo next week." Nik capped his fountain pen and leaned back in his chair. "Now, what's all this about Princess Rose?"

"It is inappropriate! She is an impressionable young girl, sheltered all her life. She should be spending more time on her studies and with her grandparents, not with these outsiders! I don't think—"

"Can you hear yourself, man? Rose is sixteen, not six. And exposure to outsiders is good, don't you think? She may not be the crown princess, but she's still a member of the royal family. She'll be dealing with 'outsiders' for the rest of her life."

Nik shook his head. *What prompted this?* Granted, Rikard was a member of the Royal Council, but since when did he take such a close interest in Rose?

"Ha. Outsiders, perhaps. But interlopers, no. The princess is far too influenced by Dr. Charette and her assistants. Why, just this afternoon I overheard them talking about university programs in the United States."

"Them who? Rose and Emily? Or Rose and Emily's assistants?"

"All of them. Today I heard them all. They are upstairs in the far end of the stacks right now, I am sure. You should listen sometime. They are encouraging her to leave home, to study abroad."

Nik stood and walked over to the little refrigerator built into his credenza and extracted a bottle of water. Leaning against the furniture, he twisted off the cap and swallowed a mouthful. "I'm not sure why that's such a bad thing. We both left. So did her parents. So did ours—or our fathers, anyway."

"Yes, our fathers. Our mothers did not. And before you start telling me that times have changed, I would ask you to think about the women in your social circle. These are the women in whose company she will be, in a few years. She will need to be able to navigate European society. She may choose to participate in Council, or take on some of Dubrovia's public relations. Not… not spend her nights in an astronomical observatory on the other side of the world, looking at the skies! What kind of career is that for a princess?"

"Seriously? You're worried about her career choice? She's sixteen! She has plenty of time to decide where she wants to go to university and what she wants to study, and what she might do after that."

"And did you have such choice? Did I? We knew what our responsibilities were. We went to the best universities, chosen for us by our parents. We studied what would be of best use to Dubrovia, what was appropriate. Not whatever took our fancy."

Rikard dropped into one of the chairs in front of Nik's desk and shook his finger. "This is all Dr. Charette's fault. She's a bad influence on the princess."

"I'm not so sure I'd call her a bad influence, but I do agree she is an influence." Nik shrugged. "Who else does Rose have to turn to? Her parents are gone. My parents are gone. Because of her condition, her grandparents are terribly protective of her, so they keep her close."

"That's my point! I know they want her to remain at home. Hasn't the king himself spoken in Council meetings about reviving our university and expanding what is offered so as to keep our young students here? Do you not think that position is driven by his desire, his and the queen's, for Princess Rose to stay and study here?"

"Quite likely. If he thought about it, though, he would realize that her university days are approaching too fast for her to be affected by anything we start now. And besides, her condition requires that she attend a school that can accommodate both her physical condition and her security."

"Unless her physical condition became a non-issue."

Nik's hands stilled on his water bottle. "What are you saying? The king and queen are not considering further surgery for the princess. It's too risky."

"I agree completely. But you might want to check on Dr. Charette. It seems she has been advising the princess on the subject. Apparently your little librarian is all for it," Rikard said, a smug look on his face.

"What? How do you know this?" Nik was stunned and angry. How dare she? It was one thing to give Rose advice about school, about travel, and yes, even about boys. He'd overheard part of one such conversation just the other day, although they'd ceased talking as he walked past them to get to his office and resumed when they thought he was out of earshot.

In those areas, Emily was good for Rose. His cousin's self-esteem had taken quite a nosedive after her accident. She rarely saw herself as others did: that she was still a pretty and vibrant girl, even if confined to a wheelchair. Having the two young men around so much, both of whom treated her as just another person and not disabled, was good for her too.

But encouraging her to opt for risky surgery, to go against the advice of older and wiser family members? That was unacceptable.

If it was true. Nik looked hard at his colleague, very aware of the other man's dislike of the archivist. "Are you sure about this? It doesn't sound like Emily. She doesn't strike me as a risk-taker."

"You can ask her yourself," Rikard replied. "In fact, I strongly suggest that you do. She should not have such influence on our princess. Such a course of action is dangerous."

He stood and reached for the signed contract. "Perhaps the king and queen should be advised. Queen Elspeth in particular was very keen on having Dr. Charette here as a role model." He snorted as he headed for the door. "Some role model, encouraging an impressionable girl to rebel against her family's wishes. It makes me question if this is how she deals with all of her students. I wonder if her supervisors are aware?"

Nik sat at his desk again as the door closed behind Rikard. He placed the water bottle on his blotter and traced rings with the condensing moisture. He questioned whether Emily would really counsel Rose to take such chances. Did his grandparents have any inkling this was going on?

He lifted the phone and called the queen's personal secretary. "Hello, Elita, would you please check the queen's schedule? I would like to speak to her on a matter of some urgency."

* * *

The queen was not amused.

Or at least Nik thought so. He'd dutifully reported Rikard's assumptions, that Emily had tempted Rose to have potentially risky surgery. Or at least investigate potentially risky surgery.

The problem was, he didn't know who angered her. Was Emily the target, for not being the role model the queen encouraged? Was Nik, for reporting a rumor and innuendo without confirming the truth of Rikard's story?

Or was the queen annoyed at herself? Nik was certainly annoyed at himself. He'd started out believing Emily was someone who could be trusted. How could a woman so shy, so retiring, counsel a young person, someone younger than her students, to take such a risk?

Unless she encouraged risks for others but not for herself. That might be a possibility, he considered as he made his way back to his suite. He didn't understand it. He always enjoyed moderate risks—fast cars, daredevil water-skiing stunts, black-diamond ski slopes—but for himself, not others.

This is when he missed his parents and his cousins. Viktor Kuliç's sudden and fatal heart attack ten years ago had thrust Nik into his father's position, first as minister of external affairs and then as prime minister, as well as forced him to take over managing the family finances. Then Stefan's death made him the accidental crown prince, a role for which he still felt woefully unprepared two years into the job.

Nik felt their absence keenly today. His father was born almost fifteen years after the king and so had taken a more... moderate, maybe? perspective on the world. Plus he had spent more time outside the country. Even as Nik himself was now responsible for foreign trade, his father had once been too. And his mother, Nansci, being younger than the queen, had also been closer to Kate—and therefore to Rose—than Elspeth was.

Emily was stepping into the role of beloved aunt. She was young; she was educated; and most important for Rose, she was here.

But was she a good aunt?

Nik hurried down the hall. Time to investigate, to find out what Emily had been telling Rose. He just hoped he wouldn't have to do too much damage control.

Chapter Twenty-One:
An audience with the Queen

I t was like a replay of her first night here. Only backwards. This time, the queen came to her.

Emily watched, bemused, as Queen Elspeth wandered around the den, Nik's office, pulling out a book here, picking up an artifact or piece of artwork there. She didn't think the older woman was nervous; she seemed to explore the space, trying to see Emily's fascination with it.

"I haven't spent much time in here in years. I remember, when I first married Filip, it was Viktor's office, before he passed away and Nikolas took on his duties." Elspeth stopped at the large golden orrery at the side of the room and nudged it to set the celestial bodies spinning around the central sun in their mechanical orbits. "I think every royal child for generations has come in here to play with this."

"I know Princess Rose used to. She said it was a happy memory she had of her father, even from when she was very young: her and her mother coming in here, spinning the planets while he was finishing up for the day."

"As did Nikolas and Stefan, in Viktor's time." She gave the mechanism one more push, then brought the planets to a halt one at a time, aligning them all in a row. "Perhaps that is why Nikolas keeps this as his working space instead of using the office up in his suite. He and his father spent a good deal of time here."

Emily made a noncommittal sound. She tried to limit the occasions she spent time with Nik in here. He rarely spoke to her about his predecessors who had used the office, other than to mention that it was traditionally the prime minister's space and was Viktor's before his. What would it be like, she wondered suddenly, to work every day in a space that held such history? It was a dream of hers, one not likely to be realized. Would you feel inspired by those who had served before, or weighted down by the continuum of responsibilities?

"I don't know, Your Majesty. In my experience, this is Crown Prince Nikolas's space, and he is protective of it. Only in the last couple of weeks have I come in to work. And my assistants don't work in here at all."

"Yes, that sounds like Nikolas. I wonder if Rose ever comes in here? There used to be some books on astronomy on those shelves." The queen waved her hand in the general direction of the fireplace.

Emily had already done a cursory examination of those shelves; she knew the books in question. "They're still there, ma'am. But they're not texts so much as journals, personal observations recorded over a number of years. I wish I could figure out where the observations had been done from, though. The one journal I leafed through sounded like they weren't made from the castle proper."

"No? Not even from the observation room?"

"I can't say for sure, but I don't think so. Princess Rose has the antique telescope she used to use with her father, plus a set of powerful binoculars. If we could figure out the location of those observations, I think she would like to see for herself how the sky has changed since the journal was written," replied Emily.

"Hmmm, yes, about Rose," said the queen.

She paused at the knock at the door. Emily opened it to find Anton holding another beautiful antique china set. A replay indeed, complete with tea.

Emily took the tray from him and brought it into the room, placing it onto the low table in front of the fireplace and pouring for both of them. As they settled themselves into the overstuffed armchairs, she racked her brain for a possible reason for the visit. Other than the occasional encounter before or after Council meetings, she hadn't seen much of Queen Elspeth since her first night. Should she give some sort of informal report? Was this purely a social visit? She opened her mouth, but the queen spoke first.

"I understand Rose talks to you about Canadian health care," she said, taking a sip and placing her cup back on its saucer.

"A bit, yes, Your Majesty. She asked about my mother, who was a nurse," Emily said carefully. Rose? Health care? This wasn't about the library at all.

"I had been given to understand her questions were more around surgeries. Did she not ask you for names of surgeons?"

"Well, she did, but I don't know any surgeons except for a couple Mom used to work with. Ma'am, might I ask what this is about?"

The queen tilted her cup back and forth, as if trying to read the answers in the tea leaves. "It has come to our attention Rose has been investigating alternative treatments for her spinal injuries. In particular, she questioned Dr. Bergner, her neurosurgeon, because she had read about some sort of experimental procedure performed in Belgium and wanted to know if it was available anywhere else. I ask you now if she spoke to you about this."

Rose had, sort of. At least she had mentioned to both Pétur and Ivan she was tired of being stuck in her chair and wanted to explore other options. And Pétur, being both softhearted and a terrible gossip, had mentioned the conversation to Emily. But Rose had also talked to Emily in confidence; how much could she tell the queen without breaking that confidence?

"Your Majesty, I know Rose is unhappy with her physical situation. And I know she doesn't like to speak about it too much because it upsets you. But when she speaks to me, or to anyone on my team, it's in confidence."

"I applaud your loyalty toward my granddaughter. But Rose is a child. She cannot make those decisions for herself. Experimental surgery is too much of a risk."

"Risk is a funny thing, Your Majesty. What seems like a terrible risk to one person might be a way of life to another. I never understood people who like to race cars or jump out of airplanes, but a lot of people seem to enjoy them as sports. As for health risks? The way my father is right now, if we heard about an experimental procedure that would give him back what he's lost this past year, I know he would want to try it. And I would like to think I would support his decision no matter what."

She took a risk herself, she knew, contradicting a reigning monarch, especially one who was such a strong supporter of her work and instrumental in getting her funding. But how could she say otherwise?

"Are you sure? Even if you might lose him?"

"I'm losing him anyway." Emily placed her cup gently down on the table. "Every day, he slips a bit farther away. That's why I go back one week in four, and why I was reluctant to take the project on in the first place. It's hard, being here right now."

The queen harrumphed. Emily didn't think she'd ever heard anyone actually make that noise before, but the older woman harrumphed again, and said, "Well. I am sorry, my dear. I did not think you had any experience with this sort of choice. But he is an adult and still able to make his own decisions, yes? Not until it is absolutely necessary will the responsibility be yours. So you can understand why we are so protective of our Rose."

"I do, truly I do, Your Majesty. Rose is very dear to me. Kate and Stefan were dear friends when I lived with them in Fredericton." She smiled, a little sadly. "I don't have any sisters or brothers. I like to think of Rose as a younger sister.

So yes, she talks to me as she might to a sister. Or maybe an aunt. I'm trying not to influence any decisions she might make about anything, not about school or surgery. But she needs enough information to be able to make those decisions."

"Well, perhaps you are right. She is sixteen, after all. While I cannot give her permission for the surgery now, we need only wait for two years and she will be able to do what she wants. I just don't want her to get her hopes up."

"Oh, I don't think she is, or at least not recklessly. She's just looking at this stage, and asking questions."

"Will you tell me, then, if she asks you questions again?"

"Your Majesty—"

"No, I'm sorry. It was wrong of me to ask that of you. Rose needs a confidant. I am glad she has you to speak to. Although, your assistants…"

Emily laughed. "Believe me, I don't think she talks to Ivan about surgery options! He is a nice young man. We were lucky to find him. By next year he'll be somewhere else, since he wants to get an advanced degree."

"Yes, I know. I wanted to address that. We spoke, when you first arrived, about the state of our university here. And the topic arose during some meetings of the Royal Council you attended. We are hoping once the library restoration is into the next phase, we can start making plans to revive the school, bring it into the twenty-first century and expand some of its programs."

She remembered. She didn't know what it had to do with her, but she certainly remembered. "Well, I don't know anything about administering a university, but I know about working at one! I'm sure Dean Smithton would be willing to talk to your chancellors, or the University of Alberta could send a team of consultants. Don't expect a fast process, though, to make such changes."

"No, I am sure it will not be. But this is our dream, you see: to make our country a place where our young people can thrive, where they want to stay. We lost too many, over the last generation or so, who went away to go to school and never returned. In fact, I think if Stefan and Kate had not perished in that accident, Nikolas would be quite happy to remain abroad, managing our business affairs. I do not think he is entirely happy here, at least not yet."

Not a subject she wanted to discuss, Nik's happiness. Or unhappiness. Or anything else. "Well, ma'am, I wouldn't know."

"No? I had thought you and my nephew were becoming close. He speaks of you, now and again, and how you are spending time together since you started your work in his office."

Emily felt the blush, the hazard of a fair complexion, start somewhere in the vicinity of her midsection and work its way up to her cheeks. "Oh. Well. I try to stay out of his way as much as possible. We talk sometimes, when we cross paths, for the most part about the library and what I'm working on, or the winery and what he's working on, nothing more personal. I wouldn't say we're close."

She had the impression Nik wasn't close to anyone since his cousin died. Oh, lots of women came and went, Helena DiSalvo being the latest in a long line. And of course there was Rikard Asanovic, who spent a lot of time passing in and out of Nik's office. Emily made sure to find somewhere else to work when the pushy councillor was present. That was one man she actively disliked.

The men's recent conversations, from the bits and pieces she had overheard, had centered around that contract they'd been hammering out. Or the social calendar of European society and the latest invitations Nik had received, although it was always Rikard who raised the subject and Nik who declined. He'd become somewhat reclusive of late, turning down parties and receptions in favor of remaining in Dubrovia.

Not that she was paying attention or anything. High-society parties and receptions were not for the likes of mid-level academics like her. Business dinners and cocktail parties, or fundraisers at the university or the hospital where her mother used to work were about her limit. So the little pang she felt when she thought about dressing up, dancing the night away? Squash it flat.

"I think you underestimate the attraction of an intelligent woman, my dear." The queen was watching her steadily. "For too long our Nikolas has been chasing fluff. It is past time for him to be thinking about settling down.

Dubrovia needs him here, not away in Europe somewhere chasing business contracts—and chasing skirts. Don't you agree?"

Oh, yikes. Discussing Nik's social life was even more uncomfortable than discussing Rose's slow journey toward independence. "Ah, Your Majesty, I couldn't say."

"Oh, you probably could, but you would not. You have tact, girl," Queen Elspeth said, standing and walking to the door as Emily rose and followed. "I am hopeful you have courage as well."

Chapter Twenty-Two:
Rikard stirs the pot

Emily released the tieback and tugged on the long drape. Finding the right balance between sun and shadow was tricky this time of day. Too much light and she ran the risk of fading the centuries-old ink in the journal on the desk. Too little and she couldn't read the washed-out scrawls on the pages.

She'd discovered this set of personal diaries one day, tucked in the back of one of the skinny document drawers in the map chest. There were a half dozen, all bound in crackling blue leather. As they seemed to be personal journals, at least they didn't have any gold leaf on the covers and spines to worry about, just the general fragility of old, dried-out leather and paper and glue. Which was enough to cause her to take great care as she eased open the cover of the second one—and found the same gibberish the first volume had displayed.

She quickly checked the other four. Sure enough, they were all unreadable. "Who writes their personal journals in code?" she muttered to herself, reaching for a pen and paper.

"Talking to yourself?" The dark voice sounded amused.

The amusement was at her expense, and she expected nothing else from him. The door to the office remained open today; the room got stuffy in the sunshine. That seemed to signal she was open to interruptions. And insults, apparently.

Rikard strolled in and threw himself down on the chair in front of the big desk. "What, nothing to say? So you only talk to yourself?"

Don't say it, don't day it, don't— "At least if I talk to myself I'm guaranteed an intelligent audience." *Damn, said it anyway.* Emily gave a mental shrug and moved on. "Is there something I can do for you, Councillor?" she asked, putting down the pen. She saw no point in trying to work while he sat with her. He'd come in for a purpose, and he wouldn't leave till he achieved it.

"I just thought I would check on your progress. In the crown prince's absence, I am in charge of your project, you know."

Not according to her contract. Minister Janko was the top of the heap, officially. And besides, keeping Nik in the loop had become an automatic courtesy since the days they had job-shadowed each other. He had given her permission to work in his office without him present as well. There had even been the occasional afternoon when they shared the space, working quietly at opposite ends of the room until one of them (usually Nik) had come up for air and suggested a break.

Emily closed the book and set it aside. She wouldn't rise to the bait. If he wanted to think he was in charge, fine. So long as he didn't interfere with her, or with her assistants, she didn't care. That didn't mean she had to take the time to give him a personal status report anytime he felt like popping in.

"The work is going well. Having Pétur and Ivan assist is a big help. We expect to finish the first phase before year-end," she replied, speaking evenly. "But you read my regular reports to Council. Is there something more you wanted to know?"

"By the end of the year? So you expect an invitation to the Christmas Ball? We do invite select staff to attend." His eyes drifted over her. "You would be expected to dress appropriately, of course."

She knew what he saw: a plain shirt (purple today, as she did love color), hair clipped up in a messy bun, minimal makeup. Black dress slacks and black ankle boots completed her outfit, her normal working clothes. Nothing fancy, but appropriate for the work she did.

Rikard was still talking. "And you would be expected to behave appropriately as well. Foreign dignitaries, celebrities, and local officials attend. Make sure you ask Marta for the staff protocol guide. That goes for the Harvest Ball in a few weeks as well, although that one is slightly less formal, with more locals and fewer foreign attendees."

"Councillor, I have no idea whether I will be attending either ball. I haven't received an invitation, and if Dean Smithton received one on behalf of the U of A, he hasn't told me about it. But I'm not going to discuss my clothes or my behavior with you," Emily said firmly. "Now, did you have a specific question about my work? If not, I'd like to get back to it."

"Oh, yes, your work. You are all about your work, aren't you? Except when you are not."

"What do you mean, when I'm not? That's what I'm here in Dubrovia for: to work."

"Yes, yes, of course. But you are not working when you spend time with Princess Rose, are you? Or with Crown Prince Nikolas?"

"Actually, most of the time when I'm with Princess Rose, I *am* working. She comes and helps out sometimes in the afternoons when she can."

"But not all the time are you working when she is with you."

Seriously? He was going to give her grief for the occasional breakfast or lunch they took together? Or the times she ran into Rose and Jacquie in the pool? "No, not all the time. Sometimes we just talk," she stated calmly. No point in getting defensive.

"And what is it you talk about?" he pressed.

"Most of it is general conversation. We share some interests, and we like to talk. Anything we have discussed in confidence is just that: confidential. I don't see why it's any of your concern."

"It's my concern when an outsider is exerting undue influence on an impressionable young girl. Do you think you are the first to try? Did you know one of her previous attendants was dismissed on the same charge?" He rose from his chair and leaned on the desk in an attempt to intimidate her.

She refused to be so easily threatened. Not on this. Emily pushed back her chair and stood herself. "First of all, I am not exerting any sort of influence on Rose. She's a friend, and the daughter of friends. Her parents were very good to me when I was about her age. I would never do anything that would go against their memories.

"Second of all," she continued, riding over his interruption. "Second of all, Queen Elspeth is very much aware of my conversations with Rose. While we might not agree on some of the topics, she recognizes our conversations are meant to help, not hurt. I'm not giving Rose advice; I'm showing her choices."

"Oh, so you expect me to believe you and the queen have regular chats, then? Who do you think you are?" he said indignantly.

"Not regular, but occasional conversations, yes. And I know who I am, and who I report to. My boss in Edmonton is Dean Smithton of the University of Alberta. On this project, my bosses are Minister Janko, Minister Bartak, and Crown Prince Nikolas. With regards to Princess Rose, I suppose you could say my bosses are the king and queen, especially the queen. Notice you aren't even on the list.

"And now," Emily said again, "I'd like to get back to work. You can sit there, if you feel the need to keep an eye on me. I expect you'll be bored in under ten minutes. Or you can leave and let me work in peace. Up to you."

Rikard pushed off the desk and stood upright, his arms crossed over his chest. "Oh, so the little mouse has a bite, does she? I wonder if you've ever shown it to our crown prince. He might not be so taken with you, and with this project, if he saw this side of you."

"I'm sure he sees what he needs to see." Damn that fair complexion; Emily hoped he thought she was flushed with anger and not blushing from… whatever this was.

"I don't think so. I think he sees what he *wants* to see. I think you have pulled the wool over his eyes. He sees a pretty face, he forgets his responsibilities."

"Forgets his responsibilities!"

"Yes, he forgets his responsibilities! And when that girl forgets her place, well, let's just say bad things can happen." He turned and strode for the door.

"You—" Emily stopped and sucked a deep breath in through her nose. She blew it out in a rush and tried to find some composure. "I don't think Crown Prince Nikolas ever forgets his responsibilities. You give me far too much credit if you think I have any sort of influence over him at all." She felt her mouth twist wryly as he hurried out. "And believe me, I know my place."

* * *

She couldn't settle. The journals sat closed on the desk; she couldn't focus on deciphering them with her mind in such a state. How could she have let Asanovic get under her skin? She knew better. He was no different from the bullies she'd been dealing with ever since she beat out the competitors for her first doctoral grant: opinionated, rude, and closed-minded.

And prone to underestimate her. Not going to happen. She'd proved herself more than capable in her academic pursuits. Now she was on her first solo professional project, she'd be damned if she let someone like him trip her up.

Rather than risk damaging the fragile diaries, then, she worked to sort through the rest of the map chest. The drawers were absolutely stuffed with the expected maps, plus architectural drawings, land claims, and all sorts of other loose documents that needed to be stored flat.

Sort by subject, sort by date? The archivist in her argued for the former: organizing like with like. The historian wanted to record the chronological progression the documents had taken, to get a sense of the people who had used this room and chosen to preserve the manuscripts now in her hands.

Emily spent several hours sorting and documenting what she found. The archivist won: maps in this pile, drawings of the castle (and other buildings; what were they?) in that pile, land claims over there. As she worked, her mind would occasionally drift back to the end of her conversation with the obnoxious councillor.

What did he mean, the crown prince was neglecting his responsibilities? It looked to her as if he were instead stepping into his role, concentrating more on local affairs in Dubrovia now than he had in the past. (She put aside the notion she was somehow the cause; she didn't believe that for a minute.) So why would Rikard Asanovic object to Crown Prince Nikolas acting like, well, like a crown prince and not so much like an international playboy?

She liked him as prince better than playboy, even if his buddy Rikard didn't. Oh, maybe that was the problem, she considered as she straightened a stack of maps threatening to cascade onto the floor. (Sorting each stack would work better if they weren't all different shapes and sizes, she thought idly. Time to find something to contain them, or at least hold them still. She searched out a couple of small figures to use as paperweights and placed them on the various piles.)

So was it about losing his drinking buddy? Or his party meal ticket? Maybe Rikard liked being the sidekick to a rich and powerful man if that meant he was also the recipient of special treatment and personal favors. Maybe there was something more in it for him when the crown prince of Dubrovia toured around as part of the European social scene.

Emily laughed at herself. Yes, and maybe she was completely out to lunch and reading far more into the man simply enjoying getting a rise out of her.

She shook her head and let her thoughts go as Rose burst through the door, wheelchair going at top speed.

"Look, look what I have for you! My grandmother is sending them out this afternoon, and I asked if I could bring you yours." She skidded to a halt inches from the table holding the precarious stacks of paper.

"Hey, watch it!" Emily laughed. "I spent hours sorting through all those."

"Sorry. But look!" The girl was practically dancing in her chair as she flourished something at Emily. "Here's yours, with your name on the front and the official seal on the back."

"Hold it still if you want me to see it." She finally managed to extract the envelope from Rose's waving hand and turned it over and over to examine both sides. It was a heavy buff-colored envelope with her full name—Dr. Emily Marguerite Charette—written in a beautiful copperplate script on the front and, yes, the official seal of Dubrovia on the back flap. "What is it?"

"Open it, open it!"

There was a letter opener on the desk, she knew. Emily used it to tease the wax seal away from the paper, then lifted the flap and pulled out the card inside. Her eyes opened wide; she read the card as Rose said, "It's your invitation to the Harvest Ball!"

Chapter Twenty-Three:
Getting closer

Emily pressed her fingers against her temples and focused again on the pages in front of her. She made it a bit of a game to occasionally take another look into the set of journals from the map chest, trying to figure out how they were encoded. Because encoded—or encrypted, her expert told her—was what they were. She was no closer to figuring out the puzzle now than when she'd found the books a couple of weeks ago.

Keeping her eyes and her mind on the book at least kept them off the man sitting behind the desk. The dark, handsome, sexy prince had been on the phone most of the morning with everyone from bottle manufacturers in the Czech Republic, to investment bankers in Scotland, to a horse breeder in Spain. She couldn't block the sound of the deep rumble of his voice, nor the scent of his woodsy-spicy aftershave, though, and both proved to be a definite distraction.

When her own phone rang, she grabbed it like a lifeline. Her heart jumped into her throat until she checked the call display to see a Swiss number, not a Canadian one. So, not her father's caregiver; instead, it was the other crypto expert she'd been trying to contact for a week.

A brief conversation got her no closer than before. Yes, he had received the scanned document sample she had sent. Yes, it was definitely encrypted, not encoded. Yes, the source language was most likely Czech. And no, he wasn't able to break it. The only new piece of information? The encryption appeared to be a variant on a book cipher, which meant unless she could locate and identify the book used as the key, her puzzle would remain unsolved.

Frustrating. She ended the call and dropped her phone with a clatter.

"Problem?" came the question from across the room.

"Sorry," Emily apologized, "didn't meant to make so much noise. No, not a problem, exactly, just not the answer I hoped for."

Nik stood and stretched, then came out from behind his desk. *Nobody should look that good in a plain white shirt and black slacks,* she thought absently as he strolled across the room and sprawled on the couch. His collar was unbuttoned; he'd ditched the tie and jacket as soon as he came into his office after his one meeting in the morning.

Once again the sight of him distracted her. She finally registered that he had said something to her. "Sorry?" she asked, blushing.

He gave her a lazy smile. "I said, you should take a break. I asked Marta to send up some lunch; the tray should be here shortly." He straightened up and patted the couch next to him. "So come and sit and tell me what has you so tied up in knots."

Besides the invitation to join him on the couch? Tempting. Stupid. Distance was good. Distance would help her keep some composure. She walked over, with every intention to aim for the chair at the end of the table. That would be the smart thing to do.

Apparently she'd given up being smart sometime today. Emily curled up on the couch—in the opposite corner, mind, but on the couch.

For just a second, a wicked grin replaced his lazy smile, so fleeting she almost thought she had imagined it. The easy, open expression returned as he said, "There, see? Now, what was the question to which you did not hear the answer you wanted?"

"I asked a colleague about Renaissance cryptography for those journals that I found in the map chest. Remember? I sent him a scan of a couple of pages. He thinks it's a book code of some sort. Those can't be deciphered unless you have the book used as the key."

They talked about codes and encryption and security and language before lunch, through lunch, and even after lunch. It was the most relaxed conversation they'd had since their visit to the winery.

Relaxed on the surface anyway. Emily remained hyper aware of Nik's every movement. His words may have been casual, but every once in a while she intercepted a glance that was anything but. Oh, she never caught him staring, but now and again she could feel his gaze travel over her, as palpable as a touch.

By the time Marta had returned to clear the debris, she felt itchy. And warm. So when he excused himself to return to his phone calls, she took the opportunity to escape as far as the other end of the office.

Putting aside the journals, she focused on the last wall of bookcases she had yet to inventory. Since Ivan and Pétur were working so diligently out in the main areas, she could focus in here. The office held a subset of the bigger collection, almost as if the generations of prime ministers had gathered what interested each of them, stocking the office with their personal favorites.

If Nik's predecessors were like him, Emily mused, this set of documents had probably wandered in here from the primary collection in, oh, about his great-great-grandfather's time. Each man had bumped the previous set farther away from the desk that sat at one end, moving the books down the shelves and eventually back into general circulation. While not quite as accurate a timeline as rings on a tree, the migration did show a picture of each man and his reading habits.

Emily struggled to keep her mind on her work. She wasn't used to being observed. And this wasn't like being watched as in "what are you doing?" It was more personal than that. More unsettling.

With her mind wandering, it was a wonder she was observant enough to notice. But something had bugged her since she'd first unlocked this particular bookcase in the corner. It looked shallower than the others. At least, the books on the shelves were a lot smaller than most of the others.

She got up off the floor where she had sat for the last little while. She needed a stretch. She'd poke around at the bookcase because it truly was different, she decided. It was the only one in a corner that didn't go all the way to the corner; it ended about a meter short, leaving a blank space of stone wall.

Standing in the corner between this case and the one on the side wall, back against the stones, was a suit of armor. She eased between it and the bookcase, trying to see where wood met masonry, and found a little gap, not quite big enough for her fingers. The bookcase itself felt as solid as the others; it didn't move when she prodded it.

Funny, though. She could see that this case was built from a different wood than the others, now that she had her nose all but pressed against it. The stonework of the back wall looked different too. Newer, maybe?

Emily glanced back at the desk. Oh, good, he was off the phone. "Nik? Can I interrupt you for a minute?"

He lifted first his head, then his eyes. She could never get used to the shock of heat she felt when his gaze crossed hers.

His eyes narrowed. "What are you doing back there?"

"I wanted to see why this bookcase is different. Do you know if there was work done on the wall? Because it's different too."

"No idea. Any changes would have been made well before my time." He rose and came toward her. "We can ask my uncle, or Tomas. There would be records of any renovations or changes."

"Good idea. I can't tell for sure from back here." Emily started to ease her way out of the corner. The armor rattled when she brushed against it, then tilted off-balance. "Hey!"

She staggered back as it came tumbling down, the upraised shield glancing off her forehead. As she slipped, she reached blindly for the closest stable thing: the side of the bookcase.

Except it wasn't stable. It moved in one direction as she fell in the other.

"Emily!"

He reached her just as she landed hard, her head ringing from the blow and his shout. She touched the back of her head, wincing, and looked at the armor in dismay. "Oh, Nik, I'm so sorry! Is it damaged? Oh, God, I hope it's insured…"

* * *

"To hell with the armor, let me see your head!"

"What?" She looked up at him, still a little dazed. "What's wrong with my head?"

"I think you're bleeding, for one. You took quite a knock there. Let me see," he said, stroking back her bangs and peering at her. "Dammit, Emily! You're going to have one hell of a bruise."

"Sorry," she winced. "I didn't do it on purpose." She started to get up.

"What are you doing? Here, don't get up till we know how badly you're hurt."

Nik ran his hands down her arms and around the back of her head to check her scalp for more bumps. If he hadn't been so worried about a possible concussion, he would have enjoyed the feel of his hands in her hair. At least until he hit the lump coming up.

She was plainly embarrassed and tried to ease away from his touch. "I'm fine. No, really. Except for the bump on my head, the only thing I hurt was my pride," Emily said.

"I'll have Marta bring a first aid kit. In the meantime, you're going to sit still where I can keep an eye on you." He scooped her up off the floor and carried her over to the couch.

"Hey! I can walk. Nik, put me down! I—"

He lowered her to the couch just as the door swung open and Anton rushed in. "Your Highness! I heard—what happened?" he cried. His eyes opened wide at the sight of Nik holding Emily, then opened even wider at the sight of the tumbled suit of armor. "Your Highness? There's—"

"Anton, good. Call your mother for a first aid kit and some ice. Dr. Charette has been injured," he said. He took a pristine white handkerchief from his pocket and pressed it to her brow. "Here, hold this. It'll slow down the bleeding."

Anton hung up the phone and came back from the desk. "Sir? There's—"

Nik focused on her, not on what his aide said. "Is Marta on her way?"

"Yes, of course, sir. She wanted to know if she should call the doctor. But, sir, there's—"

"No doctor!" protested Emily. "Honestly, I took a minor bump on the head. A little ice, maybe a Band-Aid, and I'll be fine."

"You might need a stitch or two," Nik said, lifting the handkerchief a little to peer underneath. "I'll be able to see better once we get it cleaned up."

He turned as Marta rushed in and came to a dead stop, first aid kit and bowl of ice in hand. She looked at him and Emily on the couch, looked at the suit of armor now in pieces on the floor, then looked farther into the corner. "Sir? Here are the first aid kit and the ice. But did you know there is a big hole in the wall?"

Chapter Twenty-Four:
Clues

Emily twisted her head to face the back of the room, dislodging the handkerchief Nik held against the cut. "Ow!" she hissed.

"Stop moving." He swatted at her hand as she reached for the scrap of linen. "Let me see how bad it is."

"But, but—"

"You can see later. Whatever is behind the bookcase has been there for years. It can wait ten more minutes." He reached his hand out to Marta without taking his eyes off Emily's forehead. "First aid kit?"

"Oh! Yes, sir, sorry. Here—Anton! What are you doing?" she cried.

This time Nik did look up, and swore. He shoved the handkerchief into Emily's hand, saying, "Here, hold this." Then he lurched off the couch, calling as he went: "Anton! Step back! Do not go through the opening. Don't even put your hand inside. We don't know why it opened, or what is keeping it open. It could close any minute."

The younger man froze and took a careful step back. "Sorry, sir. I just wanted to see…"

"First things first." Nik stepped over the fallen suit of armor and glanced into the dark opening. "Can you see any sort of mechanism? Without sticking your head in?" he reminded the younger man.

"No, it's too dark. But I can try—"

"No. No trying. Not yet. Before we do anything," he warned, raising his hand and shaking his head at the younger man's obvious disappointment, "before we do anything, we will secure this room and treat Dr. Charette's injury. So. Anton, close and lock the door to the library, yes? And Marta, come bring the first aid kit. Now, Emily," he finished, turning to her, "let me see that cut."

Several minutes later, butterfly bandage attached and ice pack in place, Nik let Emily off the couch with a warning. "You will not exert yourself, or that will start bleeding again. You will sit... Anton? Roll the desk chair over here," he called.

When the chair was close, he held it still for her. "Sit. You can watch what we're doing and still stay seated."

"May I at least roll closer?" Emily gave him a dirty look.

"Of course," he consented, smiling at her expression. "You are our expert on libraries, after all. I don't suppose you have any experience with secret rooms or passageways?"

"Not ones that have just appeared, no." Emily tried to peer around Anton and his father.

Nik had requested Tomas come and bring a toolbox and some lights. The king and queen were both unavailable at the moment; he had left messages for them to join the group in his office as soon as possible.

In the meantime, Tomas and Anton managed to wedge open the sliding bookshelves. They still weren't quite sure how the mechanism was controlled, whether Emily had actually triggered the opening device or just bumped into the bookcase hard enough to force it to move. There was quite a lively discussion going on between the father and son about that.

Nik placed the rolling chair where Emily had a halfway decent view into the chamber. "So you've seen something like this before?"

"I've seen a few bookcases that pivoted away from the wall, and I've seen walls with stones that pivoted out. I've never seen a secret room with a bookcase as a sliding door before."

Nik thought hard. He had no idea what might be in this little room-within-a-room. The opening was a bit smaller than the bookcase that had covered it: maybe a meter wide and a little more than two meters high, tall enough that they wouldn't need to duck to enter. He couldn't judge the depth yet. Anton wanted to go inside and measure and check it out; he was pleading his case first to his father and then to Nik.

"Tomas, are you sure that it won't slide closed?" Nik placed his hand on the older man's shoulder where Tomas knelt to study the grooves on the floor.

"Well, I cannot be sure it will not start to slide. I haven't yet discovered what made it start. But I'm sure that it cannot close all the way again. See? We placed blocks here." Tomas pointed to the wedges he and Anton had hammered into the space between the bottom of the bookcase and the stone floor. He glanced back and up at the others. "It is as safe as we can make it without getting inside to see how it works."

"Very well." Nik turned to Anton and lifted the flashlight from his hands. "I will enter and see." At Anton's wordless protest, he grinned. "Did you think I would let anyone else explore first?"

It took less than a minute for Nik to find the mechanism that controlled the door from the inside. The big counterweight that helped the bookcase slide was tripped by a lever, which was affixed to two bits of the carved wooden molding on the outside edge of the bookcase.

"I must have grabbed both of those exact spots when I fell," Emily mused. She started to rise from the chair for a better angle but froze at Nik's growl and sank back down. "I guess it takes pushing on two spots so the staff doesn't accidentally trip it when they clean."

"Or so one of us doesn't open it by accident just by moving a book on the shelves," agreed Nik. He stepped out of the opening and turned off his flashlight. "Tomas, I suggest we remove the wedges and make sure we can open and close it on purpose—from the outside." He pointed at Anton. "And I need your promise that you will tell no one of this."

"But, sir, don't—"

"No one. The king and queen will be here shortly. Other than the two of them, and the five of us, no one is to know this exists, let alone how to open it," Nik said sternly.

"Yes, sir, of course." The younger man wilted a little.

"And that should be them now," Nik said at a knock on the den's door. "Marta, would you please let them in? And if it's anyone else, tell them… I'll be available in two hours."

He was relieved to see his aunt and uncle. It was hard enough to keep a secret among so many people. If someone else—Rikard, say—had been at the door, turning him away might raise suspicion, or at least attract unwanted interest.

Queen Elspeth looked surprised at the secret opening. King Filip did not. *And isn't that interesting?*

"Did you know about this, Uncle Filip?" Nik asked, once they had made their way over and been greeted by the others.

"I knew it existed. But I never knew the secret to opening it. That knowledge was passed down through the prime minister's office, to your father, and my uncle before him."

"Do you have any idea what is inside?"

"Only in general." Filip sighed, running his hand over the back of his neck. "I lost more than a brother when your father died. I lost—no, *we* lost valuable information about our heritage." He lowered his voice so only Nik could hear. "This vault holds the personal journals of your predecessors, prime ministers and crown princes going back who knows how many generations. I hoped your father had told you about it, shown you how to open it."

"No." But Nik wasn't exactly the model prime minister's heir. Since he graduated, hell, since he started university, he'd spent far more time outside Dubrovia than within its borders. Or at least up until two years ago, when the accident that took so many lives made him crown prince. And even since, his interests had kept him focused more on international affairs than internal ones.

So many lives wasted. So much lost. He wanted to reclaim and recover what was left. "Uncle Filip, do you object to Dr. Charette working on whatever we find in here? If those journals and books," he said, jerking a thumb over his shoulder toward the hidden room, "are anything like the encrypted journals she found in the map chest, we're going to need her expertise. And perhaps her contacts with outside colleagues."

* * *

Emily couldn't wait to get into the room, get her hands on these latest discoveries. This could be a career-making event for her! Yes, they'd keep the discovery and the location of the room a secret, at least for now. And probably most of the contents would be private family items, journals and records and such. But surely she would find something that could be documented and eventually released to the general public!

She shrugged off the queen's concerns over the cut and bumps on her head. "It was my own fault. I got in behind the suit of armor to look at the back of the shelves, and when I tried to come back out I got caught on something and tipped it over. I went down when it went down." She craned her head around to see it still spread out on the floor;

everyone was still picking their way around the pieces. "I didn't damage it, did I?"

Marta was back, fussing with the ice pack Emily still held against the back of her head. "I wouldn't worry. It was made to take hits from swords and other weapons," she said. "Here, do you still need this? It has mostly melted."

"No, that's fine. Honestly, it wasn't much of a bump." Emily handed off the ice pack.

Nik turned to frown at her. "No? You went down pretty hard. You hit the front and back of your head." He looked over at his aunt. "Perhaps we should call the doctor to examine her injuries?"

"I'm fine. See?" Emily stood and pushed the rolling chair back a few feet. "I didn't lose consciousness, I'm not dizzy. I don't need a doctor." She tried to peer past him, into the hidden room. It was better than looking at him. Even when he frowned at her, looking at him made her insides jumpy.

"I must take your word. But I will ask you to please tell me if you don't feel well. Or tell Marta, if you prefer?" he asked.

"I will," she promised. "So... may I see inside now?"

He smiled at her. Oh, boy, that smile. It made him look younger, more carefree, more approachable. And more attractive. As if he needed that.

Then he held out his hand. "Of course."

She was in *such* trouble. Emily took his hand, hoping her palm wasn't damp. Prickles of sweat beaded at the back of her neck under her hair.

Nik carefully led her over and around the suit of armor and in through the opening. He clicked on his flashlight and shone it on the shelves. But he didn't let go of her hand.

Emily sucked in a breath. So many journals! Some of them looked centuries old; some were quite a bit newer. And more books! Books not duplicated out in the main library, or even in Nik's office. She moved closer to the shelves. It was all she could do to not reach for a book, to take one down and discover what was hidden here. "Oh, I wish I had my camera," she said under her breath.

"Plenty of time for that. This room isn't going anywhere." He still held on to her hand.

She moved along the shelves, gazing at the contents. "See here? I think the journals are probably in order by date. So the oldest..." She pointed back to the entrance. "The oldest should start there and get newer as we move deeper."

He moved with her, turning as she did. But he still didn't let go of her hand.

She didn't know what to make of that. Was he trying to keep her from getting too close to the books? Or had he simply forgotten he had her hand in his? Whatever the reason, she liked it, a lot. And feared it a little.

Emily made the final turn to face the side to the right of the opening, the wall that would be behind the big fireplace out in the office. She gasped and stepped toward the shelves, finally pulling her hand free of Nik's. "Oh my God. Look, Nik! Those first ones?" she exclaimed, touching the edge of the farthest, highest shelf. "Those are by Schyrleus and Hevelius, but I don't recognize the manuscripts. And these, on the next shelf? I think those are hand copies of most of the major works by Kepler and Hajek and Galileo."

"Well, I recognize Galileo and Kepler. But who are the others?" he asked. He closed the distance between them once again, standing close behind her to peer over her shoulder.

She turned to face him, gripping her hands together so tightly her knuckles were white. "They were some of the foremost central and eastern European astronomers of the 1600s. Well, Hajek was a little earlier than the others. Renaissance, anyway."

She squeezed her eyes closed for a second, then opened them again. "This is… I can't tell you how important a find this is. You may find manuscripts here that don't exist anywhere else. Hevelius's library was destroyed in a fire in 1679, or 1680 maybe; I can't remember the precise year." She turned to look at the shelves again and stepped back reluctantly. "I need to bring my camera in here before we start taking them down to examine."

"Not today." He took her by the arm and steered her out of the chamber.

"What do you mean, not today?" Emily let herself be steered, but she came to a stop as soon as they had both cleared the opening. "I can fetch my camera and be back in five—"

"Not today," he repeated. "You had a blow to the head, and I need to consult with my king and queen"—he nodded to them—"about what this might mean for Dubrovia. And to set up some additional security. If this is as important as you anticipate, we must proceed with care."

Chapter Twenty-Five:
Rose has an adventure

The café was crowded and noisy, but she didn't care. Rose sat at a tiny table squished in the corner (away from the windows, at her bodyguards' insistence) with her friend, Maria, sipping on the wonderful house coffee drink with chocolate and orange peel and whipped cream. A plate of tiny pastries, stuffed with fruit or sweetened cheese and sprinkled with powdered sugar, sat half-devoured on the table between them. *No wonder this was Mama's favorite place to stop during an afternoon of shopping in Cerina.*

Getting into the café had been a challenge, but she didn't care. She had forgotten about the three shallow steps leading up from the street-level patio into the café proper. Her two bodyguards had had a quick but intense discussion with the owner, and after much waving of hands, she was carried up the steps, one bodyguard at the handles at the back of her chair and a busboy at her footrests. The owner had scurried about inside, maneuvering tables and patrons to give her a clear route to roll through.

He beamed at her once she finally settled in place. "Your Highness! Welcome to my café! It has been long since you visited us. It is very good that you are here again!" He bustled around the little table, moving chairs, fussing with the place settings, pouring sparkling water from a bottle brought by a server, talking all the while. "I will bring you one of my special coffees, yes? Made the way your mother liked it, may she rest in peace."

He paused with his hands resting on the back of the chair across from her. "She was a great lady, and a great princess. She is missed, she and your father. You do her proud." He bounced his hands once on the chair back. "And you do us honor! I will bring your coffee now, yes?" he said as he bowed and spun away.

So she sat, and sipped her coffee, and waited for Maria.

People looked at her, even stared, but she didn't care. It didn't take long for her to realize that they weren't being rude, and they weren't staring at her chair. They were glad to see her! She would respond with a smile, a nod, and get a beaming grin in return. No one came up to her, asking intrusive questions (although the presence of two stern-faced bodyguards standing not quite behind her might have had something to do with that). It was pretty much the way she had remembered Saturday afternoons with Mama and Dad, coming down into Cerina to shop or have lunch. People were polite and respectful, but happy to see them. Now, no one seemed to care that she was in a wheelchair.

And then Maria rushed in, all apologies for being late, though Rose didn't care.

"I'm late! I'm sorry! Two years since I saw you and I still can't get here on time! Oh, Rose, I missed you so much!"

They fell into a hug, made awkward by the bulk of the wheelchair until Maria made a frustrated noise and pulled her own seat closer. She clasped Rose's hands. "Look at you! Look at us! Sitting in a café, drinking coffee like grown-ups!" She giggled, then sobered. "Oh, Rose, I'm so, so sorry. It must be so hard, losing your parents like that, and…"

"Ending up in a wheelchair?" Rose said wryly. She sighed. "Yeah, it's hard. What makes it harder is being stuck up there in the castle all the time. I mean, I love Nana and Papa, but I wish I could come back to St. Anna's for school."

"Why can't you?" Maria asked. She licked a dab of whipped cream from her spoon.

"Because the old buildings aren't wheelchair accessible. Plus I don't think my grandparents would agree."

"You should ask them. And St. Anna's would add ramps and fix bathrooms and do whatever it takes to get you back. Rose, you're our princess! Of course they'll renovate or build stuff. And if you must bring a bodyguard with you." She tipped her head toward the two standing at the wall. "Could you make sure to include the cute guy?"

"Maria! You're terrible!"

The two girls sipped coffees and nibbled their way through tiny sweets and talked and talked. Rose started to get tired, but she didn't care. She was about to suggest that they finish up and head to their next stop when she became aware of a tiny girl standing behind Maria's elbow, staring at her, cookie in one hand and her mother's sleeve in the other.

"Why do you have such a funny chair?"

"Katje!" exclaimed her horrified mother. "Oh, Your Highness, I'm so sorry. She knows better than to intrude."

"No, it's all right." Rose rolled her chair to turn sideways a little bit, and held out her hand for the child. "My chair has wheels because my legs don't work very well."

"Why don't your legs work?"

"Oh, Katje, honestly! I am so sorry. Her favorite question is 'why.' She'll go on forever if you let her. I'll take her—"

Rose shook her head. "Really, it's all right," she said to the mother. To the girl, she answered, "My legs don't work because I was in a car crash."

"Oh." That seemed to take some thought. "You can't walk or run anymore?"

"I can stand, and walk a little. But it hurts a lot, so I don't unless I have to. It's easier to go places in my special chair."

More thought. "Can't your mommy kiss it better? That's what my mommy does, when I get hurt."

"I wish she could, Katje. But my mommy and daddy died in the car crash when I was hurt."

"So you don't have anyone to kiss it better? That's sad." Katje turned and thrust her half-eaten cookie at her mother. "Here."

Then she rushed over to Rose and gave her a smacking kiss on each knee. "There! I give you kisses to make it better," she said, smiling up at Rose. She spun away again to her mother, tugging her toward the exit. "Bye! Bye!" she yelled back at Rose, waving as she skipped out the door.

Rose was on the verge of tears, and she didn't care. She was so used to the castle staff and her family tiptoeing around her like she was going to break. It was so great to be with people who talked to her like anybody else.

"Oh, Rose, that was so sweet! I love how little kids will say anything that pops into their heads." Maria laughed, turning to watch as Katje and her mother left the café.

"She didn't care about my legs," Rose said quietly.

"Well, of course she did. She kissed them better, didn't she?"

"No, that's—I mean, it didn't matter to her that I'm in a wheelchair. That my legs don't work. That I'm not who I used to be."

Maria stared at her. "Of course you're who you used to be. You're still Rose Kuliç, aren't you? Princess of Dubrovia? Granddaughter of King Filip and Queen Elspeth, cousin to the yummy Crown Prince Nikolas, aren't you?"

"Eeew, Maria, he's my cousin!"

"And you're still my best friend. Don't forget that most important fact," declared Maria. "And as your best friend, I hereby proclaim that it's time to go shopping!"

Rose's exit caused almost as much fuss as her entrance had, but again she didn't care. This time, when the proprietor fussed over the men carrying her chair over the steps, she thanked him and said she'd be back. This time, when the cute busboy winked at her, she blushed and smiled instead of ducking her head. This time, when she rolled down the sidewalk with Maria on one side and her bodyguards behind, she allowed herself to look people in the eye and nod and smile.

The dress shop had only one shallow step up from the sidewalk, more a raised doorsill. Rose eyed it, unsure if she had enough momentum to roll her way over it and through the doorway. Without missing a syllable, Maria stepped behind, grabbed the handles of her chair, and tipped her up and over.

And they were in! The girls looked around in awe. This was one of Cerina's most famous dress shops, offering everything from reasonably priced off-the-rack outfits for high school dances to custom-designed cocktail dresses and ball gowns for the most formal of events. Rose's mother had bought most of her good wardrobe there; her grandmother still did.

"Oh, Rose, look at this! This one's perfect for you for the Harvest Ball!" Maria had rushed over to a display of long dresses, touching the hem of a long, floaty dress with a sparkly bodice and sheer chiffon sleeves. The color was somewhere between lilac and lavender; the beading on the bodice made that part a little darker.

"I'm not sure my grandparents will let me wear something like that." Rose rolled over and touched the flowing skirt. "It's so pretty, though."

"Why not? It's not low cut or see-through or anything. Well, except for the sleeves, but they don't count," Maria countered.

"It's kinda grown-up."

"Well, you want them to start seeing you as more grown-up, right? This dress will help. Besides," Maria said mischievously, "I can imagine how Ivan's eyes will bug out when he sees you in it!"

Rose blushed. She could imagine it too.

The two girls wandered around, looking at some of the other dresses, while the shopkeeper and her assistant served a woman and her daughter. Soon it was their turn. Maria had chosen a simple cocktail-length dress from the rack and went into a changing room to try it on in case it needed to be altered. (Rose doubted it; her friend had always been a perfect size four.)

"Your Highness, we are very glad to have you in our store again. It has been too long since we were asked to serve a princess—not since we made a Christmas Ball gown for the former crown princess, may she rest in peace. How may we help you today?"

"Hello, Madame Amyot. My mother always came here for her special dresses. I know she loved the ones you made for her." Rose took a deep breath. "I need a gown for the Harvest Ball. One that I can stand in without tripping. I like this one," she said, wheeling back to the first dress she and Maria had seen, "but I'm not sure about the length. Or the color."

The older woman studied the dress, her lips pursed in thought. "That is a good choice. We can make it with a slightly shorter skirt, ankle length I think, but keep the fullness for when you are seated. As for color…" She raised her head and called out to one of the other girls working in the shop. "Gizella! Bring me the chiffon book from the counter, please."

She turned again to Rose. "Yes, I think a deeper purple or a blue for you. No pastels; they will wash you out. Not green either. So, let us—"

"Princess Rose? Your Highness! What are you doing here, alone?"

Rose winced at the sound of the voice coming from behind her. Helena. The last person she wanted to see, and the last person she expected to encounter in a small dress shop in Cerina. No matter how talented its dressmakers, Cerina was not known as a hotbed of haute couture.

The horrible, horrified voice grated on her ears. "Whatever was he thinking, to allow you to come here unescorted? How unsafe! Oh, my dear," continued Helena, oozing condescension and criticism together, "you must return to the castle immediately with me and my driver."

"Not safe?" Madame Amyot puffed up like an angry cat. "Of course she is safe here. Nothing bad will happen to our princess in my shop, I guarantee it!"

"And I'm not unescorted," retorted Rose. "I came with two bodyguards and a driver. And my friend Maria is—"

"Your friend? I don't think it is appropriate for you to be here with someone who calls herself your friend," Helena said, shaking her head sadly. "Now come along, dear, and I will return you to the castle where you belong."

"Hey, I don't call myself Rose's friend, I *am* her friend! We've been friends forever," Maria cried, rushing over to stand in front of Rose. "And I don't know who you are. Rose," she said, turning a little to speak to her, "do you know her? Want me to call your guards? Make them take her out of here?"

"No." Rose caught Maria's hand and held on, part to prevent her from leaving and part for courage. "I know who she is. She's Uncle Nik's ex-girlfriend."

"Oh, dear, is that all that you think of when you think of me? Well, we'll soon correct that, won't we? In the meantime"—Helena sniffed—"we should leave this little store and go back to the castle. That gown is much too old for you. If you want a new little dress, I shall ask my personal designer in Italy to create something for you. Something far better than can be found here."

"Hmmmph," snorted Madame Amyot. "I do not welcome strangers who come into my store and insult my dresses. Or my princess. I think you need to leave."

"And the gown is not too old for me. I'm sixteen. My nana—the queen—sent me here to be fitted for one. And Madame Amyot and her family have made dresses and gowns for the women of the royal family of Dubrovia for generations. She made most of my mother's clothes. I will be pleased to wear one of her dresses."

Rose exchanged a satisfied look with Madame Amyot; they both then glared at Helena. What was this all about? The only time Helena had ever paid her any attention at all was if they encountered each other at a castle dinner or reception. Which didn't happen often, because Rose didn't attend them often. And now that Uncle Nik had finally, FINALLY dumped her, Helena shouldn't be attending too many more herself.

"Well. I suppose that a small provincial designer will be adequate to supply you with a gown. After all, I'm sure you will make an official appearance and then leave. It's too much for you to be expected to stay for the entire evening."

"What makes you think that?" She hated the way Helena talked to her, or talked around her: as if she were stupid, or deaf, or completely unable to do anything. "Of course I'm staying for the whole thing. I'm making a presentation at the ball for one of the charities we support."

"Oh, well, I'm sure I don't want to offend you. I had understood, from the prince…"

"I don't think so. I don't think Uncle Nik talks to you so much anymore. He's been staying home here in Dubrovia more than traveling, and working in the library with Emily, Dr. Charette."

"Ah, yes, the library." Helena glared at Rose. "Is that where this is coming from? That little librarian? I hear she's been filling your head with nonsense, encouraging you to leave the country for school, pestering your poor grandparents about having more surgery. That is unwise, you know." She shook her head. "You are far too young to be even thinking about such things, let alone making any such decisions on your own. Apparently she's a bad influence on you. I shall speak to the crown prince again and convince him that you need better care closer to home and that you should not be allowed to spend so much time in the library."

"Emily is not a bad influence on me! She's a great influence! And a mentor! I can talk to her about school; she knows a lot of people at a lot of places."

"Of course she is a bad influence on you, dear. Look at today: I assume she encouraged you to come here by yourself? Unescorted? And meet up with this… friend, who just happens to be the cousin of one of her assistants?"

"I am NOT unescorted!" Rose shouted. "I came with two bodyguards and a driver. And they will be in here any second if you do not GO AWAY!"

Indeed, her female guard stepped inside at that moment. "Your Highness? Is everything all right? Do you need us?"

Rose was breathing hard. "Yes, thank you, I'm okay. But stay a moment. Miss DiSalvo is leaving and I want you to make sure she gets back to her car."

The guard's eyebrows lifted and came back down in an almost-frown. She looked at Helena pointedly. "Miss DiSalvo, if you could please come outside now? I think the princess and her friend would prefer to finish their shopping in private."

"Of course," Helena said smoothly. "I think I should find the crown prince. He needs to know what is going on here."

Chapter Twenty-Six:
Nik listens to Helena

"**N**ik, you know you must do something. This situation has gotten out of hand."

Nik leaned back in his chair, his hands steepled against his chin, his eyes hooded. For the past ten minutes he had watched his former lover pace around his office and listened to her describe her "chance" encounter with Rose in a dress shop down in the city.

Chance? Hardly. Helena didn't do anything by chance. If she visited that particular shop at that particular time, she had a reason. He just had to figure out what her reason was.

Now Helena sat in front of his desk, her hands clasped in her lap, looking like the perfect concerned... friend? Older sister? Aunt? He'd never been sure how she envisioned her relationship with his young cousin. As far as he could tell, Helena avoided the girl as much as possible, almost as if she saw Rose's disability as somehow catching.

So why, then, was Helena so concerned about Rose's trip into the city? Or about Rose at all?

He tuned in again as she spoke. "But to find her, all alone in that shop! Nikki, you must agree to the impropriety. Why, anything could have happened to her!"

"Cerina is not Paris, or Rome. We're not a hotbed of intrigue or crime here, Helena."

"But surely you agree she must be protected. Is she not your heir, until you have children of your own?"

"Of course. But Rose was safe among our people. They would notice a stranger." He smiled slightly. "They noticed you, did they not?"

"Well, yes, of course they did," Helena said, sounding flustered. (One more thing she never did was get flustered. Strange.) "I did not attempt to be clandestine. I made myself known to her right away. But Nikki, I saw no guards, no security. What if I had been a stranger, someone who intended to harm her?"

"The guards were in place, Helena, doing their job. If you did not see them, then they did their job well. And they saw you enter; they reported to me immediately. Rose doesn't like them hovering. Neither do I. I assume you never noticed them when I traveled around Europe, or when you attended various functions in Italy with me?"

She sucked in a gasp, her hand to her throat. "You had bodyguards? When we were together? And you did not tell me?"

"Of course I had bodyguards. I am heir to a ruling monarch. What did you expect?"

"I expected you to tell me something so important! Have you no regard for my privacy?" she said indignantly.

"I have great regard for safety and security. And your father knew. I'm surprised he didn't tell you."

"No, he… I suppose you are right. It is just unsettling to think of our private moments being, well, not so private."

"Helena, you can't have it both ways. Complete privacy and complete security are mutually exclusive. I find a

254

balance that works for me," Nik said. "And Rose was safe, I assure you."

"Well, you do what you think is best, Nikki. You always do. It just surprised me to see her in town."

Nik shrugged. "I'm glad she's getting out and about a bit. It's good for her to visit with a friend, someone she knew before her accident. Even though she may never rule, she is important to Dubrovia. She needs connections here."

Helena pounced on his statement. "I agree. She should be encouraged to strengthen those local connections. All of her relationships should be carefully monitored, however, to ensure she is less susceptible to outside influences, like that little librarian. Why, did you know the girl she spent the afternoon with is the cousin of one of the assistants to your Dr. Charette?"

"What of it? Dubrovia is not a large country, and Cerina is not a large city. You know the American expression 'six degrees of separation'? Everyone here is connected to everyone else. Sometimes those connections are closer than you find in other countries, other cities."

"But what of the influence your Dr. Charette holds over her? Are you not concerned? Princess Rose is young, impressionable. I can see how she might be dazzled by visions of attending foreign schools, living in foreign countries."

"Helena…"

"No, truly, Nikolas. You should find out whose idea it was for Rose to meet up with her friend and visit that dress shop. If not her own, then whose? If she wants a dress for the ball, why does not the palace dressmaker come to her? She's a princess. She does not need to be shopping for her own clothes. And certainly not at the same shop as her little friend."

And there it came: the snobbery that had irritated him when they were together and was no less annoying now they were not. "Madame Amyot's shop has served the royal family for generations. Rose's mother went regularly. They provide most of my aunt's wardrobe still."

"Oh, but Nik! To go to a shop? And not even to be fitted for a custom dress. She shopped off the same racks as everyone else. And with her special needs? You would think the dressmaker would be more considerate of her condition and have offered her a private room."

Helena rose to pace again. "You see? This is what can happen when she spends too much time with, well, commoners. People beneath her."

Nik rose as well. "In that case, Helena, perhaps I should be careful of the same thing?"

"Of course!"

"I should make a point of only consorting with my peers, those of similar social standing?"

"Exactly! But you—"

"Then, Helena," he said, coming around his desk and taking her elbow, steering her toward the door, "perhaps you should leave. After all, you are not my peer, are you?"

"Nikolas! How could you?" she exclaimed. Her voice shook as he reached for the door, he couldn't tell whether from anger or tears.

"Helena, in case you haven't noticed, princes are few and far between. If I socialized only with my peers, I would lead a rather lonely life. However," he said, cutting off her response, "I think you've said enough for this afternoon, don't you?"

She dug in her five-inch heels, forcing them both to a stop. "Nik, all I want is for the little princess to be safe. Can you not understand that?"

"I don't believe she was ever at risk. And I don't believe Dr. Charette is necessarily a bad influence on her. But she is an influence, I will grant you that. And I promise to look into the situation. In the meantime," he said, easing her out the door, "I need to review the contract again before I meet with your father in the morning. I expect to see you at the reception with Council tonight."

Nik closed the door firmly behind her. It took several seconds before he heard her heels click on the marble floor as she walked away. He blew out a breath and wondered what he had ever seen in her.

Chapter Twenty-Seven:
News from home

"Emily? Hey, Emily, I'm back!"

Emily heard the call from halfway across the library. She was working on a table close to the French doors, for the light and the air. The late-September sunshine was deceptive, though; the breeze had a bit of a nip. Summer had definitely eased into fall, she thought idly as Rose's wheelchair cruised across the flagstone floor and came to a stop beside her.

Rose's excursion into Cerina was a success, then. Well, good for her! It was about time for her to start picking up the pieces of her life again. And that meant venturing outside the castle, even if only as far as the city below for now.

Emily was out in the library because Nik was working in his office today, alternating between closed-door meetings and open-door drop-in sessions. Or that was how she thought of them: when his door was open, anyone and everyone seemed to stop by for a minute or ten.

Right now his door was closed. Helena DiSalvo had stalked in about twenty minutes ago. She'd made a point of stopping and catching Emily's eye with a glare and a smirk before passing through the opening and closing the door behind her.

Emily had no idea why. She was a little surprised to see the woman, but she supposed it might be about the contract negotiations, which hadn't yet concluded according to Anja, who'd heard it from Anton.

No matter. What did matter right now was Rose's excitement over her afternoon out.

"I can see that!" She laughed at the girl. "Enjoyed yourself?"

"Best day EVER! I met up with Maria when she got out of classes, and we had coffee and—oh! I almost forgot!" Rose rummaged in her ever-present bag and pulled out a small bakery box. "Here! We ate some of these. They're my favorite, and my mama's. We used to share them whenever we went into the city. I brought you some."

Emily took the box and peeked in. "Wow, they look great! Thanks," she said, placing the box on the table. "So, you met up for coffee and… what else? Did you have time to go shopping? You went to look at dresses, right?"

"We did, and it was great! I found a dress design, and Madame Amyot said she could make it in this beautiful purple chiffon in time for the ball and fix the hem so the skirt doesn't catch in my chair wheels and I can stand in it and it'll cover me okay when I sit back down," Rose said, all in one breath. "You should have come! They had lots of really nice dresses. You could have bought one for the ball too."

"Rose, I don't think—"

"You *are* coming to the Harvest Ball, aren't you? Everybody comes. It's even on a weekend that you're here and not back in Edmonton. I checked."

"Okay, yes, I'm coming to the ball. But I'm not buying a new dress. I have a couple of gowns back home, for receptions and dinners. I'm home next week; I'll bring one back with me when I come back."

"Oh, no new dress?"

Rose sounded so disappointed, Emily laughed. "No new dress. I don't get paid enough to buy something new for every event!"

"That's too bad. I saw a blue one that would look great on you. Maybe for the Christmas Ball!"

"I'm not sure I'll be at that one, Rose. Isn't it more formal? I know the Harvest Ball is open to staff, and people from the city come too. But the Christmas one is more formal, more exclusive, right?"

Rose shrugged, poking into the piles of books and documents spread out across the table. "I guess. There will be a lot more foreigners, people from all over Europe, for sure." She looked at Emily. "You'll still be here, though, right? You said that the work is going a lot faster now, with Pétur and Ivan helping. But even if you finish this part up early, you'll stay for Christmas, right?"

"Not on the day itself. I'll be home with my father for that, whether we've finished here or not. As for the ball, well, we'll see. I can't make any promises."

They chatted a bit about the books on the table, until Emily noticed Rose shifting uncomfortably in her chair. "Are you okay, Rose? I think you might have overdone it a little this afternoon."

Rose made a face. "I'm supposed to see Jacquie for a session in a few minutes. It's going to hurt. I can get in and out of the car myself now, but it twists my back some and then I get sore."

"The sooner you go, the sooner it's over. Try to convince her to finish in the hot tub today. I can meet you down there in, oh, an hour?" Emily glanced at her watch.

"Yay! I'll see you there! That'll give me something to look forward to as she's pounding on my back."

Rose spun her chair around, facing out into the rest of the room. "Oh, ick. Look who's coming out of Uncle Nik's office." She wrinkled her nose. "I hoped I wouldn't run into her again today."

Emily turned in time to see Helena clicking her way across the wide expanse of floor, making her way from the office to the exit into the gallery. "Again? What do you mean, again?"

"Oh, she came into Madame Amyot's shop while Maria and I were looking at dresses. She—Helena, not Maria or Madame Amyot—gave me a hard time about being in town unescorted. But I wasn't! I took two bodyguards and a driver. They just weren't in the shop with us. They stood right outside, though. So I don't know what her big deal was."

"Maybe she was just concerned about your safety?"

"Ha!" Rose snorted. "As if she cares about me or my safety one little bit. And she comes running to Uncle Nik to talk to him after? She must have rushed back to the castle to beat me home. No, she's sneaky. I don't know what she's up to, but it's something."

Rose waited until Helena's footsteps faded away before saying, "Hope she's gone now. At least her rooms aren't on the same floor as yours and mine! So I'll see you later?"

Emily agreed and went back to work on the books as Rose left. She had flagged these on her first pass through the stacks, weeks ago when she'd first arrived. With Pétur and Ivan working to finish up the counting, she was free to dive into the deeper study.

As usual, she lost herself in the one in front of her. The massive tome had ragged page edges and a heavy leather cover complete with gold leaf she took care not to nudge off. It appeared to be a printed book re-bound to include handwritten pages. She'd found a number of those in Dubrovia's library, various scholarly works to which earlier rulers, or their subjects, felt driven to add their own notations and drawings.

This one was a botanical study. Plants, flowers, trees, and vines were described and illustrated in intricate detail. Notes in the margins of the original printed pages thoroughly cross-referenced the later additions.

Not her area of expertise, though, so she made a mental note to fire off an email to the appropriate department head back in Edmonton. She could help with the translating, but she needed an expert to evaluate the work itself.

The ringer on her cell phone broke the quiet of the library. "Hello, Sam, how are you? I didn't expect to hear from you so early. How's Dad today?"

The news on the other end wasn't great. It rarely was, these days. Her father's general health was fairly stable at the moment, but his mental state had declined rapidly. Some sort of dementia was taking hold, and taking its toll.

Emily listened to the latest report from her father's caregiver, one hand holding her phone, the other propping up her head. Her father's condition was why she had resisted taking this project. He'd been able to convince her she should go; sitting and watching his memory disintegrate wouldn't help either of them, he argued.

She knew he was right, but it was hard, so hard, to be this far away. She wondered again if he had more of an idea of what was in store for him than he had let on. In spite of all the reading she'd done on Alzheimer's and other forms of dementia, she'd never expected things to deteriorate so quickly. It was, what, five months since his diagnosis? Already he didn't recognize her voice on the phone some days. And while he still recognized her face when he saw her, how long would that continue? Would it be this trip home, or the next, or the next, when she walked in the door and he wouldn't know her?

Had he sent her away so that she didn't have to watch him slip farther and farther away each day?

"Do I need to come home, Sam?" she asked softly.

"Maybe. I think it's time to move him to the secure ward. He got up last night and left his apartment and wandered down the hall. The night nurse caught him before he managed to figure out the elevator. But they're not set up for that level of care here; he needs to be where someone is paying attention twenty-four seven," came the response.

"I should be home for the move. How fast can you find him a bed? Do they have any vacancies?"

"Yes, as a matter of fact. I asked this morning. They could move him over as soon as next week. And you're right; he'll take it better if you're here."

"It's my weekend to come home anyway. I arrive Sunday afternoon. If there's paperwork you need to get this started, could you email it to me?"

Emily hung up after working out the details. She set her phone down and pressed the heels of her hands against both eyes. Hard. It wasn't her eyes that hurt, though; it was her heart. So many years, such a brilliant mind, and it was all falling apart. She couldn't imagine what it must feel like from the inside.

Chapter Twenty-Eight:
Nik questions Emily

Nik closed and locked his office door and started across the library. He was on his way to the upper vineyards. They were harvesting far upslope this week, and there was always something needing his attention. This time of year, he always stayed close to home. This year, it didn't feel like an imposition.

He saw Emily and pulled up short, looking at his watch. Good; it was late enough her assistants had probably finished for the day.

Helena's accusations spun through his head as he approached. Was she right? Was Emily a bad influence on his cousin? He wasn't sure whether she had any sort of influence on Rose, let alone a bad one.

He had dressed down today, expecting to be up in the hills before long. His rubber-soled hiking boots made less noise on the stone floors than dress shoes, so he managed to come within a few feet of her before she realized he was there.

The quiet allowed him to overhear her last words before she ended the call. Who was this Sam? Why was she so upset after talking to him?

Her head dropped down, her palms pressed against her eyes and elbows on the table. As he reached her side she scrubbed her hands up and into her hair, sweeping back her long bangs and dislodging the clip that had held the streaky mass up in a messy bun. Her back stiffened, and she turned to face him.

"Sorry, I didn't hear you," she apologized. "Is there something I can do for you?"

Traces of something—sadness, maybe—shadowed her eyes. Nik wanted those shadows lightened, wanted her more at her normal bright, enthusiastic self. But he wanted some answers, and he feared his questions might deepen those shadows instead.

"Yes, actually, there is. I wanted to talk to you about—you've seen Rose."

"What? How did… oh, the pastries." Emily smiled, her face lighting up as she reached for the confectionery box. "She brought me some of her favorites from the café she went to this afternoon with Maria. Want some?" she asked, lifting the lid and holding out the box.

"No, thank you. Save them for later; they're very good." He fought down the image of Emily biting into a pastry, licking traces of powdered sugar from her lips. "Rose came to you as soon as she returned?"

She closed the box and slid it back onto the table. "I suppose. She was excited about seeing her friend and buying a dress. Why? Should she have gone somewhere else first?"

"No, I—how much did she tell you about her afternoon?" He turned to lean on the table next to her chair, looking down at her.

She looked surprised, then concerned. "What's all this about, Nik?"

"I'd appreciate it if you answered the question. How much did she tell you about what happened this afternoon?"

Concern shifted to annoyance. Her face went blank as she rose from her chair and stood to face him. "What I can tell you is she spoke about drinking coffee and eating pastries and shopping with her friend. If you want to know more than that, ask her."

"Oh, come now, Emily. It's an innocuous enough question."

"Is it? Why does it feel there's more behind it? Oh, of course. Miss DiSalvo was in your office. So, you heard her side of their encounter. You know, if you want to know anything more, you should speak to your cousin. It's hearsay if I tell you what she told me."

"So they did have an encounter."

"Sure, they did," Emily answered. "But you already knew that. And you heard your girlfriend's side. If you want Rose's side, and I think you need it, ask her."

"Helena and I are no longer involved. And I'm asking you. Rose talks to you now more than anyone else. I'm trying to find out if that's a good thing or a bad thing." How had he lost control of this conversation?

"Maybe she talks to me because I don't treat her like an invalid? I had a similar conversation with Her Majesty the queen earlier. She's the one who told me my first day she wanted me to be some sort of mentor for Rose. Well, as her mentor, and as her friend, I'm not comfortable relaying private conversations."

The queen? She'd spoken to the queen about Rose? Nik felt he was three steps behind and losing ground.

He raised his hands and mentally retreated a little. "I'm not asking you to betray a confidence, but Rose is an impressionable young girl, and—"

"Oh, please," Emily snorted. "She's not that young, and she's not that impressionable. She's sixteen! And a royal, with all the political acuity you can expect from her upbringing. Up until two years ago, she was out and about in the community a lot, down in Cerina, traveling abroad with her parents. Only since the accident does everyone want to shelter and protect her. I can tell you from my perspective, she feels smothered. And smothering her will drive her out of Dubrovia faster and farther than her natural curiosity might otherwise take her."

"And you feel entitled to encourage her leaving?"

"Nik, I don't encourage her to do anything. What I talk to her about is choices. She looks to me for an outside opinion, outside experiences. I was young when I left home to go to school, remember? That's why I stayed with Stefan and Kate in Fredericton: I was too young to be at university on my own, and my parents couldn't travel with me."

"And perhaps that is why you may not be the best person to advise Rose." Nik grabbed a chair and sat down facing her. "Sit, sit." He waited for her to settle herself again. "We are concerned. Like it or not, Rose's life is more constricted since the accident. She simply doesn't have the physical wherewithal to travel as she used to. Don't you think that encouraging her to look abroad at schools is just getting her hopes up?"

"Nope." Emily shook her head emphatically. "There are a lot of schools that can accommodate students with physical disabilities. Did you know she's interested in astrophysics? Not exactly a strenuous occupation. Most of her time would be spent sitting and thinking. And using powerful telescopes, which these days doesn't always mean climbing up into observatories in the dead of night. But she can't earn an advanced degree in astrophysics here."

"Well, no, but—"

"You went away for school, didn't you? I seem to remember you were at Oxford at the same time Stefan attended the University of New Brunswick. And as for any physical limitations," she continued, warming to the subject, "you're not taking into account the possibility she might opt for more surgery and someday be able to ditch the chair."

"That is not going to happen."

"No? Well, not before she's eighteen, for sure. She made her case to the king and queen, and she knows they're not in favor. But after, when she's of age and comes into her trust? Don't bet on it. And don't get in her way, or she might not come back once she sees how far she can go."

"So you consider it advisable for her to leave Dubrovia? Leave her home, her family?"

"I think young people should stretch their wings, yes. You learn so much by studying someplace else! I also know she's strongly rooted here. We're a lot alike that way. I travel

271

and accept assignments abroad, but I'm a homebody. I like being in familiar places. Edmonton is home for me. Once I finished my degrees, I had a lot of offers from a lot of places. I went home." She shrugged. "I'm not all that adventurous."

He pounced on her comment. "Is that why you stay here in the library all the time, because you're not adventurous? I practically had to drag you out of the castle and up the mountain to the vineyards and the winery. That wasn't so much of a big adventure, was it?"

Emily squirmed in her chair. "Not a big adventure, maybe, but perhaps not such a good idea either," she retorted, blushing.

She has the most amazing skin. It showed her emotions more clearly than her features did. The question of Rose aside, he liked seeing her a little off-balance. Emily was such a private person, so different from most of the women he knew. Being just friends with a woman was new, and he realized he liked being able to tease her a little. None of the women he had dated would tolerate even this gentle ribbing.

"I disagree. I still think it was a good idea, you and me, getting to know each other again, getting a better understanding of what the other does."

"Well, maybe so. But I'm not here to sightsee, Nik. I'm here to work."

"So you didn't go into town with Rose today because you had to work? You could take a couple of hours. You can make up the time during evenings and weekends if you really feel obligated."

"Oh, no!" Emily denied vigorously. "No, this was Rose's opportunity to meet up with an old friend. I'd have been in the way."

"So you'll go to Madame Amyot's shop another time for a gown for the ball? My aunt tells me Rose delivered your invitation."

She huffed out a laugh. "Hardly. I'll be home next week, and when I return, I'll bring a dress back with me. Or maybe two—Rose wants to help me choose which one to wear."

"You'll wear a dress you've worn before?" Unheard of. Certainly all the women in his social circle wouldn't be caught dead in a repeat outfit.

"You think I can buy a new dress every time I go to a reception or a dinner or something? Some of us don't make that kind of money." She laughed, shaking her head.

"We can't allow that." He frowned at her, half-teasing and half-serious. "The Crown has an account there; just go and order a dress."

"Not on your life! Nik, you can't buy me a dress!"

"Why not?"

She sounded absolutely horrified. What was the big deal? He made it a regular practice to offer his American Express Centurion Card to his partner of the moment for a shopping spree. Surely one dress wasn't out of line. Even if she was just a friend.

"Because! It's completely inappropriate! I work for you! Sort of. Well, I work for the Crown, and you're the crown prince—close enough!" she snapped.

Emily leaped to her feet and started to gather her things from the table. She took great care with the old books, he noticed, but her own things got quite a workout as she slammed them into her messenger bag.

"I didn't mean to offend you. I thought—"

"No, you didn't think!" She whirled to face him. "Remember our conversation about how important this job is to me? How I need to worry about my professional reputation? How would it look if I started accepting expensive gifts from you? To say nothing about how it would give out the wrong idea. So no, Nik, you can't buy me a dress. You can't have the Crown buy me a dress. What you can do," she fumed, picking up her bag and starting for the door, "is forget we ever had this conversation!"

Chapter Twenty-Nine:
Helena plots

Emily shoved the key into the lock and turned it slowly till she felt the second click. Nik's office door was fussy. You had to be careful and feel the tumblers click into place or the thing wouldn't open.

And you had to be just as careful easing the key back out of the lock. The last thing she wanted was to have to call Anton to help her get unstuck; the second time it happened, he'd laughed and taken pity on her and showed her the trick. She brought the key back just past vertical, waited for the lock to sort of jump into place, and then turned it back to the first position and slid the key out. She loved old buildings, with their beautiful brass and bronze hardware, but times like this, with her arms laden with books and her heavy bag over her shoulder, she missed the electronic key cards of modern doors.

Pushing the heavy door open with her hip, she stepped inside and nudged the light switch with her elbow. At least they had modernized the lighting recently. Rocker switches were far easier to manage than the round dimmer-type switches for the gas lamps of the very first library she had worked on with her father.

As she placed the books down on the table and turned to close the door, two women appeared in the opening. "This room will do nicely," the older woman said to her companion before turning to Emily. "You will leave now. And close the door behind you."

Not likely. The younger woman was Helena DiSalvo; from the resemblance, the older woman must be her mother. She was not going to let them into Nik's office and leave them alone. She had permission to work in here this week, since Nik was up on the mountain supervising the last of the harvest from the farthest vineyards. But she didn't even bring her assistants in with her. Not in here.

"I'm sorry, but no. You can't come in here," Emily said, reaching out to halt the woman as she passed.

Signora DiSalvo looked down at the hand at her arm in distaste. Speaking in Italian to her daughter she said, "I would think they trained their staff better than this."

Helena replied in the same language, "Oh, she's not 'staff,' not exactly. She's the Canadian hired to do something with the library. You know, that project Nikki is so worried about, the one taking his funding?"

"No matter. She should not be refusing entry to the Crown's guests." To Emily, she continued in English, "You will leave now. We need the room for a private conversation."

Emily stood her ground. "No, I'm sorry. You can't use this room, or at least I can't let you use it; I don't have the crown prince's permission to allow anyone else in here. If you want a place to talk, the upper reading room is above this one. It's just up those stairs," she said, pointing to the spiral staircase in the far corner. "Or you can always use your guest suite."

Both women glared at her, then Helena huffed out a breath and said to her mother (again in Italian), "She means it. It's not worth the bother, Mamma. You can always complain to the queen later." To Emily she said in English, "We will leave, but you will hear more about this." The two turned as one and glided out the door.

Well, that was fun. Emily shook her head as she closed the door behind them. It wasn't like they could make real trouble for her, she mused as she picked up all her stuff and headed for the desk. But her relationship—friendship, whatever it was—with Nik was a little shaky at the moment. Hopefully this... incident wouldn't make it any shakier.

"Oh, God." She reached for her cell phone in a panic and texted Pétur: **You're not working in the upper reading room today, are you?** *Please, please don't let them be in that room!*

No, why? came the fast reply.

Helena and her mother are on their way up. Wanted to use Nik's office for a private chat. Sent them up there instead.

No, we're in the south stacks. Saw them go by. Heard the Ice Queen bitching. Never knew Italian could sound so nasty.

She laughed as she clicked her phone's screen off. Good; her guys were well out of the way. Time to get some work done.

Except… she could hear voices. Not just any voices, but the same female voices that had been in this room with her not five minutes ago.

Emily turned her head, trying to track the direction. There, from that wall. She walked closer to the fireplace. Yes, there were voices, the sound echoing down through the flue and into the opening, clear enough she could make out the individual Italian words.

She didn't mean to eavesdrop. And before she heard her name, she had every intention of digging her headphones out of her bag and working in her own little bubble of music.

But there's something about catching the sound of your own name spoken, especially when you know you're not supposed to, that obliges you to listen.

So she did.

Her modern Italian was a little rusty, and not every word made it down the chimney ungarbled. Enough came through, though, to get her hackles up.

"I cannot believe {unintelligible} this, this library person. Why, she works for a living, Mother! {unintelligible} nobody!"

Helena must be pacing, Emily thought; her voice was cutting in and out.

"A nobody, indeed. But pretty enough, in a common sort of way. And even if he isn't involved with her, she and this project of hers are a distraction. One you cannot afford, my dear."

That voice came through crystal clear. It was the meaning that caught her off guard. Involved with her? Nik wasn't involved with her, wasn't going to be involved with her. Because Helena's mother was right: she was a nobody.

"Are you saying I should allow this to go on? I thought the plan was for me to get him back. We need him, Mamma."

A chair scraped against the stones upstairs. Helena must be sitting with her mother now, and right by the fireplace.

"Let him have his little fling. He'll soon realize she isn't suitable to be his crown princess. He must marry someone from our circle. I have every faith he will come back to you. As for breaking them up at the proper time... didn't you say this person has some level of influence over Princess Rose? We can use that to our advantage."

"Yes, she does. They seem to have become 'friends.' It is unclear what Rose's grandparents are thinking, or Nik for that matter, to allow it, but they do spend a great deal of time together. But how can that help us?"

"Wheels within wheels, my dear. We want the young princess to no longer be in the succession at all, do we not?"

"Yes, of course. She's Nik's heir until he has children of his own," Helena confirmed.

"Until you give him children," corrected her mother. "But listen. If she were not here, if she were attending school outside the country, for example, or getting more surgery— risky surgery... Didn't you say Nikolas had been angry this Emily seemed to be encouraging young Rose to do both?"

At Helena's murmured agreement, she went on, "Well then. A string has two ends, and we can pull them both. To Rose, you become the supportive older sister. You have—well, your family has—ties to both universities and doctors in Italy. You can help her achieve her goals. And since your contacts are closer to home, so to speak, her grandparents might be more receptive to the idea."

"That might take some doing. Rose is completely enthralled with this Dr. Charette. And how does that help with Nik?"

"Even easier. To Nik, you appear horrified at the idea. Rose is an invalid; she should stay well protected in the bosom of her family. And as an invalid she is certainly not fit to be his heir. Play your cards right, my dear, and he will name *you* as his heir as soon as you are married. You won't need to wait nine months for a child to be born."

"I hope you're right. Convincing Nik will be the easy part; convincing Rose will be much harder."

"True, true. Men are easier, aren't they?" The older woman laughed. "Dangle sex in front of them and you can convince them to do most anything. Better still, deny them sex for a while, till you get what you want."

"Does Papa have the revised contracts ready to go, then? Once I convince Nik his best option is to marry me, the next logical step is to sign the exclusive distribution deal."

"Of course. And you must make sure he agrees to a substantial settlement in the prenup. And an allowance.

After all, you will want to maintain your household in Italy as well as his here. He need never know funding your household means financing the family business."

The scraping of both chairs as the women rose drowned out the next few sentences. As they walked away from the fireplace too, the sound of their voices faded. The last thing Emily heard clearly was Helena being congratulated by her mother for getting all of them invitations to the Harvest Ball. Apparently Nik didn't make a habit of inviting old flames; it must be the impending contract signing that caused the visit. The timing with the ball was simply a coincidence, one that Helena and her family were poised to take advantage of.

What should she do? Should she do anything? Emily sat frozen in indecision. If she went to Nik, would he believe her, believe Helena was still after him to marry her? Not for his own sake, and not entirely so she could be crown princess of Dubrovia (although she was sure that was a nice perk for the Italian blond). No, it was for the money, pure and simple.

No, Nik wouldn't believe her. If she hadn't heard it firsthand, she wouldn't believe it herself.

Not true, her conscience scolded. *You would readily believe Helena was up to something that nasty. But you never imagined this particular scenario.*

But Rose? Rose should be warned. The girl was so eager to travel and see the world, she might be vulnerable to assistance that wasn't really assistance at all. Emily owed it to her old friends Kate and Stefan to protect their daughter.

Chapter Thirty:
Emily confronts Helena

Emily fumed.

She was livid. She was furious. She was aggravated, she was annoyed, she was outraged, she was... How many synonyms were there for *angry*?

She had more than one target for her ire too. Helena the sneaky, Helena the devious, Helena the scheming—and Nik, who seemed to buy into her "concern" for Rose.

At least Rose was smart enough to pierce the smoke and mirrors. Rose, who had come to her, at first confused and then increasingly angry herself, as Helena kept encountering her (accidentally on purpose) and pushing a clear agenda: Rose should apply to universities in Italy, Rose should talk to doctors and surgeons in Italy, Rose should go to Italy to live to finish out her high school years. All so Helena and the rest of the DiSalvo family could look out for her. Because they considered her incapable of looking out for herself.

"She even followed me into my PT session today!" Rose said. "It was creepy, having her there watching. And every time Jacquie stepped away, she was like, 'Oh, I know a great massage therapist in Italy, we have these wonderful thermal baths in Italy, you should come with me to such-and-such a spa in Italy.' God. Like I'm going to spend even a minute with her, getting mud packs or seaweed wraps or whatever she does in her favorite spa. I was in a physio session, for crying out loud. It's not fun. It hurts. I'm not doing it for my looks. I'm doing it so maybe someday I won't need a wheelchair."

She wheeled away and back again. "And don't get me started on her ideas about school. The ones she recommended? None of them were internationally recognized universities. She talked about fashion and design programs! When I said something about physics and astronomy, she looked at me like I had two heads and asked me why a princess would need those. Apparently all a princess needs to know about is clothes."

Emily let her rant. To be honest, she was a more than a little relieved to see Rose like this. Better to be annoyed and see through the nonsense than to believe it.

But, oh, she was angry at Nik. He claimed he and Helena were no longer a couple, but they seemed to be together an awful lot. Pretty much every minute he wasn't in the hills watching over the harvest he spent shepherding the DiSalvo family—father, mother, and daughter—about and around.

She knew because she saw them. The whole castle was in chaos, what with the harvest winding down and preparations for the Harvest Ball in a few days at a fever pitch. Pétur was back in Edmonton this week, and Ivan was writing exams, so Emily was on her own. It was impossible to accomplish much in the library, with all sorts of people wandering in and out, asking questions, asking directions.

So she had taken Nik's advice and started going out and about in the countryside and the city of Cerina. She borrowed a car from the castle fleet, and discovered she loved tooling around the winding mountain roads in the convertible Audi roadster. She had spent a couple of afternoons wandering around Cerina, popping into the little shops and bookstores (they had wonderful used bookstores!) and having her lunch or coffee and a pastry, enjoying the sunshine in the cozy street-side patios.

The DiSalvos never visited the small cafés, of course. No, lunch for them meant fine dining at expensive restaurants. She saw them several times, disembarking from the big black limo they used when they visited, the one that took up the entire street and had to be parked around the corner, often in front of Emily's café of the day.

She shared a coffee with their driver more than once. Havel (the same driver who had picked her up at the airport her first day) was usually in a much better mood by the time he left to pick up the DiSalvo family after their extended lunch than he had been when he arrived after dropping them off. He was closemouthed about his passengers, but Emily got the distinct impression he was counting the days until they left Dubrovia and went home to Italy.

Today was no different, except she had cut her wanderings short and come back to the castle by midafternoon. She and Jacquie were going into Cerina that evening for a night out, and Rose wanted to give her stamp of approval on Emily's dress as well as her gown for the ball tomorrow night. (The younger woman refused to believe you could find pretty, dressy dresses in Canada.)

Emily ran the brush through her now-dry hair and contemplated pinning it up versus braiding it back as usual. Rose had other ideas.

"Oh, no, Em, leave it down. It'll look great with the neckline on that dress," Rose declared.

Emily laughed. "See? A princess does need to know about fashion."

Rose rolled her eyes. "Know about fashion, sure. Study it? Not on your life." She wheeled herself over to the dress hanging on the outside of the armoire and fingered the lacy overlay. "You don't even need jewelry with material this detailed."

"Good thing, because I don't really own any." Her voice was muffled as she pulled the dress on over her head. "You sure I shouldn't French braid my hair?"

"Nope. Leave it down. The guys will love it."

Emily's head popped out, and she reached behind to zip up the back. "Sheesh, Rose, I'm not going there to pick up guys!"

"No? Okay, but you are going to dance, right? Jacquie always complains the next day her feet hurt from dancing so much."

"Speaking of dancing… good thing you reminded me. I'll wear these," she said as she pulled out a pair of flat sandals that laced up her calves. The best of both worlds, she thought as she put them on: pretty and comfortable.

"Oooh, nice." Rose rolled over to the window and peeked out through the drawn drapes. "Huh. Look at that. Uncle Nik is arguing with the wicked witch in the garden."

"Still?" Oh, damn, she hadn't meant to say that.

"What do you mean, still?"

"When I left them they were arguing. In the library, though, not the garden."

"Do tell!" Rose dropped the edge of the curtain and came over swiftly to where Emily sat on the edge of her bed, a sandal dangling from one hand. "What were they arguing about?"

"You, mostly."

"Me? But Uncle Nik didn't seem to worry about what she said to me this past week. At least he didn't when I asked him if he could make her stop. He just about patted me on the head and told me I was overreacting."

"Yes, well." Emily bent down to lace up her other sandal, then straightened to face Rose. "It's kind of my fault."

"Go, you!" the girl said with glee. "Tell me everything that happened!"

* * *

Emily picked up the cord from her phone and headed for the stairs. If she hurried, she had enough time to recharge it before she and Jacquie left for the rest of the day.

The universe had other ideas, though, because Helena stopped her before she had a chance to cross the expanse. "I want to speak to you, Dr. Charette."

"Can this wait till tomorrow? I'm kind of in a rush…" Emily glanced at her watch.

"No, it cannot. I know you are not working this week; I saw you driving from the castle and having lunch in Cerina. So you can spare a few minutes from your busy social schedule. I have something to say to you."

"All right," she answered cautiously. "What can I do for you?"

"I spoke to Princess Rose. I am not pleased with your undue influence over her. You should be spending your time on the job for which you were hired, restoring this library." Helena looked around and made a face. "You have been here for months with little to show. The library still looks the same as it did before you arrived."

"And it won't look much different when we're done," Emily agreed. "My work isn't about how the books sit on the shelves. It's about what's in them, and how important it is to preserve that. But this isn't about the library—you don't care about that. So why don't you tell me what you came to say?"

"I do indeed care about the library, because Crown Prince Nikolas cares about the library. I can't figure out why"—she shrugged—"except of course for the funding. He has enough other things to worry about; he shouldn't need to worry whether funds are being spent inappropriately."

"Inappropriately? The Royal Council approved this project. Crown Prince Nikolas approved this project. I can assure you, funds are not being spent inappropriately!"

"Unadvisedly, then. Unwisely. But you are correct. It is not the library I wish to discuss with you, but Princess Rose."

"And how much I influence her, yes, I heard you. Not that it's any of your business, but Queen Elspeth and King Filip don't believe I have 'undue influence' where Princess Rose is concerned. In fact, Her Majesty asked me to act as her mentor the first day I arrived."

"An ill-advised or unwise decision, perhaps. You are only a temporary fixture in her life. She is much too young and impressionable to be allowed to be swayed by such a transient personage."

"Again, not that it's any of your business, but I've been friends with Rose for a long time, going way back to when I used to babysit her when she was a child in Canada with her parents," Emily retorted.

"She is still a child. And children need to be directed. Royal children in particular need to be directed by those in their peer group. You cannot help her fit into society. She will struggle enough, given her condition. She needs guidance you cannot provide."

"No? Well, you're partly right; I'm not in her social circle. I can't help her avoid the landmines she might encounter as a royal. What I *can* do, what I have been doing, is show her options for her education." She hurt to think she might be only passing through Rose's life. No, she wouldn't accept that. "And I can be her friend."

"Her friend? She does not need to look to you for friendship. If she comes to Italy, we can start to introduce her to European society, where she belongs. That's where her friends must be found."

"We disagree there. Friends are found where you look for them and are kept by working at it. They aren't only from one sliver of society. And Rose is much less of a child than you treat her."

"You are a fool if you think you are her friend. People like you, who must work for a living? You work for people like us. We are not your friends; we are your employers."

"Yes, I work for a living. I do something I love and am paid well for it. And I am proud that I support myself; I'm not a burden on society," Emily said proudly. "Or on a husband, for that matter."

Helena frowned at Emily, then brightened. "A husband?" She let out a tinkly laugh. "Surely you aren't expecting someone to be interested in marrying you? Oh, my dear, it's a good thing you have this little career of yours. I'm sure it will give you great comfort in your later years. Unless," she continued with a small frown, "unless you... oh my God! That's it, isn't it? You're here to try and catch a husband!"

Emily goggled at her. "Are you out of your mind? Where did THAT come from? I most certainly am not."

"Oh, you poor girl. He flirted with you, didn't he? The crown prince? And now you are convinced there is something more?"

"What? No! He—"

"Listen to me, Dr. Charette. He might smile. He might flirt. He might even seduce you. But all you can ever be to him is a fling, a temporary liaison, an affair. After all, he's rich, he's handsome, and he likes women. He always has. God knows he's gone through enough of them since he finished school and entered society himself. But he will settle down to his responsibilities someday. And when he does, he will choose someone from his social circle—*our* social circle—to be his crown princess. Just as Princess Rose will eventually choose from the same circle. And people like you? You can't aspire to be part of our circle. You shouldn't even try."

"That's enough." The hard voice came from behind them.

Helena whirled. "Oh, Nikki! I didn't hear you. I was just explaining to Dr. Charette—"

"I heard your explanation. I think you've said enough, don't you?" Nik turned to Emily. "I am sorry you had to hear that."

"I'm sorry I heard it too, believe me. But—"

"I will take it from here. I wish to speak to Miss DiSalvo. Would you please excuse us?"

"No, it's okay, I—"

291

"Thank you, Dr. Charette, but my conversation with Miss DiSalvo is private," he stated. He looked pointedly at the door to the hall and then back at Emily, waiting expectantly.

Oh. My. God. She'd been dismissed. Just like that. Just like… a servant. Maybe Helena was right and that's all she was here.

Emily wrapped her phone cord tighter around her hand and nodded to him, not meeting his eye, walking across the library in a daze. She made it all the way up the stairs and to her suite before she started to shake.

But Rose was there, waiting for her. So she couldn't indulge in a screaming fit the way she wanted to. Instead, she'd listen to Rose and shower and change for tonight. And not think about how much it hurt.

Chapter Thirty-One:
Nik confronts Helena

Nik led the way out the French doors into the gardens. With all the outsiders visiting this week and wandering around the public spaces in the castle, he wanted some privacy for this conversation with Helena—but he didn't want to shut himself up in his office with her either. Better to keep this discussion public but unheard.

He rounded on her as soon as they reached the paths winding through the late-blooming roses. "Why are you here, Helena? Or more importantly, what are you trying to do here?"

"My father is looking forward to speaking with you about the contracts again. We hear the harvest is particularly good this year. I would think you would want your distribution channels settled before you start bottling, no?" She shot him a coy look from under her lashes, taking his arm to walk beside him. "As for me? I am here to attend your Harvest Ball. I have been looking forward to it for months."

"You do remember we are not together any longer, don't you?"

"Oh, Nikki. I remember we were good together. So you needed some time apart? That is of no matter. I understand any woman who is in your life should expect your occasional absences. You shoulder so many responsibilities, both here and abroad. I can wait as long as it takes."

"Then you'll be waiting a long time, Helena. I made it very clear there will be no marriage."

"You must marry sometime, Nik. And the pool of suitable candidates is not that large. Besides," she said archly, "my father expects me to be on your arm tomorrow night. And we don't want to disappoint my father, do we?"

Dammit, she was right. He didn't want to disappoint her father. Not until he had a line on other distribution contracts, other markets. "All right, that answers the question of why you are here. But please address the question of what you are trying to do," he countered. He'd bring up the marriage question again once he figured out what else was going on.

"Do? Do about what?"

"Don't play games, Helena. We both know you are not stupid. You know what I'm talking about: What are you trying to do with Rose?"

"Oh, the poor little princess." Her sigh rubbed the side of her breast against his arm. Back in the spring, that would have signaled an invitation into her bed, one he would often accept. Now, it felt contrived and forced, as if she was acting out a role in a play he wanted no part of.

"The 'poor little princess' what?"

"Did you know she wants to leave Dubrovia? Oh, perhaps you did not," Helena sympathized. "I think perhaps she does not speak to you as she would to someone who is not family. She probably does not want her grandparents to realize. After all, if they are upset, they will stop her."

What was this? He knew Rose had been speaking to Emily about going to university abroad, and about looking into some surgeries. And he knew his aunt and uncle were not happy about the possibility of more surgery, but had become resigned to her exploring her scholarly pursuits. But would Rose have spoken to Helena too? Surely not; they weren't close. So how had Helena known? Nik racked his brain trying to think of a time when the two could have spoken, let alone the kind of heart-to-heart talk Helena's revelation had implied.

"Helena—"

"I can offer a solution, Nik. One that might sit better with the king and queen than letting their only grandchild go off to who knows where to study who knows what, and be with who knows what sort of people. Let her come with me back to Italy and stay with my family. She will have the experience abroad she craves, but I and my family can keep a closer eye on her than any staff you might assign." She shook her head. "At least in Italy, we understand that the children of important people need a bodyguard close by, which means in class with them. I understand that would be a problem in some foreign schools. Can you imagine? She would be completely unprotected."

"I don't think—"

She rolled right over his objection. "And her aide could stay with her too, to help with her disability. What's the girl's name, Jenny or Jacquie? So when poor Rose wasn't able to manage, Jacquie would be present to help her." She frowned. "We should hire someone who is more like a teacher's aide, though, someone who can help her understand her studies. Although fashion shouldn't be too difficult, she would of course be studying it in Italian."

What in the world—? "Have you spent five minutes with Rose? She has absolutely no desire to study fashion, I assure you. Her interests lie more along the lines of physics and astronomy." Now he knew Helena was making all of this up. Rose? Study fashion? Not likely. So what was Helena after? Or maybe the question should be, what was her family after?

"Physics and astronomy? Nonsense. Those are not suitable endeavors for a princess. If she feels she must continue her studies, then she must be guided into more appropriate directions."

He started to laugh. "Helena, what century do you live in? If Rose wants to be a scientist, why shouldn't she? She has the brains for it."

"And you know this how? Because some little librarian, some outsider, this Dr. Charette, told you so? And what is her motivation in all of this? I'm sure she wants to keep her cushy little project going for as long as she can. So why not become a major influence in the life of a sheltered young princess, one too inexperienced to see through such subterfuge?"

"If you spent any time in real conversation with Rose, Helena, you would recognize how brilliant she is. As both of her parents were. And they managed to study abroad with no mishap—and no bodyguards. So did I. So did Stefan." He stopped next to a bench and motioned for her to sit. He continued to pace in front of her. "So why the push to Italy?" And why the focus on Emily?

"Nik. You know we want to be the exclusive distributors of Dubrovian wines, which will bring our families closer together. So why should we not be willing to provide a home for your disabled cousin?"

"And this has nothing to do with you wanting a marriage out of the deal."

Helena picked up a fallen leaf from the bench beside her and spun it in her fingers. "As I said, Nik, you must marry sometime. Perhaps if we spend more time together because of Rose, you will remember what it was like when we were together."

"Oh, I remember." He stopped in front of her. "It is an experience I do not care to repeat."

"Well, then, consider this. As you assume your responsibilities as crown prince, you will spend more and more time here. You said it yourself, back in the summer: you intend to give up your—what did you call it?—your 'playboy lifestyle.' But how many women in our circle would be willing to change their lifestyle to suit yours? If you married me, you could be sure I would maintain a home in

Italy to be near my parents. I am not likely to allow myself to become bored here in the mountains."

"So this is all about a marriage, after all. You want to be crown princess of Dubrovia."

Helena shrugged. "Of course, who would not? And think of this as well. Since I would be spending time in Italy, and perhaps elsewhere in Europe, you would be free to pursue other interests."

"Other interests. Such as...?" Nik couldn't believe his ears. Was she suggesting what it sounded like? A marriage where husband and wife led separate lives? Had affairs to keep from becoming bored?

"You know very well of what I speak. Your little librarian seems to fascinate you. So why not indulge yourself? Have a fling, now or later. It won't impact the marriage contract. Or the wine distribution contracts, either."

"You must be joking. If I intended to marry you, or anyone else, I would not enter into an affair! Not now. And certainly not after my wedding. A marriage is not just a contract, Helena. It's a promise. And I keep my promises."

"Yes, so you told me." Helena stood angrily. "And you are no closer to giving me your promise, your word, now than you were months ago, are you? Well, perhaps I should have a word of my own—with my father. I told him you were taking your time in proposing. If I tell him you do not intend to marry me, he will pull those precious contracts like that," she snarled, snapping her fingers under his nose.

"Helena—" Nik pinched the bridge of his nose. It could all fall apart, and he might not be able to salvage it. "We've already been down this road. The distribution contracts cannot be tied to a marriage contract. Why do you think I removed myself from the negotiations? Business and personal do not mix."

"Business and personal ALWAYS mix in Italy, Nikolas. You would do well to remember that. You want to keep my father happy? Well, he wants to keep me happy." She started to flounce away.

Nik grabbed her elbow and spun her back to face him. "There. Will. Be. No. Marriage."

She pulled free. "Then there may not be any contracts either."

He stared at her. "Well, then, perhaps you should leave."

"Leave? What do you mean, leave?"

"If your father will not sign contracts unless a marriage goes along with them, then we might as well not prolong this. I think it best you not attend the ball tomorrow." And he would negotiate with her father another time.

"Oh, Nikki, don't be like that. If I misread your feelings for your little librarian, I apologize. It's just I can see her wanting to stay here, to extend her project, and I think she may be manipulating Rose in order to do so." (And manipulating him, was the unspoken implication. Was she?)

Helena continued, "I can leave the idea of marriage aside while you negotiate with my father. After all, it is to all our benefits to sort those out as soon as possible, yes? But if I leave now, tonight, and do not attend the ball, he will know we quarreled."

Oh, hell. She was right. "This is more than just a quarrel, Helena. No, I do not want to jeopardize the negotiations. But you must understand that—"

"Yes, yes, Nik, I heard you," she said, then stopped. He could almost see the gears turning in her head. "She will be at the ball, yes?"

"Who, Rose? Of course." What was she driving at?

"No, no, silly. Your little librarian. Dr. Charette."

"Yeeesss," he replied slowly. "So?"

"So, tomorrow you will observe her in a social setting, yes? I would think she is most comfortable buried among her precious books in the library. When you see her tomorrow night, and see all the other women as well, you will understand why I say you must choose a wife from our social circle."

"Like you, you mean," he scoffed.

"Yes, like me! But also like so many of the other women who will attend. Including your aunt, the queen. When you finally do decide to go looking for a crown princess, you must choose someone like her, someone who understands the demands of royalty, who can navigate the political waters as well as she does. And your little librarian," she finished as she turned and walked off, "isn't going to make the cut."

She was right, and she was wrong.

Nik stood still for all of three seconds. His eyes were on Helena as she walked away, but he didn't see her. Or not the way she wanted him to, at least. He saw her as... what? A reminder of the way he used to live? Perhaps, but not as a temptation to resume it, no matter what incentive she might throw at him.

Including her father's contracts, he realized. "Helena, wait!"

She spun as if she had been waiting for him to call. "Yes? Do you have something you wish to say to me?"

"Yes, I do." He strode to where she stood. "You're wrong."

"Wrong?" She wrinkled her brow in confusion; he watched as she deliberately smoothed it. God forbid Helena should ever show so much as the tiniest flaw. "Wrong about what?"

"All of it. Rose, Emily, my eventual marriage. Let's start with Rose," he said. "Rose is a brilliant sixteen-year-old with her whole life ahead of her. Yes, she is my heir, for now, but she is not the crown princess. She will not always be in the direct line of succession. And even if she were, there's nothing stopping her from going abroad to wherever she likes, to study whatever she likes. Our family will figure out whatever it takes to support her. That might mean bodyguards and it might mean physical therapists and it might mean an aide to help her around campus. Whatever it takes. But she gets to choose."

"Oh, Nik, I never meant to imply anything otherwise."

"Yes, you did. And that's the difference between your advice for Rose and Emily's. All Emily is doing is showing her choices. She's not trying to influence Rose's decision."

"And you are sure of that, how?" Helena spat.

"Because unlike you, I *have* spoken to Rose. And to Emily. And to Her Majesty Queen Elspeth. Rose will have choices. She will be guided, yes, but ultimately the decision is hers."

"I never—"

"And as for Emily, maybe you should do a little more investigating before you start making accusations. Especially about whether someone's behavior is appropriate. She is dedicated to her career. She would never act in such a manner as to put her professional reputation at risk. Her mentoring Rose was done at the queen's request."

"And her... relationship... with you is purely professional also? Because, Nik, I tell you—"

"We're friends. I realize it is difficult for you to imagine a man and a woman as friends, not lovers, but such is the case with Emily and me. And if it should ever turn into anything more, what of it? It is none of your business."

"Oh, Nik," Helena said, rolling her eyes. "Could you choose someone less suitable?"

"Suitable? Suitable by whose standards? Here is another way you are wrong, Helena. You keep saying when I eventually marry, I must choose from the very limited pool of our social circle. In the first place, my social circle seems to be less restrictive than yours. And in the second place, why must I limit my choices to European high society, or the daughters of the investors and bankers I dealt with all the time as minister of foreign trade? Stefan didn't; he married a Canadian he met at university. My father didn't; my mother was a teacher in Cerina when he met her. Even the king chose a commoner; my aunt's family runs a couple of bakeries in the south of France."

"Your mother and your aunt are the exceptions. They might come from commoner families, but they were raised to certain standards of behavior. And I would never want to speak ill of the dead, but your cousin's wife was not. She would not have made half the queen your aunt is. Perhaps... no. I will not."

"Will not what, Helena? Go on, you might as well finish what you were going to say."

"Well, since you ask. Perhaps it is best for Dubrovia you are now the heir. Crown Prince Stefan was a charming man, and his princess was pretty enough. But he was not as ambitious as you. You will push and pull and shape Dubrovia into something important. You, not your cousin," she declared. "And you need a wife who can match you."

"And you think you're the best candidate for the job?" Nik asked. He clenched his fists by his side. What he wanted to do instead was... hit that tree. Repeatedly. Or yell at someone. How dare she?

"Yes, I am. Certainly better than a little nobody who must work for a living," Helena said defiantly.

"Tread lightly," he replied softly. "I work for a living."

"Oh, good God, Nikolas, you are an international businessman. And you run a country, for all intents and purposes. You do not punch a time clock or collect a salary from someone else."

It was hard for him to believe he had wasted months on this woman. She was an expert at hiding her true colors. But once she revealed herself? No way would he resume their... whatever they had. He couldn't call it a relationship, or even a fling. Both of those required some level of emotional involvement. What he'd had for Helena, Nik realized, was merely the desire to bed her. And even that couldn't survive the vitriol she had spewed today.

"You should go." He turned away from her to head back into the garden. "I do not care whether you show up at the Harvest Ball tomorrow or not. And I also do not care if you go running to your papa and tell him to cancel the contract negotiations." He looked back as she started to sputter. "I can even be civil to you, if we are both to be in the company of that 'social circle' you are so enamored of. Because I tell you something, Helena. I feel nothing for you. Nothing at all."

Chapter Thirty-Two:
What do you want from me?

Nik paced and fumed, fumed and paced. For a change, he threw himself onto the couch in the third-floor seating area and fumed sitting down. She wasn't here. She was always here. How come the one time he wanted to find Emily to talk to her, she chose that evening to go out on the town with Jacquie?

After leaving Helena in the gardens earlier, he'd looked for his cousin. In the last few months, he'd watched Rose blossom under Emily's mentorship. But she was still a sixteen-year-old girl who had led a very sheltered life. She might be book-smart, but that didn't make her people-smart.

And the same could be said for Emily. He'd observed that himself the few times he had seen her with the Royal Council. She was fine as long as the conversation stuck to the library, her project status, or something else equally dry or academic. Turn the conversation over to more general or, heaven forbid, more personal subjects, though, and she became evasive. She didn't like to reveal much of herself.

He smiled, remembering the last Council meeting. Janko had asked her whether she planned to be in Dubrovia for the two upcoming balls. She hemmed and hawed—and blushed furiously. And she never gave him an answer.

Still restless, he rose and paced the edges of the room again. His conversation with Rose had been eye-opening to say the least. For the first time that he could tell, Rose had reacted to him as an adult. God, she reminded him so much of her father! The same studious demeanor, the same brown eyes, the same quick wit. She had her mother's quick temper, though. How had he not noticed before?

Because when you treat her like a child, she acts like one.

He rubbed his chin ruefully. You'd think he would recall his own teenage years, trying to make his parents and his aunt and uncle take him seriously. Of course, Rose wasn't nearly as wild as he had been. That was as much opportunity as temperament. Given her almost complete seclusion in the castle since her accident, it was no wonder she led such a sheltered existence.

She really lit up when she told him about her afternoon in Cerina, looking at dresses and having coffee and pastries with her old friend. He wanted to give her more opportunities to do that, he decided. Even if it meant putting a little pressure on the king and queen.

Rose hadn't been so cheery when she told him how Helena had cornered her in the dress shop, accusing her of traveling without adequate protection, taking chances where she shouldn't. Sheltered or not, Rose was far too savvy to take such a risk. She'd been raised a royal and traveled extensively with her parents before the accident. She knew what was necessary for her protection, and she accepted it. They all did.

Although traveling with a security detail hadn't saved her parents in Switzerland, when the avalanche slid down the mountain two years ago, wiping out half a kilometer of roadway and the cars sitting on it. But the guards following dug Rose out from where she'd been thrown from the broken limo before she froze to death, although they couldn't save her parents, or his mother.

Nik opened the French doors and paced onto the balcony overlooking the long front drive. He leaned on the balustrade and gazed down the long slope toward Cerina. The glow of the lights was barely visible from here; it was too far, and there were too many trees in the way, to see the city proper. What was she doing down there? All Rose had told him was that Emily had gone with Jacquie into the city to go clubbing.

Clubbing! That was an unlikely entertainment for her. Somehow she didn't strike him as the kind to go barhopping, drinking and dancing with strange men, letting them hold her close...

Enough. Thinking about it, worrying about it, wouldn't bring her home any faster. He turned and went back inside and closed the door.

And what was he doing, thinking about her in such terms anyway? Yes, they'd shared a kiss. Almost. Sort of. And afterwards she told him she wasn't interested.

No, he mused as he pulled the heavy drapes closed again, that wasn't exactly true, was it? What she said was she *could* not, because it wasn't a good idea. Not that she wasn't interested. *Well, now, that's an entirely different story. So what can I do to change her mind?*

And should he try? She was clear about not wanting to do anything that might interfere with her project. While he didn't see a problem, perhaps getting involved with the crown prince, the fellow who controls your contract, might not be looked upon with favor by her superiors back in Canada.

He'd cross that bridge when he came to it, he decided. First, you get the girl to want you. Then you deal with the consequences.

But he couldn't start if she wasn't here.

* * *

"All right, Jacquie, you need to walk up these stairs."

Emily held the other woman's arm and steered her to the main staircase. The elevator might have been faster, but they were less likely to run into anyone at this end of the hallway at this time of night. Maneuvering the giggling Jacquie over to the handrail, Emily was glad once again she'd only drank a couple of glasses of wine. Never one to drink much, she hadn't felt deprived. And thank heavens for staff drivers and cars made readily available when you called too. Two drinks were two too many on winding roads at night.

They made it up the first flight without incident, although Emily had to catch hold of Jacquie's arm at the top to turn her into the next set of stairs. "Just a few more stairs, girlfriend, and then we'll—"

She ran into Jacquie when the other woman stopped dead at the third floor. "Well, look who's here!" said Jacquie with a giggle. "Aw, did you wait up for us? How sweet!" She stumbled into the big sitting room and wove her way over to the closest couch, where she leaned unsteadily. "Look, Em! Look who I found!"

"Oh, God," Emily muttered under her breath. "We so didn't need this." To Jacquie she said, "Yes, hon, I see. Now keep going, and we'll tuck you in your bed in no time."

Nik frowned at them. "Did you two drive home like that?"

"Oh, no, Emily's not drunk! She only had… how many did you have, Em? Was it one glass of wine or two? She's kind of boring," Jacquie whispered loudly at him.

"Boring is good," Emily said as she grabbed Jacquie's arm to start her moving again. "Boring called for the driver, and boring found the car when he couldn't drive all the way into the square. And boring is going to put you to bed before you fall down."

"Aw, Em, come on! I want to visit with the pretty prince! I don't get to see him much. And he's cuter than those guys tonight, don't you think?"

"Oh, you are so going to regret this tomorrow." Emily all but shoved her down the corridor. "I don't think the prince wants to visit with you, Jacq."

"Nooo, he wants to visit with YOU!" Jacquie found that terribly funny. She laughed so hard she almost fell off her heels. "Ooops! Sorry." She giggled again. "Hey, you should stay and visit with him!"

"No, that's fine. I'll just walk you down the hall and into your room, okay?"

"Actually, I do want to speak with you." Nik followed them as far as the entrance to the far hallway.

"See?" Jacquie chortled. "Told you so! The prince wants to talk to you, Em!"

"Maybe this isn't the best time," Emily said over her shoulder as she steered her wobbling friend in the right direction.

"No, tonight is the perfect time. I will wait here until you come back, yes?" Nik said.

Emily frowned. Damn, if he stayed in the sitting room, she'd have to pass by him to reach her suite, and she'd talk to him tonight whether she wanted to or not. "I might be a while," she replied. With any luck he'd take the hint and give up for the night. She was tired, from the dancing and the late hour and generally trying to keep up with Jacquie in the city.

"I can wait."

"Oooh, he's going to wait for you! You're a lucky girl, Emily Charette! I wish I had someone waiting for me."

At least she was moving in the right direction, finally. "Say good night to Prince Nikolas, Jacquie."

"Good night, Prince! And don't worry about Emily. I'll send her right back!"

* * *

It was almost a half hour by the time Emily made her way back into the sitting room. If she was lucky, he'd have given up and...

No, no such luck. He was still there. Well, he might want to talk, but she'd had about enough company for the night. "I'm sorry. She had more to drink than usual, I think, and, well, she doesn't get out much, working here. She may have gone a little overboard."

"Yes, I noticed."

He was frowning, which might not bode well for her friend. "She didn't mean to be disrespectful. Can't you forget—"

"I'm not worried about Miss Simons. She's entitled to sample the local nightlife. Lucky for her, you looked out for her and brought her back home in one piece," Nik said dismissively. "I was more concerned about you."

"Me? Why were you concerned about me? I told you, we called for a driver, and—"

"Where were you?"

"I'm sorry?"

"Where did you go? Rose said you and Jacquie went out clubbing. I know some of the bars and clubs in Cerina extend their hours this week, for the Harvest Festival. Where did you go?"

"I don't know all the places. Jacquie asked Anton and Ivan for some names. I know we started at the festival itself in the square, but I kind of lost track after that."

"On two glasses of wine."

"Yes, on two glasses of wine. I'm not much of a drinker. I can nurse a glass of wine or a beer for hours. And the bars gave out lots of water and soft drinks." What did he care? What difference did it make if she had one drink, or two, or ten?

"And so you went to these clubs, and you danced, you and Jacquie? With any number of men, I'm sure."

Emily's irritation spiked; the back of her neck tightened up. "I'm sorry, Nik, but that's none of your business. Now, if you'll excuse me, I've been on my feet for hours and I'd like to call it a night."

"It's barely one," he said, moving toward her.

"Yes, and we drove into the city at five. I'm not used to partying for seven hours. I'm beat and I want to go to sleep. Tomorrow will be a late night too."

She circled around him on her way out of the room. Her suite was the first one down the hall. If she moved fast enough, she'd be inside with the door closed and on her way to her own bed in a matter of minutes.

Nik followed close behind her. He caught up to her at her door, grabbing her hand as she reached for the lock.

"You never leave the castle. You're always here, somewhere. In the library, with Rose, or with my aunt sometimes. But here. In the castle. So when I went looking for you, I didn't expect you to be gone." He sounded as annoyed as she felt. What was his problem? What did he have to be angry about?

"So?"

"So you've been gone a lot this week. I tried to find you the other day, but Helena said she saw you in town. And then tonight—"

Emily looked back at him over her shoulder as she jerked on the handle. "It was your idea!" she said testily, opening the door to step inside. If she was fast...

Not fast enough. He grabbed the door before she went through and held it still. "My idea? How was it my idea for you to go out dancing with Jacquie tonight?"

"Not tonight specifically. But you're the one who's been badgering me to go out and tour around, get to know Dubrovia. How better to learn about a country than to attend a local festival?"

"It seems out of character for you," Nik said defensively. "I didn't expect it. You keep such a low profile, I—"

Emily let go of the door and whirled to face him. "I can't win this, can I? When I stayed in the castle all the time, working all day every day, you gave me grief about not getting out, 'experiencing life' I think was how you put it. But I go out this week, and tonight, and you're not happy about that either. Dammit, Nik, what do you WANT from me?"

"What do I want from you? This is what I want from you." She didn't have time to take a breath before his mouth crashed down on hers.

Chapter Thirty-Three:
Lovers

Oh, God, her mouth. She tasted sweet and hot all at once. He wanted to nibble her lips forever, he wanted to take great gulping bites, he wanted, he wanted…

He wanted. Her body, stiff with surprise at first, softened and eased against his. He leaned into her, trapping her between the wall and his own body. He didn't realize his hands had come up to cup her head until his fingers ran into the little sparkly clips embedded in her hair just behind each ear.

He eased his fingers past the clips and stroked her hair. It unraveled like cool silk, flowing over and around his hands as they wandered down her spine and back up again. Nik grasped the strands in his fist, turning her head a little for better access to that marvelous mouth.

Her hands came up his chest to clutch his shirt, fingers flexing as he deepened the kiss. He thought for a split second she would push him away. He wasn't sure that hadn't been her original intent. But the longer they kissed, the longer that mouth was pressed to his, responding to his, the closer she pulled him against her.

Until she did pull her head away, long enough to gasp for air. "Oh, God, Nik! Wait! What are you doing?"

His mouth tracked across her cheek, along her jaw, behind her ear, down her neck, leaving a trail of nips and kisses. She shuddered when his tongue traced the line of her collarbone. "If you can't tell what I'm doing, *miláček*," he whispered against her skin, "I'm not doing it right."

"No, I didn't mean… Oh, Nik, wait. Oh, God. You have to stop."

Her breathless protests finally registered as she pushed him away. "Why?"

"Why?" she asked incredulously. "We're standing in the hallway where anybody might pass by, and you… you kissed me!"

"I did, didn't I?" He grinned at her. "You kissed me back."

"Well, yes, but—"

"So," he said, backing her into in her room, "you're right. We should take this somewhere more private." And he kissed her again.

* * *

Oh, God, his mouth. She'd never felt anything as intoxicating as his mouth on hers. When his tongue slipped between her lips to tangle with hers, Emily moaned and reached for him again, her hands sliding up his back to hang onto his shoulders for dear life.

Because if she let go, she'd fall over. Her knees were weak. She always thought that to be such a cliché—who knew it could happen for real?

The door clicked shut behind her, the sound jarring her out of her haze. "Nik, wait. You don't want—"

"Oh, sweetheart, I most certainly do." He rocked his hips against her, his mouth back at her neck. He hadn't lied; he did want.

"But I'm not…"

"Not what?" This time he was the one to pull away. He looked down at her, a question in his eyes. "You're not what?"

It was hard to think, with his body pressed against hers, his erection hard against her belly. It was hard to think with his eyes staring down at her, looking through her. It was hard to think with her senses scrambled by his kisses.

And oh, God, he was hard. He rocked against her again, showing her just how hard he was. And how big. Emily was no virgin, but she was pretty sure she'd never had an erection this size pressed against her, making her ache, making her want…

What did he ask? Oh, yeah. "I mean, I'm not… not beautiful, not glamorous, not sophisticated. Not like your usual women."

His eyebrows went up, and his eyes went down. She swore she sensed real heat as his gaze traveled down her body and back up. "No, you're not like the women I usually date. And thank God for that," he continued, pulling her back into his arms when she stiffened and pulled away. "But if you notice, I'm not here with one of them. I'm here with you."

"Nik, no, really, you don't want me," Emily said. She turned her head to give him better access to the hollow of her throat, where he bit gently. "Oh, God."

His chuckle rumbled through her. "You're saying that a lot." He nipped at her one last time. "And I'm sure I know who I want to be with tonight."

Tonight? Maybe that was it. He'd quarreled with Helena today; Rose was convinced they'd really come to a final parting of the ways this time. And Emily was here, she was available, she was going to melt into a little puddle at his feet any minute now.

She was nothing like his usual women. He said so himself. So maybe tonight was… what? A momentary lapse, an aberration, a sidestep on his way to finding himself a crown princess?

All of a sudden she didn't care. He was here, tonight. He was hers, tonight. She'd take it.

* * *

She was kissing him back again. Thank God; he wasn't sure he'd have been able to walk down the hall in this state if she had told him to leave. Whatever indecision had floated through her mind, whatever insecurities had caused her to doubt that he wanted her, had dissolved under the onslaught of mutual lust.

That's all it was, right? Mutual lust? It had to be. He wasn't looking for anything more, and Emily, well, he didn't know what Emily was looking for but, he doubted it was

318

him. Not in the long term anyway. And since she wasn't going to be here long term, that would work just fine for both of them. They'd have tonight, and however many more nights he convinced her to share his bed.

With one hand he reached behind her to flip the lock on the door. With the other he covered her breast, squeezing gently and then more firmly when she moaned into his mouth. "I want to see you. I need to touch you."

She stilled in his arms, then sighed. "I want to touch you too," she said softly. She looked up at him. "Nik, I want—"

"I know," he murmured, nuzzling into her neck. His hand behind her reached up and eased down her zipper. Her strapless dress clung to the curve of her breasts until he had opened it completely. It slithered down her body, leaving her standing in nothing but the tiniest of bra and panties.

It was his turn to groan. The wispy purple silk made her pale skin glow in the moonlight streaming in through her open curtains. He barely touched her, running the very tip of his finger against her flesh just at the edge of the lace. "Beautiful," he whispered. Who knew the librarian who wore Oxford shirts and plain black slacks had a thing for sexy underwear?

She shivered at his touch. He picked her up in his arms and carried her through her sitting room and into the adjoining bedroom.

This room was darker, the drapes closed against the night. Nik slid her down his body and reached for the lamp beside her bed. At her wordless protest, he stopped at the first, dimmest level.

The bed was already half turned down, ready for the night. He pulled the covers down the rest of the way, keeping one hand on her side.

* * *

It was almost as if he was afraid she would change her mind, tell him to leave or walk away. Emily wasn't sure she was able to walk anywhere herself. She knew she didn't want to. She took a deep breath and reached for him. "I want to see you too."

His skin was warm, warmer than hers, smooth under her touch except for the whorls of dark hair on his chest. She ran her hands over him, enjoying the textures, so different from her own. Muscles bunched and flexed as he unbuttoned his shirt and eased it off his shoulders, dropping it to the floor.

When she reached for his belt and zipper, he laughed a little. "Might be best if I handle that," he said, sounding strained. He toed off his shoes and socks once his pants hit the floor, leaving him in silky boxer briefs.

He sucked in a breath when she touched him, and pulled her to him for another scorching kiss. His hands were everywhere: one cupping a breast, flicking a nipple through the lace, the other running over her ass under her barely there panties. They both moaned when his searching fingers found her wet core. "Oh, God, Nik, I'm going to fall over if you keep doing that."

He scooped her up again and tossed her into the middle of the bed. "Can't have that, now, can we?"

He crawled across the bed toward her. It was like watching a panther stalk his prey, and she was the prey. He came over the top of her on his hands and knees and lowered himself until he was fully against her. His mouth came down on hers again, this time softer, more enticing: little nips and bites, followed by a stroke of his tongue to soothe.

Emily sighed when he shifted, moving his body to lie next to her, turning them both so they were face-to-face. He reached behind to open the clasp of her bra. "I want to see you. All of you." He placed open-mouthed kisses on her neck, her shoulder.

She rolled away a little, and he tugged the bit of lace out from between them and tossed it aside. She moved back in to press her naked breasts against his chest, enjoying the sensation of his chest hair against her heated skin. That brought their hips back together; she pressed against his erection, doing it again when he moaned.

"Little minx." She heard him laugh. "Want to play, do you?"

* * *

So his little librarian had a naughty side, did she? Perfect. Nik kissed his way down her body, stopping wherever she quivered or sighed, mapping out her hot spots. He circled one full breast with his mouth, kissing and licking around and around, under in the sensitive crease, over the mounded top. He teased the edges of the areola but never quite reached the nipple until she made a protesting sound.

"Nik! Please…"

"Please what, *miláček*?" He smiled against her. "Tell me what you want."

"I want… I want," she said hesitantly. "I want you to suck on my breast."

"Like this?"

"Oh, God."

His mouth worked her relentlessly, sucking and tugging on the nipple, making it stand up proud and red against the creamy pale breast. He let go with a pop. She started to protest until he merely switched to the other side and started all over again.

Nik slid his thigh between hers, pressing against her wet core and easing away. She squirmed against him, trying to gain some traction against his leg. Instead he moved his hand from pinching her erect nipple down to slide inside her barely there panties, fingering her clit, rubbing in circles, fast then slow, driving her mad, by the sounds she made.

He slid one finger inside, then two. "Oh, *dítě*, you're so hot, so tight," he groaned, his thumb still working her sensitive little button. "So wet. I need to taste you."

Nik let go of her breast and slid down her body, trailing kisses all the way. He dragged the last lacy bit down her legs and tossed it in the direction of her bra and his clothes. Lying between her thighs, his shoulders braced her legs apart as he gazed at his target.

Her curls were one shade darker than her streaky ash-blond hair, and damp now from her juices. She squeaked when he lowered his head and took a deep breath. "What are you doing?"

He grinned up at her. "Best perfume in the world." Nik closed his eyes and breathed deep again. Then he moved in.

* * *

Emily's hips arched up off the bed when his mouth made contact. Nik's arm came up to press her firmly back down, holding her still while he licked and sucked and nibbled. The pressure inside her built to an almost unbearable level. "Nik! I'm going to—"

"Oh, yeah, *dítě*, that's it, come for me," he crooned against her.

The vibrations kicked her over the edge. She keened as she came hard, harder than she ever had in her life.

He continued to lick and stroke as she came back down. When her tremors slowed to a stop, he gave her clit one last lick and slid back up her body. His mouth captured hers again for a long, slow, wet kiss. Emily tasted herself on his lips and tongue; it was probably the single most erotic thing she had ever experienced.

He drew back, his eyes dark. "You're amazing," he said, stroking her hair back from where it had covered her face as she'd flailed on the pillows.

She felt his erect penis against her leg. If anything, it was longer and thicker than before. She reached down and held on, intending to bring him inside her. "You didn't—"

"Not yet, but I will."

He rolled away and reached over the side of the bed. Her side grew cold until he came back, foil packet in hand. Good thing one of them was still thinking, because she sure wasn't. She took the condom, opening and discarding the wrapper. "Let me."

Nik hissed as she smoothed it down his length. He took her in his arms and flipped her until she was directly beneath him. All the parts lined up; all she had to do was…

Emily opened her thighs wider and moved up a tiny bit, and eased down until the very tip of his penis entered her. He was so big that even this little bit stretched her. It wasn't uncomfortable, not quite. He moved and slid in farther. The pressure, the fullness increased. Rather than making her hurt, it made her ache. She wanted all of him. Now.

She arched her back and brought her knees up along his sides, and he slid home. Pelvis to pelvis, they lay still for the barest second. Then, his eyes on hers, he started to move.

* * *

Hot. Wet. Tight.

Her muscles clamped around him as he stroked in and out, slowly at first, then faster and faster. Her eyes drifted closed. "Open your eyes, Emily. Watch me. Watch us."

He changed the angle, bracing himself up on his palms instead of his elbows, looking down at where their bodies joined. "Look."

She curved her body up to see what he saw. She whimpered at the sight, his flesh disappearing into hers and then reappearing.

Hot. Wet. Tight.

Nik plunged, faster and faster, harder and harder. Emily collapsed back on the bed, her muscles trembling, convulsing around him as she started her climb. He dropped back down to his elbows to sneak a hand between them, reaching down, aiming for her sensitive clit.

One touch, one flick of his finger against her, and she shattered. She screamed this time, his name echoing in his ears.

Hot. Wet. Tight.

He was past thought, pure sensation. Even through the condom he felt her pulsing contractions. One last thrust and he came, pouring himself into the protective sheath, shuddering, spasming.

Gasping, he rested his head against her shoulder. He rolled to his side, bringing her with him as they heaved breaths in sync and recovered from the fall.

He felt as if he had poured his soul out with his semen.

* * *

His heavy head rested against hers, pressing her into the pillow, giving her something to anchor herself to. Without that, she thought, she might well have floated up to the ceiling and out of the window.

She registered his hands, stroking down her side and back, soothing and caressing, but the sensation was a little distant. Once when she was twelve, she had broken her leg skiing. The drugs they gave her in the hospital when they set her leg had made her all light and floaty. She felt a lot like that right now, as if she'd had an out-of-body experience.

She remembered, though, the pain that had followed when the drugs wore off. And she hoped she hadn't let herself in for the same sort of pain tonight.

Chapter Thirty-Four:
The Harvest Ball

"And now, as dinner comes to a close, we are asked to adjourn into the Winter Garden for champagne and sweets while the ballroom is reset for dancing. So, on behalf of His Majesty King Filip, Her Majesty Queen Elspeth, His Royal Highness Crown Prince Nikolas, and myself, welcome to the Harvest Ball of Dubrovia!"

Emily was so proud of her! Rose had started her speech among whispers in the audience, but she finished it to rousing applause. This was the girl's first major public appearance since her accident. The muttered asides started when she rolled her wheelchair up to the center of the dais, and intensified when she stood and took two unsteady steps to the microphone. But they calmed and quieted as she started to speak. And if she was hanging on to the podium for dear life by the end, well, all the more reason to be proud of her.

As the other diners at her table stood, Emily excused herself and wound her way through the crowd toward the head table. She wanted to catch Rose and Jacquie before they went up to Rose's suite for the short break. And if she kept moving, she could avoid—

No such luck. "You skipped out on me this morning." Nik's low tones tickled her ear, warming her in places best left ignored in public.

Emily kept moving. She spared him the fleetest glance before returning her gaze to the front of the room. "Could we talk about this another time?" *Like never. Or at least not tonight.*

He grasped her elbow, slowing her down but not stopping her. "Emily, why don't we step—"

They both jumped at the voice behind them. "Your Highness! I hear the grape harvest was particularly fine this year! We should talk!" boomed a stout little man with the black, yellow, and red Belgian flag pinned to his lapel.

Emily eased her arm from his hold. "We can speak later, Your Highness. You have social obligations this evening," she reminded him as she backed away.

His frustration evident in his stiff and formal manner, Nik nodded. "Very well. Save me a dance," he said, turning to shake the hand of the man who had interrupted them. "Good to see you again, sir. Yes, we're pleased..."

She lost his voice in the buzz of conversation as she caught up to Rose and Jacquie. "Oh, Princess, you were great! I'm so proud of you!"

Rose gave a shaky smile. "I barely held on, though. I need to go upstairs so Jacquie can readjust my back and braces a bit so I can make it through the dance."

"Is there anything I can do?" Emily asked, opening the door into the hall.

"Yes, you can come up with us and explain why Uncle Nik didn't take his eyes off you during dinner!" Rose laughed as Emily swung around. "Made you look. Why don't you come up with us for a couple of minutes?" She waggled her eyebrows suggestively. "Inquiring minds want to know!"

Emily followed them down the corridor to the elevator to the family suites. "There's not much to tell."

"So he left before you got back after you dropped me off?" Jacquie reached over the wheelchair handles and pushed the call button. "He didn't look like he was going to give up and go away."

Emily shook her head slightly at Jacquie and pointedly eyed the back of Rose's head. Jacquie's eyes widened and her mouth opened in a silent O.

"Got back where? Where were you with Uncle Nik last night? I thought you went dancing down in Cerina?" The questions shot out in a rapid fire as Rose backed out of the elevator.

"We did." Jacquie swung the wheelchair around with the ease of long practice and headed them down the hallway. "Prince Nikolas was in the main hall up here when we got back." She shrugged as they stopped and Rose reached forward to open the door to her suite. "I guess he wanted to make sure you got back all right."

Tell me later! she mouthed at Emily.

The three of them worked Rose out of her dress and the braces on her back. Rose lay down on her bed and groaned in relief as Jacquie massaged her stiff muscles, loosening cramps caused by hours of unaccustomed standing and moving. "You're going to hurt tomorrow. Do you want to nap for a while? You don't have to go back down right away."

"Not a nap; I'll never want to put the brace back on if I go to sleep. I might stretch out for a little bit, though. Give me ten minutes?"

Jacquie turned to Emily the second they were back in Rose's sitting room. "Okay, spill."

* * *

"…so that's it," Emily finished.

Jacquie stared at her. "You left? Just… left? Didn't wake him up, didn't invite him to stay for another round, didn't tell him it was time to go? You just *left*?"

Emily winced as the other woman laughed. "He was sleeping, and I didn't want to wake him, so…"

"You mean you didn't want to face him," Jacquie corrected, sorting and smoothing the straps on Rose's brace.

"What should I have said? 'Gee, Prince, thanks for spending the night. Now could you leave so I can go down for a swim?'"

"You had a hot guy in your bed! Who says you had to *say* anything?" said Jacquie, her voice rising.

"Shhh!" Emily shushed her. "I don't want Rose to know that I slept with her cousin."

"No, probably not a picture she needs in her head," Jacquie agreed. "I, on the other hand, am enjoying the mental picture of Prince Nikolas in bed, thank you very much! You don't mind if I live vicariously through you, do you?"

She closed her eyes and gave a little hum of appreciation. "Okay, I'm done now." Jacquie fanned herself, ducking and laughing when Emily swatted her arm. "Seriously, though, Emily, you need to talk to him. You have to work with him for at least a couple more months. It could get sticky."

"I know. I'm a coward. This wasn't supposed to happen! I never get involved with a client. I don't DO things like this."

"You've never had a fling?"

"Not with a client! Before this I always worked with my dad. Which isn't conducive to… to… whatever this is." She glared at Jacquie, who was snickering. "It's not a fling. It's more of a one-night stand. And I don't do those either."

"Oh, honey, you may not do them, but you just did. And you're stuck here for weeks yet. So you had better figure out what you're going to say to him when we're back downstairs. He didn't look like he was going to let you escape without a little chat first." She cocked her ear, listening to the sounds coming from the next room. "And you better figure it out pretty quick, because Rose is moving around—which means we're heading back down in a couple of minutes."

"Oh, God."

* * *

Nik took one last turn around the dance floor with his aunt, his eyes scouring the edges of the room. Where was she? Emily had disappeared with Rose almost an hour ago. Rose was back, so where was Emily?

Queen Elspeth tapped him on the shoulder as the music ended. "Nikolas, it is not like you to be so distracted. You usually love to dance, even with an old lady like me."

"You're not old, Aunt Elspeth," he replied absently. He made an effort to bring his attention back to her, and smiled ruefully. "I'm sorry. I was trying to spot—"

"Dr. Charette, yes, I know. She's over near the garden doors talking to Karel Janko and his wife." The queen looped her arm through his, turning him to face that side of the room. "She looks lovely tonight, doesn't she? Not at all like some stuffy academic."

"Stuffy academic? Emily's not—"

"No, she isn't. I just wondered if you realized that."

He scrambled to say something nonincriminating. While he didn't regret a minute of last night, he had yet to figure out why it had turned out the way it did. She left him sleeping in her bed. He hadn't enjoyed waking alone.

"We've both been working in my office at the same time over the last month—well, except for this past week. I've had the chance to get to know her a little better."

"Mmmm." Queen Elspeth made a sound—of agreement or disagreement, he wasn't sure. "So she is merely a working colleague? Funny, you don't stare at the other women you work with quite like that," she commented.

"Aunt—"

"A word of advice, Niko? She may not be a stuffy academic. But our Dr. Charette is a sensitive young woman, with a tender heart. Do not break it."

"Aunt!"

"Oh, come now, Nik. Your history is no secret. She is not some piece of fluff like most of your past... partners have been."

He snorted out a laugh. "I don't think I would call Helena DiSalvo a piece of fluff."

"Perhaps not. That one is all hard edges and sharp angles, both in body and in spirit. But the relationship? That was fluff."

"You do know I ended it, do you not?" he asked cautiously. "I haven't heard from her father since. So what the implications might be for the wine contracts, I have no idea."

"Pah." The queen gave his arm a little shake, then released him. "There will be other contracts if he chooses to withdraw now. His business agreement with you should not be predicated on a crown for his daughter. If that was his target, he must aim elsewhere."

"So... what are you saying, Aunt Elspeth? And is this my aunt speaking, or my queen?" Nik took two glasses of wine from a server and handed one to her.

"In this, I am both," she said. "As your aunt, I want what is best for you. As your queen, I want what is best for Dubrovia. I do not think those are mutually exclusive goals. And I think," she continued, "that you have been too narrow in your search for a potential partner. You need not limit yourself to the circles in which that one travels." With her chin she indicated Helena DiSalvo, currently dancing with her father.

So, was his aunt suggesting that Emily might be a candidate for his princess? *Far too soon to think about anything like that,* he admonished himself as he kissed his aunt's cheek in farewell and made his way around the dance floor. *First I must find out why she left her own bed in such a hurry.*

* * *

Emily watched Nik work the room. He was a master: a handshake and a clap to the shoulder for the men, a kiss on the hand or the cheek for the women (interesting how it was the older women who got the kiss on the cheek), a turn around the dance floor for a select few. She had her fair share of dance partners herself: the councillors, occasionally their sons.

She placed her empty glass on a side table and took a glass of sparkling water from the server passing by. Tonight's ball, while more formal than she was used to, wasn't all that far off from the receptions and dinners she attended as a professor at her university, or with her parents, and then her father alone, for the various projects they had worked on. She hated them—hated the small talk, hated the undercurrents she could sense but not understand, hated the dressing up.

Her feet were killing her. She sneaked a glance at the clock behind the dais set up for the king and queen to sit on between dances. It was almost one thirty; another half hour or so and she could make a good case for ducking out. Rose had made it to midnight before she made her exit, Jacquie in tow. Emily wished she had left with them.

She wandered around the edge of the dancers, watching the rulers of Dubrovia take a turn around the floor with each other. They made a beautiful couple, in both their marriage and their reign. Very different people but very much in sync.

Emily sighed. And there was Nik, dancing with Helena. Another beautiful couple, moving smoothly to the music. His back was to her, but she could see Helena's face, a small frown playing over the woman's features. She was listening to something he was saying, visibly unhappy. Sure enough, as the dance ended, they parted and walked off the parquet floor. Not touching but still together.

Emily turned away to hide the sudden heat in her cheeks and to try to lessen the pang in her midsection. It didn't matter that a number of staff had managed to mention, oh so casually, that they were surprised to find the DiSalvo family attending this year, since Prince Nikolas was no longer dating Miss DiSalvo (and that was a good thing even if it might put a crimp in the wine distribution contracts). Even Nik had been emphatic last night that no, he and Helena were no longer a couple, that there were no personal strings tying them together. It still wasn't pleasant to watch them dance.

Last night had been amazing. Her body wanted a repeat as soon as possible. Her head told her to be cautious, that if anyone found out, her contract and perhaps her professional status would be at risk. (Was there a penalty for sleeping with your contract holder? she wondered.)

And her heart? Her heart told her that the woman he led off the dance floor was a much more suitable partner. That Emily didn't belong here. And that even if she took up with him—had an affair, a fling, whatever you wanted to call it—and was with him from now until her contract ended in a few months, eventually they would part company. Because eventually everyone left, didn't they?

Her mother, who died two years ago. Her father, whose mind slipped farther away every day. Without them to anchor her, she felt adrift, as if she didn't quite belong anywhere.

And that was the crux of it. She didn't belong here either. Oh, she knew her place in the library, but outside it, in what Nik had referred to as "the real world"? No, there she didn't quite fit, hadn't quite found her place.

That was nothing new. So she didn't belong in Dubrovia, not long term. That didn't mean she couldn't enjoy the time she had left here.

And if that meant spending some quality time with the crown prince, why not? He was handsome enough for a fairy-tale romance. And kinder and bigger hearted than she had started out believing.

She just had to remember that he wasn't *her* fairy tale.

Chapter Thirty-Five:
Discoveries

The late-afternoon sun poured through the tall windows at a sharp angle, tucking deep shadows into corners and behind furniture. Dust motes wafting up from the books and leather portfolios danced in the slanting beams. Emily carefully untied the ribbon surrounding this latest bundle of letters and eased it away from the fragile paper.

"This is a signed work by Johannes Hevelius, did you know? I did not expect to find such a thing in this backwater. The University of Leiden will be very interested in acquiring this," declared her companion.

She glanced at the older man happily puttering away at his own table several feet away. Excitement warred with greed on his face.

"Professor DeWitte, I don't think the Dubrovian government is going to be selling off any of these findings," Emily warned. She needed to keep her eye on him. The competition to find long-lost archival materials was fierce, even cutthroat. While she didn't think he'd walk off with something, or claim he had been the one to find the book, she would make sure someone in the local government or the university down in Cerina had a full inventory sooner rather than later.

Nik was right to keep this stuff locked up and out of the main library. And I should make sure Professor DeWitte's access to the observatory room is limited to when one of us can be in here with him. One more thing to add to her list of things to do. She might never work her way through these family letters and journals at this rate.

She sent a quick text to Pétur: **Come babysit the professor so I can take a quick break? I need to find out who should be the local keeper of the inventory of all this found material. Oh, and want to start the inventory?**

As the professor's comments quieted back down to a happy mutter, her ears tuned him out and her eyes focused again on the stack of letters. The top one was dated April 15, 1857, and was addressed to a state minister of Dubrovia. Emily's Italian was rusty, and this was a dialect she hadn't seen before. Pulling over her laptop, she began to puzzle her way through the stilted prose.

She managed to work her way through almost a page of formal introductions and salutations before her phone buzzed. Good, that would be Pétur. He could sit and listen to the mumbling for a while; she needed a break.

The clatter of shoes on the marble steps coming up to the observatory room were almost drowned out by the professor's sharp exclamation. "This is extraordinary! Dr. Charette! You have been through much of the castle by now, I imagine, and the surrounding countryside. Have you uncovered any evidence of a telescope here?"

"A telescope?" Emily eased the letters into a folder and sealed it before pushing away from her table. "What sort of telescope? From Hevelius's time? Mid- to late 1600s, right?"

"Yes, indeed. Look here," he said, pointing to the work in front of him. "Hevelius is talking about an out-of-the-way installation of one of his famous long scopes. There couldn't be anywhere much more out of the way than Dubrovia, could there?"

"Oh, I don't know," she replied absently, trying to read over his shoulder. "I could think of a few. What makes you think one might be here, though? I haven't seen any evidence—"

"Of course not. You weren't looking in the right places! You spend your days in the library, where it is clearly not," he huffed. He turned to face her, planting his hand in its white glove on the page under discussion. "But think, girl! This room is the observatory room! What else might the former residents and their honored guests be observing but the stars? The view is not so grand they spent their time gazing down the valley toward the town. We do not know how much of a town there was then!"

"I don't, but I'm sure someone here does. The University of Cerina has a marvelous local history section. They gave me a tour when I first arrived. Theirs is at least as extensive as anything up here at the castle. If a big telescope was installed somewhere in the town or the castle, I am sure they would have bragged about it."

"Not if it was disassembled long ago! Those long scopes were never meant to be permanent installations. They were so susceptible to weather, the astronomers of the time would take them apart to keep the lenses and the metalworks clean and maintained," he explained.

"No telescopes that I've seen. Not any lens mounts or… what else should I have looked for?"

"Metalworks where none are expected. Some sort of building or installation kept locked up to keep the commoners out. A tradition of sky watching among… I don't know, the men who work in the vineyards or herd the sheep and goats up in the hills." He glared at her. "Think outside the box; isn't that what you young people are always saying? The possibilities are endless!"

"But it's just a possibility, right? There's nothing in that book that says for sure Dubrovia had a long scope?" Emily asked.

"Well… no. Not directly. But I know of significant findings made on far less direct evidence than this! Why, likely half of all archaeological discoveries started out as a hunch, a guess." He turned back to his table. "Hmph. Some people are going to be very interested in this possibility. I would have thought the daughter of the famous Dr. Edward Charette would also be interested."

The daughter of the famous Dr. Edward Charette.

That's what she was, how they saw her. All the projects, all the accolades, all the *work*—and that's how she'd be remembered.

The daughter of the famous Dr. Edward Charette.

Was it too much to ask to be noticed and appreciated for herself? For what she brought to a project all on her own?

* * *

Nik took the stairs two at a time, Rose's plea reverberating in his mind: "Please, won't you talk to her, Uncle Nik? She'll listen to you!"

He frowned as he rounded the last corner and headed to the open door of the observatory room. Not for the first time, he wondered at the name. It didn't offer a particularly good view of the countryside; in fact, mostly what you saw from its windows was the forested hillside between the castle and the town.

Frown deepening to a scowl, he came to a stop outside the doorway. *This is ridiculous. I'm sneaking around my own home and skulking in doorways and eavesdropping.* But he paused to listen without being seen.

The only sound was the old professor mumbling to himself. Wasn't Emily working over here this afternoon too? Oh, yes, there she was. He strained his ears but couldn't make out her response.

Footsteps in the marble hallway behind him drowned out the buzz of renewed conversation within. Nik turned to see Emily's assistant trotting up the stairs. "Good afternoon, Pétur," he said, raising his hand to block the younger man's passage.

"Your Highness," Pétur acknowledged, coming to a halt. "The doc still inside?"

Nik observed Pétur, too, stopped short of the open doorway. They couldn't quite catch the two scholars conversing, but they couldn't be seen. So Pétur also wanted to listen in unobtrusively? What was going on? Time to ask some pointed questions.

"Yes, she and Professor DeWitte are working up here this afternoon. I assume you knew."

"Doc Charette texted me and asked me to come up and relieve her for a bit. Don't want to leave the professor alone with the goods. Not that we don't trust him, but…"

"But you don't trust him. Why not? He seems harmless enough."

Pétur snorted out a laugh. "Oh, sure, hail and well met, that's Professor DeWitte. Great guy if you want to buy him a round in the pub and listen to him talk about the good old days. Of course, his good old days ended around 1700." He rolled his eyes. "But trust him? With new findings we haven't had time to inventory yet? Not likely.

"You'd be amazed at how nasty the academic world is, Your Highness," he continued, edging around Nik to peer into the chamber. "Doc Charette should get credit for anything important we uncover in the collection that was in the hidden room."

"And you think this Professor DeWitte might somehow prevent that? Why is he here, then, if he will interfere with the work she's doing?" Nik turned and looked through the doorway himself. He still couldn't see the two scholars.

"We don't know for sure he'd do anything shady. And he's one of the best in the world in his particular area. But it's smart not to put temptation in his way, right? So we're careful to never leave him alone with the stuff." Pétur shrugged. "Better safe than sorry. I'm going to be doing the photographic inventory this week, and afterward she might ease off a little. Or not. I guess it depends on what they find."

"You mean, anything of real value?"

"It's all got some value, just because of its age, right? And your family wouldn't have tucked it all away in that hidden room if there was nothing special about it, even the stuff the professor isn't interested in because it's not about science."

"What else is there, if not the scientific treatises that excite him?"

"We don't know specifically yet. But the doc has got bundles of what look like old correspondence. Tons of it, actually, in layers sorted by date. By century, even. Since everybody did everything by mail, who knows what she'll find? Probably things like contracts and deeds and marriage negotiations. All personal and important to your family, but more important because it shows us a lot of Dubrovia's history."

"And identifying these letters, or rather identifying their historical and cultural significance—this is not the sort of thing her father was famous for? So Emily is supposed to be following in his footsteps and be more interested in the things our visiting professor deems important?"

Pétur shrugged. "That's right, I guess. He was all about the big discoveries," he said. "Did you ever get to meet him?"

"Not on this project, no. But I knew him years ago, when Emily attended the same university as my cousin Stefan. Did you know him well?"

"He was one of the reasons I wanted to do my graduate degree at U of A. I heard him speak when he did a guest lecture when I was an undergrad. We should go in, so Doc can take her break," Pétur said as the two of them started through the doorway.

"I'll tell you something, though," he added under his breath. He put his hand in front of Nik to stop him before they reached the two scholars.

"And what is that?" Nik asked.

"Her father? He was good, really good. But she's better."

Chapter Thirty-Six:
Distance

Nik stroked his hand down Emily's hair as she lay next to him on his bed. Less than curly, more than wavy, her hair rippled over the pillow and under his fingers. He smoothed the tangled strands, pushing the heavy mass over her shoulder to drape over her back. Snuggling after sex was new. Hell, having a woman in his bed was new. He usually went to them; it made escaping afterward easier.

But he liked having Emily in his bed. He liked holding her after they'd made love, and talking about anything and everything: the progress she'd made in deciphering whatever piece she was working on, the processing of the grapes from the harvest, whether the skiing was better in the Rockies or the Alps. It didn't matter what. It was the continuing connection that counted.

That was new for Nik. He'd never thought of himself as a continuing connection sort of man. No, he had been all about the immediate connection, the short-term gratification of sex. The sex was fabulous, but there was more to having Emily in his bed than just sex.

And he had to convince her to linger, every time. That was new for him too. Usually he ran, and the women chased.

His fingers traced lazy circles on her lower back. "So, does that happen a lot? Getting an offer for your next contract while you're still on the first one?"

Emily shrugged, which did interesting things to her anatomy where it was snugged up against his. She was tucked under his arm, her head resting on his shoulder. One leg was thrown over his, one arm draped across his chest, and her front pressed to his side. "Oh, sure. Never quite so blatantly. And most often it was whoever Dad worked for who offered him a placement after his current contract ended."

"No one ever offered you one? Wouldn't they be more interested in getting someone younger who would be employable for some time? I would have thought a university would welcome the opportunity to have a world-class archivist on staff."

She shrugged again, this time rolling away to lie flat on her back. "I'm not what they need. Most of the time, our typical clients need a historian, not an archivist. Someone like Professor DeWitte but with less emphasis on science and more on history and culture. That's what my father is famous for, but it's not what I do."

His side felt cold where she had moved away. Empty, as empty as her voice had sounded. He remembered how she had reacted—or rather, not reacted—when DeWitte had compared her to her father.

Nik switched to his side so he could see her face. He recognized her blank expression; he showed a similar mask himself whenever someone compared him to his cousin.

"You're not looking for a long-term placement? Only these short-term contracts?"

Emily closed her eyes, hiding her expression. "Not… Europe is too far away. Edmonton is home as long as my dad is there. And there aren't many positions for high-end archivists in Canada at the moment." She stirred as if to rise. "Look, Nik, I—"

"Not so fast." He rolled on top of her, pinning her to the bed, grinning down at her. "It's early yet."

Emily gave one startled squeak at his sudden move, then proceeded to try and wrestle him for control, laughing and giggling as they rolled over the bed.

Who knew sex could be so much fun? Nik couldn't remember the last time he had laughed in bed. She managed to do some serious tickling before he caught both of her wrists in one hand and yanked them over her head.

Their breathless laughter caught and held. Easy smiles morphed into smoldering looks. Nik kept his eyes on hers as he lowered his head, turning at the last second to graze his teeth along the side of her jaw.

She arched against him with a small moan. "Oh, God, don't stop."

"Not anytime soon," he murmured, working his way down her body. "This is going to take a while."

Her skin was warm and getting warmer. Nik spent some time at her breasts, nipping and teasing her nipples, alternating from one side to the other. When both were tight and hard and hot to the touch, he gave each one a last lick and blew a cool stream of air across her chest.

He gazed up at her from halfway down the bed. Emily's eyes were blurred and unfocused, her breathing fast and unsteady. Again, he held her eyes as he trailed his mouth down her belly.

Her flesh quivered. She sucked in one gasping breath when he neared her core. When his tongue circled the sensitive spot, her head snapped back and her hips snapped up. Nik braced his hands on her thighs, using lips and tongue and teeth and fingers to bring her closer to climax.

"Too much! I can't—" Her eyes were clenched tight, her head thrashing back and forth.

"Yes, you can. We can," he said. He slid up her body and into her in one motion, then stilled. "Open your eyes, Em. Look at me while I take you all the way over."

It took everything he had to stop moving, to pause before bringing them both to climax. He waited till her eyes opened again, frantic with need. He started with small thrusts, gradually going faster and harder and deeper until they were both teetering on the brink.

He didn't know what she saw in his eyes. He didn't know what he saw in hers. Nik just knew he had never felt this before, had never seen such an expression on a lover's face.

Two more hard thrusts, and Emily shattered beneath him. He followed her over the edge and into oblivion.

Hours later, she stirred and sighed. "I should go." She slid out from under the sheet without making eye contact and padded over to the chair to pull on her clothes.

"Stay." He hadn't meant to speak. And he wasn't surprised when she froze, then continued dressing.

"I can't. I need to be out of here before there's a chance I'll run into someone in the halls."

"The staff know you're here, Emily. They always know where everyone is," he reminded her, swinging his feet to the floor and reaching for the flannel sleeping pants draped over the nightstand.

Head down, pulling on her shoes, Emily replied, "It's not the staff I'm worried about. I thought more in terms of Professor DeWitte."

"I doubt the good professor is wandering the halls this time of night." Nik stood, tugging up and tying his pants. "And would it be so bad if you ran into him on your way back to your suite?" Why was she so adamant to keep their nights together secret? Shame? Embarrassment?

"It would be a disaster," she stated flatly, standing and fastening the buttons on her shirtsleeves. "I have enough trouble getting men like DeWitte to take me seriously. If he knew I'd slept with you? He'd report my unprofessional behavior to my dean in a heartbeat. I'd be lucky to work in rural Alberta, shelving books in some elementary school library."

"Oh, come now. Surely you exaggerate." Nik followed her out of his bedroom and through the sitting room beyond. "Why should he care? Why should anyone care? We are consenting adults. We have done nothing improper."

"It's the appearance of impropriety I have to worry about." Emily rested her hand on the door to the hall for a second, then turned and faced him. "I'm contracted to Dubrovia for this project. That makes you my boss, here at least. We both know you were initially against the project. But if DeWitte has any idea that we're personally involved, there are all sorts of questions he could raise. Did I sleep with you to sweeten the deal? Did you intimidate me into sleeping with you so you wouldn't oppose the project?

"Remember, in the winery? The first time you kissed me? I told you right away I had to worry about my professional reputation, and I thought this was a bad idea."

Eyes closed, she dropped her head back against the door with a small thunk. "I still think it wasn't a good idea to start. With him here in the castle, it *really* isn't a good idea to continue."

"So, you're saying... what? That you regret this? That we should stop?" Nik stalked closer till they were toe to toe. He wasn't sure if he was hurt or annoyed, or both. Baffled, mostly. She was walking away. Women never walked away.

Emily opened her eyes, glancing up at him and then away as she slid out from between him and the door. "I haven't regretted... whatever this is. At least up till now. But I think it's time we stopped, don't you? I've got maybe two months left, including a couple of rotations back to Edmonton, and then I'm gone. That gives you time to decide what the next steps for the library will be. But it won't be me managing it. You'll need a project manager, but not necessarily an archivist. And I need to get back home."

He watched in silence as she cracked open the door and slipped out, closing it softly behind her.

Home. It was all about home for Emily. Oh, she might talk about growing her international reputation, taking on projects. But at the end of the day, she was a homebody at heart. And Dubrovia wasn't home.

Chapter Thirty-Seven:
The telescope

Emily shivered as she turned away from the window and let the heavy damask draperies fall back into place. The wind had picked up, and the sky was that peculiar pewter color she associated with an imminent snowfall. Rose had assured her this morning that the beginning of November was too early for a heavy dump: they might get flurries, but no substantial accumulation was predicted. Emily wasn't so sure.

This room, with its huge north-facing windows currently rattling in the wind, was always chilly. The cheery fire snapping in the hearth couldn't counteract the tendrils of cold air that snuck in under the curtains and meandered around her ankles. She tugged down the sleeves of her sweater. "Now that DeWitte is gone and we don't need the extra security, we should move all this stuff someplace warmer, Pétur."

"Like the Bahamas, maybe?" her assistant countered. "Even Edmonton is warmer than Dubrovia this week." He continued to page through the huge book on the table closest to the fireplace. She had to laugh. He had grumbled all morning about the chill in the room until he had cajoled some of the staff to help him maneuver the heavy piece of furniture—and the rug underneath—to the warmer side of the room. He stood with his back to the blazing fire, and every once in a while he would turn from side to side, much like the cat sleeping in front of the hearth.

He was still grumbling (Pétur, not the cat), but not about the cold. "I still don't know why Professor DeWitte was so convinced there must be one of those long telescopes here someplace. We never found any evidence of one. Now, granted," he said with a sly look in her direction, "unlike you, I haven't had the privilege of seeing some of the more private areas of the castle. And I'm sure that a Renaissance telescope was the last thing on your mind when you were in the crown prince's suite—a different sort of instrument, perhaps?" He laughed at her pained expression, then patted the book he was examining. "But your overbearing Dutch friend sure wanted to take this with him, didn't he?"

"Jeez, Pétur. Could you be a little more crude?" She shook her head. "And DeWitte's not my Dutch friend. He's not my friend at all," Emily said emphatically.

She dismissed the pushy professor from her mind as she gazed around the room, mentally calculating how much more time they'd need to finish up cataloging the materials they had removed from the secret room hidden in the den. There were stacks and mounds and single books everywhere. The contents of that little room, not much more than a closet, seemed to expand tenfold once everything was moved out into the light of day and spread out over every flat surface up here. "How much longer, do you think? We've done all we can in the den, except for all of this. And we closed out the gallery last month. How close are we to finishing up in the main library?"

"Why, you in a hurry to leave? I thought you and the prince—"

"Whatever you were thinking, stop right there. There is no 'me and the prince.' Not the way you mean, at least. Not long term. You and I are going back to Edmonton at the end of this phase. If Dubrovia chooses to continue on with the next phase, they should designate someone local to head it up. So when we're done, we're done."

"You seem pretty sure about that." Pétur closed the book and angled himself to face her, leaning on the edge of his table. "You can tell me to mind my own business…"

"Mind your own business, Pétur."

"…but I know you, Em. How long have I worked for you now, three years? I've never seen you become as attached to a project or a client as this one. It'd be only natural if you wanted to stick around to see what might happen next."

Emily turned away and started loading books onto the closest library cart. "What will happen next is we're going to load this stuff up and return it to the library. We can use the upper reading room again since it's just us and no outsiders now."

"You're avoiding the subject." He started loading up his own cart.

"No, I'm changing the subject," Emily retorted, stacking books. "There's nothing to talk about. Yes, we had a fling or an affair, a thing. But it was never going to last forever. I knew that going in and so did he."

"So that's it? You just walk away?" Pétur pushed his now-full cart to the door. "Never figured you for a coward, Em."

"It's not being a coward! It's being sensible and responsible. Consider my responsibilities back in Edmonton: classes to teach, other grad students besides you, and my dad. I need to be home." Emily wheeled her own full cart down the hall after him.

"Home is where the heart is," Pétur replied loftily.

"Oh, you did *not* just say that!"

"Sure I did. And what about Rose?" They took the elevator down a floor.

"What do you mean, what about Rose?"

"Yes, what about Rose?" came a voice from beyond the partly opened elevator doors.

"Uh oh." Pétur apologized, "Sorry, Em, didn't mean to put you on the spot."

"No, that's okay. Rose, we were talking about the end of this phase of the project when Pétur and I return to Edmonton. I think he's wondering how you feel about that, right, Pétur?"

"You don't have to—"

"That's quite all right, I don't mind talking about it. I know she has to go. And I'm hoping she'll be my ticket out," Rose informed him.

"What do you mean, your ticket out?"

"You know that she stayed with my parents to attend university a long time ago, when I was little, right? Well, I want to go away to school too. But I can't manage on my own, not like this. So Emily said she'd help me find a way to go, so I can live away and study. Find me a family to stay with, if I can't stay with her," Rose explained.

She turned to Emily. "Right? It won't be till after I graduate high school. And I want more surgery on my back first. Which means I have to talk my grandparents around, or wait till I'm of age. But I'll still probably need some help, and it would be great to stay with someone you know."

"That's the deal," Emily confirmed. "My father pulled strings and called in favors fifteen years ago, and I ended up living with Rose and her parents as an undergrad. I'll do the same for Rose when she's ready."

"See? So no cause to worry on my account, Pétur."

"Guess not," he acknowledged. "So it's only the crown prince who—"

"Enough, Pétur!" Emily rolled her eyes. "Seriously, we need to get you back home and focused on your own love life and not on mine!"

"Love life?" Rose asked. "What love life?"

"I'm not discussing this." Emily nudged Pétur with her library cart. "Move again, Pétur, and let's get these into the reading room so we can fetch the rest."

"Actually, Emily, if you have a minute? I was coming to find you about something else, if you have some time." Rose bit her lip. "I wanted to ask you something."

"Sure, Rose, anytime. Did you want to come along with us while we move this stuff?"

"I'd rather have a private chat, if you don't mind."

"Of course. In your suite?" At the girl's nod, Emily pushed her cart to the side of the hall, out of the way. "Pétur, why don't you round up some staff and finish up? I'll come find you later."

She followed Rose through to her sitting room and shut the door. "What's up?"

The younger woman wheeled her chair over to her desk and fiddled with some things.

"Is something wrong, Rose?"

"Well, not wrong exactly. But, well, I wanted to hear more about the telescope that the professor was looking for when he was here."

Emily frowned. "Did he bother you? He's not known for his tact. He's like a bulldog with a bone in his teeth when he's pursuing something."

"No, not me. I don't think he noticed me. Most people don't." She shrugged. "But he asked the staff a lot of questions about whether anyone knew anything about a telescope. And it made me think about this one."

Rose lifted the case of her favorite telescope from her desk. "Remember it? My dad always told me it was an antique, but I don't know how old."

"We never did find any markings on it, did we?"

"No. And I didn't want to tell the professor about it even if it was the one he was looking for. I think he would go to my grandparents to make me give it up. He was all about how important things are to history, but I don't think he'd care how important it is to me."

"Oh, Rose! You never have to give it up. Even if that was the one he was looking for, we could get an expert in to authenticate it right here. It's your telescope. Besides," Emily said, shaking her head, "he was looking for a long scope, one ten meters long or more."

"I know. I figured that out. But…"

"But what?"

"Well, there's more to this one than we thought. Remember when it fell off the table in the library?"

Emily remembered and cringed. "Oh, God. I remember. That was the first day I met up with Nik again. And with Helena DiSalvo. And they found me crawling around on the floor under a table trying to pick up the mess I'd made. I was so afraid I'd damaged something!"

"You did, sort of. But not in a bad way!" Rose insisted, reaching her hand out to grab her arm as Emily sucked in a shocked breath. "No, no, Em, don't panic! The telescope was fine, remember? We opened up the case and looked at all the bits and pieces and nothing was broken."

"So, then, what happened?" Emily asked cautiously.

"Here, look." Rose spun back to the desk and opened the case, removing the contents and laying them out on a towel she had spread out. When the case was emptied, she held it up for Emily to see. "The telescope wasn't damaged. But here, inside the case. See this bit?"

The case had been purpose-built for the telescope. There were velvet-covered supports and clamps along the bottom. Emily watched in amazement as Rose wiggled the support for the main barrel, which came loose in her hands.

Rose lifted it up and placed it to the side. "Now watch." She pressed gently on one corner of the case bottom and the opposite corner tipped up. Alternating corners, she wiggled the base back and forth until one edge was up high enough to grab.

Emily couldn't believe her eyes. The whole bottom layer lifted to show a small cavity, about the depth of a paperback book. And in the cavity was a bundle of old papers, folded and tied with a faded green ribbon.

"Rose! What is that? What did you find?"

"I think I found a map to that big telescope."

Chapter Thirty-Eight:
To the tower

Rose's words echoed in Emily's head. "What do you mean, a map to the telescope? You found proof of a long scope here somewhere? In these papers? Wait, why didn't you tell Professor DeWitte when he asked if anyone knew anything?"

"He never asked me."

"What do you mean, he never asked you? I thought he spoke to everybody! I know he talked to the staff. He never interviewed you? And you didn't tell him, once you found this?"

Rose fiddled with the frayed ribbon. She took a deep breath and started to speak, fast enough to prevent interruptions. "He never noticed me. Most adults don't. They don't see kids, even older kids, or they think we don't pay attention and don't have anything to contribute. And since I'm in a wheelchair, it's as if he thought I was mentally disabled as well as physically disabled. When I did run into him, he talked to me like I was five. So no, he never asked me about a telescope. And I didn't find this till after he left." She nudged the lump of papers, then continued, rolling right over Emily's attempt to say anything.

"I noticed that first day when I took the pieces out that the bottom part of the case was crooked. We were so busy looking at the telescope itself, the case didn't seem important. But last week when I opened the case to use the telescope, one end of the bottom piece was sticking up even more, so I went to try to push it back in, and then the other end popped up, and no matter how much I tried to wiggle the whole base back into place, it just got looser and looser and then it popped up and almost all the way out of the case on one side."

She was on a roll now. "So I got a pencil under it and pulled it up so I could get it back in straight. But when I pulled it up... I found these papers. And I got curious because I know how excited everyone got when you found that secret room with all the journals and books in it, and I thought it was cool that I'd found something secret too. So I started reading them, sort of. A lot are in Latin, so I can't read them, but some are in Czech. The letters, at least, not the other papers and drawings. And they were personal, the letters, family stuff. I figured the papers were too. Not public like books. So I wanted to show you first, not Professor DeWitte."

Rose took another deep breath. "And I wouldn't have told him anyway. I didn't trust him. Did you know he tried to force Pétur to sign a paper that said he—Professor DeWitte, not Pétur, and not you—should be credited for finding that book he was so interested in? Because you are just a librarian and he's the historian, and he's the one who figured out who wrote it and decided it was valuable? All you did was find the place where it had been hidden away for so long. So that last day he was here, he was going on and on to Pétur about how much more important his findings are than anything you did here, and how people who live in backward places like Dubrovia don't recognize or appreciate what's all around them and how awful it is that we actually *use* the furniture and stuff in the castle instead of putting it all in museums. And I didn't want this telescope in a museum because it's the one my dad and I used together. It's mine now. So I never mentioned it to him. Not the telescope, and not the broken case, and not the papers in the secret compartment."

Her eyes shone brightly at Emily. "I don't have to give it up, do I? Even though I found these papers in the case?"

"No, of course not. Good historians are concerned about removing and preserving items that are not in use, so they aren't lost and forgotten. They don't remove personal items," Emily said absently.

She couldn't believe her ears. Or her eyes. She held her breath as Rose eased the fragile bundle from its resting place. "Careful, Rose."

"I know. The papers are pretty fragile, kind of crispy on the edges."

They both breathed easier when the papers were out and the ribbon untied. Rose unfolded the stack and turned them to face Emily. "Here. Take a look."

Emily flipped through the pages, skimming, catching dates, looking at drawings. She frowned when she came to a sketch of a metal apparatus that extended up over a crenellated wall, and replaced the page back on the stack. "Well, it might have existed at some point, but I've never seen anything like this here in the castle. There are only a couple of places where the roof isn't steep, and none of them have stone walls around a big open space like in this drawing."

"Not here, but I know where! I think," came Rose's eager answer. "See here?" She retrieved the page before the sketch and ran her finger down the crabbed writing. "Where is it, where is it... Here!"

She jabbed her finger at the phrase, then spun the pages around again. "See where it says *pták dům věž*? That means 'bird house tower.'"

"I know, but—"

"The old tower! Didn't you and Uncle Nik go up to the tower on the mountain, that day when you visited the winery?"

"We drove up to the base, when we visited the vineyards and the orchards and the sheep meadows. We never went in. I thought the upper levels weren't safe. And I know I didn't see anything like this extending over the top of the walls." She looked hard at Rose. "Are you telling me you've seen this, this metal framework, at the top? When would you have been inside and up the tower? When would anyone?"

"No, I never saw it myself. And I haven't been in the tower since I was little. My parents and I went up a few times for the spring shearing. The shepherds use part of the tower during lambing and shearing. That's how I know the tower is still in reasonably good shape. There's no heat or hot water, just bare bulbs for lights and a pump for the well."

"But the framework?"

"It might have rusted away by now, for all I know," Rose replied. "Or enough of it rusted so it collapsed and you can't see it from the ground."

Her enthusiasm was contagious, but Emily was still uncertain. "Who can we ask? If they still use the bottom of the tower, does anyone ever try to go up to the roof?"

"I don't know. I don't care! We can go check ourselves! We—"

"Oh, no. Not a chance. I'm not taking you out on the mountain, especially not with snow on the way! And not to a place where you can't recharge your chair."

"Okay, you go! It's easy to get there: past the last vineyard the road only goes to the tower. And it's not going to snow today. Well, not much."

She scooted over to her desk and grabbed some papers. "I copied some of the sketches for you. There should be some bits remaining of the base here in the center, see? Even if the rest has rusted away. And here's a map to the last vineyard gate, with distances and everything."

"Rose, I'm not sure about this…"

"No, no, look! You told me you know about winter driving and winter camping. You can take the Range Rover, the smaller one—it's easier to drive on the twisty roads. And we can ask Marta to pack up supplies so if you do get stuck overnight you'll be okay. Well, Tomas, maybe, not Marta. I don't think Marta knows about camping so much. And," she said, "I got a key for the tower door." She waved it at Emily.

"How on earth did you get that?"

"I asked. No one ever thinks I can do anything anymore, so I can get away with stuff like that." She folded up the original papers and tied them with the ribbon again. "So? What do you think? Will you go look?"

Would she go? Could she? Go up on her own, and take a chance on Rose's guesswork? If she did and found nothing, all she'd lose is a day in the library. *And a warm bed tonight. Don't forget how uncomfortable winter camping is,* her subconscious reminded her.

If the evidence did exist, this could be the find of her career, even more significant than the book by Hevelius that had DeWitte all hot and bothered.

And if she didn't go, she'd forever kick herself. How could she risk letting someone else make the discovery?

She had no alternative. "I'm in. How do we do this?"

Chapter Thirty-Nine:
Anticipating the storm

Emily straightened from her crouch and stretched. She glared at the sky as she wiped her hands on the rag she found in the back of the Range Rover with the tire chains. What happened to the beautiful blue sky of the morning? The weather had been clear, if cold and damp, until she rounded the last curve of the twisty alpine road. The final approach to the old tower took her around to the southeast side of the mountain—and into the teeth of the oncoming storm.

One look at the dark clouds, one fat snowflake hitting her cheek as she parked close to the tower door, convinced her to take the time now to take care of the tire chains. She hated trying to put them on with snow halfway up the hubcaps. She threw the rag into the SUV and grabbed the ice scraper and little folding shovel. Again, better safe than sorry. She didn't know the weather here well enough to predict how much snow might accumulate by morning. But she didn't want to have to dig her way to the car with nothing more than her hands in order to reach the tool she needed to clear the rest of the way.

It took three trips from the car to bring all her stuff inside the tower; ten minutes to get a fire going that was hot enough to catch a couple of good-sized logs; and a few extra minutes to find and flip on the main breaker and confirm that, yes, there was power so, no, she didn't need the small generator Tomas had packed for her. Emily glanced around, making sure she had everything inside she might need for the night. No matter what she found at the top of the tower, she wouldn't risk that road in the gathering dark, storm or not. Emily grabbed her camera bag and tripod and headed up the wooden stairs that wound up against the outer wall.

The door at the landing at the top was a little warped and a lot stuck. Emily bashed into it a couple of times with her shoulder before it burst open. She rubbed her arm as she crossed the single open room with a dozen or so empty bed frames, a few tables and chairs, and some bare light bulbs dangling from the ceiling with pull strings. A few windows graced the walls, covered with steel shutters sealed tightly enough to keep out everything but a heavy layer of dust. This must be where the workers stayed during lambing season, she mused as she crossed over to the next staircase and continued up.

The third floor looked like the second one, with less furniture and more dust. As she passed over to the last staircase (she hoped) the nearest shutter rattled on its hinges. *Great, the wind is picking up.*

She popped open the final door and stepped out into a little protected area. Stepping out of the alcove and into the open space, she swiped a loose bit of hair out of her eyes and shivered in the cold, damp wind.

And stared. From the ground, nothing had been visible at the top of the tower but the crenellated wall. From here, though… from here, she saw the bent and twisted remnants of metal struts that extended up from anchor points all around the circumference of the circle. None were more than about five feet high—none, that is, but the heavier central pole. And that had lost its top fitting, which was sitting down at the base, rusting into a solid lump.

This was it! This was what she'd hoped to find, what she and Rose had seen in the drawings that had stayed hidden in the telescope case for almost four centuries: what was left of a long telescope installation.

Her imagination filled in the missing pieces, repaired the broken ones, and showed her the installation in its prime: the girders stretching up overhead to meet in the middle; the lens holders that slid up and down, manipulated by servants on ladders as the scientists of the day stayed at the base with the eyepiece lens, directing the placement of the lenses and tubes.

It was clear, too, why the tower was called the bird house, although no one recalled birds being kept here. The metal framework would have looked exactly like a metal birdcage with a domed top.

Another gust of wind swirled a pile of leaves and other detritus around and around the central post. Emily looked at the threatening sky. If she hurried, she could capture some photos today and take some measurements before the light was gone. The rest would have to wait till tomorrow—and she hoped the snow would hold off.

Once she'd set up the tripod, she mounted her camera and started to shoot. The light wasn't bright enough for fine details, but she took some shots that gave the feel and the scale of the place.

The circle of uprights was bigger around than she'd expected. Without knowing how tall the central post had been, it was hard to figure out just how long a telescope would have been possible here, but she did a quick estimate of twenty meters or so. Long enough to have rivaled some of the outstanding ones of its time.

The papers Rose had found were dated to the mid-1600s. This was one whopper of a discovery, a career changer. One that would make her father proud. As she moved around the circle, taking photo after photo, her mind raced through her historian contacts. At least this sort of discovery fell out of DeWitte's area of expertise. She knew a lot of other people she could enlist.

Emily managed a solid hour before the cold and wind became too much. There was no real snow yet, but the dust whipping up was hard on her eyes and couldn't be good for the camera either.

By the time she made it inside and down all the stairs, her ground-floor refuge had warmed up nicely. She added another log to her lovely crackling fire and stood in front of it for a few minutes, grateful for its heat.

Her phone buzzed where it sat on her duffel: Rose, the very first person she wanted to tell. It was as much the girl's discovery as hers, and she'd make sure Rose was credited with the find.

"Rose? Rose! You were right! It's here. Well, the remains are. And—"

"Oh, finally, you answered! I didn't tell him, Emily, honest! I thought you would get back before he found out."

"What do you mean, get back? Even if I found nothing here, I'd be staying the night. I don't know that road well enough to risk it in the dark. And who didn't you tell?"

"Uncle Nik. He wasn't supposed to be home till tomorrow, but he drove back from the airport with Anton, and he saw that the Range Rover was gone, and Tomas told him that you'd gone up to the tower, and when he came to find out why, he got kind of mad and then quiet, and—"

"Slow down, Rose. So Tomas told him about the tower, and it made him angry that I came up here? Why? Doesn't he realize how important this place is?"

"I think he's mad because you went by yourself. I told him I wanted to go with you but—"

"You know you couldn't come with me. So he's not happy. I'll deal with that when I return, which should be sometime tomorrow. I want to bring Pétur up here to help me measure, and then—"

"No, no, listen! He's on his way there. He was so mad, he took the other Range Rover and left right away. I've been calling you for half an hour, ever since he left."

Half an hour ago? That meant she had maybe another half hour before he arrived. Maybe less. "Okay, Rose, thanks for letting me know. I guess I'll be having that conversation with him today."

"So you're not mad at me too? I had to tell him why you went to the tower. And I couldn't stop him from following you," Rose said cautiously.

"No, of course not. It's not your fault he overreacted. Look, I want to sort out my photos and give Pétur a call so he can start finding an expert to document this. I'll be back sometime tomorrow."

Emily ended the call and started transferring her photos. The awareness of Nik's imminent arrival sat in the back of her brain, in turns exasperating and annoying and intimidating—and provocative. She hadn't spent any significant time alone with him since she'd walked away from his bed several weeks before. She missed him. Missed his touch, his scent, the feel of him wrapped around her, the heat of him against her, his weight pressing her into the sheets, his mouth moving on her skin.

She didn't miss the constant fear of discovery, or his discounting those fears. He'd never understood what it might mean to her if their relationship were revealed. He had nothing to worry about. She was just one more woman to fall under his spell and into his bed. What was one more notch on the bedpost of a known playboy? Even if said playboy had been living a much quieter life since becoming crown prince.

Her professional credibility was everything. She could ill afford to damage it for the sake of a fling.

But here, no one would see. No palace staff who could unexpectedly open a door. No family members she had to avoid. There was no need to sneak from one bedroom to the other before the break of dawn.

She stopped short and stood perfectly still, counting off weeks and days in her head. Four more weeks until the Christmas Ball. Four more weeks until her project was done and she went home for good. And she'd be gone for one of those weeks. So three, really. Not a lot of time. And then she'd never see him again.

Could she risk it?

She wanted this, wanted one more night. Then she'd walk away, and learn how to live without him.

Chapter Forty:
Not your concern

Gravel sprayed behind the back tires as Nik made the last turn into the open area at the foot of the tower. He'd made the drive from the castle to the crest of the ridge in record time, racing to beat the storm, wanting, no, needing to be sure she was safe.

First things first. Find Emily and make sure everything's all right, and that she isn't in a panic about having to spend the night.

And then he'd shake some sense into her. What was she thinking, to drive up an unfamiliar mountain road, in an unfamiliar vehicle, in unfamiliar weather? What had Tomas been thinking, to not only allow the escapade but to facilitate it: providing and provisioning the Range Rover, giving Emily detailed instructions on how to drive to the tower, how to use the backup generator, what to do if she got really stuck on the mountain or in case of an emergency?

Emergency. Pah. This whole situation was turning into an emergency. His heartbeat started to smooth out once he saw her SUV parked safe and sound, but he supposed it wouldn't return to normal until he saw her in person.

And maybe not then. Lately just her presence caused his heart to beat a little faster, a little harder. Whether he wanted it to or not.

Nik let out a low growl as his hiking boots crunched on the gravel and fallen leaves to the door. It swung open as he reached for the handle.

"Oh, good, you're here! Come in and warm up for a few minutes. There's still time before it's too dark to—"

He interrupted Emily's cheery greeting, taking hold of her upper arm and steering her through the doorway and into the almost round room. "We must talk."

The room was brighter and warmer than he'd expected. Apparently she'd had enough time and enough presence of mind to start a fire before doing... whatever she had been doing in the upper reaches of the tower before he arrived. Too bad it would be nothing but a waste of wood.

"Talk? Sure. We can talk while I collect my stuff. Can I get you some coffee first?"

Emily was nattering away as if nothing were wrong, as if she was out on a pleasure jaunt instead of facing a potential blizzard in a derelict tower on the side of a mountain. Perhaps the situation had affected her more than she wanted him to think. Although she had relaxed with him in recent weeks, she still wasn't usually what you would call chatty. This babbling was not like her.

And it didn't matter. Nothing mattered except getting them down the steep and winding road before the storm hit. "Stop."

Either she didn't hear or chose not to. "Tomas insisted I bring all this stuff up here. I must admit I'm glad for the coff—what?"

"I said stop. We are not going up to the top of the tower. We are going to put out the fire and pack up the bare minimum of what you need to bring back. And then we're going to leave. Right now."

She looked up, her hands full of camera and case, her expression surprised. "What do you mean, leave? I have more work to do! I want—"

Nik strode over to the fireplace and pulled out the biggest logs. Good, they hadn't quite caught yet; they would be safe enough if he dropped them in the damp earth outside. He spoke to her over his shoulder. Gather your things, Emily."

"Hey, wait! We'll need a fire tonight!"

"No, we won't. You will pack up now, and we will leave." He dropped the smoldering logs into the metal log carrier she'd used to bring them in from the woodpile and headed for the door. "Collect your personal items right now. Leave all this gear, and someone can come for it later." He waved his hand toward the camping gear she had stacked near the fireplace.

"No, wait! Why are you doing this? I came up here to find the telescope, the one the papers Rose found said should be here. And I found it! Don't you understand? This is an important discovery, Nik! I'm not going to leave until I document what I found, so I can prove it's from Hevelius's time. It might even be one of his own."

"I am doing this because it is not safe for you to be on the mountain tonight. A storm is coming. Did you and Rose and Tomas not think to check the weather first?"

"Sure, we did. The forecast is for a few centimeters. Even if it's more than a few, so what? I know winter; I'm used to driving in snow. I put chains on the tires, I've got food and water for a few days, and I brought a cell phone and a portable generator. Did you think I'd let a little winter weather interfere?"

He returned to the hearth and dropped the carrier with a clang. "No, I was sure you would let nothing interfere. Not even common sense. Which is why I followed you up the mountain, and why you will be leaving with me now. So collect your things."

"What is that supposed to mean, about not letting common sense interfere?"

Nik grabbed her coat and stalked to where she stood defiantly. "Here, put this on," he said, thrusting it at her. "It means this is all about your career, is it not? That is the one thing you would risk everything for."

"My career? You think the only thing I care about is my career?"

"You made that perfectly clear recently." He moved around her, collecting bits and pieces and stuffing them into her messenger bag and the duffel she had left open at her feet. "But this here is not part of your precious archive."

"No, but the documents that led here sure were! Nik, don't you see how important this is? You've been on me from the beginning to justify the project, to find something of value in the library. This is it! It doesn't get much bigger than a ten-meter telescope."

"And that's important to you."

"Of course it is! It should be important to you too! This is tremendous news for Dubrovia, don't you see? You think DeWitte was excited before? Wait till he hears about this!"

Nik hefted the duffel onto his shoulder and handed her the other bag. "So this is all about winning some sort of contest with him?"

"No, that's—no. It's not about winning anything. But it is a competition, sort of. Every career is, don't you think? Well, maybe not yours. Not a lot of contenders for crown prince, are there? So yes, when I come across something that might help my career, I want to make the most of it. This is good for the project, good for the university, good for Dubrovia. And yes, good for me. Is it such a bad thing, to want to succeed?"

"And you are willing to pay the cost of course."

"What cost? I took a day, maybe two, from working on the archiving. At this point we're mostly wrapping up anyway. Pétur has everything under control. If you're concerned, I'll cut short my trip back home next week, or I'll tack a few extra days onto the end if I need to. It's not like I get paid by the hour."

"You put your safety at risk, coming up here alone. And the project as well. What would happen to your precious project if you had driven off the road?"

"The project would continue without me. No one is indispensable. Well, maybe you are, but I'm certainly not." Emily shook her head. "Dubrovia hired me because I'm the best, not because I'm the only. And what you hired me for is just about done. The only thing left on this project is some of the stuff in your office, the shelves by your desk." She shrugged. "Which is why I don't feel guilty about taking a couple of days to come up here. My work in Dubrovia is almost done. And if I discover a way to finish with something spectacular, why wouldn't I grab it?"

"But this is not part of your project. So I am returning you to the castle and the library. When the weather clears, a team of historians can come back and do whatever needs to be done to authenticate the telescope and Rose's documents. You will not be involved. It is not safe. Is that clear?"

Emily's face went white and still. He had never seen her expression so blank, or so cold. She moved slowly, as if she was in pain. "Clear enough." She took a deep breath, closing her eyes for a moment. When she opened them again she avoided his gaze.

"I apologize for overstepping my bounds, Your Highness. It won't happen again." She looked down at her hands as if she had forgotten she still held her camera, then pushed it gently into its case. "I'll turn all my photos and preliminary measurements over to… who do you want me to give it all to?"

"If you give it to me I will make sure the appropriate person receives it. In the meantime…"

"Yes, I heard everything you said. I'll go back to the castle, and stay away from things that don't concern me." She zipped her camera into her messenger bag and picked it up. Stepping carefully around him as she retrieved her duffel from his shoulder, she walked out the door.

He didn't like this withdrawn Emily. Where was the fire, the enthusiasm that drove her career? Where was the passion he had experienced in her arms, in her bed?

He followed her out of the tower, catching up to her just as she shoved her bags into the back of her SUV. "Emily, I didn't mean—"

"Yes, you did. I get it. I do. I'm here to do a job, and up here I'm not doing that job. It won't happen again." She slammed the hatch and stalked around him to open the driver's door. She turned to face him as she climbed in. "Since the last shelves remaining to be cataloged are in your office, I'll have Pétur move all the material up to the reading room so we can work on them out of your way."

Nik caught the door before it closed. "That will probably be for the best. I have meetings this week." It was a terrible idea. If she was working elsewhere, he wouldn't get to see her this week. And there didn't seem to be a lot of weeks left. "Emily…"

"Nothing more to be said, is there?" she said, tugging the door out of his hand and slamming it shut.

Chapter Forty-One:
Complications

Emily's nose wrinkled. The heavy perfume that hung in the air almost made her sneeze. Nodding to the man standing guard outside the door, she asked, "Whose perfume is that? It can't be yours, Mikel!"

"No, miss." He sniffed as well, and grimaced. "It is strong, isn't it? I am not sure if it belongs to Miss DiSalvo or her mother. They were both here. They wanted to use the reading room, but I told them they could not because of the work you are doing in there."

"I'm sure they weren't happy about that, so thank you for heading them off for me. Do you know where they happened to go? I'm done for the day, but I'd rather not run into them."

"No, miss. But their suite is on this floor, so if you want to avoid them, you might want to go down the spiral stairs and back up at the other end of the castle."

"Thanks, Mikel, I'll do that. If I had a coat, I would go out and around through the gardens," Emily said over her shoulder as she strode away.

Emily wove her way through the second-floor stacks, sticking to the inner walls and avoiding the railing that overlooked the main floor as much as possible. No point in taking a circuitous route and then blowing it by being visible over the edge. As she started down the carved spiral staircase, voices traveled up. The openwork of the wooden half walls that encased the stairway kept her hidden from those below but did nothing to muffle sound.

She stopped moving and sat quietly on the top step. She couldn't sneak past them if they were right at the bottom of the stairs. And if she went back she ran a similar risk of discovery, should one of them look up at the wrong time. Better to stay right where she was, around the curve and tucked down below the carved wooden panel.

"You foolish girl! You have not done your part. By now he should have proposed. You have been adept at capturing men's attention before this. Why is the crown prince not eating out of your hand?" an unseen speaker ranted. Emily knew immediately it came from one of the women she was trying to avoid.

"Mamma, I have been trying! It is not my fault he is distracted!"

Emily heard the whiny tones of Helena DiSalvo in full pout. The first voice must have been her mother's. *Too bad Nik can't hear them now.* Emily snickered under her breath. *That would be enough to discourage anyone. Like mother, like daughter in thirty years.*

"Distracted? Is that what you call it? I call it uninterested. You must work harder, my girl. You know how important these contracts are," reprimanded a man's voice.

Oh, great, the gang's all here. Now I'm stuck till they all decide to go somewhere else. Wonder what's so important about the contracts?

"Papa, I'm sure he'll come around eventually. This… project that occupies him will come to an end soon, Rikard says. Then he will be more focused on the winery and not on this stupid library," Helena declared. Her voice faded, as if the three of them were moving farther away, out into the library proper.

"You must make sure he is focused on you, not on the winery or the library! Enlist our friend Rikard's assistance if you cannot do it alone. He knows how delicate this final stage of negotiations is. If the crown prince should discover the other contracts…" And the voice trailed off into an indistinguishable mutter.

Wait! Come back, I need more! Emily scrambled to her feet and hurried down around the curve. She strained to hear more before she came to the bottom of the stairs, but they were gone.

Contracts? What other contracts? Nik never mentioned any other contracts. Neither had Rikard Asanovic, although it wasn't as if he said two words to her at the best of times.

Emily turned and ran back up the stairs and through the stacks. She was out of breath by the time she reached the door to the reading room again.

Mikel the guard was surprised to see her. "Miss? I thought you were done for the night? Did you forget something?"

"No, not exactly," Emily panted. She worked to get her breathing under control as she unlocked the door. "Mikel, has anyone else from outside the castle besides Miss DiSalvo and her mother tried to get in here? Or anyone from inside the castle, who wouldn't normally be in here?"

"No, miss, not while I've been here. Did you want me to check with Councillor Asanovic? As head of castle security, he would know of anyone attempting unauthorized access."

"Nooo, that's okay." She replied slowly but thought fast. The last thing Emily wanted was to alert Rikard to her suspicions. She'd just have to double her efforts to go through the last remaining materials right now.

After all, if any unknown documents had lain hidden for years, then they must be in the last few boxes of materials left to work through. This was all that was left of the books, loose papers, and bound sets of ragged pages discovered in the little secret room tucked into the corner of Nik's office.

So far what she'd sorted and inventoried had been old, dating from the seventeenth and eighteenth centuries. There was a sort of chronological organization to the shelves, so she'd started with the oldest and most fragile.

A lot of it had turned out to be personal correspondence: Kuliç family records rather than Dubrovian records. The more public material was out in the office proper, on shelves and in the big cases of document drawers that lined the outer walls of the room.

But that made sense, she thought as she walked around the reading room, turning on the lights she'd turned off not five minutes before. Put the public records out in public view, but keep the more confidential documents hidden away.

Problem was, there was still a lot of material to go through. And she was on her own: Pétur was back in Edmonton, and Ivan, their local student help, probably didn't qualify for the sort of security clearance necessary to handle sensitive materials.

"Not that I do either," she muttered, seating herself at her worktable and reaching for the closest pile. "But at least I don't have any sort of hidden agenda."

Chapter Forty-Two:
The big argument

Nik hung up the phone as she walked in. "What can I do for you tonight, Dr. Charette?" He motioned for her to approach.

His voice was guarded, his stance neutral. This was not the passionate lover of a couple months prior. It seemed that once their... fling had ended, she'd become nothing more than a business acquaintance to him.

She could deal with that. It was what had she expected. "I'm here to deliver the last of the documents and translations. We'll send the final report to you in a couple of weeks." Emily eased herself down into one of the big leather chairs in front of his desk.

"And do you count your effort here as a success? Time well spent?"

"Yes, I do," she replied firmly, lowering her messenger bag to the floor and leaning it against a chair leg. "We finished the first stage before schedule and under budget. We'll provide a plan to move forward, and some recommendations on hiring for the rest of the work. You've had one visiting scholar here. And since he made a significant discovery, I expect others to come knocking at your door soon."

"There have been several inquiries, yes. But I was thinking more about whether you consider this a personal success as well as a professional one. Whether you would do anything differently, if you had to do it again."

Not going there. Oh, no, not going there at all. Emily stayed silent. What could she say? She didn't regret her time with Nik, only that it was ending on a less-than-positive note.

"So, you are leaving us." It was a statement, not a question.

"Yes. That was always the plan, right? I come here for six or seven months, do the initial inventory, and leave you with recommendations for how to proceed with the next phase," she said defensively. "What else is there?"

"What else, indeed?" he asked, rolling his pen through his fingers. "But you were not truly here for six months, were you?"

"I'm sorry?"

"Three weeks out of four, only, were you here. So we paid you for six months but we really had you for three-quarters of that time."

"Oh, no," she retorted. "You paid for a project, a piece of work. My availability and my travel time were factored into the schedule we presented, and Dubrovia accepted. You are *not* going to quibble now over my trips home."

"Quibble? No. I do not quibble. But can you honestly say that your many trips home were not disruptive to the work?"

"Yes, I can! When I couldn't be here, Pétur was. And even when one of us was back in Edmonton, we kept working. Not all the work had to be done on-site. So no, our trips home did not disrupt anything." Getting angry was better than feeling hurt, right?

"You never explained why the schedule was arranged in such a way. What was so crucial it took precedence over such an important project?"

"I thought the library wasn't important to you?" Emily fired back, then raised her hand and shook her head. "Sorry, that was uncalled for. But the reasons I traveled home are my own, and not relevant to the work here."

"If you insist." He shrugged. "I suppose it does not matter now, does it? After all, you are shortly to leave us, without so much as a backward glance. Moving on to the next big thing, are you?"

"Probably not. Projects like these don't come along every day." She shrugged herself. "And you'll get your office back. You should be glad; you can focus on your own projects again. Which brings me to—"

"And what about the princess? What about Rose?"

Emily looked at him blankly. "What about Rose?"

"Do you not think she will miss you after you leave? The two of you grew close, these past few months."

What about you? Will you miss me after I leave? "Rose will be just fine. She's tougher than you give her credit for. And since she's looking at Canadian neurosurgeons, she might end up in my neighborhood for a while."

"We are not looking at Canadian neurosurgeons. To my knowledge, my aunt and uncle are investigating doctors in

Europe, specifically in Italy. Salvatorio DiSalvo recommended several."

Nik raised his eyebrows at her expression. "Oh, come, now, Dr. Charette. What possible reason could you have for objecting to their recommendations? What have the DiSalvos ever done to you, to make you dislike them so?"

"Not to me, so much, but to Rose. Do you listen to the way they speak to her? It's like they think she has the mental capacity of a three-year-old. She's in a wheelchair; she's not stupid."

"I think you exaggerate. Helena and her family do not know Rose as well as you, that's all. Which brings me back to my point: What about Rose, when you leave?"

"We'll miss each other, of course. But I think more than missing my company, she'll miss having someone she can count on unconditionally, someone with only her best interests at heart without another agenda."

She spoke right over his attempt to interrupt. "No, I don't have any concrete evidence! I just don't trust them. Not where Rose is concerned, and not where Dubrovia is concerned. And neither should you."

"You cannot be serious. The DiSalvo family has been more than cooperative. They open doors for our wines, they help promote us as a tourist destination, and now they make recommendations for doctors for my cousin. These are all good things for Dubrovia, for my family. Why should we not trust them?"

"I don't know!" Emily stood and paced away, then back. "I don't know, okay? I can't give you any concrete evidence. But everything you say they've done for you, they have an ulterior motive for. Nothing is done in service to Dubrovia, or to you. It's all in their interests."

Nik rocked back in his chair and gave her a cold, level gaze. "I concede the self-interest in the wine distribution. A commercial contract is supposed to benefit both sides, or what is the point? But what have they to do with Rose, other than offer a connection to a different doctor?"

"I don't know! I just... When Rose was hurt, the succession was changed, right? Because the doctors couldn't be sure if she'd ever regain consciousness, right? But when she did, the title of crown princess still didn't go to her."

She felt his eyes track her as she paced, as he swiveled back and forth in his desk chair. It was nothing like the focused gaze of Nik the attentive lover. The absolute concentration behind this stare made her feel like a bug under a microscope.

She kept going, stumbling over her words, knowing the more she spoke the more she lost him, unable to help herself. "So there's possibly some confusion about the succession. Dubrovian law isn't clear; I know your Council and the king and queen scrambled to get something in place to get you back here to become crown prince, next in line for the throne."

No response from Nik. It was like talking to a wall, or a closed door. She continued, "Not that Rose would ever challenge your title. She doesn't want to rule, not as she is. But that's the point, isn't it? What happens if she gets her surgery and her spine is repaired and there's no longer any physical reason for her not to rule? What then?"

"Then nothing. The succession change was permanent, not temporary. And that negates your argument the DiSalvos harbor ill intent toward Rose, does it not, if they are recommending doctors to help her overcome her disability?"

"Maybe. Maybe not. They talk about their influence. What if the doctor is in their pocket?" At his disgusted look, she backtracked. "Okay, we won't go that far. But Rose is pretty vocal about wanting to travel, to go to school someplace else, and that's one reason why she's petitioning for the surgery. So if they help her leave, a potential obstacle is removed from your path."

"There is no obstacle! Even if you could wave a magic wand and completely cure her, she is no longer next in line for the throne! And why should that make a difference to Salvatorio DiSalvo anyway?"

"Because if his daughter becomes your crown princess and then your queen, his grandchildren eventually inherit. How far would he go to make that happen?"

Nik stood so quickly, his chair scooted back on its wheels till it collided with the bookshelf behind him. "Enough! This is ridiculous. Without any sort of evidence, this is all speculation, bordering on slander. Frankly, I expected better of you."

"You haven't seen—all right." She raised her hand to defuse his anger. "We'll let that go. If you won't listen about Rose, though, let's talk about Dubrovia and your precious wine."

"You are trying my patience, Dr. Charette."

"I'm sorry, but you need to hear this." Emily rose and walked to the bookcases lining one side of the room. She was grateful they were on the side that right now he was not.

"Remember that day in here, the first day I saw what was behind these doors?" She hooked her fingers on the brass filigree and rattled the screen that closed in the shelves. "I noticed you had a lot of books about Italy. You also told me at one point most of the stuff in here"—she waved her hand to indicate the room at large—"was collected by your father and his predecessors."

"Yes, I remember. So? Our ties to Italy span several generations. What is your point?"

"My point is this. Dubrovia has long-standing ties to Italy, yes, but not necessarily to the DiSalvo family. I'm sure, with your business background, you explored other options for distributing the wine, right? Some other Italian companies?"

"We explored many options, of course. Dr. Charette, I struggle to understand why this is any concern of yours," he said, walking over to frown at her.

"And you never came across any correspondence from your father's tenure as prime minister, or your great-uncle's? Nothing pointing you to any specific family?" She slipped out from between him and the bookcase to return to her chair and pick up her messenger bag.

"There was nothing in this office when I came into my role, no. Not that it would make a difference. We are very close to finalizing the agreements with DiSalvo Distributing. And since this project is concluding, perhaps I will be able to return my focus to where it belongs."

He followed her over and leaned on the desk near where Emily was pulling files and folders out of her bag. "So, that is all, then? These are the last of the documents from the little room? I can take them now."

She held on to the portfolios as he reached for them. "Yes, but... Look, Nik," she said, deliberately using the informal address to get his attention. "You were against this project from the beginning. And I know the scientific and historical discoveries didn't quite meet your expectations for finding something of value in the library during the inventory. So maybe," she said, dropping the big stack onto his desk with a thump, "maybe these will."

He made no move to inspect them. "What are those?"

"Those," Emily said, closing her messenger bag and slinging it over her shoulder, "are documents I was able to decipher once I discovered that the encryption key is one of those books on Italy from your bookcase. Your father's earliest journal had a note tucked into the binding, naming the book and explaining the code key. These are some preliminary contract negotiations for wine distribution from the late seventies and early eighties."

"From the eighties? We barely had a wine industry then." Nik poked at the stack as she walked to the door.

"Your father thought ahead. But he died ten years ago, didn't he? So he never had the chance to see what you made of the winery, and he never had the chance to close this deal."

Just before shutting the door behind her, Emily said over her shoulder, "I know my opinion doesn't count for much. But before you sign anything final with the DiSalvos, do your country a favor and read through those."

Chapter Forty-Three:
Nik returns to Dubrovia

Nik blew into the castle on a gust of wind from the winter storm raging outside, all ice and fury. And like the last of the autumn leaves skittering around the courtyard in the gale, people—staff, councillors, guests, and the usual hangers-on—parted before him and eddied behind him in his wake.

He was a force of nature.

He was a man on a mission.

A mission with multiple objectives, he thought, sending his gaze over the heads of the crowd in search of…

There. He changed direction and headed toward Minister Janko. If the older man was out in the main hall, the Council session had ended for the morning, and his uncle the king would be taking his midday meal before resuming the afternoon session.

As he strode through the milling crowd, he fired orders at his aide. "Anton, set up accommodations for the Marabellas. It will be Sebastiano and his wife, plus whatever staff they bring. They arrive later today. We're tight on space here in the castle, so see what you can do. And make sure they receive the official invitation to the Christmas Ball. Oh, and schedule a meeting with Salvatorio DiSalvo for after this afternoon's Council session," he said, never breaking stride.

"Yes, sir. Did you want me to confirm if His Highness is available now?" Anton dodged around a strolling couple to catch up with his boss.

"No, I'll head on up once I speak to… Minister Janko! A word?"

* * *

Several hours later, a very satisfied Nik rose from his desk to greet Salvatorio DiSalvo and his wife and daughter. He hadn't expected the whole family for what was to be a business meeting, but perhaps this was for the best. This way he would prevent any misunderstandings when he gave them his news.

As Anton closed the door behind the maid who'd brought a coffee service, Nik greeted the family, got them settled in armchairs and on the sofa with drinks, and stood leaning against the crackling fireplace.

"Well, my boy, you cut it fine, didn't you? The ball is tonight. I'm surprised you weren't here yesterday, greeting your guests as they arrived. Isn't that usually the crown prince's duty?" the jovial Italian reprimanded. He settled back into the couch next to his wife, the picture of smug contentment.

"Business took me out of the country. You know how it is. Their Royal Highnesses, and Council as well, understand when demands elsewhere interfere with more pleasurable duties here."

"No matter, no matter. You're here now. And since you requested this meeting, can I assume you want to say something to me, before the ball? And perhaps to my daughter as well?"

Yes, but not what you think. "I do indeed have something to say. Mostly to you, sir, but it affects all of you. I wanted to tell you, before you hear from anyone else: I just returned from Italy, where I revived an old, pre-existing contract and signed an exclusive wine distribution partnership with the Marabella family."

"What? You signed with someone else? I thought we had a deal!" DiSalvo leaped to his feet. "How could you do this? What were you thinking?"

"As always, I think about what is best for Dubrovia. And I thought about what my father would have done, since it was his notes on the original negotiations I found."

"Your father?! Pah. He has been dead these ten years. What has he to do with what you do now? What did he ever do or say about your actions?"

"You are right. I was not a very attentive son in my younger years. And my father did not expect to die before I came to my senses and returned to Dubrovia to train under him," Nik agreed. "But that does not negate the value of what he did. It only meant it was much harder for me to uncover what he started to put in place. Stefan was here, after all, and I'm sure he was well informed about these old contracts."

"Old contracts? They were statements of intent, at best. Nothing was ever signed, or I would have known. So they were not valid then, and they are not binding now," blustered DiSalvo.

"So you admit that you knew about them? Then you know while they might not stand up in a court of law, they are binding all the same. Or do you not consider your word your bond? Mine is. You can ask your daughter. I keep my promises. And I make no promises I do not intend to keep."

DiSalvo twisted in his seat to confront his daughter. "Why did I not know about this? How could you have missed those papers?"

"Papa, I—"

"No! No excuses! This was your one task, Helena, yours and Rikard's: to make sure he signed with us, giving the DiSalvo family those exclusive rights. All you had to do was keep him focused on you. But you couldn't even do that, could you?"

"Maybe if you had told me what this was all about, I might have found something!" Helena jumped to her feet. "But no. I was the distraction, you said. Tell you what was he was up to, what we talked about, you said. And I did, did I not? But never a word from you about what questions to ask, or what to look for. And if Rikard knew, he never saw fit to tell me either. Not that I was ever in here unescorted, but still."

She pointed at Nik. "And it is NOT my fault he fell for that little mouse. Who could believe the world-famous playboy Nikolas Kuliç would get all caught up in a… a… librarian! Someone with no social standing whatsoever."

"Stop. My relationship with Dr. Charette is not up for discussion. And it has nothing to do with these contracts." Nik set his drink down on the mantel.

"Oh, Nikki, if you believe that, you are more of a fool than I thought you were," Helena replied sadly. "And even if you want to keep denying your feelings for her, you must realize she is in love with you! Why else would she give you those documents?"

"Because that was her job? Of course she turned over those documents. She was here to find anything of value that might be hidden in the library. She also reported finding scientific papers and instruments from the 1600s. Are we going to discuss the potential value of those to Dubrovia as well?"

"Fool." The whisper barely carried.

"Enough!" roared DiSalvo. He stood and shook his finger at his daughter. "Enough from you. And you!" he said, whirling to confront Nik. "You can still fix this. If you marry Helena we can set those contracts aside in favor of her marriage agreement. I will contact my lawyers immediately, before the ball, and—"

"No."

"—we can… What do you mean, no?"

"No. There will be no marriage, there will be no setting aside of valid contracts. No."

"I can't believe this! After all the time and money I've invested in pursuing this, do you think I am going to quietly let it drop? My daughter is right about one thing: you are a fool."

"I have no control over what you spend your time and money on. And if I am a fool, perhaps it is a good thing that we will not be doing business together. Or become related by marriage."

Nik took a step away from the fireplace. "So. Now that you understand the situation, may I ask whether you intend to remain for the ball?" He shrugged. "It is entirely up to you, of course, although don't expect any assistance from Rikard Asanovic. He has been relieved of his duties as councillor pending an investigation. I have vetted the guest list; there might be other potential partners—in business and in marriage—that you want to pursue. It might be a bit uncomfortable for you to do so tonight, however. Sebastiano Marabella and his wife Ysabel will be in attendance."

DiSalvo sucked in a breath. "You worked fast. Well. We had a gentleman's agreement, but since you chose not to honor it, then—"

"Honor? Do not speak to me of honor! Remember I said I read my father's notes on the matter. You were aware of these older negotiations, but you chose to attempt to undermine them with new contracts. Whose honor is compromised? If Dr. Charette had not uncovered them, I would have broken my father's word. Inadvertently and unknowingly, but broken it all the same. Because of her actions, I was able to salvage the work he did before he died. I think he would be proud of the end result."

"Dr. Charette again! Do not pin your hopes on that one. She might have delivered the documents to you, but she did not stay around long enough to harvest the results." He took his wife's arm and jerked his head at Helena. "We are leaving. Now."

"Wait!" Nik rounded the coffee table and stepped into DiSalvo's path. "What are you talking about?"

"Ha! So you don't know, do you? She's gone. Left. Flew home the day you left for Italy, apparently. Couldn't even be bothered to stay for the ball thrown by the country who hosted her for, what was it, six, seven months?" He maneuvered around Nik and moved for the door again. "You could have had my daughter as well as a decent contract. I hope you are happy with your new partners. Too bad they don't have a marriageable daughter."

Nik stood stunned and silent as the three sailed out the door. Anton edged his way into the room past them. "Sir? I have made the arrangements for Signor and Signora Marabella to stay here in the castle."

"What? Sorry. I was caught up. They're to stay here in the castle? Where did you find room?"

"Sir, that is what I wanted to tell you right away. They'll be in the suite Dr. Charette—"

"Did you know she was gone? No, of course not. You were with me." Outside he was as smooth and cool as ever. Inside, now, inside was another story.

"Sir, I... No. Not until tonight, when I asked about rooms for the Marabellas. I think—"

"When did she leave?"

"About an hour after we flew to Italy. Sir, do you want me to reach her by phone? It's midmorning there. I can—"

"No. There is no need. She left nothing outstanding from the library project, correct? Then there is no reason. I'm sure if Dr. Charette or the University of Alberta find any reason to contact us, we will hear from them. And you said you made the arrangements for the Marabella family, yes? Then there is nothing more I need from you at the moment."

He didn't hear Anton's reply, or the door closing softly behind him. Nik turned blindly to his desk and the decanter behind it on the table. Coffee was not going to be enough.

Why had Emily left? He cast his mind back to the night she had deposited those old contracts on his desk. Yes, they had disagreed about the DiSalvo family (and in hindsight, she was right). But that couldn't have been enough to drive her away. Could it?

Chapter Forty-Four:
Aftermath

Hours later, he still had no answer. His best source of information would be Rose, of course, as she and Emily were close. But his cousin had been busy getting ready for the Christmas Ball; preparing for and attending social events requiring formal dress were so much more difficult from a wheelchair, he knew.

And then he got caught up in the ball himself. The Marabellas arrived and had to be welcomed and introduced to the king and queen, the Royal Council members and their wives, and the various other dignitaries and important persons, both Dubrovian and foreign, who were attended this evening.

He did catch the occasional glimpse of the DiSalvos. The pinched expressions of Helena's parents told him while they might be trying to lobby against the new contracts, they weren't succeeding. Helena herself looked like she wore a blank mask, her face expressionless, her posture stiff.

As the evening wound down, Nik worked his way through the departing crowd, shaking hands, accepting congratulations on the new contract announcement. He discovered Rose tucked along the side, watching everything.

"You're a hard girl to track down, Rose," he commented, settling into a chair at her side.

"I just came back downstairs. I went up to my room for a little while after Ivan left, so Jacquie could adjust my brace," she replied. She fidgeted in her wheelchair, adding, "My back has been bothering me."

"I can tell." He studied his young cousin. It wasn't like Rose to complain; if she volunteered the information, she was in pain. "What can you do?"

"Not much." She squirmed again. "I went through a growing spurt and Dr. Bergner says my spine stretched. Things are moving around, and something got pinched, and it hurts."

"What does that mean?" Nik frowned. He hated to see her uncomfortable.

"It means," she said, "I don't want to talk about my back. I want to talk about why you're so grumpy. Aren't you happy? You announced the new contract. Council is thrilled the Marabellas came to the ball so they could meet everybody. Nana and Papa are happy you made it back in time. Helena and her parents are pissed off and will probably leave early tomorrow morning. Best night ever. What is there to be grumpy about?"

"I'm not grumpy. I'm tired, but I'm not grumpy."

"No? You should see your face. If that's your happy face, I would hate to see you when you thought you were grumpy."

"I am not grumpy. Could we change the subject, please?" He sighed, exasperated. He turned to the server hovering at his elbow. "Another champagne, please. And no," he said, frowning at Rose, "none for you."

"I know," she grumbled. "Ginger ale for me for another year. So," she said as the white-coated waiter moved off to fetch their drinks, "if you don't want to talk about your grumpy face, what did you want to talk about? Nana said you looked for me earlier."

"I wanted... I wondered if you had heard from Dr. Charette since she left Dubrovia. All Anton found out was she left for Edmonton the same morning I left for Italy." Nik winced inside. So now he was reduced to asking his teenage cousin for gossip.

"So it IS about your grumpy face!" Rose crowed. She schooled her expression at his glare. "Sorry, Uncle Nik, I don't know much more than that either. Jacquie heard from Anja, who heard from Marta that Emily was upset about something, and she asked Tomas how fast he could get her home. He booked her a flight for that afternoon. She left in such a hurry that she only took a little of her stuff; Marta and Anja packed up and shipped the rest. It left the day after she did."

She gave him a hard look. "Do you know what upset her? Did you guys have a fight?"

Not that it was any of her business, but: "A fight? No. We had a professional disagreement." He was sure of that. So why had she run?

"Okay, if you say so. Maybe something happened at home, then."

"At home? What, at her university? Do they not close over the Christmas holiday season as ours does?"

411

"Sheesh. Didn't you guys ever talk about anything? Her father lives there, and he isn't doing so well, I don't think. So maybe, Uncle Nik, she didn't leave because of you at all."

That never occurred to him, he thought, sheepish. "And you have not heard from her?"

"No, I haven't! Have you?" Rose twisted to face him, and froze abruptly. "Oh, that's not good."

"What, that neither of us…" He finally registered the expression on her face. It wasn't her *I'm giving my uncle a hard time* smirk. This was pain he saw. "Rose? What happened?"

Her breathing became shallow and erratic. Nik looked around wildly, just short of panic. Where was Jacquie? Where were his aunt and uncle? "Hold on here, Rose, until I can find—"

"No, don't leave me, Uncle Nik!" Her hand latched on to his arm with a strength he didn't think she possessed. "It might pass. Sometimes it does. But I don't think I should be alone right now, in case it doesn't."

He moved behind her chair and flipped off the brakes. "Then we will have to find some help, will we not? And you can speak more of these pains you've been having."

As they moved across the floor to the nearest exit, Rose alternated between telling him about her latest issues with physiotherapy and smiling and nodding at the last few party-goers. Her condition had deteriorated while he had been away, and her grandparents now considered surgery for her.

Not what he expected to hear. Before he left for Italy, Rose was fine. Why now?

By the time he rolled her out the door and down the corridor, she was grimacing in pain. Running over the bumpy edge of a rug in the great hall elicited a gasp and moan she failed to hide.

"Stop, Uncle Nik! It hurts too much. I need—"

"You need a hospital, Rose." Nik changed direction, pulling out his cell phone as he headed toward the front door. "Anton? Get the king and queen down to the entry. And call up a car, and call ahead to the hospital. It's Rose."

Chapter Forty-Five:
Going back

HOUSE FOR SALE C/S
    The big blue and white sign caught Nik's eye as soon as their car pulled up across the street. Then he saw the van with the name of a moving company.

He must have made a noise because Rose (who hadn't seen either sign or van) asked, "Uncle Nik? What's the matter? Are we where we should be?"

"We are, Rose," he answered grimly, "but it looks like Emily is not."

"What do you mean, she's not here?" Rose scrambled across the seat to peer out of the window on his side of the car. "She has to be here. She's not teaching this term, Pétur said. Where else would she be?"

Nik thought back on his conversation yesterday with Emily's TA. Yes, Pétur confirmed, Dr. Charette had returned to Edmonton in December. No, she wasn't teaching again this term. What else? Something about her father, he was sure.

He swore under his breath as he fished out his phone and dialed, praying the call would not go to voice mail. Luck was with him as the younger man answered on the second ring.

"Mr. Tumason, Pétur, this is Nikolas Kuliç again. I am calling... Yes, I realize now Dr. Charette is not here. I thought to find her at home since you said she is not teaching this semester… Wait, what do you mean she has taken an indefinite leave? What—"

"Indefinite leave?" Rose yanked on the phone he held to his ear. "Let me talk to Pétur!"

"Hold for a moment, if you would," Nik said, covering the phone with his other hand. "Rose, if you will wait, I will get to the bottom of this."

"But, Uncle Nik!"

"Hush," he said, then returned to the call. "My apologies. Princess Rose is most anxious about Dr. Charette. We have not heard from her since she returned to Edmonton in December."

He kept his eyes on the fidgeting Rose as he conversed with Pétur. "I see. Well, no, actually, I do not see. You say she… Yes, I understand. But… When, do you know? What? But where is she now? Wait, let me write this down."

Nik took note of the instructions fired rapidly into his ear, writing furiously on the pad Rose dug out of her purse. "Yes, I'm sure we'll find it. Yes, I understand why you cannot call her and tell her we are on our way. No matter; we will see her in a few minutes."

Ending the call, he stared at his notes for several seconds, Rose fairly vibrating next to him. Before she could reach her boiling point, he spoke to their driver, rattling off an address.

Once the car pulled out, he said, "We arrived just in time, Rose. Emily is leaving Edmonton today. Pétur either could not or would not tell me her destination. We must move quickly to catch her."

* * *

The cold March wind crept under her coat and poked through her gloves as Emily kicked her way through the remnants of yesterday's snow squalls. She was tired of winter; she was tired of the snow and the cold and the dark; she was tired of being alone. She was just tired.

Fourteen weeks. Some days it felt like it had all happened so fast, and some days it felt like forever. One minute she was arguing with Nik about some old documents, and the next she was standing at her father's grave to say goodbye before getting on a plane and leaving Edmonton.

For how long, she didn't know. She was about to take an enormous leap of faith: packing up everything she owned, selling the house she grew up in, leaving her life here and flying to... Well. She wondered what her reception would be when she arrived. She'd heard exactly nothing from Nik since that day in December. But they hadn't parted on the best of terms.

Even Rose was silent. For fourteen weeks. Emily knew she hadn't explained, then or since, why she'd left so abruptly. She'd never shared the details of her father's health with anyone in Dubrovia, had she? And she hadn't explained about the call, that terrible day: how his degeneration escalated so unexpectedly; how a fall in the night resulted in a broken hip; how the broken hip necessitated a trip to Emergency; how the trip to Emergency stretched into admission to hospital with pneumonia from which he never recovered.

At some point during her first week home, she stopped checking her phone all the time. Most of her days were spent at her father's bedside, and she turned her phone off in the hospital. The only people she spoke to were the caregivers: doctors and nurses, many of whom she knew from her mother's last bout with cancer.

Eventually Pétur gave up and stopped calling every few hours, although he made a point of stopping in every other day or so. After a while, she figured he came to make sure she ate and slept. She didn't do much of either for weeks.

What she did do was think. She thought about her life, and her parents. About how she'd finally accomplished what she thought she wanted: eager students, great opportunities to advance her career, the respect of her peers. About how she'd worked so hard to achieve so much and somehow it didn't seem important anymore.

Because she had no one to share it with. Even if her father had survived, had somehow recovered enough from this last round of treatment to be released from hospital, he would have gone back into long-term care. He never would have come home again.

And now home wasn't the home she remembered. It was just a house. No one she cared about lived there with her. So what was the point of staying?

Emily came to that conclusion the day of her father's first seizure, New Year's Eve. She didn't feel at home in her own home anymore.

It felt like an itch under her skin, barely noticeable most of the time, then flaring up into an unbearable intensity at the oddest moments. She felt it in the darkest hours of the night, when the hospital corridors were quiet and empty.

She kept vigil those nights. They moved a bed into her father's room for her. She left only to eat and shower (when Pétur made her), and spent her days watching her father breathe. His final directive refused any life support except basic nutrition: no pain medication, no extraordinary measures, not even oxygen. And so he hung on, not recovering but not dying, for weeks.

Those weeks gave her plenty of time to think: about herself, about Dubrovia, about Nik. She hadn't realized until she was back in Edmonton how much she had fit in in Dubrovia. She had never expected to. Living in a castle, with servants and staff around, was never a childhood wish.

So where was the fit? More thinking brought her to the people who'd accepted her almost as part of the family. Having Rose in her life again, getting to know her as more than a child, was an unexpected bonus.

And then there was Nik. That last night—*No, be honest, Em, it went back to the day at the tower.* She still wasn't altogether sure why he had turned on her. She was honest from the start about how much the project would boost her career. And in the end, Dubrovia benefited the most. The discovery of first the book and then the telescope put the little country on the map.

She had no idea whether anything would ever come of the contracts—well, notes for contracts—that she turned over to Nik before she left. And there had been a very loud silence from that side of the ocean ever since.

But it came down to her and Nik, didn't it? Even though there wasn't such a thing as "Emily and Nik."

But there might have been. If I were braver. If I admitted to myself I wanted... What? What did she want?

She wanted him. She wanted him to look at her the way her father had looked at her mother: as if the sun and moon rose and set where she stood.

As Emily watched her father slip slowly toward his inevitable end, she made a decision. No more hiding. No more protecting her heart to the point of shutting herself off. No more turning herself into a washed-out academic (heaven knows, she ran into enough of them at faculty meetings).

She would reach for what she wanted. She'd go to Dubrovia and fight for Nik. And if he didn't think he wanted her, well, she was smart, and she was determined, and she'd figure it out. She loved him. What else could she do?

Weeks later here she stood, at her father's new headstone, right next to her mother's. The house had conditionally sold. Everything she owned was packed up, ready to go with her this afternoon, or into storage until she could send for it. (And thank heavens for Pétur, who'd offered to handle that step for her. "Anything to smooth the course of true love," he'd said.) Her plane tickets were in her ever-present messenger bag, along with her laptop.

No phone, though. She returned her university-issued phone to the dean this morning. That would be her first purchase once she hit Europe: a phone with a local SIM card.

Emily knelt and placed the bouquets down on the graves: star lilies for her mother, red and yellow tulips for her father. "I'm leaving for Dubrovia today. I'm not sure when I'll be back. But anyway, I know you're not really here, and I believe you're together somewhere."

She pulled out a tissue and blew her nose inelegantly (was there any other way?). She kissed her fingers and reached out to touch each headstone. "Wish me luck. I miss you."

A car stopped somewhere behind her while she stood at their graves. That wasn't so unusual. Every time she'd visited in the six days since the funeral, there was a steady stream of visitors to various parts of the cemetery. But this time the low-voiced conversation between her cab driver and whoever just arrived caught her attention.

Emily turned around in time to see her cab start up and drive away. "Hey, wait!" she yelled. When he didn't stop, she turned her wrath on the driver of the other car. "Did you tell him to leave? Why would you do that?"

The driver didn't answer, just opened the back door of the car. The big black car. The limo, now that she looked at it.

The limo's passenger stepped out.

And her heart skipped a beat or two. "Nik?" she whispered. She almost didn't have enough breath for that much sound. "Nik, what are you doing here?"

He smiled and shook his head. "You were gone. We came to find you."

"We?"

He reached into the car and helped out… Rose? A Rose who stood, no canes or crutches in sight. A Rose who walked toward her, hesitantly on the snow and ice, but walked. On her own.

Oh, her uncle followed right behind her, ready to lend a steadying hand if she needed it. But she didn't.

Emily froze in place for all of two seconds. She burst into motion, sliding to a stop in front of Rose, flailing her arms to keep her balance as she hit a slippery patch.

Then they were both laughing, and crying, and talking, asking, telling each other how: how they (Rose and Nik) came to find Emily because Rose had had her surgery after all (and almost three months of physio, thank you very much), how Emily came home to take care of her father in his last days. Then Rose was asking wasn't she going to come back to Dubrovia with them? Because Rose really, really wanted her to.

At that, Emily drew back, wiping her eyes. She turned to Nik without letting go of Rose. He leaned on the car, watching, an indulgent smile on his face.

"Nik? Is that what you want too?"

His gaze never left hers. "Rose, why don't you get back in the car?"

"Oh, come on, Uncle Nik! I want to know what Emily is going to do! And—"

"Rose, I think Emily and I need to talk, don't you? And you need to get off the snow before your balance gives out and you fall." He nodded to the driver, who came around to help Rose back to the car.

"Nik?"

"You didn't call." He stalked closer.

"No, I—"

"I know now why you left Dubrovia as you did. But for weeks I had no idea what I had done to drive you away." When she started to protest, he touched her lips with his fingers. "I only knew I had to find you and bring you home."

Emily closed her eyes. The feel of his touch, after so long? It was enough to make her melt. Even if she hadn't been on her way to him, she'd follow him anyw—

Her eyes snapped open. "Did Pétur tell you where to find me?"

"Well, yes. But he—"

"Did he also tell you where I was going?"

"No, we never got that far."

And then she started to laugh. After weeks of mourning, watching her father slip away, the joy bubbling up inside might have had a slightly hysterical edge. But it was joy nonetheless. "To Dubrovia. I was going to Dubrovia. I have tickets in my pocket for an overnight flight to London.

I was going…" She took a deep breath. "I was going to Dubrovia to tell you I love you, I'm in love with you, and that if you didn't love me yet you would, I'd figure out a way, and—"

It was impossible to talk while he kissed her.

THE END

ACKNOWLEDGMENTS

Writing a book is, for the most part, a solitary endeavor. Publishing one is not. I have people to thank:

For cover art: Su Kopil of Earthly Charms http://www.earthlycharms.com/.

For beta reading: Bonnie Taylor Wachowicz of https://taylormadetime.com.

For copyediting: Jessica Gardner of Jessica Gardner Editing http://www.jessicagardner.co/.

For book coaching in the early stage: Paula Chaffee Scardamalia of Divining The Muse http://www.diviningthemuse.com/.

And, as always, the biggest thanks you can imagine go to my husband Tom. Thanks for the meals, the support, the laughs, and the life we've made together. You're my Happy Ever After.

ABOUT THE AUTHOR

Win Day is a storytelling geek who loves to read and write about strong men and savvy women. Her first novel, *On a Whim*, won the RWA Contemporary Chapter's Stiletto contest in two categories: Best Contemporary Short and Best First Book. *Treasure in the Library* is her second published novel.

Born and raised in New Jersey, Win moved to Canada after working as an engineer in an overseas oil refinery, where she met her husband, Tom. The two have been married for thirty-six years, and have two sons who are all grown up and living on their own. Win and Tom currently live in Calgary, Alberta, Canada.

A member of her local chapter of Romance Writers of America, Win divides her time between building custom WordPress websites for authors, and writing both fiction and nonfiction. She learned long ago that she needs both the technical and the creative to keep her brain busy and her heart happy!

When she isn't writing or working on a website, Win enjoys traveling to warm places (she's solar powered!), cooking (and eating!), and curling up on the couch with a good book. And listening to all sorts of music.

Win believes that everyone deserves their Happy Ever After. And if you're not living yours right now, duck into a book. Someone else's story can give you the hope you need, and show you what's possible.

FIND WIN ONLINE

Writing website: http://www.windaywrites.com/

Visit and sign up for information about new releases!

Facebook: https://www.facebook.com/WinDayWrites/

Twitter:https://twitter.com/WinDayWrites
(@WinDayWrites)

Email: Win@WinDayWrites.com